THE
MARBLE COLLECTOR

Cecelia Ahern was born and grew up in Dublin. She is now published in nearly fifty countries, and has sold over twenty-four million copies of her novels worldwide. Two of her books have been adapted as films and she has created several TV series. She and her books have won numerous awards, including the Irish Book Award for Popular Fiction for *The Year I Met You*.

For more information on Cecelia, her writing, books and events, follow her on Twitter @Cecelia_ Ahern, join her on Facebook www.facebook.com/CeceliaAhernofficial and visit her website www.cecelia-ahern.com, where she would love to hear from you.

Also by Cecelia Ahern

THE
MARBLE COLLECTOR

cecelia
ahern

HarperCollins*Publishers*

HarperCollins*Publishers*
1 London Bridge Street
London SE1 9GF

www.harpercollins.co.uk

Published by HarperCollins*Publishers* 2015
1

A catalogue record for this book is available from the British Library

ISBN: 978-0-00-750182-3

This novel is entirely a work of fiction.
The names, characters and incidents portrayed in it are the work of
the author's imagination. Any resemblance to actual persons, living
or dead, events or localities is entirely coincidental.

Typeset in Sabon LT Std by Palimpsest Book Production Ltd, Falkirk, Stirlingshire

Printed and bound in Great Britain by Clays Ltd, St Ives plc

MIX
Paper from
responsible sources
FSC
www.fsc.org   FSC® C007454

FSC™ is a non-profit international organisation established to promote
the responsible management of the world's forests. Products carrying the
FSC label are independently certified to assure consumers that they come
from forests that are managed to meet the social, economic and
ecological needs of present and future generations,
and other controlled sources.

Find out more about HarperCollins and the environment at
www.harpercollins.co.uk/green

For my Sonny Ray

I saw the angel in the marble and carved until
I set him free.

Michelangelo

PROLOGUE

When it comes to my memory there are three categories: things I want to forget, things I can't forget, and things I forgot I'd forgotten until I remember them.

My earliest memory is of my mum when I was three years old. We are in the kitchen, she picks up the teapot and launches it up at the ceiling. She holds it with two hands, one on the handle, one on the spout, and lobs it as though in a sheaf-toss competition, sending it up in the air where it cracks against the ceiling, and then falls straight back down to the table where it shatters in pieces, murky brown water and burst soggy teabags everywhere. I don't know what preceded this act, or what came after, but I do know it was anger-motivated, and the anger was my-dad-motivated. This memory is not a good representation of my mum's character; it doesn't show her in a good light. To my knowledge she never behaved like that again, which I imagine is precisely the reason that I remember it.

As a six-year-old, I see my Aunt Anna being stopped at

the door by Switzer's security as we exit. The hairy-handed security guard goes through her shopping bag and retrieves a scarf with its price tags and a security tag still on it. I can't remember what happened after that, Aunt Anna plied me with ice-cream sundaes in the Ilac Centre and watched with hope that every memory of the incident would die with each mouthful of sugar. The memory is vivid despite even to this day everyone believing I made it up.

I currently go to a dentist who I grew up with. We were never friends but we hung out in the same circles. He's now a very serious man, a sensible man, a stern man. When he hovers above my open mouth, I see him as a fifteen-year-old pissing against the living room walls at a house party, shouting about Jesus being the original anarchist.

When I see my aged primary school teacher who was so softly spoken we almost couldn't hear her, I see her throwing a banana at the class clown and shouting at him to *leave me alone for God's sake, just leave me alone,* before bursting into tears and running from the classroom. I bumped into an old classmate recently and brought the incident up, but she didn't remember.

It seems to me that when summoning up a person in my mind it is not the everyday person I think of, it is the more dramatic moments or the moments they showed a part of themselves that is usually hidden.

My mother says that I have a knack for remembering what others forget. Sometimes it's a curse; nobody likes it when there's somebody to remember what they've tried so hard to bury. I'm like the person who remembers everything after a drunken night out, who everyone wishes would keep their memories to themself.

I can only assume I remember these episodes because I have never behaved this way myself. I can't think of a moment when I have broken form, become another version of myself that I want and need to forget. I am always the same. If you've met me you know me, there's not much more to me. I follow the rules of who I know myself to be and can't seem to be anything else, not even in moments of great stress when surely a meltdown would be acceptable. I think this is why I admire it so much in others and I remember what they choose to forget.

Out of character? No. I fully believe that even a sudden change in a person's behaviour is within the confines of their nature. That part of us is present the whole time, lying dormant, just waiting for its moment to be revealed. Including me.

1

PLAYING WITH MARBLES

Allies

'*Fergus Boggs!*'

These are the only two words I can understand through Father Murphy's rage-filled rant at me, and that's because those words are my name, the rest of what he says is in Irish. I'm five years old and I've been in the country for one month. I moved from Scotland with Mammy and my brothers, after Daddy died. It all happened so quickly, Daddy dying, us moving, and even though I'd been to Ireland before, on holidays during the summer to see Grandma, Granddad, Uncle, Aunty and all my cousins, it's not the same now. I've never been here when it's not the summer. It feels like a different place. It has rained every day we've been here. The ice-cream shop isn't even open now, all boarded up like it never even existed, like I made it up in my head. The beach that we used to go to most days doesn't look like the same place and the chip van is gone. The people look different too. They're all wrapped up and dark.

Father Murphy stands over my desk and is tall and grey and wide. He spits as he shouts at me; I feel the spit land on my cheek but I'm afraid to wipe it away in case that makes him angrier. I try looking around at the other boys to see their reactions but he lashes out at me. A backhanded slap. It hurts. He is wearing a ring, a big one; I think it has cut my face but I daren't reach up to feel it in case he hits me again. I need to go to the toilet all of a sudden. I have been hit before, but never by a priest.

He is shouting angry Irish words. He is angry that I don't understand. In between the Irish words he says I should understand him by now but I just can't. I don't get to practise at home. Mammy is sad and I don't like to bother her. She likes to sit and cuddle. I like when she does that. I don't want to ruin the cuddles by talking. And anyway I don't think she remembers the Irish words either. She moved away from Ireland a long time ago to be a nanny to a family in Scotland and she met Daddy. They never spoke the Irish words there.

The priest wants me to repeat the words after him but I can barely breathe. I can barely get the words out of my mouth.

'*Tá mé, tá tú, tá sé, tá sí . . .*'

LOUDER!

'*Tá muid, tá sibh, tá siad.*'

When he's not shouting at me, the room is so quiet it reminds me it's filled with boys my age, all listening. As I stammer through the words he is telling everybody how stupid I am. My whole body is shaking. I feel sick. I need to go to the toilet. I tell him so. His face goes a purple colour and that is when the leather strap comes out. He lashes my hand with leather, which I later learn has pennies sewn into the layers. He tells me he is going to give me 'six of the best' on each hand. I can't take the pain. I need to go to the toilet. I go right there and then. I expect the boys to laugh but nobody does. They keep their heads down. Maybe they'll laugh later, or maybe they'll understand. Maybe they're just happy it's not happening to them. I'm embarrassed, and ashamed, as he tells me I should be. Then he pulls me out of the room, by my ear, and that hurts too, away from everyone, down the corridor, and he pushes me into a dark room. The door bangs closed behind me and he leaves me alone.

I don't like the dark, I have never liked the dark, and I start to cry. My pants are wet, my wee has run down into my socks and shoes but I don't know what to do. Mammy usually changes them for me. What do I do here? There is no window in the room and I can't see anything. I hope he won't keep me in here long. My eyes adjust to the darkness and the light that comes from under the door helps me to see. I'm in a storage room. I see a ladder, and a bucket and a mop with no stick, just the head. It smells rank. An old bicycle is hanging upside down, the chain missing. There's two wellington boots but they don't match and they're both for the same foot. Nothing in here fits together. I don't know why he put me in here and I don't know how long I'll be. Will Mammy be looking for me?

It feels like forever has passed. I close my eyes and sing to myself. The songs that Mammy sings with me. I don't sing them too loud in case he hears me and thinks I'm having fun in here. That would make him angrier. In this place, fun and laughing makes them angry. We are not here to be leaders, we are here to serve. This is not what my daddy taught me, he said that I was a natural leader, that I can be anything I want to be. I used to go hunting with him, he taught me everything, he even let me walk first, he said I was the leader. He sang a song about it. 'Following the leader, the leader, the leader, Fergus is the leader, da da da da da.' I hum it to myself but I don't say the words. The priest won't like me saying I'm the leader. In this place we're not allowed to be anybody we want to be, we have to be who they tell us to be. I sing the songs my daddy used to sing when I was allowed to stay up late and listen to the sing-songs. Daddy had a soft voice for a strong man, and he sometimes cried when he sang. My daddy never said crying was only for babies, not like the priest said, crying is for people who are sad. I sing it to myself now and try not to cry.

Suddenly the door opens and I move away, afraid that it will be him again, with that leather strap. It's not him but it's the younger one, the one who teaches the music class with the kind eyes. He closes the door behind him and crouches down.

'Hi, Fergus.'

I try to say hi but nothing comes out of my mouth.

'I brought you something. A box of bloodies.'

I flinch and he puts a hand out. 'Don't look so scared now, they're marbles. Have you ever played with marbles?'

I shake my head. He opens his hand and I see them shining in his palm like treasures, four red rubies.

'I used to love these as a boy,' he says quietly. 'My granddad gave them to me. "A box of bloodies," he said, "just for you." I don't have the box now. Wish I had, could be worth something. Always remember to keep the packaging, Fergus, that's one bit of advice I'll give you. But I've kept the marbles.'

Somebody walks by the door, we can feel their boots as the floor shakes and creaks beneath us and he looks at the door. When the footsteps have passed he turns back to me, his voice quieter. 'You have to shoot them. Or fulk them.'

I watch as he puts his knuckle on the ground and balances the marble in his bent forefinger. He puts his thumb behind and then gently pushes the marble; it rolls along the wooden floor at speed. A red bloodie, bold as anything, catching the light, shining and glistening. It stops at my foot. I'm afraid to pick it up. And my raw hands are paining me still, it's hard to close them. He sees this and winces.

'Go on, you try,' he says.

I try it. I'm not very good at first because it's hard to close my hands like he showed me, but I get the hang of it. Then he shows me other ways to shoot them. Another way called 'knuckling down'. I prefer it that way and even though he says that's more advanced I'm best at that one. He tells me so and I have to bite my lip to stop the smile.

'Names given to marbles vary from place to place,' he says, getting down and showing me again. 'Some people call them a taw, or a shooter, or tolley, but me and my brothers called them allies.'

Allies. I like that. Even with me locked in this room on my own, I have allies. It makes me feel like a soldier. A prisoner of war.

He fixes me with a serious look. 'When aiming, remember to look at the target with a steady eye. The eye directs the brain, the brain directs the hand. Don't forget that. Always keep an eye on the target, Fergus, and your brain will make it happen.'

I nod.

The bell rings, class over.

'Okay,' he stands up, wipes down his dusty robe. 'I've a class now. You sit tight here. It shouldn't be much longer.'

I nod.

He's right. It shouldn't be much longer – but it is. Father Murphy doesn't come to get me soon. He leaves me there all day. I even do another wee in my pants because I'm afraid to knock on the door to get someone, but I don't care. I am a soldier, a prisoner of war, and I have my allies. I practise and practise in the small room, in my own little world, wanting my skill and accuracy to be the best in the school. I'm going to show the other boys and I'm going to be better than them all the time.

The next time Father Murphy puts me in here I have the marbles hidden in my pocket and I spend the day practising again. I also have an archboard in the dark room. I put it there myself between classes, just in case. It's a piece of cardboard with seven arches cut in it. I made it myself from Mrs Lynch's empty cornflakes box that I found in her bin after I saw some other boys with a fancy shop-bought one. The middle arch is number 0, the arches either side are 1, 2, 3. I put the archboard at the far wall and I shoot from a distance, close to the door. I don't really know how to play it properly yet and I can't play it on my own but I can practise my shooting. I will be better than my big brothers at something.

The nice priest doesn't stay in the school long. They say that he kisses women and that he's going to hell, but I don't care. I like him. He gave me my first marbles, my bloodies. In a dark time in my life, he gave me my allies.

2

POOL RULES

No Running

Breathe.

Sometimes I have to remind myself to breathe. You would think it would be an innate human instinct but no, I inhale and then forget to exhale and so I find my body rigid, all tensed up, heart pounding, chest tight with an anxious head wondering what's wrong.

I understand the theory of breathing. The air you breathe in through your nose should go all the way down to your belly, the diaphragm. Breathe relaxed. Breathe rhythmically. Breathe silently. We do this from the second we are born and yet we are never taught. Though I should have been. Driving, shopping, working, I catch myself holding my breath, nervous, fidgety, waiting for what exactly to happen, I don't know. Whatever it is, it never comes. It is ironic that on dry ground I fail at this simple task when my job requires me to excel at it. I'm a lifeguard. Swimming comes easily to me, it feels natural, it doesn't test me, it makes me feel free. With swimming, timing is everything. On land

11

you breathe in for one and out for one, beneath the water I can achieve a three to one ratio, breathing every three strokes. Easy. I don't even need to think about it.

I had to learn how to breathe above water when I was pregnant with my first child. It was necessary for labour, they told me, which it turns out it certainly is. Because childbirth is as natural as breathing, they go hand in hand, yet breathing, for me, has been anything but natural. All I ever want to do above water is hold my breath. A baby will not be born through holding your breath. Trust me, I tried. Knowing my aquatic ways, my husband encouraged a water birth. This seemed like a good idea to get me in my natural territory, at home, in water, only there is nothing natural about sitting in an oversized paddling pool in your living room, and it was the baby who got to experience the world from below the water and not me. I would have gladly switched places. The first birth ended in a dash to the hospital and an emergency caesarean and indeed the two subsequent babies came in the same way, though they weren't emergencies. It seemed that the aquatic creature who preferred to stay under the water from the age of five could not embrace another of life's most natural acts.

I'm a lifeguard in a nursing home. It is quite the exclusive nursing home, like a four-star hotel with round-the-clock care. I have worked here for seven years, give or take my maternity leave. I man the lifeguard chair five days a week from nine a.m. to two p.m. and watch as three people each hour take to the water for lengths. It is a steady stream of monotony and stillness. Nothing ever happens. Bodies appear from the changing rooms as walking displays of the reality of time: saggy skin, boobs, bottoms and thighs, some dry and flaking from diabetes, others from kidney or liver disease. Those confined to their beds or chairs for so long wear their painful-looking pressure ulcers and bedsores, others carry their brown patches of age spots as badges of the years they have lived. New skin growths appear and change by the day. I see them all, with the full understanding of what my body after three babies will face in the future. Those with one-on-one physiotherapy work with trainers in the water, I merely oversee; in case the therapist drowns, I suppose.

In the seven years I have rarely had to dive in. It is a quiet, slow swimming pool, certainly nothing like the local pool I bring my boys to on a Saturday where you'd leave with a headache from the shouts that echo from the filled-to-the-brim group classes.

I stifle a yawn as I watch the first swimmer in the early morning. Mary Kelly, the dredger, is doing her favourite move: the breaststroke. Slow and noisy, at five feet tall and weighing three hundred pounds she pushes out water as if she's trying to empty the pool, and then attempts to glide. She manages this manoeuvre without once putting her face below the water and blowing out constantly as though she's in below-zero conditions. It is always the same people at the same times. I know that Mr Daly will soon arrive, followed by Mr Kennedy aka the Butterfly King who fancies himself as a bit of an expert, then sisters Eliza and Audrey Jones who jog widths of the shallow end for twenty minutes. Non-swimmer Tony Dornan will cling to a float for dear life like he's on the last life raft, and hover in the shallow end, near to the steps, near to the wall. I fiddle with a pair of goggles, unknotting the strap, reminding myself to breathe, pushing away the hard tight feeling in my chest that only goes away when I remember to exhale.

Mr Daly steps out of the changing room and on to the tiles, 9.15 a.m. on the dot. He wears his budgie smugglers, an unforgiving light blue that reveal the minutiae when wet. His skin hangs loosely around his eyes, cheeks and jowls. His skin is so transparent I see almost every vein in his body and he's covered in bruises from even the slightest bump, I'm sure. His yellow toenails curl painfully into his skin. He gives me a miserable look and adjusts his goggles over his eyes. He shuffles by me without a good morning greeting, ignoring me as he does every day, holding on to the metal railing as if at any moment he'll go sliding on the slippery tiles that Mary Kelly is saturating with each stroke. I imagine him on the tiles, his bones snapping up through his tracing-paper-like skin, skin crackly like a roasted chicken.

I keep one eye on him and the other on Mary, who is letting out a loud grunting sound with each stroke like she is Maria Sharapova. Mr Daly reaches the steps, takes hold of the rail and lowers himself slowly into the water. His nostrils flare as the cold hits him. Once in the water he checks to see if I'm watching. On the days that I am, he floats on his back for long periods of time like he's a dead goldfish. On days like today, when I'm not looking, he lowers his body and head under the water, hands gripping the top of the wall to hold himself down and stays there. I see him, clear as day, practically on his knees in the shallow end, trying to drown himself. This is a daily occurrence.

'Sabrina,' my supervisor Eric warns from the office behind me.

'I see him.'

I make my way to Mr Daly at the steps. I reach into the water and grab him under his arms and pull him up. He is so light he comes up easily, gasping for air, eyes wild behind his goggles, a big green snot bubble in his right nostril. He lifts his goggles off his head and empties them of water, grunting, grumbling, his body shaking with rage that I have once again foiled his dastardly plan. His face is purple and his chest heaves up and down as he tries to catch his breath. He reminds me of my three-year-old who always hides in the same place and then gets annoyed when I find him. I don't say anything, just make my way back to the stool, my flip-flops splashing my calves with cold water. This happens every day. This is all that happens.

'You took your time there,' Eric says.

Did I? Maybe a second longer than usual. 'Didn't want to spoil his fun.'

Eric smiles against his better judgement and shakes his head to show he disapproves. Before working here with me since the nursing home's birth, Eric had a previous Mitch Buchannon lifeguard experience in Miami. His mother on her deathbed brought him back home to Ireland and then his mother surviving has made him stay. He jokes that she will outlive him, though I can sense a nervousness on his part that this will indeed be the case. I think he's waiting for her to die so that he can begin living, and the fear as he nears fifty is that that will never happen. To cope with his self-imposed pause on his life, I think he pretends he's still in Miami; though he's delusional, I sometimes envy his ability to pretend he is in a place far more exotic than this. I think he walks to the sound of maracas in his head. He is one of the happiest people I know because of it. His hair is Sun-In orange, and his skin is a similar colour. He doesn't go on any traditional 'dates' from one end of the year to the other, saving himself up for the month in January when he disappears to Thailand. He returns whistling, with the greatest smile on his face. I don't want to know what he does there but I know that his hopes are that when his mother dies, every day will be like Thailand. I like him and

CECELIA AHERN

I consider him my friend. Five days a week in this place has meant I've told him more than I've even told myself.

'Doesn't it strike you that the one person I save every day is a person who doesn't even want to live? Doesn't it make you feel completely redundant?'

'There are plenty of things that do, but not that.' He bends over to pick up a bunch of wet grey hair clogging the drains, which looks like a drowned rat, and he holds on to it, shaking the water out of it, not appearing to feel the repulsion that I do. 'Is that how you're feeling?'

Yes. Though it shouldn't. It shouldn't matter if the man I'm saving doesn't want his life to be saved, shouldn't the point be that I'm saving him? But I don't reply. He's my supervisor, not my therapist, I shouldn't question saving people while on duty as a lifeguard. He may live in an alternative world in his head but he's not stupid.

'Why don't you take a coffee break?' he offers, and hands me my coffee mug, the other hand still holding the drowned rat ball of pubic hair.

I like my job very much but lately I've been antsy. I don't know why and I don't know what exactly I'm expecting to happen in my life, or what I'm hoping will happen. I have no particular dreams or goals. I wanted to get married and I did. I wanted to have children and I do. I want to be a lifeguard and I am. Though isn't that the meaning of antsy? Thinking there are ants on you when there aren't.

'Eric, what does antsy mean?'

'Um. Restless, I think, uneasy.'

'Has it anything to do with ants?'

He frowns.

'I thought it was when you think there are ants crawling all over you, so you start to feel like this,' I shudder a bit. 'But there aren't any ants on you at all.'

He taps his lip. 'You know what, I don't know. Is it important?'

I think about it. It would mean that I think there is something wrong with my life because there actually *is* something wrong with my life or that there is something wrong with me. But it's just a feeling, and there actually isn't. There *not* being something wrong would be the preferred solution.

What's wrong, Sabrina? Aidan's been asking a lot lately. In the same way that constantly asking someone if they're angry will eventually make them angry.

Nothing's wrong. But is it nothing, or is it something? Or is it really that it *is* nothing, *everything* is just nothing? Is that the problem? Everything is nothing? I avoid Eric's gaze and concentrate instead on the pool rules, which irritate me so I look away. You see, there it is, that antsy thing.

'I can check it out,' he says, studying me.

To escape his gaze I get a coffee from the machine in the corridor and pour it into my mug. I lean against the wall in the corridor and think about our conversation, think about my life. Coffee finished, no conclusions reached, I return to the pool and I am almost crushed in the corridor by a stretcher being wheeled by at top speed by two paramedics, with a wet Mary Kelly on top of it, her white and blue-veined bumpy legs like Stilton, an oxygen mask over her face.

I hear myself say 'No way!' as they push by me.

When I get into the small lifeguard office I see Eric, sitting down in complete shock, his shell tracksuit dripping wet, his orange Sun-In hair slicked back from the pool water.

'What the hell?'

'I think she had a . . . I mean, I don't know, but, it might

17

have been a heart attack. Jesus.' Water drips from his orange pointy nose.

'But I was only gone five minutes.'

'I know, it happened the second you walked out. I jammed on the emergency cord, pulled her out, did mouth-to-mouth, and they were here before I knew it. They responded fast. I let them in the fire exit.'

I swallow, the jealousy rising. 'You gave her mouth-to-mouth?'

'Yeah. She wasn't breathing. But then she did. Coughed up a load of water.'

I look at the clock. 'It wasn't even five minutes.'

He shrugs, still stunned.

I look at the pool, to the clock. Mr Daly is sitting on the edge of the pool, looking after the ghost of the stretcher with envy. It was four and a half minutes.

'You had to dive in? Pull her out? Do mouth-to-mouth?'

'Yeah. Yeah. Look, don't beat yourself up about it, Sabrina, you couldn't have got to her any faster than I did.'

'You had to pull the emergency cord?'

He looks at me in confusion over this.

I've never had to pull the cord. Never. Not even in trials. Eric did that. I feel jealousy and anger bubbling to the surface, which is quite an unusual feeling. This happens at home – an angry mother irritated with her boys has lost the plot plenty of times – but never in public. In public I suppress it, especially at work when it is directed at my supervisor. I'm a measured, rational human being; people like me don't lose their temper in public. But I don't suppress the anger now. I let it rise close to the surface. It would feel empowering to let myself go like this if I wasn't so genuinely frustrated, so completely irritated.

To put it into perspective here is how I'm feeling: seven

years working here. That's two thousand three hundred and ten days. Eleven thousand five hundred and fifty hours. Minus nine months, six months and three months for maternity leave. In all of that time I've sat on the stool and watched the, often, empty pool. No mouth-to-mouth, no dramatic dives. Not once. Not counting Mr Daly. Not counting the assistance of leg or foot cramps. Nothing. I sit on the stool, sometimes I stand, and I watch the oversized ticking clock and the list of pool rules. No running, no jumping, no diving, no pushing, no shouting, no nothing . . . all the things you're not allowed to do in this room, all negative, almost as though it's mocking me. No lifesaving. I'm always on alert, it's what I'm trained to do, but nothing ever happens. And the very second I take an unplanned coffee break I miss a possible heart attack, a definite near-drowning and the emergency cord being pulled.

'It's not fair,' I say.

'Now come on, Sabrina, you were in there like a shot when Eliza stepped on the piece of glass.'

'It wasn't glass. Her varicose vein ruptured.'

'Well. You got there fast.'

It is always above the water that I struggle, that I can't breathe. It is above the water that I feel like I'm drowning.

I throw my coffee mug hard against the wall.

19

3

PLAYING WITH MARBLES

Conqueror

My neck is being squeezed so tightly I start to see black spots before my eyes. I'd tell him so but I can't speak, his arm is wrapped tight around my throat. I can't breathe. I can't breathe. I'm small for my age and they tease me for it. They call me Tick but Mammy says to use what I have. I'm small but I'm smart. With a burst of energy, I start to shake myself around, and my older brother Angus has to fight hard to hold on.

'Jesus, Tick,' Angus says, and he grips me tighter.

Can't breathe, can't breathe.

'Let him go, Angus,' Hamish says. 'Get back to the game.'

'The little fucker's a cheat, I'm not playing with him.'

'I'm not a cheat!' I want to shout, but I can't. I can't breathe.

'He's not a cheat,' Hamish says on my behalf. 'He's just better than you.' Hamish is the eldest, at sixteen. He's watching from the front steps of our house. This statement is a lot, coming from him. He's cool as fuck. He's smoking a cigarette. If Mammy knew this she'd slap the head off him, but she can't see him now, she's inside the house with the midwife, which is why we've all been turfed out here for the day until it's over.

'Say that again,' Angus challenges Hamish.

'Or what?'

Or nothing. Angus wouldn't touch Hamish, older than him by only two years but infinitely cooler. None of us would. He's tough and everyone knows it and he's even started hanging out with Eddie Sullivan, nicknamed The Barber, and his gang at the barbershop. They're the ones giving him the cigarettes. And money too, but I don't know what for. Mammy's worried about him but she needs the money so doesn't ask questions. Hamish likes me the most. Some nights he wakes me up and I've to get dressed and we sneak out to the streets we're not allowed to play on. I'm not allowed to tell Mammy. We play marbles. I'm ten but I look younger; you wouldn't think I play as well as I do, most people don't, so Hamish hustles them. He's winning a packet and he gives me caramels on the way home so I don't tell. He doesn't need to buy me off but I don't tell him that, I like the caramels.

I play marbles in my sleep, I play when I should be doing homework, I play when Father Fuckface puts me in the dark room, I play it in my head when Mammy is giving out to me, so I don't have to listen. My fingers are moving all the time as if I'm shooting and I've built up a good collection. I have to hide them from my brothers though, my best ones anyway. They're nowhere near as good at playing as me, and they'd lose my marbles.

We hear Mammy bellow like an animal upstairs and Angus loosens his grip on me a bit. Enough for wriggle room. Everyone tenses up at the sound of Mammy. It's not new to us but no one likes it. It's not natural to hear anyone sound like that. Mattie opens the door and steps out even whiter than usual.

He looks at Angus. 'Let him go.'

Angus does and I can finally breathe. I start coughing. There's only one other person Angus doesn't mess with and that's our stepdad, Mattie. Mattie Doyle always means business.

Mattie glares at Hamish smoking. I get ready for Mattie to punch him – those two are always at it – but he doesn't.

Instead he says, 'Got one spare?'

Hamish smiles, the one that goes all the way to his green eyes. Daddy's green eyes. But he doesn't answer.

Mattie doesn't like the pause. 'Fuck you.' He slaps him over the head, and Hamish laughs at him, liking that he made him lose his temper. He won. 'I'm going to the pub. One of you come get me when it's out.'

'You'll probably hear it from there,' Duncan says.

Mattie laughs, but looks a bit scared.

'Are none of you keeping an eye on him?' He gestures to the toddler crouched in the dirt. We all look at Bobby. He's the youngest, at two. He's sitting in the muck, covered in it, even his mouth, and he's eating grass.

'He always eats grass,' Tommy says. 'Nothing we can do about it.'

'Are you a cow or wha'?' Mattie asks.

'Quack quack,' Bobby says, and we all laugh.

'Fuck sake, will someone ever teach him his animal sounds?' Mattie says, smiling. 'Right, Da's off to the pub, be good, Bobby.' Mattie rustles Tommy's head. 'Keep an eye on him, son.'

'Bye, Mattie,' Bobby says.

'It's Da, to you,' Mattie says, face going a bit red with anger.

It drives Mattie mad when Bobby calls him Mattie, but it's not Bobby's fault, he's used to us all calling Mattie by his name, he's not our da, but Bobby doesn't understand, he thinks we're all the same. Only Mattie's first boy, Tommy, calls him Da. There's Doyles and Boggs in this family and we all know the difference.

'Let's get back to the game,' Duncan says as Mammy screams again.

'He's not allowed to play unless he takes his turn again,' Angus says angrily.

'Fine, he will, calm down,' Hamish says.

'Hey!' I protest. 'I didn't cheat.'

Hamish winks at me. 'You can show them.'

I sigh. I'm ten, Duncan is twelve, Angus is fourteen and Hamish is sixteen. The two Doyle boys, Tommy and Bobby, are five and two. With three older brothers I'm always having to prove myself, and even when I'm better than them, which I am at marbles and they can't stand it, then I have to work even harder because they think I'm a cheat. I'm the one who teaches them the new games I've read about in my books. I'm better than them. They all hate it but it drives Angus mental. He hits me whenever he loses. Hamish hates losing too but he's figured out how to use me.

We're playing Conqueror; me, Duncan and Angus. Angus wouldn't let Tommy play because he's the worst, he's so bad he just ruins the game. When my older brothers aren't around I teach Tommy how to play; I like doing that, even though he's diabolical. That's the word Hamish uses for everything. I use my worst marbles, just the clearies for him because he chips them and everything. Tommy's sitting on the steps away from Hamish. He's afraid of Hamish. Tommy knows that Hamish and his da don't get along so he thinks he has to defend his da when he's not there. He's only five but he's a tough little shit, scrawny and pale like his da too. The lads call him Bottle-washer because he's so skinny and wiry.

What happened to put me in the headlock was that Angus threw the first marble, then Duncan shot his marble at Angus's. It hit and that's why Angus got mad in the first place. Duncan captured Angus's marble then threw another to restart the game. I hit Duncan's, captured his then threw another to restart.

Angus threw his taw and missed mine.

Duncan aimed at Angus's corkscrew, not because it was closer but because I know he could tell Angus was already getting angry and wanted to wind him up. Anyway he missed and it was my turn. I had two targets; I could have chosen Duncan's opaque, which I don't much want because everyone has them – that's marbles that are just one colour – or Angus's Popeye corkscrew, which I've had my eye on for a long time. Angus says he won it in a game but I think he must have stolen it from Francis's corner shop. I've never seen anyone with one like that. I've only ever seen a picture of one in my marble book, so I know that his is a three-colour special called a snake corkscrew. It's a double-twist and has a green-and-transparent clear with filaments of opaque white. It has tiny clear bubbles inside. I found it in his drawer a few days ago and he caught me snooping and kicked me in the balls to let it go. I didn't drop it though, I know better than to let it get scratched, but watching him play with it hurts more than the kick in the goonies did. He should be keeping it in a box, safe so it doesn't get ruined.

I decided to do a move I'd been working on and impress them all by putting a spin on my marble and hitting both marbles in the one throw. I threw my taw and it hit Duncan's opaque first like I planned, then Tommy shouted and they all looked at Bobby who had a snail in his mouth, shell and all. Angus rushed over to grab it from him and chucked it across the road. He opened Bobby's mouth wide.

'The snail is missing from the shell. Did you eat it, Bobby?'

Bobby didn't answer, just waited for a clatter, his big blue eyes wide. Bobby's the only blond. He gets away with murder because of those blue eyes and blond hair. Even Hamish doesn't hit him half as much as he wants to. But anyway when they were all busy wondering about where the slug part of the snail went, nobody was looking when my taw hit Angus's marble as well, which meant that I could capture both marbles in the one throw. They looked back at me to see me holding two of them in my hand, and that's when Angus accused me of cheating and wrapped me in a headlock.

Free now of the headlock I have to respond to the cheating allegations by trying to repeat the move, which should be fine, I know I can do it, but I can't when they think that I'm a cheat. If I can't do it again it proves to them that I cheated. Hamish winks at me. I know he knows that I can do it, but if I don't win he might not take me out tonight. My hands start to sweat.

Mammy screams again and Tommy's eyes widen.

'Baby?' Bobby asks.

'Nearly there, pal, nearly there,' Hamish says, rolling up another cigarette, cool as fuck. Seriously, when I grow up I want to be just like him.

Mrs Lynch's door opens – she's our next-door neighbour – and she comes out with her daughter, Lucy. Lucy's face is already scarlet when she sees Hamish. Lucy is holding a tray with a mountain of sandwiches all piled up, I can see strawberry jam, and Mrs Lynch has diluted orange in a jug.

We all pile on top of the food.

'Thanks, Mrs Lynch,' we all say, mouths full and devouring the sandwiches. With Mammy in the throes of it we haven't eaten since dinner yesterday.

Hamish winks at Lucy and she kind of giggles and runs inside. I saw them together late one night, Hamish had one hand up her top and the other up her skirt, and she'd one leg wrapped around him like a baby monkey, her thick white thigh practically glowing in the dark.

'That mammy of yours will keep going till she gets that girl of hers, won't she?' Mrs Lynch says, sitting down on the step.

'I've a feeling it's a girl this time,' Hamish says. 'Her bump's different.'

Hamish is serious; for all his trouble he notices things, sees things that none of the rest of us do.

'I think you're right,' Mrs Lynch agrees. 'It's high up all right.'

'It'll be nice to have a girl around,' Hamish says. 'No more of these smelly bastards to annoy me.'

'Ah, she'll be the boss of you all, wait'll you see,' says Mrs Lynch. 'Like my Lucy.'

'She sure is the boss of Hamish,' Angus mutters, and gets a boot in the stomach from Hamish. Chewed-up jam sandwich fires out of his mouth and he's momentarily winded and I'm glad: payback for my headlock.

Hamish's green eyes are glowing, he really does look like he wants a girl. He looks like a big softy thinking about it.

Mammy wails again.

'Won't be long now,' Hamish says.

'She's doing a fine job,' Mrs Lynch says, and she looks like she's in pain just listening. Maybe she's remembering and I feel sick thinking of a baby coming out of her.

The midwife starts chanting, as if Mammy's in a boxing match and she's the coach. Mammy's squealing like she's a pig being chased around with a carving knife.

'Final push,' Hamish says.

Mrs Lynch looks impressed with Hamish's knowledge. As the eldest he's sat through this five times; whether he remembers them all or not, he's definitely learned the way.

'Okay, let's finish this before she comes out,' Angus says, jumping up and wiping his jam face on his sleeve.

I know Angus wants to prove me wrong in front of everyone. He knows Hamish likes me and just because he's too weak to hit Hamish, he uses me to get at him instead. Hurting me is like hurting Hamish. And Hamish feels that way too. It's good for me but bad for the person who treats me bad: last week Hamish punched out a fella's front tooth for not picking me for his football team. I didn't even want to play football.

I stand up and take my place. Concentrating hard, my heart beating in my chest, my palms sweaty. I want that corkscrew.

The midwife is screaming about seeing the baby's head. Mammy's sounds are terrifying now. The piggy's being slashed.

'Good girl, good girl,' Mrs Lynch says, chewing on her nail and rocking back and forth on the step, as if Mammy can hear her. 'Nearly over, love. You're there. You're there.'

I throw the taw. It hits Duncan's marble just like I planned and it heads to Angus's. I want that corkscrew.

'A girl!' the midwife calls out.

Hamish stands up, about to punch the air but he stops himself.

My marble travels to Angus's corkscrew. It misses but nobody's looking, nobody's seen it happen. Everyone is frozen in place, Mrs Lynch goes still. Waiting; they're all waiting for the baby to cry.

Hamish puts his head in his hands. I check again. Nobody is looking at me, or my taw, which went straight past Angus's, it didn't even touch it.

I take a tiny step to the right but they're still not looking. I reach out my foot and push my marble back a bit so that it's touching Angus's Popeye corkscrew. My heart is beating wildly, I can't believe I'm doing it, but if I get away with it then I'll have the corkscrew, it'll actually be mine.

All of a sudden there's a wail, but it's not the baby, it's Mammy.

Hamish runs inside, Duncan follows. Tommy grabs Bobby from the dirt and carries him into the house. Angus looks down at the ground and sees his marble and my marble, touching.

His face is deadly serious. 'Okay. You win.' Then he follows the boys inside.

I pick up the green corkscrew and examine it, finally happy to have it in my hand, part of my collection. These are incredibly rare. My happiness is short-lived though as my adrenaline begins to wear off and it sinks in.

There's no baby girl. There's no baby at all. And I'm a cheat.

4

POOL RULES

No Jumping

'Sabrina, are you okay?' Eric asks me from across his desk.

'Yes,' I say, keeping my voice measured while feeling anything but. I have just fired my mug at the concrete wall because I missed a near-drowning. 'I thought there would be more pieces.' We both look to the mug sitting on his desk. The handle has come off and the rim is chipped, but that's it. 'My mum fired a teapot up at the ceiling once. There were definitely more pieces.'

Eric looks at it, studies it. 'I suppose it's the way it hit the wall. The angle or something.'

We consider that in silence.

'I think you should go home,' he says suddenly. 'Take the day off. Enjoy the solar eclipse everybody's talking about. Come back in on Monday.'

'Okay.'

Home for me is a three-bed end of terrace, where I live with my husband, Aidan, and our three boys. Aidan works in Eircom broadband support, though it never seems to work in our house. We've been married for seven years. We met in Ibiza when we were contestants in a competition that took place on the bar counter of a nightclub to see who could lick cream off a complete stranger's torso the quickest. He was the torso, I was the licker. We won. Don't for a moment think that was out of character for me. I was nineteen, and fourteen people took part in front of an audience of thousands, and we won a free bottle of tequila, which we subsequently drank on the beach, while we had sex. It would have been out of character not to. Aidan was a stranger to me then, but he's a stranger to that man now, unrecognisable from that cocky teenager with the pierced ear and the shaved eyebrow. I suppose we both changed. Aidan doesn't even like the beach now, says the sand gets everywhere. And I'm trying to stay off dairy.

It is rare that I find myself alone in the house; in fact I can't remember the last time that happened, no kids around asking me to do something every two seconds. I don't know what to do with myself so I sit in the empty silent kitchen looking around. It's ten a.m. and the day has barely started. I make myself a cup of tea, just for something to do, but don't drink it. I stop myself just in time from putting the teabags in the fridge. I do things like this all the time. I look at the pile of washing and ironing but can't be bothered. I realise I've been holding my breath and I exhale.

There are things that I need to do all the time. Things that I never have the time for in my carefully ordered daily routine. Now I have some time – the whole day – but I don't know where to start.

My mobile rings, saving me from indecision, and it's my dad's hospital.

'Hello?' I say, feeling the tightness in my chest.

'Hi, Sabrina, it's Lea.' My dad's favourite nurse. 'We just

got a delivery of five boxes for Fergus. Did you arrange it?'

'No,' I frown.

'Oh. Well, I haven't shown them to him yet, they're sitting in reception, I wanted to wait to speak with you first, just in case, you know, there's something in there that might confuse him.'

'Yes, you're right, thanks. Don't worry. I'll come get them now, I'm free.'

And that's what always seems to happen. Whenever I get a minute to myself away from work and the kids, Dad is the other person who fills it. I arrive at the hospital thirty minutes later and see the boxes piled in the corner of reception. Upon seeing them I know immediately where they've come from and I'm raging. These are the boxes of Dad's belongings that I packed after Dad's home was sold. Mum had been storing them, but she's obviously chosen not to any more. I don't understand why she sent them here and not to me.

Last year my dad suffered a severe stroke, which has led to his living in a long-term care facility, giving him the kind of skilled care that I know I could not have given with three young boys – Charlie at seven, Fergus at five and Alfie at three years old – and a job. Mum certainly wouldn't have taken on the role either as she and Dad are divorced, and have been separated since I was fifteen. Though right now they're getting along better than they ever have, and I even think Mum enjoys her fortnightly visits with him.

There are those who insist that stress does not cause strokes, but it happened during a time when Dad was the most stressed in his life, coping with the fallout of the financial crisis. He worked for a venture capital company. He scrambled for a while, trying to find new clients, trying to win old ones back, and all the while watching lives fall apart and feeling responsible for that, but it wasn't sustainable. Eventually he found a new job, in car sales, was trying to move on, but his blood pressure was high, his weight had ballooned, he smoked heavily, didn't exercise, and drank too much. I'm no doctor, but he did all of these things because he was stressed, and then he had a stroke.

His speech isn't easy to understand and he's in a wheelchair, though he's working on his walking. He's lost an enormous amount of weight, and seems like a completely different man to the man he was in the years leading up to his stroke. The stroke caused some memory problems, which enrages Mum. He seems to forget all the hurt he caused her. He has been able to wipe the slate clean of all of their problems and arguments, their heartache and his misdemeanours – of which there were many – throughout their marriage. He comes out of it smelling of roses.

'He gets to live like none of it happened, like he doesn't have to feel guilty or apologise for anything,' Mum regularly rants. She was obviously planning on him feeling bad for the rest of his life and he went and ruined it. He went and forgot it all. But even though she rants about the Fergus before the stroke, she visits him regularly and they talk like the couple they both wish they'd been. About what's happening in the news, about the garden, the seasons, the weather. It's comforting chat. I think what angers her most is the fact that she likes him now. This sweet, caring, gentle, patient man is a man she could have remained married to.

What has happened to Dad has been difficult, but we haven't lost him. He is still alive and in fact what we lost was the other side of him, the distant, detached, sometimes prickly side of him that was harder to love. The one that pushed people away. The one that wanted to be alone, but have us at the end of his fingertips, just in case, for when he wanted us. He is quite content where he is now; he gets along with the nurses, has made friends, and I spend more time with him now than I ever have, visiting him with Aidan and the boys on Sundays.

I never know what exactly Dad has forgotten until I bring something up and I watch that now all too familiar fog pass over his eyes, that vacant look as he tries to process what I've just said with his collection of memories and experiences, only to find it coming back empty, as if they don't tally. I understand why Nurse Lea didn't bring the boxes directly to him; an overload of too many things that he can't remember would surely upset him. There are ways to deal with those moments, I gently sidestep them, move on from them quickly as though they never happened, or pretend that I've gotten the details wrong myself. It's not because it upsets him – most of the time it goes by without drama, as if he's oblivious to it – but it upsets me.

There are more boxes than I remember and, too impatient to wait until I get home, I stand there in the corridor and use a key to pierce through the tape on the top of the box and slice it open. I fold back the box, curious to see what's inside. I expect photo albums, or wedding cards. Something sentimental that, far from conjuring beautiful memories, starts Mum spouting about everything that was taken from her by her own husband. The dreams that were shattered, the promises that were broken.

Instead I find a folder containing pages covered in hand-writing: my dad's looping swirling letters, that remind me of school sick notes and birthday cards. At the top of the page it says *Marbles Inventory*. Beneath the folder are tins, pouches and boxes, some in bubble wrap, others in tissue paper.

I open some of the lids. Inside each tin or box are deliciously colourful candy-like balls of shining glass. I look at them in utter shock and amazement. I had no idea my dad liked marbles. I had no idea my dad knew the slightest thing about marbles. If it wasn't for his handwriting in the inventory, I would have thought there was a mistake. It is as if I have opened a box to somebody else's life.

I open the folder and read through the list, which is not as sentimental as it first seemed. It is almost scientific.

The pouches – some velvet, others mesh – and the tin boxes are colour-coded and numbered with stickers, to save confusion, and adhere to the colours on the inventory.

The first on the list is a small velvet pouch of four marbles. The inventory lists them as *Bloodies* and, beside that, *(Allies, Fr. Noel Doyle)*. Opening the pouch, the marbles are smaller than any others I can see offhand and have varying red swirls, but Dad has gone into detail describing them:

Rare Christensen Agate 'Bloodies' have transparent red swirls edged with translucent brown on an opaque white base.

There is a cube box of more bloodies, dating back to 1935 from the Peltier Glass Company. These are appropriately colour-coded red and are listed together with the velvet pouch. I scoop a few marbles into my hands and roll them around, enjoying the sound of them clicking together, while my mind races at what I've discovered. Pouches, tins, boxes, all containing the most beautiful colours, swirls and spirals, glistening as they catch the light. I lift some out and hold them up to the window, examining the detail inside, the bubbles, the light, utterly enchanted by the complexity within something so small. I flick through the pages quickly:

. . . latticinia core swirls, divided core swirls, solid core swirls, ribbon core swirls, joseph's coat swirls, banded/coreless swirls, peppermint swirls, clambroths, banded opaques, indian, banded lutz, onionskin lutz, ribbon lutz . . .

A myriad of marbles, all of them alien to me. What is even more astonishing is that in other pages of his handwritten documents he has included a table charting each marble's value depending upon how it measures up in terms of *size, mint, near mint, good, collectable.* It seems that his humble box of bloodies are worth $150–$250.

All of the prices are listed in US dollars. Some are valued at fifty dollars or one hundred, while the two-inch ribbon lutz has been priced at $4,500 in mint condition, $2,250 in near mint, $1,250 in good condition and collectable is $750. I know next to nothing about their condition – all of them appear perfect to me, nothing cracked or chipped – but there are hundreds of them packed away, and pages and pages of inventory. What Dad appears to have here are thousands of dollars' worth of marbles.

I stop and think. All around me are the sounds and smells of the care home and it transports me from the parallel marble world back to reality. I was worried about him being able to pay for his hospital costs but if his pricing is correct, then he has his nest egg right here. I'm always worried about those bills. We have no way of knowing when he might need another operation or new medicine, or a new physio. It's always changing, the bills are always climbing and the proceeds from the sale of his apartment didn't go far after paying his mortgage and numerous debts. None of us had known that he was in such a bad financial state.

His writing is impeccable, a beautiful flowing script; he hasn't made one mistake and if he did I imagine he started the page over. It is written with love, it has taken great time and dedication, research and knowledge. That's it: it's written by an expert. It's the writing of another man, not the one who now grasps the pen with great difficulty, but neither does it fit with the father I knew, whose only hobby seemed to be watching and talking about football. Wanting to take my time to go through the boxes at home, I pack everything away again and Gerry, the porter, helps me carry them to my car. But before locking them in the boot, I hesitate and take out the small bag of red marbles.

Dad is sitting in the lounge, drinking a cup of tea and watching *Bargain Hunt*. He watches the show every day: people searching for items at markets and then trying to auction them for as much as possible. Maybe there have been hints of his passion all the way along and I missed them. I think of the inventory and wonder if I should go back for it. As I watch him staring intently at the pricing of these old objects, I wonder if in fact he does remember exactly what is in those boxes after all. He sees me before I have time to think about it any further and so I go to him, to his smiling face. It breaks my heart how happy he is to receive visitors, not because he's lonely but because he could often be so irritated by others before, unless it was to convince them to buy something from him, and he now can't get enough of people's company, for nothing in return.

'Good morning.'

'Ah, to what do I owe this pleasure?' he asks. 'No work today?'

'Eric let me off early,' I explain diplomatically. 'And Lea called me. She said it was an emergency, that you were revving up the inmates, trying to organise a breakout again.'

He laughs, then he looks down at my hands and his laughter stops immediately. I'm holding the bag of red marbles. Something passes on his face. A look I've never seen before. As quickly as it arrived, it's gone again and he's smiling at me, the confusion back.

'What's that you've got there?'

I open my hand, reveal the red marbles in the mesh bag.

He just stares at them. I wait for him to say something but nothing comes. He barely blinks.

'Dad?'

Nothing.

'Dad?' I put my free hand on his arm, gently.

'Yes,' he looks at me, troubled.

I loosen the drawstrings on the mesh purse and roll them into the palm of my hand. As I move the marbles in my hand they roll and click together. 'Do you want to hold them?'

He stares at them again, intently, as though trying to figure them out. I want to know what's going on inside his head. Too much? Everything? Nothing? I know that feeling. I watch for that sliver of recognition again. It doesn't come. Just bother and irritation, perhaps that he can't remember what he wants to remember. I stuff the marbles in my pocket quickly and change the subject, trying to hide my disappointment from him.

But I saw it. Like a flicker of a flame. The ruffle of a feather. The flash of the sea as the sun hits it. Something brief and then gone, but there. When he saw the marbles first, he was a different man, with a face I've never seen.

5

PLAYING WITH MARBLES

Picking Plums

I'm home from school, a fever, the first and only day of school I've ever missed. I hate school; I would have wanted this any day at all in the whole entire year. Any day but today. The funeral was yesterday – well, it wasn't a proper one with a priest, but Mattie's pal is an undertaker and he found out where they were burying our baby sister, in the same coffin as an old woman who had just died in the hospital. When we got to the graveyard, the old woman's family were finishing up their funeral so we had to wait around. Ma was happy it was an old woman she was being buried with and not an old man, or any man. The old woman was a mother, and a grandmother. Mammy spoke to one of her daughters who said that her ma would look after the baby. Uncle Joseph and Aunty Sheila said all the prayers at our ceremony. Mattie doesn't say prayers, I don't think he knows any, and Mammy couldn't speak.

The priest called round to the house beforehand and tried to talk Mammy out of making a show of herself by

41

going to the grave. Mammy had a shouting match with him and Mattie grabbed the brandy from the priest's hand and told him to get the fuck out of his house. Hamish helped Mattie get rid of them, the only time I've seen them on the same side. I saw the way everyone looked at Mammy as we walked down the street to the graveyard, all dressed in black. They looked at her like she was crazy, like our baby sister was never really a baby at all, just because she didn't take a breath when she came out. Even though they're not supposed to, the midwife had let Mammy hold her baby after she was born. She held her for an hour, then when the midwife started to get a bit angry and tried to take her from Mammy, Hamish stepped in. Mattie wasn't there and he took over, he lifted the baby out of Mammy's arms and carried her down the stairs. He kissed her before he gave her back to the midwife, who took her away for ever.

'She was alive inside of me,' I heard Mammy say to the priest, but I don't think he liked hearing her say that. He looked like it was a bit disgusting for him to think of things living inside of her. But she did it anyway, made up her own funeral at the graveyard, and it was cold and grey and it rained the whole time. My shoes got so wet, my socks and feet were soaking and numb. I sneezed all day, couldn't breathe out of my nose last night, the lads kept thumping me to stop me snoring and I spent the whole night going from hot to cold, shivering then sweating, feeling cold when I was sweating, feeling hot when I was cold. Crazy dreams: Da and Mattie fighting, and Father Murphy shouting at me about dead babies and hitting me, and my brothers stealing my marbles, and Mammy in black howling with grief. But that part was real.

Even though I feel like my skin is on fire and everything

around me is swirling, I don't call Mammy. I stay in bed, tossing and turning, sometimes crying because I'm so confused and my skin is sore. Mammy brought me a boiled egg this morning and put a cold cloth on my head. She sat beside me, dressed in black, still with a big tummy looking like she has a baby in there, staring into space but not saying anything. It's kind of like when Da died but this is different; she was angry at Da, this time she's sad.

Usually Mammy never stops moving. She's always cleaning, cleaning Bobby's nappies, the house, banging sheets and rugs, cooking, preparing food. She never stops, always banging around the place, us always in her way and her moving us out of the way with her legs and feet, pushing us aside like she's in a field and we're long grass. Now and then she stops moving to straighten her back and groan, before going back to it again. But today the house is silent and I'm not used to that. Usually we're all shouting, fighting, laughing, talking; even at night there's a child crying, or Mammy singing to it, or Mattie bumping into things when he comes home drunk and swearing. I hear things that I've never heard before like creaks and moaning pipes, but there's no sound from Mammy. This worries me.

I get out of bed, my legs shaking and feeling weak like I have never walked before, and I hang on tight to the bannister as I go downstairs, every floorboard creaking beneath my bare feet. I go into the living room, joined on to the kitchen, tiny at the back of the house like they forgot it and added it on, and it's empty. She's not here. Not in the kitchen, not in the garden, not in the living room. I'm about to leave when I suddenly see her in black sitting in an armchair in the corner of the living room that only Mattie ever sits in; so still I nearly missed her. She's staring into space, her eyes red like she hasn't stopped crying since yesterday. I've never seen her so still. I don't remember it ever being just me and her before, just the two of us. I've never had Mammy to myself. Thinking about it makes me nervous: what do I say to Mammy when there's nobody around to hear me, to see me, to react, to tease, to goad, to impress? What do I say to Mammy when I'm not using her to get a rise out of someone else, to tell on someone, or know if what I'm saying is right or wrong because of their reactions?

I'm about to leave the room when I think of something, something I want to ask, that I would only ask if it was just me and her, with no one else around.

'Hi,' I say.

She looks over at me, surprised, like she's had a fright, then she smiles. 'Hi, love. How's your head? Do you need more water?'

'No thanks.'

She smiles.

'I want to ask you a question. If you don't mind.'

She beckons me in and I come closer and stand before her, fidgeting with my fingers.

'What is it?' she asks gently.

'Do you . . . do you think she's with Da?'

This seems to take her by surprise. Her eyes fill and she struggles to talk. I think if the others were here I wouldn't have asked such a stupid question. I've gone and upset her, the very thing Mattie told us not to do. I need to get myself out of it before she yells or, worse, cries.

'I know he's not her da, but he loved you, and you're her mammy. And he loved children. I don't remember loads about him but I remember that. Green eyes and he always played with us. Chased us. Wrestled us. I remember him laughing. He was skinny but he had huge hands. Some other das never did that, so I know he liked us. I think she's in heaven and that he's minding her and so I don't think you need to worry about her.'

'Oh, Fergus, love,' she says, opening her arms as tears run down her face. 'Come here to me.'

I go into her arms and she hugs me so tight I nearly can't breathe but am afraid to say. She rocks me saying, 'My boy, my boy,' over and over again, and I think I might have said the right thing after all.

When she pulls away I say, 'Can I ask you another question?'

She nods.

'Why did you call her Victoria?'

Her face creases again, in pain, but she composes herself and even smiles. 'I haven't told anyone why.'

'Oh. Sorry.'

'No, pet, it's just that nobody asked. Come here and I'll tell you,' she says, and even though I'm too old, I squeeze on to her lap, half on the armchair, half on her. 'I felt different with her. A different kind of bump. I said to Mattie, "I feel like a plum." Says he, "We'll call her Plum, so."'

'Plum!' I laugh.

She nods and wipes her tears again. 'It got me thinking about my grandma's house. We used to visit her: me, Sheila and Paddy. She had apple trees, pears, blackberries, and she had two plum trees. I loved those plum trees because they were all she talked about, I think they were all she thought about – she wouldn't let those trees beat her.' She gives a little laugh and even though I don't get the joke, I laugh too. 'I think she thought it was exotic, that growing plums made her exotic, when really she was plain, plain as can be, like any of us. She'd make plum pies and I loved baking them with her. We stayed with her on my birthday every year, so every year my birthday cake was a plum pie.'

'Mmm,' I say, licking my lips. 'I've never had plum pie.'

'No,' she says, surprised. 'I've never baked it for you. She grew Opal plums, but they weren't reliable because the bullfinches ate the fruit buds in winter. They used to strip those branches clean and Nana would be crazy, running around the garden swatting them with her tea cloth. Sometimes she'd get us to stand by the tree all day just scaring them away; me, Sheila and Paddy, standing around like scarecrows.'

I laugh at that image of them.

'She gave the Opal more attention because it tasted better and it grew larger, almost twice the size of the other tree's plums, but the Opal made her angrier and didn't deliver every year. My favourite plum tree was the other tree, the Victoria plum. It was smaller but it always delivered and the bullfinches stayed away from that one more. To me, it was the sweetest . . .' Her smile fades again and she looks away. 'Well, now.'

'I know a marble game called Picking Plums,' I say.

'Do you now?' she asks. 'Don't you have a marble game for every occasion?' She prods at me with her finger in my tickly bits and I laugh.

'Do you want to play?'

'Why not!' she says, surprised at herself.

I'm in such shock I run up the stairs faster than I ever have to get the marbles. Once downstairs she's still in the chair, daydreaming. I set up the game, explaining as I go.

I can't draw on the floor so I use a shoelace to mark a line and I place a row of marbles with a gap the width of two marbles in between. I use a skipping rope to mark a line on the other side of the room. The idea is to stand behind the line and take it in turns to shoot at the line of marbles.

'So these are the plums,' I say to her, pointing at the line of marbles, feeling such excitement that I have her attention, that she's all mine, that she's listening to me talking about marbles, that she's possibly going to play marbles, that nobody else can steal her attention away. All aches and pains from my fever are gone in the distraction and hopefully hers are too. 'You have to shoot your marble at the plums and if you hit it out of line you get the plum.'

She laughs. 'This is so silly, Fergus.' But she does it and she has fun, scowling when she misses and celebrating when she wins. I've never seen Mammy play like this, or punch the air in victory when she wins. It's the best moment I've ever spent with her in my whole life. We play the game until all the plums are picked and for once I'm hoping I miss, because I don't want it to end. When we hear voices at the door, the shouting and name-calling as my brothers return from school, I scurry for the marbles on the floor.

'Back to bed, you!' She ruffles my hair and returns to the kitchen.

I don't tell the others what me and Mammy talked about and I don't tell them we played marbles together. I want it to be between me and her.

And in the week that Mammy stops wearing black and bakes us plum pie for dessert, I don't tell anybody why. One thing I learned about carrying marbles in my pockets in case Father Murphy locked me in the dark room, and going out with Hamish and pretending to other kids that I've never played marbles before, is that keeping secrets makes me feel powerful.

6

POOL RULES

No Diving

Mid-morning and back home, I lug Dad's boxes into the middle of the living room floor and separate two I already know, boxes of sentimental and important items that we had to keep. I move them aside to make way for the three that are new to me. I'm mystified. Mum and I packed up his entire apartment, but I did not pack these boxes. I make myself a fresh cup of tea and begin emptying the same box I opened earlier, wanting to pick up where I left off. It is peculiar to have time to myself. Taking care and time, I start to go through Dad's inventory.

Latticino core swirls, divided core swirls, ribbon core swirls, Joseph's coat swirls. I take them out and line them up beside their boxes, crouched on the floor like one of my sons with their cars. I push my face up to them, examining the interiors, trying to compare and contrast. I marvel at the colours and detail; some are cloudy, some are clear, some appear to have trapped rainbows inside, while others have mini tornadoes frozen in a moment. Some have a base glass colour and nothing else. Despite being grouped together under these various alien titles I can't tell the difference no matter how hard I try. Absolutely every single one of them is unique and I have to be careful not to mix them up.

The description of each marble boggles my mind too as I try to identify which of the core swirls is the gooseberry, caramel or custard. Which is the 'beach ball' peppermint swirl, which is the one with mica. But I've no doubt Dad knew, he knew them all. Micas, slags, opaques and clearies, some so complex it's as though they house entire galaxies inside, others one single solid colour. Dark, bright, eerie and hypnotic, he has them all.

And then I come across a box that makes me laugh. Dad, who hated animals, who refused every plea for me to get a pet, has an entire collection of what are called 'Sulphides'. Transparent marbles with animal figures inside, like he has his own farmyard within his tiny marbles. Dogs, cats, squirrels and birds. He even has an elephant. The one which stands out the most to me is a clear marble with an angel inside. It's this that I hold and study for some time, straightening my aching back, trying to grasp what I've found, wondering when, what part of his life did this all occur. When we left the house did he watch us drive off and disappear to his 'farmyard animals'? Tend to them privately in his own world. Or was it before I was born? Or was it after he and Mum divorced, filling his solitude with a new hobby?

There is a little empty box, an Akro Agate Company retailer stock box, to be precise, which Dad has valued at a surprising $400–$700. There's even a glass bottle with a marble inside, listed as a Codd bottle and valued at $2,100. It seems he didn't just collect marbles, he also collected their presentation boxes, probably hoping to find the missing pieces of the jigsaw as the years went by. I feel a wave of sadness for him that that won't happen now, that these marbles have been sitting in boxes for a year and he never knew to ask for them because he forgot that they were there.

I line them up, I watch them roll, the movement of colours inside like kaleidoscopes. And then when every inch of my carpet is covered, I sit up, straighten my spine till it clicks. I'm not sure what else to do, but I don't want to put them away again. They look so beautiful lining my floor, like a candy army.

I pick up the inventory and try once more to see if I can identify them myself, playing my own little marble game, and as I do so, I notice that not everything written on the list is on my floor.

I check the box again and it's empty, apart from some mesh bags and boxes which are collectable for their condition alone, despite there being no marbles inside them. I flip the top of the third box open and peer inside, but it's just a load of old newspapers and brochures, nothing like the Aladdin's cave of the first two boxes.

After my thorough search, which I repeat two more times, I can confirm that there are two missing items from the inventory. Allocated turquoise and yellow circular stickers, one is described as an Akro Agate Company box, circa 1930, the original sample case carried by salesmen as they made their calls. Dad has priced it at $7,500–$12,500. The other is what's called World's Best Moons. A Christensen Agate Company original box of twenty-five marbles, listed between $4,000–$7,000. His two most valuable items are gone.

I sit in a kind of stunned silence, until I realise I'm holding my breath and need to exhale.

Dad could have sold them. He went to the trouble of having them valued, so it would make sense for him to have sold them, and the most expensive ones too. He was having money troubles, we know that; perhaps he had to sell his beloved marbles just to get by. But it seems unlikely. Everything has been so well documented and catalogued, he would have made a note of their sale, probably even included the receipt. The two missing collections are written proudly and boldly on the inventory, as present as everything else in the inventory that sits on the floor.

First I'm baffled. Then I'm annoyed that Mum never told me about this collection. That objects held in such regard were packed away and forgotten. I don't have any memory of Dad and marbles, but that's not to say it didn't happen. I know he liked his secrets. I cast my mind back to the man before the stroke and I see pinstripe suits, cigarette smoke. Talk about stock markets and economics, shares up and down, the news or football always on the radio and television, and more recently car-talk. Nothing in my memory banks tells me anything about marbles, and I'm struggling to square this collection – this careful passion – with the man I recall from when I was growing up.

A new thought occurs. I wonder if in fact they're Dad's marbles at all. Perhaps he inherited them. His dad died when he was young, and he had a stepfather, Mattie. But from what I know about Mattie it seems unlikely that he was interested in marbles, or in such careful cataloguing as this. Perhaps they were his father's, or his Uncle Joseph's, and Dad took the time to get them valued and catalogue them. The only thing I am sure of is the inventory being his writing; anything beyond that is a mystery.

There's one person who can help me. I stretch my legs and reach for the phone and call Mum.

'I didn't know Dad had a marble collection,' I say straight away, trying to hide my accusatory tone.

Silence. 'Pardon me?'

'Why did I never know that?'

She laughs a little. 'He has a marble collection now? How sweet. Well, as long as it's making him happy, Sabrina.'

'No. He's not collecting them now. I found them in the boxes that you had delivered to the hospital today.' Also an accusatory tone.

'Oh.' A heavy sigh.

'We agreed that you would store them for him. Why did you send them to the hospital?'

Though I didn't recognise the marbles, I do recognise some of the other boxes' contents as items we packed away from Dad's apartment before putting it on the market. I still feel guilty that we had to do this, but we needed to raise as much money as possible for his rehabilitation. We tried to keep all the precious memories safe, like his lucky football shirt, his photographs and mementos, which I have in our shed in the back garden, the only place I could store them. I didn't have room for the rest, so Mum took them.

'Sabrina, I was *going* to store his boxes, but then Mickey Flanagan offered to take them and so I sent him everything.'

'Mickey Flanagan, the solicitor, had Dad's private things?' I say, annoyed.

'He's not exactly a random stranger. He's a kind of friend. He was Fergus's solicitor for years. Handled our divorce too. You know, he pushed for Fergus to get sole custody of you. You were fifteen – what the hell would Fergus have done with you at fifteen? Not to mention the fact you didn't even want to live with *me* at fifteen. You could barely live with *yourself*. Anyway, Mickey was handling the insurance and hospital bills, and he said he'd store Fergus's things, he had plenty of space.'

A bubble of anger rises in me. 'If I'd known his solicitor was taking his personal things, I would have had them, Mum.'

'I know. But you said you had no space for anything more.'

Which I didn't and I don't. I barely have space for my shoes. Aidan jokes that he has to step outside of the house in order to change his mind.

'So why did Mickey send the boxes to the hospital this morning?'

'Because Mickey had to get rid of them and I told him that was the best place for them. I didn't want to clutter you with them. It's a sad story really: Mickey's son lost his house and he and his wife and kids have to move in with Mickey and his wife. They're bringing all their furniture, which has to be stored in Mickey's garage, and he said he couldn't keep Fergus's things any more. Which is understandable. So I told him to send them to the hospital. They're Fergus's things. He can decide what to do with them. He's perfectly capable of that, you know. I thought he might enjoy it,' she adds gently, as I'm sure she can sense my frustration. 'Imagine the time it will pass for him, going down memory lane.'

I realise I'm holding my breath. I exhale.

'Did you discuss this walk down memory lane with his doctors first?'

'Oh,' she says suddenly, realising. 'No. I didn't, I . . . oh dear. Is he okay, love?'

I sense her sincere concern. 'Yes, I got to them before he did.'

'I'm sorry, I never thought of that. Sabrina, I didn't tell

you because you would have insisted on taking everything and cluttering your house with things you don't need and taking too much on like you always do when it's not necessary. You've enough on your plate.'

Which is also true.

I can't blame her for wanting to rid herself of Dad's baggage, he's not her problem any more and ceased being so seventeen years ago. And I believe that she was doing it for my own good, not wanting to weigh me down.

'So did you know he had a marble collection?' I ask.

'Oh, that man!' Her resentment for the other Fergus returns. The past Fergus. The old Fergus. 'Found among other pointless collections, I'm sure. Honestly, that man was a hoarder – remember how full the skip was when we sold the apartment? He used to bring those sachets of mustard, ketchup and mayonnaise home every day from whenever he ate out. I had to tell him to stop. I think he was addicted. You know they say that people who hoard have emotional issues. That they're holding on to all of those things because they're afraid of letting go.'

It goes on and I allow 90 per cent of it to wash over me, including the habit of referring to Dad in the past tense as though he's dead. To her, the man she knew is dead. She quite likes the man she visits in the hospital every fortnight.

'We had an argument about a marble once,' she says, bitterly.

I think they had a fight about just about everything at least once in their lives.

'How did that come about?'

'I can't remember,' she says too quickly.

'But you never knew he had a marble collection?'

'How would I know?'

'Because you were married to him. And because I didn't pack them up, so you must have.'

'Oh please, I can't be called to account for anything he has done since we separated, nor during our marriage for that matter,' she spouts.

I'm baffled.

'Some of the items are missing,' I say, looking at them all laid out on the floor. The more I think about it, and hearing that they were in the possession of his solicitor, the more suspicious I am becoming. 'I'm not suggesting Mickey Flanagan *stole* them,' I say. 'I mean, Dad could have lost them.'

'What's missing?' she asks, with genuine concern. The man she divorced was an imbecile, but the nice man in rehabilitation must not be wronged.

'Part of his marble collection.'

'He's lost his marbles?' She laughs. I don't. She finally catches her breath. 'Well, I don't think your dad had ever anything to do with marbles, dear. Perhaps it's a mistake, perhaps they're not your father's, or Mickey delivered the wrong boxes. Do you want me to call him?'

'No,' I say, confused. I look on the floor and see pages and pages covered in Dad's handwriting, cataloguing these marbles, and yet Mum seems to genuinely know nothing.

'The marbles are definitely his and the missing items were valuable.'

'By his own estimation, I'm guessing.'

'I don't know who valued them, but there are certificates to show they're authentic. The certs for the missing marbles aren't here. The inventory says one item was worth up to twelve thousand dollars.'

'What?' she gasps. 'Twelve thousand for marbles!'

'One box of marbles.' I smile.

'Well no wonder he almost went bankrupt. They weren't mentioned as assets in the divorce.'

'He mightn't have had them then,' I say quietly.

Mum talks like I haven't spoken at all, the conspiracy theories building in her head, but there's one question she's failed to ask. I didn't pack them and she didn't know about them, but somehow they found their way to the rest of Dad's belongings.

I take Mickey's office details from her and end the call.

The marble collection covers the entire floor. They are beautiful, twinkling from the carpet like a midnight sky.

The house is quiet but my head is now buzzing. I pick up the first batch of marbles on the list. The box of bloodies that I showed to Dad, listed as 'Allies'.

I start to polish them. Kind of like an apology for not ever knowing about them before.

I have a knack for remembering things that people forget and I now know something important about Dad that he kept to himself, which he has forgotten. Things we want to forget, things we can't forget, things we forgot we'd forgotten until we remember them. There is a new category. We all have things we never want to forget. We all need a person to remember them just in case.

7

PLAYING WITH MARBLES

Trap the Fox

I was supposed to be keeping my eye on Bobby. That's exactly what Ma said when she left the house, in her usual threatening tone. 'You keep your eye on him, you hear? Don't. Take. Your. Eye. Off. Him.' Every word a prod in the chest with her dry cracked finger.

I promised. I meant it. When she's looking at you like that you really mean whatever you're saying.

But then I got distracted.

For some reason Ma trusted me with keeping my eye on him. It might have been something to do with the little chat we had about Victoria when the others were at school and we got to play the marble game together. I think she's been different to me since then. Maybe not, maybe it's all in my head, maybe it's just that it's different to me. I'd never seen her play like that before; a bit with the babies, but not down on the floor like she was with me, skirt hooshed up, her knees on the carpet. I think Hamish has noticed it too. Hamish notices everything and maybe that

makes me a bit more cool to him too – Ma trusting me
with things and not slapping the head off me as much as
she usually would. Or maybe she's like this with me because
she's grieving. I learned about grieving from a priest. I might
have done that after Da died but I can't remember. I think
it's just for adults.

Ma hates priests now. After what he said to her when
Victoria died, after Mattie and Hamish chased him out of
the house. She still goes to Mass though, she says it's a sin
not to. She drags us to Gardiner Street Church every Sunday
to ten o'clock Mass, in our best clothes. I can always smell
her spit on my forehead from when she smooths down my
hair. Sunday morning smells of spit and incense. We always
sit in the third row, most families stick to the same place
all the time. She says Mass is the only time she can get
peace and all of us will shut the fuck up. Even Mattie goes,
smelling of last night's drink and circling in his chair like
he's still pissed. We're always quiet at Mass because my first
memory of Mass is Ma pointing up at Jesus on the cross,
blood dripping down his forehead and nails sticking out of
his hands and feet, and her saying, 'If you say one word in
here, embarrass me, I'll do that to you.' I believed her. We
all do. Even Bobby sits still. He sits with his bottle of milk
in his hand as the priest drones on, his voice echoing around
the enormous ceilings, looking at all the pictures on the
walls of a near naked man being tortured in fourteen
different ways, and he knows this isn't a place to fuck about.

Ma is at school with Angus. He's in trouble because he
was caught eating all the communion wafers when he was
doing his altar boy duties, locking them away after Mass.
He ate an entire bag of them, three hundred and fifty to
be precise. When they asked if he had anything to say for
himself, he said he asked for a drink because there were

60

dozens stuck to the roof of his mouth. 'My mouth was dry as a nun's crotch,' he'd whispered late at night when we were all in bed and we'd almost pissed ourselves laughing. And then when we were all almost asleep, the giggles finally gone, Hamish whispered, 'Angus, you know you haven't just eaten the body of Christ, you've eaten the whole carcass.' And that set us all off again, forcing Mattie to bang on the wall for us to shut up.

Angus loves being an altar boy, he gets paid for it, more for funerals, and when he's in class the priest passes by his window and gives him the thumbs up or down to let him know what he's needed for that weekend. If it's a thumbs up it's a funeral, and he'll get more money, if it's a wedding, he gets less. No one wants to be an altar boy at a wedding.

Duncan is at Mattie's butcher shop, plucking feathers off chickens and turkeys as punishment for cheating in a school exam. He says he wants to leave school like Hamish did but Ma won't let him. She says he's not as smart as Hamish, which doesn't make much sense to me because I thought it was the smart ones that do better at school, it's the dumb ones that should leave.

Tommy's playing football outside and so it's my job to look after Bobby. Only I wasn't watching him. Not even God could watch Bobby all the time, he's a tornado, he never stops.

While he's playing on the floor with his train, I take out my new Trap the Fox game that I got for my eleventh birthday. It's from Cairo Novelty Company and the hounds are black and white swirls and the fox is an opaque marble. I don't see Bobby grab the fox but from the corner of my eye I see him suddenly go still; he's watching me. I look at him and see the opaque in his hand, close to his mouth.

He does it while giving me that sidelong cheeky look, his blue eyes twinkling mischievously like he'd do anything just to get a rise out of me, even if it means his death.

'Bobby, no!' I shout.

He smiles, enjoying my reaction. He moves it closer to his mouth.

'No!' I dive at him and he runs, the fastest little fucker you've ever seen on two legs. All chub and no muscle at one hundred miles an hour, weaving in and out of chairs, ducking, diving. Finally, I have him cornered, so I stop. The marble is against his lips.

He giggles.

'Bobby, listen,' I try to catch my breath. 'If you put that in your mouth, you'll choke and die, do you understand? Bobby all gone. Bobby. Fucking. Dead.'

He giggles again, tickled by my fear, by the power he has over me.

'Bobby . . .' I say, warning in my voice, moving slowly towards him, ready to pounce at any moment. 'Give me the marble . . .'

He puts it in his mouth and I dive on him, squeezing his pudgy cheeks, trying to push the marble back out. Sometimes he just holds things there. Stones, snails, nails, dirt . . . sometimes he just puts stuff in his mouth like it's a holding room then spits it out. But I can't feel a marble in his mouth, his cheeks are all squidge, all flesh, mixed with his spit and snotty runny nose. He makes a choking sound and I prise open his mouth and it's empty. Just little white milky fangs and a squishy red tongue.

'Fuck,' I whisper.

'Uck,' he repeats.

'HAMISH!' I yell. Hamish is supposed to be out working, or looking for a job, or doing whatever it is that Hamish does now that he's out of school, but I heard him come home, bang the door closed and bang his way up the stairs to our room. 'HAAAYYY-MIIIIIISH!' I yell. 'He ate the fox! Bobby ate the fox!'

Bobby looks at me, startled by my reaction, by my fear and he looks like he's about to burst into tears any second. That's the least of my worries.

I hear Hamish's boots on the stairs and he bursts into the room. 'What's wrong?'

'Bobby swallowed the fox.'

Hamish looks confused at first but then sees my game on the table and understands. As Hamish goes towards Bobby, Bobby really looks as if he's going to cry. He tries to run but I grab him and he squeals like a pig.

'When?'

'Just now.'

Hamish picks Bobby up and turns him upside down. He shakes him as if trying to shake the coins from his pockets like I've seen him do with lads before. Bobby starts to laugh.

Hamish puts him back on his feet again and opens his mouth, sticks his fingers inside. Bobby's eyes widen and he starts retching, vomits up some foul-smelling porridge.

'Is it there?' Hamish asks, and I don't know what he's talking about until he gets down on his knees and looks through the vomit for the marble.

Before Bobby has a chance to cry, Hamish takes hold of him again and starts squeezing him and shaking him, poking him in the belly and ribs. Bobby giggles again, despite the lingering smell of vomit, trying to dodge Hamish's finger, thinking it's a game, as we both get increasingly annoyed.

'Are you sure he ate it?'

I nod, thinking he'll turn me upside down next.

'She's going to kill me,' I say, my heart pounding.

'She won't kill you,' he says, unconvincingly, like he's amused.

'She told me not to play marbles with Bobby around, he always tries to eat them.'

'Oh. Well then, she might kill you.'

I picture Jesus on the cross, the nails through his hands and wonder why nobody ever wondered if Mary had done it. If maybe the biggest miracle of all wasn't Mary getting pregnant without ever touching a mickey, but Jesus's ma getting away with nailing him to a cross. If I ever end up on a cross, the first person anyone will suspect is my ma and she won't bother with the fourteen stations, she'll just get straight to it.

'He seems grand though,' Hamish says as Bobby grows bored of us inspecting him and resumes playing with his train.

'Yeah but I have to tell her,' I say, nervously, heart pounding, body trembling. I'm thinking of thorns in my head, nails in my hands, a rag around my mickey and my nips out for everyone to see. She'd do it somewhere public too, like Jesus on the hill, for everyone to see, maybe my schoolyard or on the wall behind the butcher counter. Maybe hanging me off one of those giant meat hooks, so everyone who comes in for their Sunday roast can see me. *There he is now, the lad who took his eye off his baby brother. Tsk, tsk, tsk. Two pork chops, please.*

'You don't have to tell her,' Hamish says calmly, going to the kitchen and grabbing a rag. 'Here, clean up his puke.'

I do.

'What if the fox gets trapped somewhere inside of him?' I ask. 'And he stops breathing?'

He considers that. We look at Bobby playing. Blond and

white pudge crashing a train into the leg of a chair over and over, talking to himself in his own language where his tongue's too big for his mouth and the words won't come out properly.

'Look, we can't tell Ma,' Hamish says finally. He sounds all grown up, and sure of himself. 'Not after Victoria, she'll go . . .' He doesn't need to say what Ma will do, we've seen enough to guess.

'What will I do?' I ask.

It must be the way I ask, I hear the baby in my voice, which he sometimes hates and wants to thump out of you, but instead he goes soft. 'You don't worry. I'll sort it out.'

'How?'

'Well, it went in one way, only one way it can come back out. We'll just have to keep an eye on his nappy.'

I look at him in shock and he laughs, that chesty cigarette laugh that's already starting to sound like Mattie even though he's only sixteen and Mattie is ancient.

'How are we going to get it out?' I ask, following him around like a little dog.

He opens the fridge, scans it, then closes it, unimpressed. He taps his finger on the worktop and looks around the small cubby kitchen, thinking, his brain in full action. I'm shitting myself but Hamish thrives on this stuff. He loves trouble, he loves it so much he wants my trouble to be his trouble. He loves finding solutions, spurred on by a count-down of how many minutes remain till our lives will be made hell. Most of the time he doesn't find the solutions, he causes bigger problems trying to fix things. That's Hamish. But he's all I've got right now. I'm as useless as tits on a bull, as he tells me.

His eyes settle on the freshly baked brown bread that Ma has left to rest on the bread board, covered in a red-and-white checked tea cloth. She baked it fresh this morning and it filled the house with the best smell.

'Ma told me not to touch it.'

'She also told you not to take your eyes off Bobby.'

That's me told. That nervous flutter again in my tummy, visions of a crown of thorns and being forced to carry a cross through the street, though maybe in Ma's case it would be a load of dirty washing. That's her cross to bear she always says. That and the six of us boys.

'And just in case the bread's not enough to flush it out . . .' Hamish says, taking a bottle of castor oil from the cupboard and grabbing a spoon. He throws off the towel and picks up the bread. 'Oh, Bobby,' he sings, dancing the bread in the air in Bobby's face. Bobby's eyes light up.

An hour later I've changed two of the most indescribably wettest shits I've ever seen and there's still no sign of the fox.

'You've really trapped that fox, haven't you, buddy?' Hamish says to Bobby and laughs hysterically.

He offers another slice of brown bread and spoon of castor oil to Bobby and Bobby says, 'No!' and runs away. I don't blame him and I'm glad. I'm literally up to my elbows in shitty terry cloths. I don't know how Ma cleans them but I've boiled up some water and have steeped them for as long as I could, burning my hands in the process, tried rubbing the parts together to get the stains off but nothing. I still think I get the better end of the deal as it's Hamish that sifts through the poo first with a knife before handing it to me to deal with. If I wasn't so terrified about Ma coming home and finding the bread gone and a marble stuck inside her precious baby then I'd be able to laugh like Hamish is.

It is when Hamish is looking through Bobby's third crappy nappy that I hear the key in the door. Ma's home and my world ends. My heart thuds and my throat closes up like it's the end of my world.

'Hurry up,' I whisper and Hamish sifts through the poo faster.

The front door opens, Hamish dashes out the back door, and Ma and Angus are greeted by a naked-from-the-waist-down Bobby who's demonstrating tumbles on the floor, his pudgy legs crashing into everything as he follows through.

'Everything all right?' Ma asks, stepping into the room.

Angus is behind her, quiet, one red cheek like he's been slapped, hands in his pockets, shoulders hunched, and I can tell she's had a good go at him. He looks at me suspiciously. Hamish is in the back garden sifting through the poo. Or at least I hope he is; part of me thinks he's nipped out the backyard door into the alleyway and left me to deal with this mess on my own.

A grin works its way on to Angus's face, he knows that I've done something, I must look guilty. He'd love it if I got caught out. Convinced I'm about to get it, that the spotlight will be taken off him for a while, he grins at me.

'What's wrong, Tick?'

'What on earth?' Ma asks, looking at Bobby who's on tumble hyper-drive. Then she sees the empty bread plate on the table, crumbs everywhere and out the window I see Hamish with a shitty hand in the window, a white marble between his fingers and a great big smile on his face. My relief is immense but now I've to deal with the brown bread situation.

'Bobby ate some, I'm sorry,' I say quickly. Too quickly. She suspects there's more to it.

'My brown bread!' Ma shouts. 'That was for tea. I told you not to touch it!' she yells. Hamish appears beside me and dumps the soiled terry cloth in my hands, slips the marble in my pocket, his hands now clean.

'Sorry, Ma, that was my fault,' Hamish pipes up. 'I told Fergus I'd watch Bobby for him, but I must have taken my eye off him because he ate it. You know what he's like with putting things in his mouth.' When Ma's not looking, when she's staring at her half-eaten loaf, devastated, he looks at me and winks.

Ma shouts a tirade of angry abuse at Hamish and all the time I think I should interrupt and confess to it all but I don't. I can't. I'm too chicken.

Ma sees the nappy in my hand, and the boiling water outside filled with cloths, and her expression changes so I can't read it. 'How many did you change?'

'Three,' I say nervously.

She surprises me then by laughing. 'Oh, Fergus,' she laughs, then ruffles my hair and kisses the top of my head. She goes outside to the toilet to flush the faeces, laughing as she goes, and I see Hamish watching her, sadly.

I ask him later when the others are asleep why he did that for me, why he helped me and then took the blame.

'I didn't do it for you. I did it for her. She doesn't want to be disappointed in you, she's used to it with me.'

Ma was right about Hamish being smart because when he gave me a calculating look in the eye and said, 'You owe me one,' I knew that he meant it and that he had me over a barrel. I don't know if he always had what we did next planned, and that's why he took the blame for the brown bread, knowing I'd have no choice but to do what he'd ask me to do, or if he thought about it after. Either way that was the beginning of our marble adventures, or misadventures, and brown bread incident or not, I would have gone anywhere with him.

But that pretty much describes Hamish. He was willing to go through any amount of shit to save my arse.

8

PLAYING WITH MARBLES

Eggs in the Bush

It's three a.m. and I'm out with Hamish. He often comes to get me during the night, but these days it's different, no nudging, kicking, or hand across the mouth so I won't scream with fright as I used to do when he woke me in the middle of the night. Instead he has to throw stones against the window to wake me up. He hasn't been living at home for a few months now since Ma threw him out. She found out he was working for The Barber, but that's not why she threw him out. Mattie and him had a massive fight, where they thrashed the house walloping each other. Hamish even put Mattie's head through the glass of the good cabinet – glass everywhere and he had to get three stitches. Tommy pissed his pants even though he said he hadn't.

So Hamish is out of the house. At twenty-one years of age Ma says he should be out of the house anyway, married and working. Even though he's out I still see him. We can't hustle people any more like we used to, I'm fifteen now and everyone knows I'm the best marble player around, or one of them; there's a new fella on the scene, Peader Lackey. People like to watch us play against each other, The Barber sets it up in his barbershop at night. He likes to entertain his people, he has meetings in the back, in his office and while that's going on he has drinks and smokes in the shop, cards, marbles, women, you name it. Hamish says The Barber would bet on a snail race. Not to his face, obviously. You don't want to piss off The Barber. If you do, and you go in for a cut and a shave, you can end up with a lot more damage done.

The Barber gives me a few bob for showing up, Hamish takes most of it. Still it's the same as with the caramels when I was ten: I'd do it for free then and I'd do it for free now. People place bets on who'll win and Hamish is the tote. You better watch out if you don't pay up, Hamish commands a lot of respect, with him being close to The Barber, and the ones who don't pay are looking for trouble, which they get.

But Hamish didn't wake me up tonight, I find him in the alleyway behind our house, bent over and looking for pebbles. I sneak up on him and kick him in the arse and he jumps like The Barber has a hot blade to his neck.

I break my shit laughing.

'What the fuck are you doing up?' he says, trying to play it all cool but his pupils are all wide and black.

'None of your business.'

'Ah that's how it is, is it?' he grins. 'Heard you've been getting fresh with one of the Sullivan girls. Sarah, is it?'

'Might have been.' It always surprises me how Hamish knows everything. I haven't told anyone about Sarah, kept it right to myself – not that there was anything to tell, she won't do much till her wedding day, said as much herself.

70

She's sweet enough, but I didn't meet her tonight. I was meeting her sister Annie, who's a lot less sweet. Two years older and she caught me up on what her baby sister wasn't sharing. My legs are still shaking from it, but I feel alive, like a man, like I can do anything. Which is probably a bad place to be in when Hamish is involved.

He motions for me to follow but doesn't tell me about what we're out to do. I figure it's a game of marbles somewhere that he's set up with an audience to bet, which is what it usually is. On the times it's not, it's about visiting the lads who haven't paid up. We go to the school, climb over the back wall and get to the dorms easy. Hamish already knows a way in, and when we climb in a window I send a jar of marbles on a desk spilling all over the floor. I expect Hamish to clock me one but instead he pisses himself laughing. None of the brothers come, thankfully. It's one thing getting a clatter on school time, it's quite another to get it when you shouldn't even be there. Hamish is laughing like a maniac, and slips on the marbles, and that's when I smell the drink on him. I get a bit worried then.

Two boys sit up in their beds, sleepy. They're fifteen, same age as me, but I look younger.

'Get up, you faggots,' he says, hitting them both over the heads. He uses shoelaces and school ties, anything he can find, to tie their hands behind their backs, their ankles to chair-legs and tells them we're going to play a little game.

While he's messing around with them I tidy the marbles up from the floor, and take a look at them. The collection has no value, just a bunch of opaques, cat's eyes, swirls and patches, nothing mint, nothing collectable. This surprises me because I know one of the lads is a rich boy. Daddy's a doctor, drives a fancy car, I would have been expecting a little bit better than this. I root through the jar and find gold. It's a two-colour, peerless patch made by Peltier. It stands out because the edges are curved instead of straight and it's my lucky day because he has three of them with picture marbles on, that's with black transfers of one of twelve different syndicate comic characters fired on the marble. I've never seen these before. The young lad watches me studying it. He's right to be worried. He's got three of them, Smitty, Andy and, can you believe it, Annie. Annie is red on white with the black transfer. It's kind of like fate. I'm not a cruel bastard, I only pocket one: Annie.

Eggs in the bush, Hamish tells them we're playing. It's a guessing game, which requires no skill whatsoever. The kind of game we play when the family go on a long journey, not that we go anywhere much. It's too expensive and Ma says we're a bloody nightmare and that she can't take us anywhere. We usually end up getting split up and going to different members of her family for a week. Two years in a row I've gone to Aunty Sheila, who has two girls and only lives around the corner. Back sleeping on her floor again, I have no good memories of being there and they're the worst summer holidays ever, except cousin Mary was friends with Sarah Sullivan and that's how I met her. It was worth pretending to be the nice kind gentleman cousin for a week.

Back to the game, and a player picks up a number of marbles and asks the other players to guess a number. If they guess correctly they get to keep the marbles, if they get it wrong, they have to pay the questioner the difference between the number guessed and the number held. Except Hamish puts his own spin on the game. Every time they get it wrong, the difference in the amount guessed and the amount held is how many times he lands a punch to their face and body. It stops being fun really quickly. We've gone collecting money a few times before, scared lads a few times, usually it's just enough for them to see Hamish in their room at night, knowing he's been sent by The Barber, but never this – or at least, never this bad. Hamish is wired. He punches too much, too hard, those boys are bleeding and crying and tied to the chairs.

I try to tell him that's enough and he fires himself at me, pulls my hair so hard on my head I think my scalp's about to come off. The alcohol from him smells worse now, and his eyes are bloodshot, like it took a while to hit him. What I mistook in the alley for a fright and then joy at seeing me was something else. He roughs them up a little more and one of the boys cries really loudly for help, his nose bleeding, his eye all shut up. I don't get any satisfaction from it, they're only kids, and it's not even that much money. Hamish gets his hands on their savings and takes it all, then we're out of there. We walk back to the house in silence; he knows I disapprove and Hamish hates that. Although he tries to be the big man, what he really wants is for everyone to like him. But he has never known how to make that happen.

He doesn't walk me back to the house, just leaves me at the alley entrance. I think he's going to walk away without a word, but he's got more to say.

'So, The Barber told me to tell you not to win tomorrow night.'

'What?'

'You heard me. Don't win.'

'Why?'

'Why do you think? He's got something going with someone. You lose, he wins a packet. You might get a bit of it.'

'Who am I playing?'

'Peader.'

'I'm not losing to Peader, no way.'

'Lookit, you have to.'

'I don't have to do anything. I don't work for The Barber, you do, and I'm not losing for anyone.'

He grabs my collar and pushes me hard up against the wall, but I'm not afraid, I just feel sad. I see a bully, my brother, where I once saw a hero.

'You be here at eleven tomorrow night, okay? Or else.'

'Or else what? You won't be my brother any more, Hamish?' All of a sudden, I'm furious. Furious with the way Hamish hit those boys, furious with the way he's implicated me in it, furious that he thinks he can still tell me what to do and I'll do it, no questions asked. 'You going to slap me around like you did with those lads tonight? I don't think so. You think Ma will ever let you set foot in the house again if you do that?'

He shifts uneasily. I know he wants to come home more than anything. He's a homebird, though he has a funny way of showing it. He's the kind of fella that teases a girl senseless if he fancies her, who treats you bad if he wants to be your friend, who hangs around his family and acts the prat when really he wants to be invited inside.

'The Barber will come after you,' he threatens me.

'No he won't. The Barber's got better things to be doing than worrying about me and a marble game. He just uses it as a distraction to whatever he's doing in that room. He uses you to cause a distraction, Hamish, that's all. Has he ever asked you into that back room? He won't even bother coming after you, he'll get someone else to do it for him. He doesn't care about you. I'm not losing for him, I'm not losing for you. I'm never losing, full stop.'

It must be the way I say it because he gets it straight away, he believes me, he knows he's nothing to The Barber, has always tried to make himself more important than he is, like pulling the stunt he pulled tonight. I've revealed him and he hates it. He knows there's nothing he can do to talk me out of it, or into it.

When I walk down the alleyway and get close to the house I suddenly feel a slap on the side of my head. It stings. I think it's The Barber at first, not him but one of his boys. Instead it's Sarah and she's crying.

'Jesus, Sarah, what are you doing out here at this hour?'

'Is it true?' She's crying. 'Did you and Annie . . . do it?'

By the next day I can forget about Annie, I can forget about Sarah and I can forget about Hamish.

The guards come round looking for Hamish, but Hamish has already legged it. He's luckier to have escaped the wrath of Ma than anything the guards would have done to him. Everyone thinks I know where he is but I don't. I tell them I don't and that I don't care either. It's true too. He went over the line last night and I can't back him up on that one. For the first time, I can't. It should make me feel sad but it doesn't, it makes me feel tougher, stronger, like if I can *think* I'm better than Hamish then that practically gives me superpowers. I've never thought of myself as better than Hamish and I spend the day puffed up with something like pride.

That night in bed the lads and I are whispering, we have to because Ma is so close to the edge any one of us will get it over nothing. Duncan says a lad he knows who works on the docks saw Hamish getting on a boat going to Liverpool.

And now I feel less like a superhero. I didn't think our meeting would be the last. I wanted a chance for us to make it up, for him to say sorry, for him to see what a big man I was. The lads talk about what Hamish will do in England, having a laugh picturing him in situations, but all I do is lie in the dark and see him working his way through England to Scotland, some old-fashioned image of him climbing across the land with a stick, finding some of Da's family to settle down with, living on the farm I can't remember any more, working the land like Da did. The thought helps me drift off to sleep, but no less worried, no less guilty, and feeling none of the superpowers I'd felt only moments earlier.

I get a warning from the guards for being a stupid kid in the wrong place at the wrong time, being influenced by my older brother. As a gesture I give the rich boy that Hamish beat up his Annie marble, much as it pains me to do it. But I win it back off him a few weeks later. That and the whole comic collection. Whenever I see those marbles they remind me of the night I became a man with Annie and the night that I went one way and Hamish went another. And sometimes when I really want to go the other way, Hamish's way, when life is just begging me to do it, I take them out as a reminder and it quietens the voice.

I don't see Hamish for a long time, and when I do, the sight of him is enough to tell me never to cross to the other side, ever. But seeing a dead body will do that to most people.

9

POOL RULES

No Ball Games

Armed with the new information from Mum, I hop in the car and drive to Virginia. I get parking on the street, outside Mickey Flanagan's office, which is between a closed-down DVD rental store and a not-yet-open Chinese takeaway. The window on to the street is covered in frosted glass and his name stencilled in black on the front. Mickey's secretary, her name badge says Amy, sits behind a protective screen, with holes punched in the glass in a circular design either for her to breathe or for us to talk. It's only when I go to speak that I realise I've been holding my breath. I must have been doing that all the way to Virginia because my chest feels tight.

'Hello, I'm Sabrina Boggs.' I made an appointment as soon as I hung up the phone to Mum and they kindly squeezed me in, though now that I look around the empty waiting room I'm not sure much squeezing was necessary.

'Hello.' She gives me a polite smile. 'Please take a seat, he'll be with you as soon as he can.'

The waiting area is beside the frosted glass. I sit between a water cooler and a waxy-looking potted plant. The radio is on to hide the usual uncomfortable silence in a waiting room, more talk about today's total solar eclipse, which has commanded every news station and talk show for the past week: what can we expect to see, where can we expect to see it, how to look at the sun, how not to look at the sun, where best to look at the sun. I'm all eclipsed-out. Aidan is taking a half-day this afternoon to collect the boys from school, then they're going to a campsite, one of the official areas for watching the total eclipse. He'll be joining his brother and his kids, whose new money-making scheme has been to invest his savings in solar eclipse glasses, which he's been selling the past few weeks at hiked-up prices. My boys have been so excited about it all week, wearing the glasses, making versions of solar eclipses with cereal boxes, Styrofoam and balls of string, decorating their bedrooms with glow-in-the-dark moons. It helps that it's a Friday night in May and we're having good weather so everyone can show interest and actually be able to see the sky. I'm not disinterested in sky-gazing but I'm not a camper and so I have a night to myself.

'I'm just not a camper,' I'd said to Aidan when he'd told me of his plans last week.

'You're not a *happy* camper,' he'd replied, watching me. I knew he was watching me though I pretended I didn't, continuing to make the school lunches. His comment had irritated me, but I didn't want to let it show. Count to five in my head, butter, ham, cheese, bread, slice. Next. He was still watching me when I jammed the raisins into the lunch boxes.

'This is a natural phenomenon,' a scientist is saying on the radio. 'In some ancient and modern cultures, solar eclipses have been attributed to supernatural causes or regarded as bad omens. It was frightening for people who were unaware of the astronomical explanation, as the sun seems to disappear during the day and the sky darkens in a matter of minutes.'

'I totally believe in all of that,' Amy says suddenly from behind her screen. 'I had a boyfriend once who used to go totally mental when there was a full moon.' She screws her finger into her temple. 'Locked me in a wardrobe, threw my shoes in the toilet. Accused me of saying things when I hadn't even opened my mouth, of moving things I didn't even know he owned, like "*Me*, did you touch my chessboard?" and I'd be like, What chessboard? And I hated being called *Me*. It's Amy. Isn't it weird that he called me *Me*, like he wanted *me* to be a part of *him*? Weird stuff. If I'd stayed, I'm sure he would have killed me like he killed that rat.' She looks at me to explain. 'He kept it for three days in the basement, torturing it.'

I picture a rat being waterboarded.

'Days like today scare me. Especially when dealing with the public. You wouldn't believe the calls we get. Freaks. The word lunatic comes from it, did you know that?'

I nod but she continues anyway. 'Lunar. Lunatic. It brings out the worst in people: violence, mentalness, you name it. I have a friend who works as a paramedic and she says full moon days and nights are her busiest. People just flip out. It's to do with the tidal effect and the water in our bodies,' she says. She's quiet for a moment, thinking. 'Though I think there really was something wrong with George. He was mental on days when you couldn't even see the moon.'

I think of me throwing the mug against the wall at work. Of saying to Eric, '*The moon made me do it.*' It would be ridiculous of course but not so far out for me. I've always had difficulty sleeping during full moons. Not so much pounding headaches as too many thoughts. Too many thoughts too quickly, all together, like the moon acts as a signal tower for my brain. Everything flowing all at once instead of slowly filtering. I think of me sitting here today, on a quest to find Dad's marbles, and wonder if this is lunacy after all. The moon made me do it. But I don't care what's making me do it. I'm doing it and if I need the moon to urge me on, then I'll take it.

I think of how excited the boys will be if the day actually darkens. If the clouds don't cover the perfect sky first and ruin everyone's chances of witnessing it. I wonder where I'll be, what I'll be doing during it, and hope it will coincide with my discovery of Dad's marbles, Scooby-Doo style, in Mickey Flanagan's house, using the veil of darkness to sneak in unnoticed and steal them back from his safe behind the oil painting in the walnut-panelled study.

'It's a new moon today,' Amy continues. 'Also known as a dark moon, because it's just a black circle. You know how crazy people go when it's a full moon, now imagine a black full moon. I mean, we should really have just stayed inside today and locked the doors. Who knows what will happen?'

She leaves us hanging on that thought.

The phone rings and we both jump, and then laugh. 'He'll see you now.'

I enter Mickey Flanagan's office, feeling anxious about what I'm here to do, and am faced with a short bald Humpty-Dumpty-like man with a welcoming face. We met just after Dad's stroke, to discuss how to manage Dad's affairs, but we've had nothing but the occasional electronic correspondence since. Each time I see an email from Mickey

I worry that the money's run out, that Dad's rehabilitation will have to come to an abrupt end. I've avoided every type of meeting with him since to avoid discussing that inevitability. Mickey struggles to his feet, bumping his belly off the edge of the desk and comes round the desk to shake my hand warmly, before returning behind his desk.

I'm nervous. I pull the plastic folder with Dad's inventory out of my bag and prepare myself for my questioning. If he has taken the marbles, I know that he won't admit his theft right away, maybe he won't admit it at all, but I'm hoping my appearance will rattle his conscience at least. I've thought of every possible scenario, I've heard his every possible answer: *I had to sell them, he hadn't paid me for months, do you expect me to work for free?* Or *of course I sold them, we had an arrangement, see this contract here, he is paying me through the sale of his marbles.* I've thought about it all, but my answer will be the same. Get them back.

'Nice to meet you, Sabrina, how's your dad doing?' he asks, concerned.

'How's he doing?' I ask, feeling my legs starting to tremble, my whole body in fact, including my tongue. My lip starts to twitch, which irritates me and makes me even more frustrated and angry. I want to be able to say what I want to say without impediment. I need to be emotion-free but it has bubbled up inside of me so quickly, the mere question *How's he doing?* acting as the trigger, that my emotion clouds my clarity. This feeling reminds me of the dream I have when I'm trying to explain myself to someone, always a different person, but chewing gum gets stuck in my mouth and the more I pull it out the more it keeps forming, stopping the words.

I clear my throat. 'Sometimes he doesn't even remember

yesterday. But then he'll tell you a story with pinpoint accuracy from when he was a child, so clear and vivid, it's like you're back there with him. Like today, this morning he told me about being at the All-Ireland final in 1963 when Dublin beat Galway, when he was a boy. He remembered every single little thing, explained in so much detail I felt like I was there with him.'

'Well that's a day to remember,' he says politely, good-natured.

'And then he'll forget something that is or once was apparently incredibly important to him.' I clear my throat again. Make the segue, Sabrina. 'Like his marbles. Up until today I didn't even know he had marbles. But he has hundreds of them. In fact, probably thousands if I was to count. Some of them are valuable, but regardless of the price all of them are important, or otherwise why would he have taken the time to do all this?' I fumble to pass over the inventory with trembling fingers. He goes through each page, from the page to my face, up and down, over and over again.

'Mickey,' I start, 'there's no way for me to say this politely. You had these marbles in your possession until yesterday. There's a part of his collection missing. Do you know what happened to my dad's marbles?'

He looks surprised, freezes with the inventory still in his hand. 'Goodness, no!'

'Mickey. I really need to know. I'm not accusing you of stealing them, I mean, obviously there could have been an arrangement with someone, with Dad maybe, where you were given permission to take them. Whatever happened, I don't need to know. I just want to find them so I can get them back and complete the collection.'

'No. No, I didn't take them and there was no arrangement with anyone, not your dad.' He straightens up, and is firm. 'As you know, the boxes were delivered to me *after* his stroke and, as you say, he doesn't remember owning them so he couldn't have instructed me to do anything with them, nor would I have so much as laid a finger on them.' He is genuine, also clearly annoyed to be accused of such a thing, but he is being professional about it. 'You have my word on that, Sabrina.'

'Could anyone have had access to them in your house? Was there ever a break-in?' I try to soften the accusation of his nearest and dearest. 'The marbles that were taken were the most expensive marbles, it seems somebody went through the inventory and chose them.'

He gives me the courtesy of appearing to think about it before answering. 'I can assure you that neither I nor anybody who was in my home is responsible for the missing marbles. I never opened the boxes. They were sealed on arrival and still had the same seal when they left. They were kept in the garage for the past year and they were out of sight and out of reach in all that time.'

I believe him. But I'm stuck because I don't know where else to go after this.

Mickey hands me back the inventory and I just stare at it, at Dad's lovely loopy handwriting, seeing, *Sabrina could not come to school today because she had a doctor's appointment.* I see handwritten birthday cards. I see scribbled notes around the house.

I purse my lips, my cheeks still a little pink with embarrassment for the accusation, no matter how politely I tried to put it.

'Well there's one other thing. Apart from wanting to find them, it would help to know who brought them to you. Mum and I packed up everything from the apartment and we never saw these boxes before.'

He frowns, genuinely confused. 'Is that so? You didn't have help? Movers or family members?'

I shake my head. 'It was just the two of us.'

He takes his time thinking about it. 'I'm not sure if you know how I came to store your dad's things.'

'Mum said that you kindly offered. I didn't have the space for them and she . . . well, she's obviously moved on.'

'The thing is, I didn't kindly offer,' he says politely, a twinkle in the blue eyes that glow from his big moon face. 'Your mother hasn't been entirely honest with you, but I'm going to be, particularly as you have come here with these . . . concerns, and rightly so, as the boxes were in my possession for the past year.'

I squirm in my chair, embarrassed now, when before I was determined.

'Your uncles, Fergus's brothers, expressed dissatisfaction with Gina keeping your dad's things. They felt that the boxes weren't safe in Gina's hands, given her feelings towards your dad. But Gina was suspicious of why they wanted the boxes, as they and Fergus weren't close in her opinion, and so we all came to the arrangement that the boxes would be kept safe by a third party. Both parties were satisfied that I was neutral enough to be trusted with them. It's not the usual thing for me to do, but I was fond of Fergus and so I did. Unfortunately my personal circumstances have changed and I no longer have the space to store his things.'

I nod along quickly, trying to kill my earlier embarrassment and surprised that Mum didn't share this with me. Did she think he wouldn't tell me? I was oblivious to all of this family drama while setting up Dad in the rehab. I was just focused on him getting better, going from the hospital to his apartment, to work, taking care of the kids, completely exhausted, like a walking zombie. I took photos of Dad's furniture and sold it all online, delivering couches across the city, meeting people on George's Street at five a.m. to hand over a coffee table. I think of the days it took to sort the items to keep from the items to sell, seeing how my dad lived, his private things, all of it so simple really, apart from the sickening stashes of chocolate bars, the disturbing collection of DVDs that you never want to imagine your dad watching, but no grand revelations. No sign of any person other than my father in the whole place.

I went through every room, every cupboard, every drawer and I sold every single one of those cupboards that wasn't stuck to the floor or wall. Of all the boxes I taped shut, I never came across these marbles. Somebody else packed them, and sent them to Mickey's home, and if it wasn't me or Mum, then who?

'I don't know how else I can help you, Sabrina.'

Me neither.

'My only thought is that they weren't in the boxes before they were delivered to me, but of course if it was just you and your mam who packed everything up then I don't know what to think.'

But it's glaringly obvious. He's being polite, but if it wasn't me then it had to have been Mum, who has already lied to me about why the boxes ended up with Mickey in the first place.

So many secrets, so many things I didn't know. What else don't I know?

10

PLAYING WITH MARBLES

Bounce About

I see Hamish again when I'm nineteen years old. It's the last thing I would have expected: to get on a plane and leave Ireland for the first time in my adult life, since arriving on a boat when I was five, for this reason.

Ma receives a visit from a garda, who received a phone call from the Irish embassy to say that Fergus Boggs has been found dead in London, and that somebody needs to go and identify the body.

'London? But Fergus is here!'

Ma shouts and yells the house down, everybody runs to her, everybody that doesn't run to her runs looking for me. I'm sitting in the pub having a pint and playing Bounce About when I should be at work in Mattie's butcher shop with the other lads. I've just started and they have me doing the worst jobs, like washing away guts, which when hungover on the first week sent me racing to the toilet to vomit. It doesn't make me queasy now, just bored, and I find a few pints at lunchtime gets me through it in the afternoons. I'm more interested in the kind of meat that Mattie's buying, I'd like to get into that side of things, sourcing better kinds of meat, it's something I want to talk to him about, but I know he won't listen until I do at least a year of stinking, stenching time in the back.

Angus finds me at the pub and grabs me, tells me to say nothing, he doesn't want to hear it, and drags me down the road to the house. I think I'm in trouble for stepping out of the shop for a pint when I should have been having a sandwich in the backyard. Duncan meets us at the front door, which is wide open. Mammy is holding court in the living room, surrounded by worried women, tea and scones. Three-year-old Joe is on her knee, bouncing up and down, big eyes worried and scared by Ma's hysterics. Everyone parts for me like I'm the prodigy child she's always wished for. She looks at me coming towards her like I'm an angel, with so much tenderness and love, I'm shitting myself and don't know what the fuck is going on.

She puts Joe down and stands up. He clings to her leg. Ma reaches out to my face, her hands hot from the gallons of tea, her skin rough from a lifetime of cleaning and scorching. Her face is softer than I've ever seen it, her eyes piercing blue. I suppose I've seen it when she looks at her babies, when I caught her when I was younger when she didn't know anyone was looking as she breastfed, as her eyes and the baby's connected to each other like they were having a silent conversation. I just never remember her looking at me like this.

'My son,' she says tenderly, flooded with relief. 'You're alive.'

Which brings a sudden snigger out of me because I have no idea where this is coming from, all I know is I was dragged out of the pub for this nonsensical drama. Mrs

Lynch tuts and I want to deck her because this spurs Ma on.

Ma's look of serenity fades and she slaps me hard across the face. I mustn't look sorry enough because she does it again.

'Okay, Ma,' Angus says, pulling me away. 'He didn't know. He didn't know.'

'I didn't know what?'

'A garda called by—'

Ma is helped to her seat, the grieving queen bee.

'He said that Fergus Boggs was found dead. In London,' Angus says. He slaps me hard on the shoulder, squeezes me, 'But you're not dead, you're grand. Aren't ya?'

I can't reply, my heart is hammering. I know it then, I just know it. Hamish. No one else would have picked my name and he wouldn't have picked anybody else's name either. It was always me. Me and him. Him and me. Even if we didn't know it at the time, I know it the moment I think he's dead, feel his loss now more than when he upped and left.

'Lighten up, everybody, will you?' Duncan says and the women relax, get the joke, suddenly see the funny side in what has happened.

But Ma doesn't laugh. And I don't laugh. Our eyes meet. We both know.

I fly over on my first flight. Windy conditions and we bounce about the place, my mind completely off Hamish as I hang on for dear life and think about what a strange fate it would be, me dying going over to see if a fella who called himself me is dead.

Mrs Smith's son Seamus is living in London and it's been arranged that I can stay with him for a few nights. I don't know what Seamus told his ma about his new life but I don't imagine it's this. Sharing one damp Victorian room with six other lads isn't my idea of making it big in London, so I stay out as late as I can on the first night to avoid having to sleep on that floor. I avoid the Irish bar they all tell me to go to in case I'm forced to join up, and instead, after asking around in an English accent, I find a place called the Bricklayer's Arms that advertises marble games. But first I walk the streets for hours knowing that every minute that passes is a minute closer to seeing Hamish, and sometimes I want the time to slow down, and other times speed up.

I strike up a game of marbles with some locals, just a game of Bounce About, like I'd been doing earlier, as if I was picking up where I left off. I can't believe it's the same day and I'm in a different country waiting to identify the body of someone claiming to be me, feeling like a different person.

The game is for two to four players but three of us play until the third guy vomits on himself and then falls asleep in the corner with his own piss leaking down his leg. It's just me and a fella named George then, who calls me Paddy like he doesn't know it's an insult. It's okay because I beat him hands down. It doesn't involve huge skill – you throw marbles, not shoot them. The medium-sized marbles are called bouncers; the first player throws his forward, the second player tries to hit it, and so on. It's about as much as he can handle, he's had so much to drink. If a bouncer is hit, the owner pays the thrower one marble, but you can't take the bouncer, which is a problem because George's bouncer is the only marble I'm interested in. Bouncers get away with murder that way.

It's a Czechoslovakian bullet-mould marble, it has a frosty finish to it. George tells me something about an acid bath.

I ask him if I can buy it and he says no, but he gives it to me instead. I've told him about why I'm here and who I think I'm going to see and he feels sorry for me, says he had to view a body once that had been chopped up into bits and I wonder if it was an official identification at all, or something to do with his lifestyle. I even wonder if he was the one who had to chop it up into bits. His story doesn't scare me off, though, oddly, the gift of the marble does make me feel a little better. I pocket the bullet and after getting lost for almost two hours, fall into Seamus Smith's shithole bedsit at four a.m., stepping over bodies to reach my space, one guy going at himself till all hours thinking nobody can hear him.

Four hours later I'm at the morgue looking at Hamish's dead naked body on a slab. The coroner just shows me his face but I pull the sheet down more. Hamish has a birthmark on his belly button shaped like Australia; nothing really like Australia, but then that would have ruined the joke. 'Want to see down under?' I hear Hamish say to the girls, so clearly, like his lips could have moved. I smile, remembering him, everything good about him and the coroner looks at me, angry, like I'm smiling because I'm glad he's dead.

'I was just thinking of something funny he used to say,' I explain.

Then he looks at me like he doesn't care, he's just here for the scientific part, not the emotional bit.

I feel the Czech bullet-mould in my pocket.

'Was he shot?' I ask. I always thought if Hamish was going to go before old age, that's what he'd prefer. Like a cowboy, he loved those films.

'No. Do you see a bullet hole?' he asks, like he's defending himself, like I'm accusing him of missing the evidence.

'No.'

'Well then.'

'What happened to him?'

'The police will tell you.' He covers Hamish's face again. I haven't seen Hamish for four years but I'll never know how much he changed in that time because he was so bloated and bruised I could barely recognise him. I know it's him all right, but I couldn't begin to tell what he looked like as an older Hamish. They think he'd been in the water for two days, probably more, because his body floated to the surface, and decomposition had begun. The police officer that I talk to afterwards says something about the skin on his foot falling off like a sock, but that's when I tune out. The part I remember more than anything else is that nobody had reported him missing.

Fergus Boggs was drunk. He had drunk far too much when he bothered the two bouncers of Orbit nightclub on Saturday night. When they turned him away they say he got aggressive. I have no reason not to believe them, it sounds like any of the Boggs boys so far, even little Joe has a meltdown when you tell him no, lying on his stomach and kicking his shoes off regardless where we are. As the youngest, Ma rarely tells him no. One bouncer got so frustrated with Fergus that he told him he'd let him in the side door so the boss wouldn't see him get in so drunk, and without paying. Instead he took him to the dark alley and beat the lights out of him. With a broken nose and a broken rib, Fergus Boggs stumbled along until he tripped, fell into a river and drowned. He was twenty-five.

Seamus Smith is waiting for me when I come out of the morgue. He's smoking a cigarette and looking shifty, his hands shoved into tiny pockets in a leather jacket.

'Is it him?' he asks.

'Yeah.'

'Fuck.'

He takes out a packet of cigarettes and hands me one. I appreciate him bringing me to the pub from there because I don't remember anything from the cigarette onwards. The next day me and Hamish get the boat together for the second time as I bring him home.

The police officer wasn't pressing charges against the bouncer who 'bounced him about a little' because the police agreed Fergus was being a nuisance and the bouncer didn't mean to kill him, it was Fergus's inebriation that led to his drowning. Bouncers get away with murder that way.

11

POOL RULES

No Pushing

When I opened the box of marbles, I opened up a can of worms.

I don't know if I sensed it when I looked at them, when I held them in my hands and my eyes scanned the inventory, but I knew it when I saw the way Dad's face changed as soon as he set eyes on the bloodies. And it's confirmed even further by learning of the messiness my family created simply by the decision of where to store boxes. I don't know what to do next. It's the moon, I've too many thoughts, can't process them all at once. Breathe.

Once outside Mickey's office I call Mum, fuming inside.

'How's Miss Marble getting on?' She laughs at her own joke. 'Did you see Mickey Flanagan yet?' I hear the anxiety in her voice and I wonder if she's afraid of me discovering her lie.

'Which of Dad's brothers didn't want you to store the boxes?' I ask.

She sighs. 'Mickey told you. Oh, love, I didn't want him to tell you.'

'I appreciate that, Mum, but if I'm going to find these marbles, I need the truth?'

'You're really going to look for these missing *marbles*? Sabrina, love, is everything okay? With you and Aidan? Are you still going to counselling?'

'Yes, we're fine,' I say, as if on autopilot. I should never have mentioned the counselling to Mum, now she thinks everything I say and do is a result of our couple counselling, which I'm going to for Aidan's sake. I'd be perfectly content not to bother. But I've been saying that a lot lately without really thinking about it. Are we fine? I change the subject back. 'Tell me what happened with the boxes and Dad's brothers.'

She sighs, knowing she has no choice but to address it, and as she speaks I hear the anger. Not at me but at him, at the situation last year. 'Angus called me, but it was really all of them that had the problem. They'd heard we'd been around at Fergus's apartment. They didn't want me with his belongings. They were fine with you having them, but I told them you had no space. You know the rest.'

I try to picture Angus. I was never particularly close to my uncles and aunts, I never saw them much because Dad didn't. While growing up I saw them at the odd family event but we never stayed long, Dad was always uptight, somebody would always say something to annoy him and we'd leave early. Mum never protested, she hated his family events too, somebody would always end up in a fight, a drunken cousin flipping over a table of drinks in a fight with a girlfriend, or sisters-in-law who couldn't keep their sharp tongues to themselves. There was always drama at a Boggs–Doyle event and we rarely went. We spent most of the time popping in, or as Dad would say, 'Let's show our faces.' That's all he ever wanted to do with his family, show his face. Perhaps that's all he did with us too, because who is this man I'm learning about?

Angus is the oldest of the brothers, a butcher, so not the one with a van. I think Duncan has the van, but that's not to say they weren't all in on it. It's been a long time since I've seen them all. I haven't been dragged to a family do since I was eighteen, and I didn't invite them to my wedding. Aidan and I had a small one in Spain with twenty guests.

Do I really want to visit Angus to ask him what happened last year? Why didn't you want my mum to store Dad's things? Did you want them for yourself so you could steal Dad's marbles? What a ridiculous line of questioning. And do I really blame the brothers for not wanting Mum to keep their brother's things? They were absolutely right and I only see that now. At any moment Mum could have decided to throw them on a bonfire, fuelled by wine and a bitter memory of something Dad did to her to make her life a misery, even though she's now happily remarried.

'Did you know about him having a marble collection?' I ask her again, firmly. 'Did you pack them away in his apartment?'

'Not at all. I told you that yesterday.'

There is enough annoyance and hurt in her voice for me to believe her.

'And if I had come across them when we were packing them up, I would have thrown them straight in the skip,' she says defiantly. 'A grown man with marbles, honestly.'

I believe her, but it makes me wonder what she came across in the apartment that I didn't, that she considered not worth keeping. Maybe she wasn't the right person to help me out at the time. And why am I only thinking of all this now? Guilt is eating away at me. I was busy, I was stressed, I was worried. I should have handled it all better. Perhaps I should have invited his brothers to join us, see if there was anything they'd like, from his past. Perhaps that's why they were angry with Mum, I didn't include them in anything. I just took over, thinking I knew everything there was to know about him.

'Mum, have you remembered what your marble fight with Dad was about?' I refuse to let that one go. I know she was holding out on me and I need to know as much as I can right now. No more secrets.

'Oh, I can barely remember now . . .' She goes quiet for a moment and I think that's the end of her answer, when she suddenly continues. 'We were on our honeymoon, that much I remember. He went wandering off on his own, like he always did, no explanation, then came back after spending months' worth of our savings on some ridiculous marble.'

I slide the inventory out of the folder as I'm driving, keeping a close eye on the road. I cast my eyes over the list.

'Was it a heart?'

'I can't remember the design.' She goes quiet. 'Actually, yes, I think it was. It drove me insane that he would spend all of our money on it. We spent three days in Venice unable to eat a thing, I remember sharing a can of Coke one day because we hadn't the money for anything else. Silly eejit,' she says softly. 'But that was your father all over. By the way, how did you know it was a heart?'

'Oh. I just . . . guessed.'

I run my finger over Dad's handwriting: '*Heart – damaged. Condition: collectable. Venice '79.*'

So it wasn't Mum who packed up the marbles, or took from them. I think I've established she would have wanted nothing to do with them.

Access. I have to think who had access to the boxes. It wasn't Mickey, it wasn't his family. There's no way of me ever really knowing that for sure, but I have to trust him. Access. Contacting the delivery company from last year seems a long shot: Excuse me, did you ever happen to steal some items you were delivering last year? Maybe Mickey is wrong about the marbles not being in the box when they arrived at his house. Maybe they were taken yesterday, and yesterday's delivery driver isn't a long shot.

'Can I help you, Sabrina?' Amy asks gently as I walk back into the waiting room.

I try to compose myself. *The moon made me do it.* 'I received a delivery from Mickey yesterday, from his home to my dad's hospital, and I was trying to figure out who delivered it. Do you know anything about it?'

'Know about it? I spent an entire weekend in that garage, unpaid, arranging deliveries. Not my job, but tell that to Mickey.'

My heart leaps a little, feeling a bit of hope. 'Were the boxes sealed before you sent them?' I ask lightly, not wanting to offend her.

'Oh God,' she groaned. 'Yes they were and they were very carefully stored, I can tell you that, but don't tell me something was broken, or missing.'

'Well, yes, actually something was missing.'

'Oh, Looper.'

'Pardon?'

'Sorry, it's Looper. The delivery guy. To explain, yes absolutely the boxes were sealed when I got to them, and I was under strict orders not to open them either. Mickey wouldn't want me seeing in his stuff – yours weren't the only ones in there, by the way. There was a bunch of stuff that had to go. Old furniture, clothes, all in storage that hadn't been touched in years, covered in dust. Anyway, I used Looper to deliver them, Mickey's nephew. He's had so many complaints, but I have no choice but to use him. Mickey's trying to help out family, you know how it is. It's between you and him, I'm afraid, I can't get involved, but I can give you his contact details.'

'Yes please,' I say happily, feeling that perhaps all is not lost. I'm getting places.

'Do you know your way around here?' she asks, handing the address over reluctantly.

'No but I have satnav.'

Amy bites her lip. 'Satnav won't even know where you're going,' she says. 'It's pretty remote.'

'It's okay, I have time,' I say, moving towards the door. For the first time in I don't know how long, I feel a surge of excitement.

'Just be careful, he's not really a people person, and particularly on a day like today –' she gestures towards the sky – 'days like today are made for people like him,' she adds before I close the door.

I drive to the address Amy has provided, and I look up at the sun and wonder if there's anything in what Amy said. Is today the day we're doomed? Or is today the day I've finally lost it myself, going on a hunt for some lost marbles that I've no real proof ever really existed in the first place. Just a handwritten inventory from I don't know how many years ago. About to approach a man named Looper in the middle of nowhere and accuse him of stealing.

After driving up and down a few random streets, satnav giving up almost as soon as I pass the town limits, much as Amy warned, I find the right place. Looper, a concerning name in itself, lives in a small bungalow, a Seventies-style build, which has been badly maintained and looks completely run-down. The front yard is covered in car parts, tyres, engines, car hoods, random items strewn about the place. There's a white van on the front drive, beneath it a pair of legs stick out wearing filthy stone-washed jeans and workman's boots. A nearby radio blares AC/DC. I pull up outside the front gate and can't get any further as it's heavily padlocked with a sign saying 'No Trespassing – guard dogs on duty', alongside a picture of two snarling dogs.

I get out of the car and stand at the gate wondering if I have finally lost it.

'Excuse me,' I call to the pair of legs, loudly. 'Looper!'

The legs finally move and slide from under the van. A young man climbs up. He's got long greasy hair that grows from a well receded hairline, despite his youth, is wearing a white vest covered in oil, sweat and grease and who knows what else. He's more chunky than muscular but he's tall and big, like an oaf, something that wouldn't look out of place in Middle-earth.

He stares at me, wiping a tool on his T-shirt, taking me in, slowly, bit by bit. He stares at the car, then back at me and then slowly saunters towards me with the wrench in his hand, as though he's got all the time in the world and he's giving great academic thought as to whether to whack me with it. He doesn't come to the gate, stops a few strides short. He licks a snake-like tongue over his lips as he looks me up and down. Smacking sounds like I'm his next meal.

'Are you Looper?' I ask.

'Maybe. Maybe not. Depends on who's asking.'

'Well . . . I am.' I smile. A wobbly one.

Looper doesn't like this hint of a smile, he thinks he's being made fun of, doesn't like this, isn't sure why, doesn't understand. Confusion makes him feel less of a man so he behaves like more of a grunt. He hacks up a golly, spits it on the ground in clear protest.

'You're the delivery man around here?'

'The one and only. You got a job for me? 'Cos I've got a job for you . . .' He gropes his crotch and sneers.

I step back, revolted. 'Are you Mickey Flanagan's nephew?'

'Who's asking?'

'Me. Again,' I say flatly. 'I'm a client. He sent me here.' *He knows I'm here, I will be missed. Don't kill me!* 'Did you do a delivery yesterday to Dublin for your uncle?'

'I do a lot of deliveries to Dublin.'

I sincerely doubt that. 'Specifically, a hospital.'

'That where you live?' he sneers, revealing that the few teeth he has are a greenish colour. He looks me up and down, like a cat would a mouse. He wants to play. His eyes are unusual, a murky colour with not much going on in them or behind them. The thought of this man in possession of my dad's precious marbles makes me sick. I wouldn't trust this guy with anything. I look around, mostly for help, for a witness in case it all goes wrong, for a rescuer in case Looper does what I'm thinking he wants to do. There are acres upon acres surrounding the house. A burned-out car sits in the middle of one unfarmed field.

Looper follows my gaze to the fields that stretch into the distance. 'Pain in my hole. Spuds is all it was ever good for. Daddy was a farmer. Them developers offered him a fortune, he said no, says he's a farmer what else would he do? Then he went and fucking died and left it to me and no one is interested in buying it now. It's a waste of space.'

'Why don't you farm it?'

'I've my own thing going on here. My garage and delivery business.'

Nothing in this yard vaguely resembles a business.

'Want to come inside? I'll show you around.'

I look in the open front door and see mayhem in the house, dirty, piled-up, cluttered mess. I shake my head. I don't want to pass the gate.

'You brought five boxes from Mickey's garage to my dad's home. Some things are missing from the box and I'm wondering if you could . . . help me.'

'You calling me a thief?'

'No, I would like your help,' I stress. 'Did you stop off anywhere? Anybody else have access to your van?'

'I put them in the van and drove them to Dublin. Simple as.'

'Did you open the boxes? Could something have fallen out?'

He smiles. 'Tell you what, I'll answer your question if you give me a kiss.'

I back away.

'Okay okay!' he laughs. 'I'll answer your question if you shake my hand.'

That's bad enough, but I'll play along. I want him to answer my question.

Looper steps forward. Hand extended. He puts the wrench in his back pocket and raises his hand to show he's weapon free.

'Come on. If you shake my hand, I'll answer your questions. I'm a man of my word.'

I look at the hand suspiciously. I reach out and as he takes my hand, he pulls my arm roughly, pulling me towards him and grabs the back of my neck, and pulls my head close for a kiss. His lips touch mine and I'm stuck in that position. I close mine tight, not letting a part of him get into me. I try to move but I can't, his hand stays at the back of my neck. I lift my hands to his chest to push him away but he's too strong and I feel panic rising. Finally he pulls back and licks his lips and howls with laughter.

I wipe at my face furiously, wanting to run to my car. My heart pounding, I look around for help, but he's not coming after me for any more, he's standing back laughing.

'You didn't answer my question,' I say angrily, wiping my lips roughly. I refuse to leave now without an answer, or even better, without the marbles. This will not be a wasted trip.

Looper looks at me, wrench back in hand, amused. 'I picked up your boxes from Mickey's, pulled over on the motorway and had a look through them. Nothing good in it so I sealed them up again and drove to Dublin.' He shrugs unapologetically. 'Papers and some kids' marbles don't do it for me. I didn't take a thing. I suggest you look elsewhere.'

And I actually believe him. He wouldn't have the brains to have looked through the inventory. It's a book and I doubt he's ever read a book in his life. He also wouldn't have the common sense to recognise or link the items on the list to the marbles in the boxes. The person who picked the two most expensive items spent time going through the list, and the marbles, not just a quick pull-over on the road. They took the two most expensive, which would have taken time to discover as the list does not go from low to high, it is categorised by the names of the marbles.

'Was it worth it?' he winks as I storm back to the car. 'Did I help?' he calls after me.

I start up the engine and drive away. Yes, he helped.

Looper didn't take the marbles. Those marbles weren't in the box when they left Mickey Flanagan's house. I'm absolutely sure of that now. And they weren't in the boxes when they reached Mickey's house. So I have to go back. Back to last year. Maybe even further than that.

12

PLAYING WITH MARBLES

Moonie

'Fergus, it's time!' Nurse Lea says brightly as she enters my room with a great big smile on her face. She's always smiling, she has two big dimples in her cheeks, like holes, big enough to fit marbles in; maybe not average-sized marbles, but miniature ones would slot in there quite nicely and never budge. She's a young girl, a country girl, from Kerry. She sings everything and you can hear her laugh from the nurses' desk all the way down the corridor to my room at the end. My spirits are usually up but she has the ability to lift them even higher. If I've had a tough day in physio – and there are plenty of those – she always arrives with a smile on her face, a steaming mug of coffee and a cupcake. She makes them herself and hands them around to everyone. I tell her if she put as much effort into her boyfriends she'd have them eating out of her hand, but she's single and always has stories of disastrous dates to share with me.

I have a soft spot for her. She reminds me of Sabrina.

Or how Sabrina used to be before she had the boys. Now she's distracted, obviously, by three little boys on hyper drive. We start a conversation and never finish it, a lot of the time we barely get the chance to finish the sentence. She's scattier than she used to be; she used to be sharp, like Lea. She's always tired, she's put on weight too. My ma was always as tough as old boots, the only time I recall her softening is when she'd had more than one brandy, which was rare, maybe twice a year. She was rake thin, always running after the seven of us, and after her pregnancies she always managed to get her figure straight back. Maybe if I'd known my ma before she'd had us I'd see a change in her too, maybe she had a carefree spirit before us and the pressures of life and motherhood changed that. God knows I changed in my life; I'm in here now. I can't imagine her ever carefree, not even in photos, they're posed rigid and uptight-looking. Arms down by your sides, no physical contact, glum faces to the camera, which I expect was felt to be the best face forward. There is one photo-graph though, one which I keep close to me at all times, of Ma, on the beach, taken by Da, in Scotland. She's sitting on a towel on the sand, leaning back on her elbows, her face lifted to the sun, her eyes closed. She's laughing. I don't know how many times I've studied it and wondered what she's laughing at. It's a sexy pose, provocative, though I'm sure she didn't intend it to be so. Hamish is a baby and sits by her toes. She's probably laughing at something Hamish has done, or something Da said, something innocent that resulted in this look. It's odd, I know, to keep provoca-tive photos of your ma, psychotherapists would have a field day with it, but it lifts me.

When I picture Sabrina in my mind I see a screwed-up face, worried.

'Are we watching a 3-D film?' I ask Lea, teasing her about the funny glasses that she's wearing.

'I have a pair for you too,' she says, taking a pair out of her pocket and handing them to me. 'Stick them on.'

I put them on and stick out my tongue and she laughs.

'Did you forget, Fergus, the solar eclipse is today?'

I'm not sure if I'd forgotten it, as I don't remember ever knowing it.

'We have a perfect sky to see it, not a cloud anywhere. Of course we're not in the perfect place, they keep going on on the radio about the best path to stand in, but the sun is the sun, sure wherever you stand you'll see it. I've made cupcakes for everyone. Vanilla cupcakes. I wanted to make chocolate but Fidelma, my new flat mate – remember I told you about her, the Donegal nurse? She's a pig, she ate all the Cadbury bars in the fridge,' she fumes. 'Four of them. The large ones. I've put Post-its all over the flat now, "Don't touch this", "Don't eat this". Just looking at her makes me mad. And remember that new plasma TV I got from my neighbour who was throwing it out? She hasn't a clue how to use it, keeps feckin' using the wrong remote controls. Found her pointing the gas fire remote control at the TV screen.'

We both laugh at that. She gives out but not in an angry way, it's humorous, it's all with a smile on her face, and that strong sing-song voice. It's lovely, like a bird chirping outside your window on a sunny May day. She tells this story while she helps me up out of my reading chair and into the wheelchair. Lea is with me most days, but when she's not the others have a different style, which is difficult to adjust to. Some are quieter, trying to be respectful, or lost in their heads with whatever's going on in their own lives, or they're too bossy and talk at me, reminding me of my ma barking at me when I was a boy. They're not rude, but Lea just has the magic touch. She knows to talk me through it, talks about other things like what we're doing isn't happening. You want that from a person who has had to wipe your arse and clean your balls. The silence with the others makes me realise it's really happening. Tom next door can't stand her. 'Does she ever shut up?' he grumbles. He says it so loud I'm sure she's heard, but it doesn't stop her. But that's Tom, he wouldn't be happy unless he had something to complain about.

She wheels me out into the sunshine, to the small lawn that we sit out on on sunny days like today. Everyone is gathered outside and looking up at the sky with these ridiculous plastic glasses. The radio is on, Radio One, a live commentary of what we're about to see, like they've been doing all week. I've never heard so much about numbras and penumbras and then fellas on talking about voodoo stuff with the full moon, though that I believe. Sabrina could never sleep as a little girl whenever there was a full moon. She'd always come into our room, crawl into our bed, curl up in the middle of me and Gina, and lie there awake, sighing loudly, tapping on my shoulder, my face, anything to wake me up to have some company. Once I brought her downstairs and made her a hot chocolate and we sat in the dark kitchen, lights off, and watched the moon, her wide awake, staring at the moon as though hypnotised by it, as though having a silent conversation with it, me falling asleep in the chair. Gina came down and shouted the head off me, it was a school night, it was three a.m., what did I think I was doing? That was that.

I think of her now on nights when I see the full moon, wonder if she's up, sitting in her kitchen having a hot chocolate, long curls down her back, though the curls are gone now of course.

Everyone is in flying form, excited about the natural phenomenon. Lea is telling me about the date she was on last night as she applies sun cream to my face and arms. My legs are covered up. She went to the cinema with a garda from Antrim. I tut.

'You can't talk at the cinema,' I say. 'Never go to the cinema on a first date.'

'I know, I know, you told me that when he asked me and you're right, but we went for drinks afterwards and believe me I was glad of the two hours not talking, he was such an eejit, Fergus. My ex-girlfriend this, my ex-girlfriend that. Well, tell you what, fella, you can have your ex-girlfriend. I'm off.'

I chuckle.

'I'll get you a cupcake, which one do you want? I've some with jellies, marshmallows, I had Maltesers but Fidelma ate them too,' she says with a grin.

'Surprise me,' I say. While she's gone I look around and see that there's lots of visitors today. Children run around the grass, one has a kite, though no matter how fast he runs it won't take off from the ground, no wind today. There's not a cloud in the sky, it's a beautiful indigo blue, with wispy white swirls. This triggers something and I try hard to remember but I can't. This happens sometimes. A lot. And it frustrates me.

'Here you go.' She returns with a plate of two cupcakes and a soft drink.

I look at them, feeling a bit confused.

'Don't you want them?' she asks.

'No, no, it's not that,' I say. 'Is my wife coming?'

She stiffens a little, but pulls up a chair and sits down beside me.

'Do you mean Gina?'

'Of course I mean Gina. My wife, Gina. And Sabrina, and the boys.'

'Remember the boys are going off camping with their dad today? Aidan was to bring them to Wicklow with their cousins.'

'Ah.' I don't remember that. Sounds like fun for them. Alfie will no doubt go hunting for worms, he likes that. Reminds me a bit of Bobby when he was little, except instead of eating them like Bobby did, he likes to name them. He once made me keep Whilomena worm in a cup for an entire day. 'But what about Sabrina? Where is she?' I picture that screwed-up worried face, frowning in concentration like she's trying to solve a problem, or remember the answer to something that she's forgotten. Yes, that's what it is. Always as though she has forgotten something. If the boys are all off on their jaunt then she must be alone. Unless she's with Gina, but Gina is very busy these days, with Robert, her new husband. Of course, that's why Lea looked at me in that way, I must stop calling Gina my wife. I sometimes forget these things.

'Sabrina was here this morning, remember? I think she had some stuff to take care of, but she'll be back in to visit tomorrow as usual, I'm sure.'

I feel around my pockets.

'Can I help you, Fergus?'

Lea again, always at the right time.

'My phone, I think I left it in my room.'

'I think it's getting close to the eclipse now. Will I get it for you after? I don't want you to miss it, being on the phone.'

I think of Sabrina and I have an overwhelming feeling for her not to be alone. I see her as a little girl again, her serious pale face lit up by the white light.

'Now, please, if you don't mind.'

I feel like I've blinked and Lea is back. I was lost in a thought but now I can't remember what that thought was. Lea's breathless and I feel bad for nearly making her miss the eclipse. Of course she's excited about a thing like that. She should have gone on a date to watch it, if she could have got the time off, and I'm selfishly glad she didn't. The others would have waited until after the eclipse to get my phone.

I dial Sabrina's number.

'Dad,' she answers immediately, on the first ring. 'I was just thinking about you.'

I smile. 'I picked up on your thoughts. Is everything okay?'

'Yeah, yeah,' she says, distracted. 'Hold on, let me move away for a minute so I can talk.'

'Oh. You're not alone then?'

'No.'

'Good. I was hoping you weren't. I know Aidan and the boys are camping.' I feel foolishly proud of myself for sounding like I remembered such a fact, when I didn't. 'Where are you?'

'I'm sitting on the hood of a car in the middle of a field in Cavan.'

'What on earth?'

She laughs and it's light.

'Are you there with friends?'

'No. But there's plenty of people around watching it. It's one of those official viewing places.'

Silence. There's more to it, and she's not telling me.

'I'm just travelling around a bit, looking for something.'

'You lost something?'

'Yes. In a way.'

'I hope you find it.'

'Yeah.' She sounds distant again. 'So how are you? Are you in a good spot to see the eclipse?'

'I'm great. I'm sitting outside on the lawn with everyone eating cakes and drinking fizzy drinks, watching the sky. I don't think we're in the correct path, whatever it's called, but it's keeping us all busy. I was thinking though while waiting, something today reminded me of an incident when you were two.' It was Lea's smile that triggered the memory, Lea's dimples that would fit miniature marbles, and I thought of the marbles because of the pouch in Sabrina's hand this morning. 'Don't think I ever told you about it.'

'If I did something bad then I'm sure Mum told me.'

'No, no, she never knew about this. I didn't tell her.'

'Oh?'

'She had to go out on an errand one day, a doctor's appointment, or maybe it was a funeral, I can't quite remember, but she left you with me. You were two. You managed to get your hands on some marbles that you found in my office.'

'Really?' she sounds surprised, interested, so eager, surprisingly so as that isn't the high point of the story. 'What kind of marbles were they?'

'Oh, tiny ones. Miniature ones. It's getting darker here, is it happening there too?'

'Yes, it's happening here. Go on.'

'Is that a dog I hear howling?'

'Yes, the animals are getting nervous. I don't think they're happy with the situation. Tell me more, Dad, please.'

'Well, you put the marble up your nostril. Right or left, can't remember which.'

'I what?' she asks. 'Why would I do that?'

'Because you were two years old, and why not?'

112

She laughs.

'Well, I couldn't get the bloody thing out. I tried everything I could, so eventually I had to bring you to A&E. They tried tweezers, tried to make you blow your nose, which you couldn't do, you kept blowing out through your mouth until eventually Dr Punjabi, an Indian man that I subsequently had a few dealings with, did a kind of CPR. He blew into your mouth and pressed your nostril closed and pop, out it came.'

We both laugh. It is dusk now, everyone around me is looking up, glasses on and looking like wallies, me included. Lea sees me and gives me an excited thumbs up.

'When your mam got home that day you told her that an Indian man kissed you. I pretended I had no idea what you were talking about, that you'd seen it on a cartoon or something.'

'I remember that story,' she says, breathless. 'Our next-door neighbour Mary Hayes said that I told her I kissed an Indian man. I never knew where it came from.'

'You told the entire street I think.'

We laugh.

'Tell me more about the moonie,' Sabrina says.

I'm taken aback by her question. It unsettles me and I don't know why. I feel uncomfortable and a bit upset. It's all very confusing. Perhaps it's got to do with what's happening up there in the sky. Maybe everybody feels like this right now. I gather myself.

'The moonie marble,' I say, conjuring up the image in my mind. 'An appropriate story for today, perhaps that's why it came to mind. I was looking for a particular type, but couldn't find it, could only get the miniature ones. A box of two hundred and fifty of them, like little pearls, and they came in a wonderful glass jar, like an oversized jam jar. I don't know how you got your hands on one. I left you for a moment, I suppose, or wasn't watching when I should have been.'

'What did the marble look like?'

'You don't want to know about this, Sabrina, it's boring—'

'It's not boring,' she interrupts, voice insistent. 'It's important. I'm interested. Tell me about it, I want to hear.'

I close my eyes and picture it, my body relaxing. 'A moonie marble is a translucent marble, and I suppose what I like about it is that when a bright light casts a shadow on it there's a distinct fire burning at its centre. They have a remarkable inner glow.'

And it's odd, and I feel so odd, in this unusual moment when the sun has faded, disappeared behind the moon in the middle of the afternoon, that I realise why it is exactly that I hold on to my ma's photograph. It's because, just like the moonie, you can see her fire burning at her centre, and that in anything and anyone is something to behold, to collect and preserve, take it out to study when you feel the need of a lift, or reassurance, maybe when the glow in you has dimmed and the fire inside you feels more like embers.

'Dad? Dad, are you okay?' she's whispering and I don't know why she's whispering.

The moon has passed the sun entirely and the daylight has returned again. Everyone around me is cheering.

I feel a tear trickle down my cheek.

13

POOL RULES

No Peeing in the Pool

I'm sitting on the hood of my car, in a field where I've pulled over to view the eclipse. A clever local farmer has charged two euro to everybody to effectively park and view the eclipse on his land. Every car hood is filled with people wearing ridiculous glasses. I've just hung up the phone to Dad and there is a lump in my throat but I'm ignoring that and flicking manically through the pages of Dad's marble inventory. I stop suddenly.

Moonies.

He has many but I run my finger down the list and find what I'm looking for.

Miniature moonies (250) and there is the mention of the glass jar too, in mint condition. Below that is *'World's Best Moon' a Christensen Agate Company single-stream marble* and Dad's description: *A translucent white opalescent marble, has tiny air bubbles inside and a slightly bluish tinge to it. Courtesy of Dr Punjabi.*

Everyone is cheering around me as the sun has appeared

again in its total form. I don't know how long the entire thing took, a few minutes maybe, but everyone is hugging and clapping, moved by the event and on a natural high. My eyes are moist. It was the tone of Dad's voice which startled me and moved me the most. It had completely altered, it sounded like another man was talking to me. Somebody else shone through and told a story, a secret story about him and me as a child, but it wasn't just that, it was a marble story. In the thirty years of my life I don't recall that word passing his lips and now, while I'm on this . . . quest and while I watch a natural phenomenon, I feel overwhelmed. I take my eclipse-viewing glasses off to wipe my eyes. I must drive directly to Dad now, talk to him about the marbles. It didn't feel right to raise the issue before when he clearly didn't remember, but perhaps the bloodies triggered more memories today.

I exhale slowly, deliberately, and hear Aidan's voice from a previous conversation.

'What's wrong?'

'Nothing,' I snap.

'You sighed,' he says, demonstrating it. It's heavy and slow, and sad. 'You do it all the time.'

'I wasn't sighing, I was just . . . exhaling.'

'Isn't that what sighing is?'

'No, it's not. I just . . . doesn't matter.' I continue making the school lunch in silence. Butter, ham, cheese, bread, slice. Next.

He bangs the fridge closed. I realise I'm not communicating again.

'It's just a habit,' I say, making an effort to communicate, not to snap, not to be angry. I must follow the counsellor's rules. I don't want to be in the spotlight again this week for all of my bad faults. I don't want to be at counselling

116

at all. Aidan thinks it will help us. I, on the other hand, find that silence and tolerance is the best way forward, even if the tolerance is on the edge, particularly when I don't know what the problem is, or even if there is one. I'm just told that my behaviour points to the fact that there is. My behaviour being one of silence and tolerance. It's a vicious circle.

'I hold my breath and then I release it,' I explain to Aidan.

'Why do you hold your breath?' he asks.

'I don't know.'

I think he's going to get in a huff again, because he'll think I'm holding something back, some enormous secret that doesn't exist but which he thinks does. But he doesn't say anything, he's thinking about it.

'Maybe you're waiting for something to happen,' he says.

'Maybe,' I say without really thinking it through, adding the raisins to the lunch box, just happy he's not in a huff any more. Argument avoided, I don't have to worry about the eggshells that surround him. Or maybe they're around me.

But I think about it now. Yeah, maybe I am waiting for something to happen. Maybe it will never happen. Maybe I will have to make it happen myself. Maybe that's what I'm doing now.

My phone rings and I don't recognise the number.

'Hello?'

'Sabrina, Mickey Flanagan here. Can you talk?'

'Yes, of course. I'm just on my way home, I pulled in to watch the eclipse.' I wonder if he knows about my trip to his nephew. I hope not. Accusing him was one thing, accusing a nephew would be a double insult. Even though it turns out he did open the boxes.

117

'Ah, a remarkable thing wasn't it? I went home to watch it with my better half, Judy. We were talking about you and the marbles.' He pauses and I know something is coming up. 'We were talking about your boxes and Judy remembered that they didn't all come together on the same day in the single delivery.'

'No?' I sit up straighter, slow the car down.

'The first boxes came in one van with my delivery fella, just like I arranged with the family. But Judy reminded me just now that a few days later a few more boxes arrived, I forgot about it but Judy didn't. She remembers because I hadn't told her that I was storing anything for anyone and she only found out when a woman arrived to the house with three more boxes. Judy had to call me at the office to check. Wasn't sure if the woman was a loo-lah making it up.'

'A woman?'

'That's right.'

'A delivery woman?'

'No, Judy doesn't think that she was. And Judy's good like that. Even though it was a year ago, she's perceptive. Sharp memory. She wasn't driving a van, just a car. She doesn't know anything about the woman at all, they didn't talk much. She thought maybe she was a neighbour, or a colleague.'

'And this woman delivered *three* boxes?'

'She did.'

Which would have to make it the boxes of marbles. Wouldn't it? Again I think of Mum, and wonder if for some reason she's holding back, if she hadn't wanted me to see these three boxes.

'One other thing,' he adds in a rush and sounds embarrassed by the minor detail. 'Judy said she was a blonde woman.'

118

My mother is not blonde. I think of my aunts but dismiss it quickly; I haven't seen them for years, they could have purple hair for all I know, or had blonde hair last year and no hair now. I have more questions, but really it's all he can help me with.

'Good luck, Sabrina,' Mickey says. 'I hope you find them. It sure would put my mind at ease.'

14

PLAYING WITH MARBLES

Steelies

Commies. The poor boy's marble. They were the first kind of marble. Made of clay, not always round and perfect but they were cheap and common, and they were what got every child playing outside during World War I. Then the aggies and porcelain came along, and glass marbles that were prettier, no two alike. Glass is my preference. But there are also steelies. I have a few of them too. Steelies are chrome-coated solid metal, like knights in battle, and they make deadly shooters. They're heavy and fast and send opponents' marbles flying out of the ring. That's me today. I'm surrounded by glass and porcelain, maybe even a little clay, but I'm the steelie. I'm twenty-four, it's my wedding day and I'm sending all the men in Gina's life out of the ring.

Iona parish church is the venue for the big day. Gina's local church where she was baptised, received first confession, first communion as a little bride, was confirmed and took the pledge and now finally to get married. The same priest who carried out all those landmark events in her life marries us today and looks at me in the same way he has since the moment we met.

He fucking hates me.

What kind of family has a priest as a family friend? Gina's kind of family. He buried her dad, comforted her ma on many late nights of free whisky and advice and he looks at me now like the bastard who's taking his place in the family clan. I said it to Gina. Told her he was looking at me oddly. She said it's because he's known her since she was born, he's protective, he's fatherly. I didn't say so but I think it's the look of a father who needs to be locked up and given a good beating.

Gina says I'm paranoid about most of her friends not liking me. Maybe I am. I think they look at me funny. Or maybe it's the fact they're so polite, like I can't figure out who they really are, because they're not shouting across from me at the table or pinning me down and telling me what they really think, that makes me suspicious of them. There was no politeness in my family, no smokescreens. Not in my house, not in my school, not on my street. I know where I stand with them, but the priest doesn't like me and I know it. I know it from the way that he looks at me when Gina's not looking. Two men, two stags who at any moment want to crash heads, tear each other's antlers off. I was glad Gina's dad is dead, so I wouldn't have to deal with that male-ownership bullshit, the fella who's 'stealing' the daughter away, but I didn't expect to have the issue with the family priest.

And the family doctor.

Jesus, him too. What kind of family has a family doctor? Gina's kind of family.

When we were sick, Ma had her own ways of getting us

better. Baking soda and water for sunburn, butter and sugar for a cough, brown sugar and boiling water for constipation. I remember I'd a lump on my knee so Mattie dipped it in boiling water then hit it with a book; simple, it disappeared. A pimple on Hamish's nose was cut off with scissors then treated with aftershave. Iodine for cuts. Gargled salt water for throats. Rarely were we on antibiotics. Rarely were we with a doctor for enough time as to strike up the friendship Gina and her ma have with their GP. No family doctor and definitely none that would care who the fuck we marry. But that's Gina's family. Even worse, or better, I'm not sure, I'll be part of their family. I can hear Hamish chuckling. I hear it as I fix my tie in the toilet and prepare for the reception that Gina's grandda is paying for.

'Best day of your life?' Angus asks cheekily, taking a piss beside me in the urinal, disturbing my thoughts.

'Yeah.'

I'd asked Angus to be my best man, wished Hamish was here to do it even though he'd be a thousand times more risky and send every family anything running from the reception with his speech. No, that's wrong. Hamish was subtle. He wasn't like the rest, he observed, knew how to hustle, judge the atmosphere and then make his move. It didn't mean he wouldn't do anything wrong, but at least he'd think about it beforehand, not shoot out the first thing that came into his head like the others. Five years since he died and he's still alive in my head. But Angus was the closest thing to Hamish and if I didn't involve my family in the wedding in some way there'd be blue murder. If I'd really had the choice I'd have asked my mate Jimmy, but it's complicated there. Shame, really, seeing as he's the person I most enjoy talking to.

I talk to him more than anyone else. We're always talking

about something, as long as the something is about nothing. I could do that all day with him. He's the same age as me, he's into marbles too, that's how we met, and we play marbles a few times a week. Only grown man I know who does. He says he knows a few others, we joke about putting a team together, going for the International title. I don't know. Maybe we actually will some day.

It felt odd, not telling Jimmy about today. Friends would do that, wouldn't they? Not us though. He doesn't exactly spill the beans on himself though either; just enough for me to figure it out eventually, but he can be so bloody cryptic. I like it this way. Why? I've asked myself that a lot. I like it when I can keep myself to myself. I can control what people know about me. The boy from Scotland who moved to Dublin for everyone to talk about, slept on the floor for a year with everyone talking, before moving to Mattie's house after a quick marriage with everyone talking – and they were right to, Ma's baby Tommy came 'early'; then us as kids, wild as anything; and then, much later, after Hamish died, the talk, everybody talking about what he did or didn't do. Everyone summing him up in one phrase or one word or one look like they knew him, but they never did and never could. Not like I did. I don't even think my other brothers knew Hamish like I did. And I wanted to get away from all that. All that talk. I wanted to be who I wanted to be, because I wanted to. No reasons, no talk. Hamish did it, but he left the country, I don't know if I could do that.

Get me away from all of them but not too far. They drive me crazy but I need them. I need to see them at least, from afar, know that they're all right.

If I'd wanted to marry a girl I'd fingered when I was fourteen I'd have stayed put but I didn't. I was twenty-three years old, ready for marriage, and leaving my home turf to meet the likes of Gina was better. Not that I travelled far. Fifteen minutes' walk away. Just a new community is all. And we didn't come from nothing either. Lived on a farm in Scotland till the age of five, Ma met Da when she moved there to be a nanny, then after sleeping on Aunty Sheila's floor, we moved to a nice house too, terraced house on St Benedict's Gardens, around the corner from our stomping ground Dorset Street, Mattie's family home that he got to keep when his ma and da kicked the bucket. Mattie does grand with the butcher's, all of us working there now, giving every penny that we earn to Ma, until marriage. But it's not where you're raised, it's how you're raised, and Gina's ma raised her differently to how Ma raised us. Raising men is different, I've heard Ma say when her and Mrs Lynch were talking about her girls.

I wanted someone better than me. I didn't know until later that was because *I* wanted to be better, like she'd rub off on me. Not more money but the politeness, the fucking genuine way she cared about what absolute tosspots were saying. We both lost our das at a young age so you can't say she had a sheltered life, no child should have to live through that, but everything she did was within three streets of her house. The same for her friends. School, shops, work. Her da ran a button factory, they lived in one of those big houses in Iona, plenty of room for lots of children that they didn't get to have because he died, dropped dead of a heart attack one day. Her ma turned their house into a guest house, they do well on match days with Croker nearby, and Gina works there with her. Always the perfect hosts. Polite. Welcoming. Every time I meet them it's as if they're standing at their guest desk, no matter where they are.

I knew Gina's da died and I used that to chat her up. I

used my da dying to get her, making up a load of old crap about how much I missed him, felt him around me, wondered if he was looking down on me and all that type of thing. I've learned that women love that stuff. It felt kind of nice to be that lad talking like that but I've never felt Da around me. Not once. Not ever. Not when I needed him. I'm not bitter about that, Da's dead, dead's dead, and when you're dead you'd think you'd want to just enjoy being dead without having to worry about the people you left behind. Worrying is for the living.

Hamish, though, I don't know, sometimes I think it with him, about him hanging around. If I'm about to do something that maybe I shouldn't, I hear him, that smoker's laugh that he had at sixteen, or I hear him warning me, the sound of my name coming through teeth clamped tight together, or I feel his fist against my ribs as he tries to stop me. But that's just my memory, isn't it? Not him actually meddling, helping me out, like he's a ghost.

I could have talked to Gina about Hamish but I didn't. I chose Da. Easier to make stuff up that way. It doesn't make me a liar, or a bad person. I wouldn't be the first lad to get a girl just out of saying things she wanted to hear. Angus got Caroline when he pretended for six weeks to have a broken leg after she ran into him on her bicycle. She kept visiting, feeling all guilty and every time she was coming he'd run in from playing football in the alley and leg it to the couch and put his leg up on cushions. We all had to go along with it. I think Ma thought it was funny, though she didn't smile. But she didn't tell him to stop either. I think she liked Caroline visiting. They used to talk. I think Ma liked having a girl in the house. Angus got her in the end. Duncan, too. He pretended to like Abba for an entire year. Him and Mary even had it as their first dance on their wedding day before he told her that night, drunk, that he hated it and never wanted to hear it again. She ran to the toilet crying and it took four girls and a make-up kit to get her out.

On our first proper date I took Gina to an Italian restaurant on Capel Street. I thought she'd like something exotic like that even though pasta wasn't my thing. I told her about playing marbles then and she laughed, thinking I was messing.

'Ah come on, Fergus, seriously, what do you really play? Football?'

It was then. I didn't tell her, for a few reasons. I was embarrassed that she'd laughed. I felt uncomfortable in the restaurant, the waiters made me nervous, were watching me like I was going to rob the knife and fork. The prices on the menu were more than I thought they'd be and she'd ordered starter *and* main course. I was going to have to think of something before she went for dessert. Anyway when she laughed, I thought, yeah maybe she's right, maybe it's stupid, maybe I won't play any more. And then I thought I can still play and have her, and that's the way it went, thinking it's no big deal keeping them separate, it's not as if I'm cheating on her, though I had a few times by then. Waiting for a virgin wife, I had to be relieved a few times by Fiona Murphy. I swear she knew how desperate I was as soon as she'd see me. I didn't bring Gina to my local, too many reasons, Fiona Murphy being one of them and every other girl I was with. Fiona literally had me in the palm of her hand. Her da had a job in the Tayto factory and she always had cheese-and-onion breath. But now that I'm married I'll have to change all that. A vow's a vow.

I've been with Gina for one year and she hasn't met my family much in that time. Enough times to not cause outrage on either side, but I know it's not enough. Short visits, quick visits. Pop into the house, drop by a party. Never let her get to know them, because then she'd get to know me, or the me she might think I am. I want her to know me through being with me.

'There's some drama going on with one of Gina's brides-maids,' Angus says. 'The one with the kegs for tits.'

I laugh. 'Michelle.'

'She says her boyfriend just got up and left the church, saw him leaving before she'd made her grand entrance.'

I make a face. 'That's a bit harsh.'

'All the girls are in the toilet trying to fix her make-up now.'

I make a face again. But I'm not really listening to Angus, I'm concentrating more on what I'm about to say. The right thing in the right way.

'Angus, you know the speech.'

'Yep, got it right here.' He takes it out of his pocket, a few pages, more pages than I was hoping for, waves it in my face proudly. 'Spent all summer writing this. Spoke to a few of your old school friends. Remember Lampy? He had a few tales to tell.'

Which made sense as to why Lampy apologised to me after the ceremony.

Angus tucks it back into the inside of his pocket. He taps it to make sure it's safe.

'Yeah well . . . just remember that, er, Gina's family and friends are . . . well, you know, they're not like us.'

I know they're the wrong words as soon as I say them. I know from the look on his face. It has been glaringly obvious they are not 'like us' all day. They're quieter for a start. Every second word isn't a swear word. They use other words to express themselves.

128

I try to backtrack. 'It's just that, they're not *exactly* like us. You know? They've a different humour. Us Boggs and Doyles, we have a different way. So I was just wondering if you could go easy in the speech. You know what I mean? Gina's grandparents are old. Very fuckin', you know, religious.'

He knows. He looks at me with absolute contempt. The last time I saw this look on his face, it was followed with a head butt.

'Sure,' he says simply. Then he looks me up and down like he has no idea who I am, as though it's not his own brother standing in front of him, in a puddle of piss. 'Good luck, Fergus.' Then he walks out of the toilet leaving me feeling like absolute shit.

His speech is boring. It is the most mind-numbingly boring speech in history. No jokes, just all formality. He didn't reach into his pocket for his speech, all those hand-written pages that I know he spent weeks on and probably practised all night. It is hands down the worst speech ever. No emotion. No love. I could have asked a stranger on the street to do a better job. Which maybe is his point. A stranger, who doesn't even know me.

Gina's ma, the family doctor and the family priest all think he is 'terrific'.

Ma's dressed in the same outfit she wore to Angus's wedding. Something else to Duncan's wedding a few months ago and then back to this dress for mine. It's pea green, a coat, a shift dress and low heels. A sparkly clip in her hair. Her best brooch. Da gave it to her, I remember it. A Tara brooch with green stones. She's wearing make-up, powder that makes her paler and red lipstick that's stuck to her teeth. She isn't dancing. I remember her dancing all night at Angus's. Her and Mattie do a good jive, the only time

I ever see them physical with each other. At Duncan's we had to carry her home. Here, she's sitting down, stiff back, a glass of brandy in front of her, and I'm wondering what Angus said to her. Mattie's watching the girls dancing, tongue running along his lips, like he's choosing from a menu. Ma and Mattie are alone at the round table. All of my brothers and their other halves headed off early with Angus; I assume he'd told them what I said. Something like telling him not to be a Boggs, pretend to be someone else. But that wasn't exactly what I'd said, was it?

That's fine with me though. I can relax more without them. No one is going to go flying across the room and smashing into a table because of a funny look or an intimated tone.

I go over and sit with Ma and we have a chat. Then as we're talking she slaps me hard across the cheek.

'Ma, what the . . .?' I hold my stinging cheek, looking around to see who's seen. Too many people.

'You're not him.'

'What?' My heart starts to pound. 'What are you talking about?'

She slaps me again. Same cheek.

'You're not him,' she says again.

The way she looks at me.

'Come on.' She throws her purse at Mattie, and he jumps to action, eyes off the dancing girls, tongue back inside. 'We're going.'

By midnight my family are all gone.

'Long way to get home,' Gina's ma says, politely, as if trying to make me feel better, but it doesn't.

I tell myself I don't care, I can dance, I can chat, I can relax with them all gone. The hard man, the unbreakable, unbeatable steelie.

15

PLAYING WITH MARBLES

Hundreds

She's never been for a massage before and so as soon as we arrive at the hotel in Venice she goes straight to the spa. She's glowing, excited, I can tell she feels grown up. We were married yesterday and we still haven't had sex. We partied hard until three a.m., in spite of all the Boggs and Doyles leaving early, the sing-song was in full swing when we left and then we both collapsed in a heap on the bed and had to get up an hour later for a six a.m. flight. Definitely no time for sex, particularly sex for the first time. For her obviously, not me. I sit on the double bed and bounce up and down. I've waited for her for a year, I suppose I can wait for the length of a massage. She thinks I'm a virgin too, I don't know what got it into her head, I never claimed I was, but that's how all the people in her life are. They're the following-those-rules type of people and she got it into her head that I am too. I just went along with it, save myself the trouble.

I know how I want to do it with her. The first time. I've

thought about it. I want to play Hundreds with her. You draw a small circle on the floor. Both players shoot a marble towards the circle. If both or neither marble stops in the circle then we shoot again. If only one stops in the circle that player scores ten points each time the marble stops in the circle on subsequent throws. Gina never wears a bra, she doesn't need to, and always wears a tight tank top and flares. She doesn't wear make-up, freckles across her nose and cheeks, freckles on her chest bone. I think about kissing them all. Most of them I've kissed already. The first player to reach one hundred points is the winner and the loser hands over a predetermined number of marbles. Only in our game, which will involve white wine because now we're married and grown up, whoever doesn't make it to the circle will have to strip off an item of clothes. She's never played marbles before, she'll keep missing, I'll miss just enough times too to make her comfortable. By the time I reach one hundred, I want her in the circle, naked. But this won't happen, I know. This is just what's kept me going this year while I do the gentlemanly thing and wait. I've never mixed marbles and sex before, and although Gina laughed the first time I told her I played marbles, I want to do this with her, with my wife.

Gina is worth the wait. She's gorgeous, any fella I know would do the same. She's too good for me of course. Not too good for the me that she knows, but for the me that she doesn't know. The part of me she knows is some man I've concocted over time. He's good with people, patient, polite, interested. He doesn't think everyone she introduces him to is up themselves and he wouldn't prefer to top himself than have a conversation with them. It's better being him, he makes life easier for him and me. But he's not me. I try to keep her away from my family as much as I can; whenever her and Ma talk I break out in a cold sweat. But Ma will never say anything, she knows the deal, knows that I'm in way over my head, but she wanted me to marry her just as much as I do so she could tick me off her list, another of her boys taken care of. Gina's only met Angus briefly, at the wedding; he's living in Liverpool and he can stay there, but Duncan, Tommy, Bobby and Joe are okay in small doses. She just thinks they're always busy. Good enough.

She knows one of my brothers died, thinks Hamish drowned. Well he did, but she thinks it was some freak accident. I plan on keeping it that way. Hamish's problems were his own but I don't want him bringing that into my new life. Gina's sweet, she's naïve, and she judges people. She'd hear a thing like that and she'd look at me different. She'd probably be right. Not that I'm trouble, I'm always on the right side of the law, but I'm not the lad who promises to play croquet with her granddad. Thank God her dad's dead and her granddad's not far from it.

I chose Venice for the honeymoon. I've wanted to come here since I saw a documentary about the Murano glass factory, an entire island dedicated to making glass is an island I want to if not live on, at least visit. I don't have much money, in fact we have very little to spend here at all, but I'm not leaving this country without a pocket full of marbles one way or another, whether I have to beg, borrow or steal. This honeymoon is being funded by Gina's granddad who couldn't help but step in when he heard we were going to Cobh for our honeymoon. *Pick anywhere you want,* he said. *Anywhere in the world.* Gina was hoping for a week in Yugoslavia because that's where one of her friends went on honeymoon, but I managed to talk her into three days in Venice instead. Yugoslavia we could maybe some day afford by ourselves, Venice we couldn't. Venice is a real escape, an adventure in another world. She bought it, because I meant it. I don't care about her grandda helping me out, giving me money. I'll take any helping hand offered, it doesn't hurt my pride. If I don't have it, I don't have it; if someone wants to give it, then I'll take it.

I pace the small room; it's not the most luxurious hotel, far from it, but I appreciate being here at all. I'd sleep anywhere and I can't wait to get out and explore.

I thought I'd be knackered from last night but I'm hopping. I'm eager to get moving. I don't know how long a massage is but I'm not sitting here in this room when there's a world out there waiting for me. I don't think Gina will want to spend much time looking at marbles, not in the way I want to, so I take my moment now and slip away. I don't have to go far before I see the most incredible marbles I've ever seen in my life. They're contemporary art marbles, definitely not for playing with, they're for collecting. I'm in such awe that I can't move from the front window. The salesman comes outside and practically pulls me in, he can see the lust written all over my face. Problem is I have the lust for them but not the money. He answers question after question that I throw at him about every aspect, allows me to examine the works of art under a 10x loupe so I can see the skill of the artist. They are clear handmade glass marbles with elaborate designs captured inside. One is clear with a green four-leaf clover trapped deep inside, another is a goldfish that looks like it's swimming in bubbles, another has a white swan in a swirl of blue sea. There's a vortex, a swirl of purple, green, turquoise, green storms that cork-screw to the very centre of the marble. It's hypnotising. Another is of an eye. A clear marble with an olive green eye and black pupil, red veins trickle around the sides. I feel like it's watching me. Another is called 'New Earth' and it's the entire planet, every country created inside, with clouds on the outer layer. It's a work of pure genius. The entire planet captured in a four-inch marble. This is the one I want but I can barely afford one, let alone the collection. The cost of one is the amount of money I have for the entire three days.

It takes everything I have to walk away and it's the walking away that fires the salesman into action. The best negotiator is the one who is always willing to walk away and he thinks I'm hustling him, which I'm not, I would sell my house for this collection if I had a house. We have to live with Gina's mother for a year while we save up for a deposit for a house. To even be thinking about buying any of these marbles is pure ludicrous and I know it. But. I feel alive, the adrenaline is rushing through my body. This is the only good side of me, the best side of me and she doesn't know it. Looking at these marbles, I vow right here to be faithful to her and I don't mean not sleeping around, but to let her see the real me for the first time. Show her this marble, show her the biggest and best part of me.

I buy a clear marble with a red heart inside. It has cork-screw swirls of deep red, like drops of blood captured in a bubble. I bargain hard and pay almost half of what he was asking for. It's still too much money but it's not just a marble for me, it's for Gina, an offering of who I truly am. It means more to me than the ceremony yesterday and words that I didn't feel in my heart. This means something to me. This is the scariest, bravest thing I have ever set out to do in my adult life. I'm going to give her this heart, my heart, and tell her who I am. Who she's married.

The seller wraps the heart in bubble wrap, then places it in a burgundy velvet pouch, pulled closed by a gold plaited tie and glass beads that I can't help but admire. Even the beads on the pouch are beautiful. I push it deep into my pocket and return to the hotel.

When I get back to the room I can see she's been crying but she tries to hide it. She wears a bathrobe which is tied tightly at her waist.

'What's wrong? What happened?' I'm ready to punch someone.

'Oh nothing.' She wipes her eyes roughly with the sleeve of her towel until the skin around them is red raw.

'It wasn't nothing, tell me.' I feel the anger pumping through my veins. Be calm or she won't tell you. Be the patient, understanding fella who listens, don't go thumping people. Not yet.

'It was just so embarrassing, Fergus.' She sits on the bed and looks tiny on the big bed. She's twenty-one years old. I'm twenty-four. 'She touched my . . .' Her eyes widen and the anger leaves me and I feel a laugh rising.

'Yeah? Your what?' My fantasy game of Hundreds comes to mind. She's on that bed, in the robe, my wife.

'It's not funny!' She throws herself down, covers her face with a pillow.

'I'm not laughing.' I sit down beside her.

'You look like you're going to,' she says, voice muffled. 'I just didn't know a massage was so invasive. I didn't wait all this time to have sex to have a four-foot Italian mama maul me before you.'

And on that I have to laugh.

'Stop!' she whinges, but I can see her smile buried beneath the pillow.

'Did you like her hands on you?' I tease her, my hand travelling up her leg.

'Stop it, Fergus.' But she means the teasing, not the

touching, because for the first time she's not stopping me. I have to do it now though, I have to show her the marble now, so that it's me that she meets, it's me that she makes love to for the first time, not him.

I stop my own hand from travelling and she sits up, confused, hair all in her face.

'I want to give you something first.'

She moves her hair away from her face and she looks so sweet, and so innocent right at that moment that I take a mental picture of it. I don't know it now but I'll try to recall it in the future at the moments when I feel like I've lost her, or hate her so much I can't help but look away from her.

'I went for a walk around. And I found something special for you. For us. It's important to me.' My voice is shaking and so I decide to shut up. I take the pouch out of my pocket, remove the heart from the pouch, my fingers trembling. I feel like I'm giving a part of myself to her. I've never felt like this before. You married me yesterday but today is the first time you've met me. My name is Fergus Boggs, my life is marked by marbles. I unwrap the bubble wrap and I hold it out in my palm. Her reaction first, then my explanation. Let her take it in, drink in her drinking it in.

'What is this?' she says, her voice flat.

I look at her in surprise, heart pounding in my throat. I immediately start to backtrack, back-pedal, hide in my shell. The other me starts warming up in the wings.

'I mean, how much was it? We said we wouldn't buy each other anything here. We can't afford it. No more gifts, remember? After the wedding? We agreed.' She's barely looked at it, she's so annoyed. Yes, we did agree, we promised each other, but this is more than a piece of jewellery, it means more to me than the ring she loves so much on her finger. I want to say that but I don't.

'How much did this cost?'

I stutter and stammer, too broken and hurt to reply honestly. I'm caught between being him and being me, I'm unable to focus on being one.

She is holding it too roughly, too harshly, she moves it from one hand to the other too carelessly, she could easily drop it. I feel tense watching her.

'I can't believe you wasted your money on this!' She jumps up from the bed. 'On a . . . on a . . .' She studies it. 'A toy! What were you thinking, Fergus? Oh my God.' She sits down again, her eyes filling up. 'We've been saving for so long. I just want to get away from living with Mum, I want it to be just you and me. We budgeted for this trip so carefully, Fergus, why would you . . .?' She looks at the marble in her hand, confused. 'I mean, it's sweet, thank you, I know you were trying to be kind, but . . .' Her anger starts to calm but it's too late.

She places her hands on my cheeks, knows that she has hurt my feelings though I don't admit to it. I will take it back I tell her, I will gladly take it back, I never want to see it again ever in my life, to be reminded of this moment when I offered my real self and I was rejected. But I can't bring it back because she drops it, by accident, and its surface is scratched, meaning it will never have a perfect heart again.

16

POOL RULES

No Bombing

On my journey back from Cavan to Dublin I can't help myself slipping into my mind. My driving is clumsy, I have to apologise to other drivers too many times, so I lower the window for the fresh air and sit up.

Aidan is on loudspeaker in the car. I needed to call him, to root myself with my life. Talk to somebody real.

'So you're looking for the missing marbles now?' he asks after I fill him in on everything that's happened so far today, apart from the mug-throwing incident, and I hear the squeals of delight as the kids have a water fight in the background.

'I don't even know if it's about the missing marbles any more,' I say, suddenly deciding. 'Finding out about Dad seems to be much more important than finding the actual marbles. It started with them and it opened up more questions, big gaping holes that I need to fill. There is a side to Dad that I never knew, there is a life he led that he kept from me and I want to discover it. Not just for me. But if *he* can't remember it, how can he ever know that part of himself again?'

Aidan leaves a long silence and I try to read it. He thinks I'm crazy, I've finally lost it, or he's jumping around with jubilance that I'm newly energised. But his response is calm, measured.

'You know best, Sabrina. I'm not going to tell you not to. If you think it will help.'

He doesn't need to say any more, I understand what it means. If it will help me and, as a consequence, us.

'I think it will,' I reply.

'Love you,' he says. 'Try not to let any more men kiss you.'

I laugh.

'Seriously. Be careful, Sabrina.'

'I will.'

The kids shout down the phone to me, *love you, miss you, poo poo, wee wee head*, and then they're gone.

A blonde woman delivered the marbles. I will delay my visit to Dad for now. I need to find the blonde woman who delivered the marbles, the woman who knows the man that I don't, and there is only one woman I can think of who fits that description, who agreed to meet me as soon as I called.

She's sitting in the darkest corner, away from the window, the light, the buzz of the rest of the café. She looks older than I remember, but then she is older than I remember. Nearly ten years have passed since we've seen each other, almost twenty since I saw her first. She's still blonde, her hair one week over its last needed colour, the greys and brown showing at the roots. Ten years older than me she is forty-two now, I always thought she was so young, but so much older than me. Too young for him, but still much older than me. Now we could look the same. She looks bored as she waits and I wonder is the boredom hiding the nervousness beneath, anxiety that I feel as soon as I see her. She sees me walking towards her and she fixes her posture, lifts her chin in that proud move and I hate her all over again like I always did. That self-righteous bitch who thought everything she wanted was automatically supposed to be hers. I try to calm myself, not allow the anger to bubble over.

I saw her with Dad when I was fifteen years old. It was before my parents separated. He introduced me to her less than a year later. I was supposed to think they'd just met, that this was the beginning of a beautiful new relationship for him, that I was to be supportive and happy but I knew that he'd been with her all along. For how long I don't know, but I never said a word. He hadn't just lied to Mum, he had lied to me too, because he looked at me and said the same words. Lies.

They were drunk at lunchtime when I saw them and every time I pass the same restaurant to this day I get the same feeling in my stomach and see them all over again. People don't know that they do that to people when they do the things they shouldn't. Hurtful things are roots, they spread, branch out, creep under the surface touching other parts of the lives of those they hurt. It's never one mistake, it's never one moment, it becomes a series of moments, each moment growing roots and spurting in different directions. And over time they become muddled like an old twisted tree, strangling itself and tying itself up in knots.

I was off school early to go to the dentist, one of my many train-track appointments to try to get to the bottom of my internal cheek bleeding as they scratched and scraped as I talked and chewed. I remember my mouth throbbing as I walked down the road, tears in my eyes

141

from frustration because another cruel boy made another cruel joke at school that day and I was tired of laughing and pretending I didn't care. It was then that I saw Dad. In a fancy restaurant in town, one of the expensive ones with tables outside that I was too embarrassed to walk by. At fifteen, feeling eyes on me from every corner of the street, my head was bowed, my cheeks already pink, my walk self-conscious, but I couldn't help it. When you try hard not to look at something it means you'd have to poke your own eyes out to stop you from looking at that something. So I looked up at all the eyes that I was afraid were looking at me and laughing, and I saw him. I actually stopped for a moment and somebody crashed into the back of me. It was only for a second and I moved again, but I saw enough. Him and her in a table by the window, drunk face, drunk eyes, quick kiss, hands groping under the chair. I didn't say anything to Mum about it because, well, they were so bad at that stage I thought maybe she knew, thought that the woman was the reason, or at least one of the reasons for things being so bad. I never said a word about seeing them together, even when I was introduced to her months later in that fake made-up rehearsed introduction as if they'd just recently met. I always hated her.

Regina.

It made me think of the word Vagina. She was just that. Every time I heard her name, every time I had to say her name, I was all the time hearing and saying Vagina. I called her it once by mistake. She laughed and said, 'What?' but I pretended she'd misheard. She giggled to herself thinking her hearing odd and funny.

And now here I am face to face with Vagina. And I have to ask her for her help, something I hate to do but it's necessary. She is the only lead I have, she is the only woman I know that was in Dad's life for the longest amount of time who could have had access to his personal belongings, his apartment, the blonde woman who delivered the marbles to Mickey Flanagan's house, who could help solve this mystery.

We don't hug or kiss when greeting, we're not old friends, not even acquaintances, not even enemies. Just two people who got twisted together.

She works at the hair salon next door to the café we're in, the same hair salon that Mum and I have avoided going to for almost twenty years. I called her from the car, after Mickey's phone call, and don't know what I was expecting but I'd come up with a few guesses. She could straight out tell me to never call her again. She could politely pawn me off, suggest a date in the future that kept changing. I didn't expect the instant agreement to meet. She was about to take a coffee break, she could meet me in thirty minutes. I wasn't prepared for that. Twenty minutes on the phone with Aidan explaining it all and I'm still not prepared.

'I really appreciate you agreeing to meet with me on such short notice,' I say, as I sit down and take off my coat, feeling like that awkward fifteen-year-old again with her eyes on me as I clumsily hang up my coat on the back of the chair. 'I'm sure it came as a bit of a surprise to you.'

'I was waiting for you to call,' she says, matter-of-factly. 'No, not waiting. Expecting,' she says. She's wearing an oversized black cardigan pulled down past her hands like she's cold, but it's not cold, it's a beautiful day and I realise she's nervous.

'Why's that?' I ask, picturing Mickey Flanagan's wife on the phone, grasping the receiver in two hands in her house, in urgent hushed tones telling her, *She knows, Regina, Sabrina knows that you were here and that you delivered the marbles. She's on her way to you now.*

'I don't know,' she says thoughtfully, taking me in. 'You were always an interesting little one. You always looked like you had a lot of questions but never asked any of them. I used to wait for you to ask, but you never did.'

'I don't think I was looking at you in any particular way because I wanted to ask you questions,' I say, and her smile drops a little. 'I knew you and Dad were together before they separated, I saw you both in a restaurant long before . . .' I pause for her reaction. 'I had a hard time listening to your lies. I could tell you both enjoyed it.'

This gives her a surprise, a little jolt, and she sits upright. Then she smiles. 'So is that what this is about? Letting me know I didn't pull the wool over your eyes?' She asks it as though she's amused, not an ounce of apology or disgust with herself. I don't know why I expected there should be.

'No, actually.' I look down, add a sugar to my cappuccino, stir it, take a sip. Centre myself. I'm here for a reason. 'As you know, there are a few things that Dad doesn't recall.'

She nods, genuinely sad.

'So sometimes I have to contact people in his life to see if I can fill the holes.'

'Ah,' she says, humble now. 'Anything I can do to help.'

Breathe. 'Did you know about his marble collection?'

'Did I know about his, what now?'

'Marble collection. He had a collection. And he played marbles too.'

She shakes her head, her forehead wrinkled in a frown. 'No. I never, we never . . . marbles? The things that children play with? No. Never.'

My heart drops. I thought. I really thought . . . 'Did you deliver boxes to a house in Virginia last year?'

'Last year? Virginia? Cavan? No, why would I . . . I

haven't seen Fergus for almost five years, and even when we were together we were more off than on. We weren't exactly platonic. We just met up occasionally when, you know . . .'

I don't want to know their reasons for meeting, I don't need to hear it, it's clear already. I'm so disappointed, I just want to grab my coat and go. There is no point to the remainder of this conversation, no point in finishing my coffee.

Maybe she senses this. Tries her best to be useful. 'Do you know one of the reasons why Fergus and I broke up for good?'

'Let me guess,' I say wryly. 'He cheated on you.'

She takes it well, it makes me not want to throw any more at her as I feel it cheapened me and not her.

'Probably. Though that wasn't the reason. He was so secretive. I never quite knew exactly what he was doing or where he was. And not because he didn't answer a question but because he'd answer it and somehow I'd realise that, after listening to him, I still didn't know. He was vague. I don't know if it was deliberate, but to pin him down was to confuse him, annoy him, seem like a nag, which I never wanted to be, but he had the ability to make a person a nag, because he never answered, he never really explained. He didn't understand why I needed to know so much. He thought there was something wrong with me. I did wonder if he was cheating on me. And the thing is, I didn't care, we didn't have that kind of relationship, but it bothered me that I couldn't get answers. So I started following him.' She takes a timely sip of her tea, enjoying it as I hang on her every word. 'And I realised after a very short time that he was not as exciting as he seemed. He was going to the same place all the time, or at least most of the time.'

'Where?'

'He was going to a pub.' She arches her eyebrow. 'He loved to drink. Boring, isn't it? I was hoping it was something else. I followed him for two weeks. And one time . . . oh my God, it was so funny, he almost caught me!' She starts laughing and I can tell she's settling down for a long chat. But I don't have the time.

I finish my cappuccino.

'Regina,' I say, hearing Vagina in my head. 'Which pub was he going to?'

She stops, realising I'm not here to listen to her detective stories into my father's behaviour. She's back to how she was when I entered. Bored. Unhappy. Disappointed nothing in her life lived up to anything it could have been. Waiting for the people she hurt in the past to make an appearance and spice up her life, make her feel powerful.

'One on Capel Street.'

'My dad wasn't an alcoholic,' I say to her, though I don't really know this. I don't know his life in detail but I think I'd have known that, wouldn't I?

'Oh I know that,' she laughs, and I feel stupid, my cheeks burn. 'My daddy was an alcoholic. Believe me, I couldn't spend two minutes with one. But they had some things in common. Fergus lied about most places he went to. About visiting his mother, about going to the pub, about going to watch matches, about being at meetings, or being away for a weekend. He didn't lie because he was going somewhere more exciting or more daring, or to be with another woman. The life he escaped to was not exotic. He was sitting in a pub. He didn't even need to lie to me, I wasn't trying to pin him down.' She leans in, hands clasped, matter-of-fact, eyes alight like she's enjoying every moment of the revelation. 'Sabrina, your dad lied *all the time*. He lied because

146

he wanted to, because he liked to, because he got some kind of buzz out of it. He lied because that's the kind of person he chose to be, and that was the kind of life he chose to live. And that's it.'

'What was the name of the pub?' I ask, refusing to believe her explanation. I know that Dad lied, but he lied for a reason. And I want to find out what that reason was.

Regina looks as though she's trying to decide whether to tell me or not, like a cat playing with a mouse, one last game with me before she knows I'll never see her again. 'The Marble Cat,' she says finally.

'Aidan,' I say loudly, pulling the car out of my parking space.

'How are you doing?' he asks.

'Just met with Regina,' I say confidently, feeling like I'm flying now.

'Vagina? I didn't think you'd go through with it. I thought that woman gave you nightmares?'

'Not any more,' I say confidently. 'Not any more.'

'So where to next?' he asks.

'A pub on Capel Street. The Marble Cat. I think I'm close to something.'

He pauses. 'Okay, baby, okay. If you think it will help.'

He sounds so uncertain, so nervous but too afraid to express it, that we both laugh.

17

PLAYING WITH MARBLES

Cabbaging

I'm lying on a picnic blanket though I can still feel the bumpy ground beneath me, earth and broken rock. I'm roasting in my suit. My tie is off, my sleeves rolled up, my legs feel like they're burning in my black pants beneath the heat of the summer sun. There's a bottle of white wine beside us, half of it already drunk, I doubt we'll make it back to the office at all. Friday afternoon, the boss probably won't return from lunch as usual, pretending to be at a meeting but instead sitting in the Stag's Head and downing the Guinness, thinking nobody knows he's there.

I'm with the new girl. Our first sales trip together, this one took us to Limerick. I'm helping her to settle in, though she's currently straddling me, and slowly opening the buttons on her silk blouse. I'd say she's settling in just fine.

No one will see us, she insists, though I don't know how she can be so sure. I'm guessing she's done this before, if not here, somewhere like this. She leaves the blouse on, a salmon peach colour, but undoes her strapless bra which falls to the blanket. It topples off the blanket and on to the soil. Her panties are off already, I know this because my hands are where the fabric should be.

Her skin is a colour I've never seen before, a milky white, so white she glows, so pale I'm surprised she hasn't sizzled under the sun's blaze by now. Her hair is strawberry blonde, but if she'd told me it was peach I would have believed her. Her lips are peach, her cheeks are peach. She's like a doll, one of Sabrina's china dolls. Fragile. Delicate looking. But she's not fragile, nor angelic; she is self-assured and has a glimmer of mischief in her hazel brown eyes, an almost sly lick of her lips as she sees what she wants and takes it.

It is ironic that we are lying in this cabbage field on a Friday afternoon, the day when my ma would serve us up cabbage soup. The word soup was an exaggeration, it was hot water with slithery slimy over-boiled strips of cabbage at the bottom. Salty hot water. The money would always run out by Friday and Ma would save for a big roast on a Sunday. Saturday we would be left to our own devices, have to fend for ourselves. We would go to the orchard and laze in the trees eating whatever apples we could, or beg and bother Mrs Lynch next door, or we'd rob something on Moore Street, but they were quick catching on to us so we couldn't go there much.

It is doubly ironic that we're lying in this cabbage field because in a game of marbles the banned practice of moving your marble closer to the target marbles is called 'cabbaging', which is cheating. This is no great coincidence, of course. I tell her this fact as we pass the fields; not of my involvement, no, only the men I play with know this and nothing much else about me. I simply share the term with her as we pass fields of cabbage, me in the passenger seat, her driving – on her insistence, which is fine with me as I'm drinking from the wine bottle, which she occasionally reaches for and takes a swig from. She's wild, she's dangerous, she's the one who will get me in trouble. Maybe I want this. I want to be found out, I don't want to pretend any more, I'm tired. Maybe the mere mention of a marble term is the beginning of my undoing. She looks at me when I say it, then slams her foot on the brake, spilling my wine, then does a U-turn and heads back the way we came. She pulls in beside the cabbage field, kills the engine, gets out of the car, grabs a blanket from the back seat and heads for the field. She hitches her skirt up to climb over the wall, high up on her skinny pale thighs, and then she's gone.

I jump out of the car and scurry after her, bottle in hand. I find her lying on the ground, back to the soil, looking up at me with a satisfied grin on her face.

'I want a part of this cabbaging business. What do you think, Fergus?'

I look down at her, drink from the bottle of wine, and look around the field. There's no one around, passing cars can't see.

'You know what it means?'

'You just told me: cheating.'

'No no, what it means exactly, is when you shoot from an incorrect spot.'

She arches her back and spreads her legs as she laughs. 'Shoot away.'

I join her on the blanket. Gina's at home in Dublin, at Sabrina's parent–teacher meeting, but despite the thought of her, this opportunity really doesn't offer much of a challenge to me and my morals. This electric peach girl isn't the first woman I've been with since I married Gina.

Apart from the day baby Victoria was stillborn and I

cheated at Conqueror to win Angus's corkscrew marble on the road outside of our house, I have never since cheated in a game of marbles in my whole life. I don't need reminding from anyone, not even as I enter her and she cries out, that in the marble world I am a man of my word, a perfect rule-abiding man, but the man without the marbles? His whole life has been about cabbaging.

18

PLAYING WITH MARBLES

Foreign Sparkler

'Hello,' I hear a woman say to me suddenly. She's in a chair beside me. I wasn't aware of her before now, not even of an empty chair, but all of a sudden there she is.

The sun is back out again, eclipse over, everybody's eclipse glasses are off, mine too though I don't recall doing that either. I feel like my ma, in her final years, dithery and forgetful with her glasses, when she was always previously spot on. I don't like this part of ageing, I always prided myself on my memory. I'd a good head for names and faces, could tell you where and how I knew them, where we first met, the conversation we had and if it was a woman, the clothes that she was wearing. It works sometimes like this, my memory, but not always. I know that comes with age and I know the stroke contributed to it too, but at least I'm here being looked after, not at work having to remember things and not being able to. That happens to people and I wouldn't like that.

'Hello,' I say to her politely.

'Are you okay?' she asks. 'I notice you seem a bit upset. I hope you didn't get a bad phone call.'

I look down and see I'm still holding the mobile phone. 'No, not at all.' But was it? Who was it? Think, Fergus. 'It was my daughter. I was worried about her, but she's okay.' I can't quite remember what we talked about, I got lost in a daydream after that but my feeling is that it's fine, she's fine. 'Why do you think I was sad?' I ask.

'You had tears on your cheeks,' she says, softly. 'I sat here because I was concerned. I can leave if you like.'

'No, no,' I say quickly, not wanting her to leave. I try to remember why I would have been so sad speaking to Sabrina. I look over at Lea, who's watching me, worrying, and then up at the sky and I remember the moon, the miniature marbles that would fit in her dimples and then I remember the marble up Sabrina's nose and tell the concerned lady the story. I chuckle, picturing Sabrina's bold face as a two-year-old, red cheeks, stubborn as anything. No to everything and everyone. She could do with learning that word now, running around after three boys all the time.

The lady's eyes have widened as though in fright.

'Oh, don't be alarmed, we got the marble out. She's fine.'

'It's just that . . . the marble story . . . do you . . .' She seems flustered. 'Do you have any more marble stories?'

I smile at her, amused; what an unusual question, but it's kind of her to show interest. I wrack my brain for marble stories, not imagining that I will have any, but I'd like to please her and she seems eager to talk. There it is again, the haze, the shutters of my mind firmly down. I sigh.

'Did you grow up with marbles, as a boy?' she prompts.

And then a sudden memory pops up, just like that. I smile. 'I'll tell you what I do remember: growing up with my brothers. There were seven of us, and my ma, who was a tough woman, introduced a marble swearing jar. Any time someone swore they had to put a marble in the jar, which in our house was the worst kind of punishment. We were all marble mad.' Were we? Yes, we were. I laugh. 'I remember my ma lining us up in the room, wooden spoon in her hand and pointing it in our faces. "If one of you fucking swears, you'll have to put one of those fucking marbles in here. Do you hear?" Well, sure, how could we keep a straight face to that? Hamish started laughing first, then I went. Then it was all of us. I don't remember Joe there, if Joe was born at all, I don't remember him around much. Probably too young. And that was it, in the first minute of its inception there were six marbles in the jar. They were our least favour- ites, of course, clearies that were chipped and scratched, Ma hadn't a clue. And even though we didn't own those marbles it would still bother us, me anyway, seeing them sitting up high on a shelf so that we couldn't touch them.'

'What did your mother do with them?' she asks, eyes glistening like there's tears in them.'

I study her for a bit. 'Your accent. It's peculiar.'

She laughs. 'Thank you very much.'

'No, not in a bad way. It's nice. It's a mix of something.'

'Germany. And Cork. I moved there in my twenties.'

'Ah.'

I look down at her hands. No wedding ring, but a ring on her engagement finger, that she keeps playing with. Rolling it back and forth on her finger.

She sees me looking and stops fiddling with it.

'What did your mother do with the marble jar? Did you ever get them back?'

'We had to earn them.' I smile. 'Every month we'd have the chance to earn them back. One person would win them all, which was a game in itself, though I don't think Ma saw it like that. I wouldn't be surprised if a few of us swore a few times on purpose just to up the stakes of the game. We would have to help out around the house. Do the washing, cleaning, and then Ma would decide who deserved to win.'

'Controversial,' she laughs.

'It was. We had some terrible scraps after those days. Sometimes it wasn't worth winning or you'd get your head kicked in, you'd end up giving back the marbles they owned in the first place. But if you could tough it out, they were yours.'

'Did you ever win them?'

'Always.'

She laughs. A musical laugh.

'I won them every month for the first few months because Ma used to give me a note; I'd bring it to the chemist, and then I'd carry a brown paper bag back to the house. Never knew what was in it till my brothers told me I was carrying lady pads. They ripped into me so much I never did anything to help again.'

'You lost out on your marbles.'

'Not mine. I figured out I should just not swear in front of Ma.'

We both laugh.

'We've talked before,' I say, suddenly realising.

'Yes,' she says, a sad smile that she tries to hide. 'Several times.'

'I'm sorry.'

'That's okay.'

'You're visiting someone here,' I say.

'Yes.'

We sit in silence, but it's a comfortable silence. She has her shoes off, and she has nice feet. Bright pink toenails. She fidgets with her ring.

'Who are you visiting?' I ask. It's not grumpy Joe, I never see her with him. It's not Gerry or Ciaran or Tom. It's not Eleanor or Paddy. In fact I don't recall seeing her speaking with anyone other than me and the nurses. Though my recollection of that doesn't count for much. Not these days.

'You've never asked me that before. You've never asked who I'm visiting.'

'I'm sorry.'

'Don't be.'

'You're visiting me, aren't you?'

'Yes.'

Her eyes are bright, she's almost breathless. She's beautiful, there's no doubt about that, and I study her hard, her green eyes . . . Something in my mind stirs, then stops again. I don't even know this lady's name. To ask now would feel rude, because she looks at me so intimately. She's still fiddling with her ring, looking down. I look at it more closely.

There's a piece of what looks like a marble embedded in a gold band, a transparent clear base with a ribbon of white and bright-coloured stripes on white in the centre. It is a machine-made marble from Germany. I know this instinctively. I know this and nothing else. No wonder she asked about the marble-story. She has a fascination with them.

'Did I tell you the marble-swearing-jar story before?' I ask.

'Yes,' she says softly, big beautiful smile.

'I'm sorry.'

'Stop saying sorry.' She places her hand over mine, the one with the ring. Her skin is soft, and warm. Another stir. 'You never told me it here, though.'

I run my finger over her fingers and over the marble. Her eyes fill with tears.

'I'm sorry,' she says, swiping quickly at her eyes.

157

'Don't be. It's incredibly frustrating to forget, it must be an entirely other thing to be the forgotten.'

'You don't always forget, and those days are the most wonderful days,' she says, and I see a sweet woman who holds on to the smallest hope.

'Foreign sparkler,' I say suddenly, and she gasps. 'That's what this marble is.'

'That's what you called me sometimes. Fergus,' she whispers, 'what is happening to you today? This is wonderful.'

We sit in silence for a moment.

'I loved you, didn't I?' I ask.

Her eyes fill again and she nods.

'Why don't I remember?' My voice cracks and I become agitated, frustrated, I want to stand up from my wheelchair and run, stride, jump, move, for everything to be the way it was.

She turns my face to her, one hand below my chin, and she looks at me with warmth and I remember my ma's face when I was summoned to her one day when she thought I was dead, and I think of Bounce About and I think of a pub in London and a man named George who called me Paddy, handing me a Czech bullet and of seeing Hamish dead. All in a flash.

'Fergus,' she says, her voice bringing me back, calming me. 'I'm not worried about you not remembering. I'm not here to remind you of anything. The past is the past. I just have been hoping that I will be lucky enough that you will fall in love with me again, a second time round.'

This makes me smile, instantly stops my agitation because, of course, it's beautiful. I don't know her and I know everything about her at the same time. I want to love her and for her to love me. I take her hand, the one with the ring and I hold it tight.

19

PLAYING WITH MARBLES

Slags

I arrive home from the airport feeling rough, but feeling exhilarated, still on a high, the adrenaline racing around my veins shouting for 'more!'; a night of partying preceded an early morning flight to get back in time for Sabrina's thirteenth birthday party. Her first year as a teenager. Gina has arranged a marquee and private catering for forty people, mainly her family, thankfully none of mine could come. Or at least that's what I told Gina; I only asked Ma to come but after Mattie's recent heart operation she's afraid to leave his bedside. Gina didn't mind, I think she's happy none of my family could make it, and she wasn't surprised either, it's nothing new. We're not the closest of brothers. We were until I met Gina, then I separated her from my family, always thinking she was too good for them. After sixteen years I'm beginning to see that was a stupid idea; there are times, occasions when I'd like them to be here. When Sabrina did something, or said something and I wished they'd been there to see. Or a family day out when the waiter trips up, or a twat friend of Gina's says something and nobody but me can see he's a twat, I know they'd agree with me and I wish they were there. I could imagine a wisecrack from Duncan, the intensity from Angus, the way he took over at protecting me after Hamish went, as if he knew something, as if he knew he had to. Little Bobby's charm, attracting all the ladies – we called him our 'bit bait'. I think of Tommy looking out for Bobby all the time, still watching out for the slugs and snails in his path, and Joe the baby, the one who came long after we lost Victoria, sensible Joe, who looks at me, Angus, and Duncan like we're somebody else's family, not his, never fully able to connect with us, as we'd all moved out of the house as he grew up. He listened to stories from locals about Hamish and thought of him like a monster, the boogie man: if he wasn't careful, Hamish would come and get him; if he wasn't careful, he'd end up like Hamish. Hamish, the ghost in our home that was always there, sleeping in our room, eating at our dinner table, the echoes of him in every single room, his energies absorbed into everything around us, into all of us.

We didn't talk like that about him though, neither did Ma. Hamish was funny, Hamish was strong, Hamish was brave. The best way to be the best you can be is to be dead. Ma mollycoddled Joe, made him a bit soft. Not in a sweet way, like most younger kids are, but in a way that made him worry, that made him fragile, that made him think he should be looked after more. She was afraid he'd hurt himself, she was afraid he'd get lost, get sick, die at any moment. Too dark out, too wet out, too hot out, too far away, too late, too early – No, Joe, just stay in with Ma and you'll be grand. He's a worrier, serious, thinks about everything twenty times before he thinks about it again. Safe. Has a boyfriend and lives with him in a new apartment on the quays, pretends to us he doesn't, walks around with a coffee cup and a briefcase. I see him sometimes if I'm driving to town in the mornings. Gina would like Joe, he's doing well for himself, something with computers, but Joe doesn't like me. I miss them sometimes, when I least expect it, but I'm glad they're not here today.

Sabrina greets me at the door, appearing happy, wearing too much make-up in a too short skirt with heels on for the first time. She's letting her top fall off her shoulder, showing off her bra-strap – the new bra that Gina bought her a few weeks ago. She doesn't look good, not to me, not even to me and I'm her dad, I'm supposed to think she's perfect in everything, blinded by fatherly love. Not today. It's a birthday lunch, the weather's not great for April, it's a grey day and Sabrina looks dressed for a garden party in Spain. The material of her skirt is flimsy and nearly see-through, a cheap silk of some sort, I can see the goosebumps on her skin.

When she smiles at me it's a full mouth of metal and my heart melts. My goofy, awkward beautiful daughter looks better in her pyjamas and spot cream all over her face curled up on the couch and watching *Family Fortunes*, than this yoke.

'You look like crap,' she says, giving me a hug. I freeze. If she thinks that then Gina will most definitely think it too. She'll analyse it, dissect it, ask me a thousand paranoid questions with her claws dug into me, and I'll have to deny everything. I have to get to the shower before she sees me. I can hear her in the kitchen, busy talking about prawn cocktails, her voice louder than everyone else's. The marquee has taken over our tiny back garden, the side of it pushed up against the garden wall so that a corner of the shed roof is digging through the canvas, looking like it will pierce it, and somebody's skull, at any moment. Gina is dressed and ready and beautiful as always, still, after all this time, talking and organising everybody like she lives in the Hollywood Hills. We don't. I couldn't give her what I know she longed for, which was the upbringing she had. Now that Sabrina is thirteen she's talking about going to work. I don't think she will, in fact I know she's bluffing, it's all just to say to me, 'You're not giving me what I need. You're not making enough money.'

I'll have to sit in that tent for the next few hours listening to people ask me, 'What are you doing now, Fergus?' like I change jobs faster than my underwear. I haven't found it easy staying put anywhere, but think I'm on to something now. Truth be told I'm not the best at managing my own money, but I know that now and I've copped on. I'm a good salesman, a great one; it all came from Mattie's butcher's shop, when I did my best to get out of cleaning guts and odd jobs that nobody else wanted to do. I started looking into getting better meat, I started advising Mattie on how best to sell it too. And it worked. Quickly found myself out of the back of the butcher's and upstairs in the office, focusing on sales. Then when I married Gina I felt it was time for me to leave Mattie, take my skills elsewhere, which I did to much success. Mobile phones, mortgages, and now a friend wants to hire me for this new company. I just need to understand the markets, which I do. I'm not good at managing my own money, doesn't mean I'm not good at making it for other people. I just need a qualification to convince people to believe me. I've enrolled in an evening course in town twice a week and then I'll be a bona fide venture capitalist.

'What's in there? My present?' She jabs at the bag in my hand and I pull it away sharply from her.

'Sorry,' she says, face suddenly serious, a little afraid, and steps back.

'Sorry, love, I didn't mean to, I just . . .' I keep my bag behind my back. I need to hide it somewhere fast before Gina wonders the same thing. A night away from her and she'll be in her element of paranoia.

I rush upstairs to the spare bedroom that's also used as my home office. From the way it looks I assume her ma is staying over, a multitude of candles, flowers, shampoo, shower gels, everything she'd need for a night away, she's just short of adding a chocolate to her pillow. I pull the desk chair over to the wardrobe and stand up. The marbles are at the top, at the back, deep in the wardrobe. I can barely reach them myself I've hidden them so well and it's exactly where I'm going to stuff this bag until I have time to empty it later.

I hear footsteps on the stairs and I literally can't get the bag in there fast enough. I'm pushing it but to no avail. If I'd used my common sense I would take the offending objects out separately, but I'm panicking. I'm sweating, can smell the black coffee smell from my armpits, feel the alcohol seeping from my pores from a night of partying. She's too close. I close the wardrobe and jump down from the chair, travel bag still in my hand, chair still beside the wardrobe.

The door opens.

Gina stares at me, looks me up and down. I know it, feel it in my gut, more than any other time and it's come close a lot of times, but I know the moment has come.

'What are you doing?'

'Just want to check up on something for work.'

I'm sweating, my chest is heaving with panic and I try to control it.

'For work,' she says flatly.

Her eyes are dark, her face fierce, I have never seen her look like this before. I feel it slipping away and I'm almost relieved but at the same time I don't want it to go.

'Where did you stay last night?'

'The Winchester.'

'Where?'

'King's Cross.'

'For the Strategic Technology Forum.'

'Yeah.'

'Yes, that's what I thought you told me. So I called. Looking for you. There was no booking in that hotel under your name, no forum. No nothing. Unless you were at an Indian wedding, Fergus, you weren't there.'

She's shaking now, voice and body trembling.

'You were there with one of your slags, weren't you?'

This throws me. She's never accused me of that before. Not directly. She has hinted as much with questions and uncertainty but has never come right out and said it. It makes me feel disgusting, the way she looks at me, for the way I've made her feel, reduced her to this version of a woman I've never met. It's over, it's over, she's got me. I give up – or do I? I never give up. One more try. Don't go without a fight.

'No, Gina, look at me . . .' I take hold of her shoulders. 'I was there all right, the conference was in another hotel. It wasn't booked under my name because work booked it through a travel agency and it's probably under their name. I don't know which one, but I can find out.' My voice is too high-pitched, it's weak, it's breaking, it's giving me away. With marbles you never have to speak, your voice can't deceive you.

'Get your hands off me,' she says, voice quiet and threatening. 'What's in the bag?'

I swallow. 'I can't . . . nothing.'

She looks at it and I'm afraid that she's going to grab it, open it, reveal the truth. She's right, I wasn't in The Winchester. I wasn't at a work forum. I was in the Greyhound Inn, Tinsley Green in West Sussex, but I wasn't with another woman. It is where I've been on the same day for the past five years for the World Marble Championships. In my bag are two trophies, the first trophy I've won with my team, and the second is for best individual player. The team is Electric Slags, named after the Christensen Agate transparent-coloured base marbles with opaque white swirls. 'Electric' because Christensen Agate slags are much brighter than those produced by any other manufacturer, the rarest colour being peach. I named the team this because it's a marble that I bought after my liaison in the cabbage field. The marble reminded me of the cream of her skin, her peach hair and lips and the moment in the cabbage field five years earlier, a reminder that my marble life was my secret, my way of cheating. Naming the team after that was branding myself, I think with a mixture of pride and detestation, recognition and acknowledgement of who I am, a cheat with a title, who wanted to take his secret marble-playing further. It was an instant hit with my team-mates, they'd no idea of the real meaning. The marble world is no different to the world of people, it too has its reproductions and fakes, and slags were an attempt to mimic hand-cut stones. Gina is my hand-cut stone, always was, always will be, while my cabbage-field lover and I were only ever slags and we both knew it.

It was a coincidence that Gina used the word slag. She had no idea, I'm certain. My teammates, five other men, know nothing about my personal life, nothing beyond the games we play together and the banter that allows men to avoid any real personal discussion. We've got together five years in a row to win the world championships, this is the first time Ireland have ever won and I can't tell anyone about it. There's a small article in the paper today about the Irish win, accompanied by a grainy photo of the team, me deliberately hiding at the back, you can't make me out. *Electric Slags win for Ireland.* And then of course mention of the best individual player, me, who scored the winning throw.

The game we played was Ring Taw, where forty-nine target marbles are placed on a six-foot raised ring. The surface is three inches off the ground and is covered in sand. The marbles are half an inch in diameter and can be glass or ceramic. Of course we used glass. Two teams of six players get a point each for each marble they knock out of the ring. The first team to knock out twenty-five marbles from the ring is the winner. Electric Slags beat Team USA to become the world champions; apart from Sabrina's birth, the second greatest day of my life. A moment I will no doubt remember for ever.

How can I tell Gina now? What would I say? For the past sixteen years I've been lying to you about a hobby of mine. It's been a huge part of my life, but you know nothing about it. Women or no women, that in itself is a betrayal. It's also weird, embarrassing. If I'm hiding a hobby, what else am I hiding? It's gone on too long to explain, to go back. Why is it easier to lie? Because I promised Hamish. Sneaking out into the night from the age of ten, it was our secret. A secret kept from Ma that we were hustling, a secret from players that I was good. I don't know why, but I kept that secret, like a pact with Hamish, a connection to him. We're the only two, of people who matter in our lives, who know. Just you and me, Hamish. But Hamish is gone and Gina is here and I can't carry on like this for the rest of my life. It will drive me mad, it is already starting to. I feel the pressure more than ever before. I'll tell her. It will be difficult for a while, she won't trust me, but she hasn't for some time anyway. But I'll tell her. Now.

'I'll show you,' I say, taking the bag from behind my back and unzipping it, my fingers shaking like you wouldn't believe. Even in the final moments of the most important game of my life, my fingers were rock steady.

'No!' she says suddenly, afraid, stopping me, hand held out.

I want to tell her it's not what she thinks it is, though I don't know what she thinks it is, but it can't be this.

'No. If you say you were there, you were there.' She swallows hard. 'Everyone will be here in fifteen minutes, please be ready.' She leaves me, the zip open on the bag, the metal of the trophy shining for me to see. If she'd just looked down.

Later that evening, mask back on, sweat washed off, prawn cocktail and chicken Kiev polished off, pavlova waiting to be eaten, I go in search of Sabrina. I find her curled in a ball on the couch, crying.

'What's wrong, love?'

'John said I look like a slag.'

I take her in my arms, the tears washing away the too much make-up. 'No, you're not that. You'll never be that. But all of this –' I look down at her outfit. 'It's not you, love, is it?'

She shakes her head miserably.

'Remember,' I feel a lump in my throat, 'just always remember to be you.'

20

POOL RULES

No Outdoor Footwear

The Marble Cat is smart black-framed pub on Capel Street with Kilkenny flags suspended on beams from the frame. It's inviting, advertising its daily specials – root vegetable soup and Guinness brown bread and Dublin Bay prawns – on a blackboard outside, unlike some of the others which wish to shut out the world and light and lock the door behind. It's four p.m. on Friday and it's not yet bustling with end-of-day workers ready to let their hair down and unload their stress for the weekend. The pub is separated into the pub and lounge. I choose the lounge, always less intrusive. Three men sit up at the bar, staring deeply into their pints; there are a few empty stools between each of them, they are not together but occasionally converse. Two other men in suits, eating soup and bread rolls, talk shop but there is no one else in the place.

A young barman stands behind the bar, watching the racing on TV. I approach the bar and he looks at me.

'Hi.' I keep my voice down and he comes closer. 'Could

I speak to the manager, please? Or anybody who has worked here a long time?'

'Boss is here today, in the bar. I'll get him.'

He disappears through the opening to the pub next door and after a few moments the space is filled by an enormous wide man.

'Here's the marble cat himself,' one man at the bar says, suddenly coming alive.

'Spud, how are ye?' he says, shaking his hand.

He's enormous, over six feet and broad, and it's then when I look around the walls of the pub that I realise who he is. Photographs, trophies, framed jerseys, newspaper articles of All-Ireland finals and wins cover every inch of the walls. Black-and-yellow stripes – the cats – and I realise suddenly what the pub name refers to, part of it at least. Kilkenny hurlers are famously called The Cats, a term which refers to anyone who is a tenacious fighter. I can see him smashing into other players, hurley in hand, before helmets and protective gear, pure solid. A marble man. He leans on the bar to get closer to my level though he's still towering, elbows on the varnished wood.

'They call you the marble cat?' I ask.

'They call me lots of things. Glad it was that one that stuck.' He returns the smile.

'You don't know this fella?' Spud pipes up. 'Six All-Ireland medals in the seventies. Kilkenny's star player. Nothing like him before, nothing like him since.'

'How can I help you?' he asks, turning away from Spud to end the chat.

'My name is Sabrina Boggs.' I watch his face for recognition, Boggs isn't a common name, but there's nothing. 'My dad is having memory problems, and I wanted to help fill in the gaps for him. He used to drink here. He was a regular.'

'Well you're in luck, because I know every single person that comes through that door, especially the regulars.'

'He played marbles, I thought that's why he chose to come here, but you're not a marble pub,' I laugh at myself.

'Kilkenny is called the Marble City,' he explains kindly. 'The footpaths of the city streets were paved with limestone flagstones and on wet winter evenings they glistened. Hence the name.'

I bet he's told this countless times to American tourists.

'A very dark grey limestone was quarried just outside of the city at a place called the Black Quarry. Between you and me,' he speaks out the side of his mouth and looks around, 'I wanted to give the pub that name, but the money men reckoned the Marble Cat would be better for our pockets.'

I smile.

'But we did play marbles here at one time, you'll be pleased to know. A small group used to come in. What is his name?'

'Fergus Boggs.'

He frowns immediately, then shakes his head. He looks at the men at the bar. 'Spud, you know a fella named Fergus Boggs, played marbles here?'

'Not here,' Spud says, without thinking about it, eyes back in his pint.

'He would have been here five years ago,' I explain, wondering if Regina's story is to be trusted.

I've piqued his curiosity, I can tell. 'Sorry, love, we only had a small marble team in here. Spud, who's here, Gerry, who's in there,' he points to the bar, 'and three other fellas. No Fergus.'

'Show her the winners' corner,' Spud shouts proudly.

The Marble Cat chuckles and lifts the bar counter. He towers over me. 'Let me give you a tour. I don't think Spud wants me to show you any of my walls of fame, but down here is the Electric Slags' corner.'

Feeling disappointed that they've never heard of Dad, I follow him through the bar to the far corner. Spud hops off his stool and follows us.

There is a glass display cabinet on the wall, inside are two trophies. 'This is the trophy they won at the World Marble Championships back in . . .' he searches his pockets for his glasses.

'Ninety-four,' Spud says immediately. 'April.'

The Marble Cat rolls his eyes. 'The second trophy is for Best Individual Player. Spud didn't win that – I can tell you that without needing my glasses,' he teases, still patting down his pockets.

'And over here is where we got a mention in the paper.' Spud points to the framed newspaper cutout and I move closer to view the photograph.

'If you look close you'll see Spud has hair,' the Marble Cat says.

To be polite I move closer. I follow the line-up and suddenly my heart pounds. 'That's my dad.' I point him out in the line-up.

The Marble Cat manages to locate his glasses and moves his face closer to the frame. Then suddenly he booms, 'Hamish O'Neill! That's your dad?'

'No, no,' I laugh. 'That's wrong. His name is Fergus Boggs. But that's him. Definitely him. Oh my God, look at him, he's so young.'

'That's Hamish O'Neill,' the Marble Cat says, prodding Dad's face with his thick finger. 'And he was a regular. Sure I know him well.'

Spud steps in now too. 'That's Hamish,' he says defensively, looking at me as though I'm a liar.

I'm stunned. My mouth opens but nothing comes out. My head is racing, too many questions, I'm too confused. I study the photo myself to see if it's Dad at all, maybe I'm the one who's wrong. It was almost twenty years ago, maybe it's somebody that looks like him. But no, it is him. Are they messing with me? Is this a joke? I study them, and their faces are as serious as mine.

'She says her dad is Hamish,' the Marble Cat says to Spud, excited, his voice booming through the pub so that the two men in suits are listening now.

'I heard her.' Spud narrows his eyes at me.

The Marble Cat laughs, his laughter filling the whole place. 'Gerry!' he yells into the bar next door. 'Get in here, you'll never guess who is here!'

'I know who's in there and I'm not going anywhere near him. Not until he apologises!' a man yells back grumpily.

'Well then you'll be a long time in there,' Spud yells back.

'Ah would you ignore your feud for a few minutes. What is it, a year now?' the Marble Cat hollers. He walks to the bar, there in three long strides, and shouts through the doorway that leads from the lounge to the bar. 'Hamish O'Neill's *daughter* is here.'

I hear a string of expletives and everyone laughs. Then Gerry appears in the bar, beer in hand, faded jeans, leather jacket. A few men are behind him, they've followed him through to take a look at me.

'Hamish is your da?' one of the men asks.

'No. Fergus Boggs . . .' I say quietly.

The Marble Cat finally recognises my discomfort and tries to calm down what he has revved up. 'Okay, okay, let's take this over here.' He leads me to the nearby table. 'Dara!' he yells as if he's back on the pitch. 'Get this woman a drink! I'm sorry,' he says to me. 'What's your name?'

'Sabrina.'

'Get Sabrina a drink!' he yells and then to me, quieter: 'What will you have?'

'Water, please.'

'Ah have something stronger, you look like you need it.'

I feel like I need it too, but I'm driving.

'Sparkling water.'

They all laugh.

'Just like your da,' Gerry says, joining us, the other men slinking back to the darkness they came from. 'Never drank when playing. Said it affected his throw.'

They laugh again.

'Gerry, call Jimmy, he'd love to see this,' the Marble Cat barks at him.

I try to interject, more people isn't necessary, I'm feeling overwhelmed and dizzy as it is, but they talk over me, like excited kids. Spud starts to explain in detail how his team the Electric Slags won the championship, almost throw by throw, setting up the scene, describing the tension between the Americans and the Irish, and then how Dad threw the winning throw. They're talking over each other, interrupting, fighting, debating, Gerry and Spud absolutely unable to agree on anything, even the slightest detail such as the weather, while I listen, feeling stunned, thinking this all must be a mistake, a misunderstanding. They must be talking about another man. Why was Dad calling himself Hamish O'Neill?

Then Jimmy arrives, twenty years older and with less hair than in the photograph, but I recognise him. He shakes my hand and sits down, seeming quieter and perhaps a bit stunned himself, having been dragged out of wherever he was to be here.

'Where's Charlie?' Spud says.

'On holiday with his missus,' Gerry explains to me, like

I know who Charlie is, but I should, he too is in the photograph, a member of the Electric Slags.

'Peter passed away last year,' the Marble Cat says.

'Liver cancer,' Gerry says.

'Shut up, you – it was the bowel,' Spud corrects him, elbowing him in the ribs, which makes Gerry spill his drink and they go at it again.

'Lads, lads,' the Marble Cat tries to calm them.

'I preferred it when you two weren't talking,' Jimmy says. I smile.

'So you're his daughter?' Jimmy asks. 'Well, it's a pleasure to meet you.'

'She says his name was *Fergus*,' Gerry says excitedly, as though Dad's name was the most exotic he's ever heard. 'I told ye, lads. I always knew it. Something didn't add up with our boy. Spud always said he was a spy, better not to ask him questions in case we got killed.'

They laugh, apart from Jimmy, and Spud who looks at me in all seriousness. 'I did. Was he a spy? I bet you he was.'

They try to quieten him and it turns into a debate: remember the time he did this, remember the time he said that, until they finally shush and look at me.

I shake my head. 'He did a few different things . . . mostly sales.' I try to think of everything about him, to prove that I know him. 'He started in meat, then later mobile phones, mortgages . . .' My voice sounds as though it's coming from very far away, I don't even trust my knowledge any more. Did Dad do any of those jobs or were they all lies?

'Oh yeah, travelling salesman, I heard that before,' Spud says, and they shush him like he's a child.

'His last job was as a car salesman. My husband bought a car from him,' I say pathetically, proving to myself that Dad was in fact *something* that he said he was.

Gerry laughs, hits a stunned and disappointed Spud in the chest. 'You should see your face,' he laughs.

'I could have sworn he was a spy,' Spud continues. 'He was so cagey. His right hand wouldn't know what his left hand was doing.'

'Come on now,' Jimmy says softly, and they realise I'm here, and this is new to me, and they pipe down.

'When's the last time you saw him?' I ask.

They look at each other for the answer.

'A few months ago,' Gerry says.

'It wasn't,' Spud snaps. 'Don't be listening to him, he can't remember what he had for breakfast. It was more than that. Over a year ago. With that woman.'

My heart beats faster.

'So in love. Jaysus,' Spud shakes his head. 'He never introduced us to a soul in all the years and then all of a sudden he shows up with a woman. Blonde. What was her name?'

'German,' Gerry says.

'Yeah, but what was her name?'

'And Irish,' Gerry continues. 'Funny accent. Funny woman.' He tries to think. 'You must know her?'

'I don't.' I clear my throat.

'It was Cat,' Jimmy says.

They all agree on that.

Cat?

'But she could be using a different name too, for all we know,' Spud says. 'She could be a spy. German one.'

They all tell him to shut up.

'Why Hamish?' the Marble Cat asks me, leaning in intently. 'Why did he call himself Hamish O'Neill if his name was Fergus Boggs?'

I search my mind but there's nothing that links to that name. 'I have absolutely no idea.'

Silence.

'I only found out yesterday that he ever played marbles.'

'Mother of divine!' Gerry says. 'So you didn't know about us? The Electric Slags? He never talked about us?'

I shake my head.

They look at each other in surprise and I feel like apologising on his behalf. I know how they feel. Were they not important enough to him?

'Well, maybe you're right about one hand not knowing what the other hand was doing, Spud.'

'Did you say I'm right, Gerry? Jaysus! And I've witnesses and all.'

'So where is he?' Gerry asks. 'It's been a year and none of us have heard from him. Can't say we're too happy with him about that.'

'How is he?' Jimmy asks quietly.

Breathe.

'He suffered a stroke last year which affected his movement and memory. He's been in hospital under full-term care since then. We didn't realise that it had affected his memory as hugely as I think it did now, but recently I've discovered some things about my dad that I never knew, like the marbles, and I'm quite sure he doesn't remember ever playing them. Obviously I don't know everything about his life to know what he remembers or not, that much is quite clear . . .' I try to control my voice. 'He had, has, a lot of secrets, I don't know what he's keeping a secret and what is a lost memory.'

Jimmy looks sad. They all do.

'I can't imagine Hami— your da, not knowing about marbles. They were his whole life,' Gerry says.

I swallow. Then what was I?

'Not his whole life,' Jimmy corrects him. 'We don't know about the rest of his life.'

'Well we never bloody knew. But I figured the rest of his life at least knew about us,' Gerry says, annoyed.

'You would think,' I say, agreeing with him, sounding a little more snappy than I intend.

There's a silence. A respectful, understanding one, which becomes uncomfortable. I would rather they were bickering.

'Tell me what my dad was like when he was playing marbles,' I say, and then I can't shut them up.

'Sabrina,' Jimmy calls after me when I'm outside.

I have tears rolling down my cheeks and him catching me is the last thing I want. I thought I'd make it to the car at least, but I don't. I don't know if I can hear any more. Who was my dad? Who is my dad? This man that I grew up with that everybody seems to think something differently of. The words of Regina haunt me: He's a liar. Simple as that. As if that answers everything. Does it? No. Does it hurt? Yes. Why did he lie to me? His own daughter. How foolish and stupid I feel for letting him in on my life, on all aspects of my life, even the moments I had marriage troubles. He was always so caring, yet he wouldn't share a thing with me. I feel used, irritated, and even worse I can't storm into the hospital and have it out with him. The man in there simply doesn't remember. How convenient for him. I sound like Mum now, this silent rant in my head. I try to calm myself, forget about it all until I'm in private.

Jimmy takes me by the arm and leads me down the road. We stop by a door beside a tools and hardware shop and Jimmy takes out a set of keys and lets himself in. I follow him upstairs to a studio apartment above the shop. It's basic and I think he must live alone, but then I see a bucket of toys.

'For the grandkids,' he says when he sees me looking. 'I take them every Friday, when my daughter's at work.'

He fills the kettle and boils it. He watches me for a while, concerned.

'It's hard, what you're going through.'

I nod. Trying to pull myself together.

'I know a little bit about that feeling. Your dad made me feel like that too. On his wedding day.'

He has my full attention but he doesn't start talking until he's poured us both a cup of tea and as much as I want to urge him to speak, I know it would be impolite. In his own time. A plate of pink Snacks comes out. Then finally.

'I was a guest on his wedding day. A first proper date with a girl I half-liked. Michelle. She was a bridesmaid, begged me to go to the wedding. Figured there'd be free food and drink, so why not? So I went. Iona Road Parish Church. I remember it well. Big church, all decked out fancy. Her friend Gina was marrying Fergus Boggs. That's all I knew. Wore my brother's suit, showed up, sat down. Didn't know a soul. Or at least, I didn't think I would. But all of a sudden a good friend of mine arrives, and I'm chuffed that I know someone. He's looking pretty dapper too, in a light blue tuxedo suit. Flares. We all wore them then. He walks all the way to the top of the aisle. Stands there, waits. *Is that the best man?* I ask the fella next to me. *Who? Him? No, that's the groom*, the fella says. *Hamish O'Neill is the groom?* says I. Yer man starts laughing. *Are ye at the wrong wedding? That's Fergus Boggs.* I'd swear the floor went from under me. Or like he'd punched me in the stomach. Couldn't breathe, couldn't get any air. I felt . . . well, I felt like you do now probably, but not as bad for me. He wasn't my dad. But he was my pal. For two years we'd hung around. Hamish O'Neill. Couldn't figure it out.'

'Did you confront him?'

'Never did.'

'Why?'

'I thought about it. Stayed away from him for a while. Easy enough, he was away on honeymoon, then working extra hours to save up to buy a house, that much I knew. But odd thing is, when he was gone, someone came into the pub looking to set up a marble team. Charlie, you didn't meet him, he was away. He'd heard there were two of us in the Marble Cat who played. I told him I was interested, wasn't sure about the other. Had no intention of telling him. But then Hamish . . . Fergus, came back, phoned me to meet for a game and a pint. I told him about Charlie wanting to set up the team and we arranged to meet. We met in the Marble Cat, it was up to me to introduce him to Charlie. I thought about it, it could have been my moment to catch him out, show him I knew, but instead I said, Charlie, this is Hamish, Hamish this is Charlie. And that was that.'

'I don't know how you could do that,' I say, shaking my head. 'If I'd known I couldn't have hid it.'

'Look, none of us are perfect. I certainly don't claim to be. We all have our . . . complications. Thing is, the man must have had his reasons. That's what I always told myself. I thought it would be best to let him tell me, or I'd figure those reasons out. Over time, like.'

'And did you?'

He smiles. A sad smile. 'Well, I am now, aren't I?'

'You and everybody else,' I say, angrily.

'He was a good man, as simple as that. Hamish O'Neill, Fergus Boggs or whoever he says he was, it doesn't matter. He was just him. He was fun, sometimes he was grumpy, I don't think he changed his personality, no way a man could do that over forty years. I don't think he was pretending to be someone else. He was just the same man with a different name. That's all. It really didn't matter to me about the name. He was a good man. He was a loyal friend. Was there when I needed him; I'd like to think I was there when he needed me. Didn't have to tell me why or what was wrong. We just played marbles. Shot the breeze and I don't think that a single conversation we had was pretend or made up, it was all real. So your dad is your dad, who he was, who he is – he's the same man you've known all along.'

I try to take that on board but right now I just can't. 'You didn't try to find him when he disappeared last year?'

'Nah, I'm no stalker, or private investigator,' he laughs. 'We'd stopped being a marble team for nearly ten years. We played together sometimes, but we didn't compete. Too difficult to get the lads together, then with Peter getting sick . . .'

'But you were his friend. Did you not wonder where he went?'

He thinks about that. 'He doesn't talk about marbles now at all?'

'Today was the first day. I showed him a few bloodies and I think something happened, they triggered something. I don't think he remembered them before.'

He nods, sadly. 'People come and go. Lots of my friends have died,' he says. 'Happens when you get to this age. Cancer, heart attacks . . . it's depressing really. You ask about someone, hear that they've gone. Think of someone you haven't seen in a while and hear that they're dead. Open the paper and see an obituary for someone you once knew. It happens at my age. The way I see it is, when I stopped hearing from him, my pal Hamish O'Neill died too.'

This brings tears to my eyes again. 'Maybe he'll want to see you.'

'Maybe,' he says, uncertainly. 'It would be nice to see him. We didn't share everything, but we shared a lot.'

I thank him for the tea and I make a move to go. It's six p.m., I've nowhere to be but I need to leave. I'm not finished yet.

Jimmy leads me downstairs to the door to the street and before he opens it he turns to me. 'He slipped up sometimes, you know. The lads might not remember now, but they definitely noticed it at the time. We used to talk about it: what's Hamish on about now? Who's he on about? Usually it was when he'd had a few. He'd mention names – by mistake, I think. He didn't seem to notice. I think he confused things then, what he'd told us and what he hadn't. I'm sure it got to him in the end.'

I nod and plaster a smile on my face, not feeling any sympathy for Dad right now.

'You know there was only one other time that I ever saw him as happy as when he was with that woman, Cat. Couldn't figure out what it was then, but it makes sense to me a little bit later in my life.'

'What was it?'

'He came practically dancing into the pub one day, bought everyone a drink. *Jimmy*, he says, taking my head in his hands. *Today is the happiest day of my life.* It took something happening in my life to realise what it was that made him like that. When I had my first baby. Happiest day of my life, went dancing into the pub just like your da had. And I knew then what had happened to him. I knew he'd had a baby. April time about thirty years ago. Maybe a little more.'

My birthday. 'Is that true?' I ask, unable to wipe the smile off my face.

'On my grandkids' lives,' he says, holding up his hands. I'll take that.

21

PLAYING WITH MARBLES

Cat's Eyes

The best thing about having had to sell my car is meeting her. The bills were totting up, the income wasn't, the car had to go. Thirty grand would go a long way. It took a while to make that decision, what's a man without a car, but then when I made it, I never looked back. A financial advisor with no money, no car, and no clients. I was always going to be the first to go; subsequently the company folded, I didn't feel any joy. We're all in the shit together. More fellas like me, looking for the same kind of jobs.

I'm a salesman, have been all my life, it's what I do best, it's all I know. Today is my first day as a car salesman. I'm trying to feel positive, though I feel anything but. I'm fifty-six years old and I don't have a car to get to my job as a car salesman – not that the boss knows that, but he'll figure it out soon enough when he sees me huffing and puffing up the hill from the bus stop to work every morning. My doctor has been at me to exercise, my cholesterol, my blood pressure, everything is bad news. Every envelope I open is bad news. I'm officially a granddad and even little Fergus likes to remind me that I'm fat Granddad as he jumps on my belly. At least these short walks to and from the bus stop will give me some movement.

She's standing alone at the bus stop, trying to figure out the timetable. I know she's trying to figure it out because she's wearing her reading glasses, is chewing on her lip and looks confused with a screwed-up face. It's endearing.

She sighs and mutters to herself.

'Can I help you?'

She looks around in surprise like she thought she was alone. 'Thank you, I can't understand this thing. Where is today? Is this today?' She points with a manicured pink fingernail. 'Or is this today? I'm looking for the number 14 bus, am I even in the right place? And this, you can't read this at all, because some clever person decided to tell the world with a Sharpie that Decko is a fag. I mean, this is no big deal, I know some very happy fags. Decko might be extremely lucky, but not if he wants to get on the number 14 on a Monday morning. Then Decko will be a miserable fag.'

I laugh, it explodes right out of me. I adore her instantly. I study the timetable for some time, not because I'm concentrating, but because I want to be near her, because she smells beautiful. She finally looks at me, lowers her leopard-print reading glasses and I'm faced with the most stunning pair of eyes which illuminate her entire face, make her glow from within.

I must be making my feelings quite obvious because she smiles, in a flattered, knowing way. 'Well?'

'I have absolutely no idea,' I say, which makes her throw her head back and laugh heartily.

'I love your honesty,' she says, taking off her glasses

and letting them fall down on a chain to her chest, which is incredibly large and inviting. 'You're new to the bus too?'

'Relatively. I just sold my car. All I know is that I'm to get on the seven fifty bus and stay on it for eighteen stops. My daughter. She likes to make sure I'm safe.'

She smiles. 'My car is the reason I'm here too. Yesterday morning it decided to give up. Poof! just like that.'

'I can sell you a new one.'

'You sell cars?'

'Today is my first day.'

'Then you are doing rather well so far, and not even in the office,' she laughs.

Together we try to figure out how to pay the driver, who won't take our money but insists on us dropping it into a machine. She lets me go first, which means I take a seat first and I'm left wondering will she sit or pass me by. Praise the lord she sits beside me, which makes me feel warm.

'My name is Cat,' she says. 'Caterina, but Cat.'

'I'm Fergus.' We shake hands, her skin is smooth, soft, she's not wearing a wedding ring.

'Scottish?'

'My dad was. We left when I was two, moved to Dublin. What about you? Your accent is peculiar.'

She laughs. 'Thank you very much. I'm from Black Forest in Germany. The daughter of a good forester. I moved to Cork after university, when I was twenty-four.'

She is addictive, I'm interested in everything about her and I forget the first-day nerves and relax completely in the seat, almost missing my stop. I ask her too many personal questions but she answers and asks back. I tell her too much about me – my debts, my health, my failures – but not in a gloomy way, in an honest way, in a way that we can both laugh.

Leaving her on the bus is like a bubble bursting, I don't have the time or the courage to ask her for her phone number. I almost miss the stop. She presses the bell just in time. The bus pulls in, everybody is waiting for me to squeeze my way out of the seat to get off, all eyes on me. I can't ask her out, it's too rushed, too panicked. I get off the bus feeling enraged.

I spend the first few hours of my first day of work feeling like a spare part that can't quite find its place. The other men aren't too impressed by my hiring. They know I'm a friend of the garage owner, Larry Brennan. It's one of the only favours I had left in my life and the only way I could get a job after five months out of work. We grew up together and he couldn't say no. Probably wanted to, but he couldn't.

As an unpopular man on the floor it is difficult to get to the customers. They jump in before me, manage to somehow distract my clients and poach them. It's dog eat dog.

'No, I want him,' I hear a familiar voice in the afternoon when I feel like I want to go home and eat an entire box of Roses.

And there she is. My colourful, vivid, larger than life, foreign sparkler. On my first day, I make my first sale.

Rather unprofessionally I use her number from the paperwork to call her and ask her out. She is more than happy to hear from me and tells me she wants to cook for me. I go to her apartment on Friday night with a bouquet of flowers, a bottle of red and a clear mission. Tell her everything.

No more secrets. No more separation of my life. I've

come to hate the man I've become. No more secrets. Not with Cat. This is my chance at a fresh start.

Her apartment is a sweet set-up, two bedrooms, one for her and her remaining daughter that she's trying to get rid of. The walls are filled with her own paintings, drying on the windowsill are painted vases and paperweights, with lilac and pink flowers crawling upward, swirls and spirals on the paperweights. I study them while she prepares the food in the tiny kitchen, which smells delicious.

'Oh, I've just started a painting class. Painting on glass, to be specific.'

'It's different to paper?' I ask.

'Indeed, and it costs seventy-five euro to know about it,' she teases.

I whistle.

'Do you have any hobbies?'

It's an easy question, such an easy question for so many people. But I pause. I hesitate, despite my mission I'd firmly decided on all week while waiting for this evening.

Because of my hesitation, she stops what she's doing. She moves to the opening that joins the kitchen to the open-plan dining and living area, oven gloves still on. Those green eyes meet mine.

I feel short of breath suddenly, like I'm admitting some-thing huge. Feel sweat break out on my brow. Do it, Fergus. Say it.

'I play marbles. Collect marbles.' It is not a full sentence, I don't even know it means anything, but I'm gripping the back of the kitchen chair and she quickly takes me in, my posture, my nerves and she smiles suddenly.

'How wonderful. When do you play next?'

'Tomorrow.' I clear my throat.

'I would love to come and see. Can I?'

Taken aback, I agree.

'You know, I was playing with marbles myself today.' She smiles, and has the cop on to talk while I try to compose myself again. 'Yes, I'm a vet. And some very clever people came up with the idea of using a glass marble to keep mares out of heat. Today I put a thirty-five-millimetre glass ball into the uterus of a mare. First time for me, and for the horse. But do you know what? I think she's been learning from these ping-pong clubs: she popped it straight back out again. Expelled it immediately. Got it right second time round, though. You know, the company I got them from call them "mare-bles"!'

I laugh, totally surprised by the ease of her taking my news, then by her own marble story.

'I'll get you one,' she says, going back to the oven. 'I bet you don't have one of them in your collection.'

'No,' I laugh, a little too hysterically. 'No I don't.'

'So tell me about your marbles, tell me about your collection.'

And so I begin at the beginning with Father Murphy and the dark room with my bloodies, and then I can't stop. I tell her about Hamish and the hustling, I tell her about my brothers, I tell her about the world championships. We drink wine, and eat roast lamb, and I tell her about the games, about my team Electric Slags, I tell her the pubs I play in and how often. I tell her about Hamish, all about Hamish, and I tell her about my collection. I tell her about the marble swearing jar, I tell her about the cheating, I tell her that Gina and Sabrina have never known and I try, with difficulty, to explain why. We drink more wine, and we make love and I tell her more as we lie naked in the dark beside each other. It's like I can't stop. I want this woman to know who I am, no secrets, no lies.

I tell her about my brothers, how I pushed them away and will never forgive myself, and moved by my story she says that she will cook for them, and I say no, that is too much, I couldn't, we all couldn't. But she is an only child and has always wished for a big family. So over the course of the next few months, she cooks for Angus and Caroline, then Duncan and Mary, Tommy and his date, Bobby and Laura, Joe and Finn. And it's a success, so we do it again, with her friends.

She asks me what was it that struck me about her, that had me hooked on her so quickly – because we were like that, addicted to each other. I say it was her eyes. They're like cat's eyes. Ironically. More specifically foreign cat's eyes, mostly made in Mexico and the Far East. Most cat's eyes are single colour four-vane and the glass has a light bottle-green tint to it. The outer rim of her eyes are bottle rim, the inside almost radioactive they're so bright.

'So what am I worth, in mint condition?' she teases me one morning in bed. 'Me at twenty-one, before my babies, perhaps?'

'You're in mint condition now.' I climb on top of her. 'Look at you . . .' I lift her arms above her head, hold her down. 'You're beautiful.' We kiss. 'But you have no collectable value whatsoever,' I add, and we both erupt with laughter.

She tells me that when I revealed to her my marble-playing hobby she knew from my face that just saying it was a big deal. She said I looked like it was life or death, that for whatever reason it had taken a lot for me to say it, and if she said the wrong thing I would be gone and she didn't want me to leave.

The first gift she gives me is a mare-ble, painted by her, of course.

The only regret I have, each day I spend with Cat, is that I haven't completed the perfection; I have not tied up all of my loose ends. This part will take me time, the part where I introduce Sabrina to Cat. It's not because I don't think they will get along – I know they will – but Cat knows about me, the real me, the marble persona, and Sabrina and Gina are completely unaware. To tell Sabrina about it would be to tell her that I cut her and her mother out of a part of my life for so long, that I effectively lied to the two people who were closest to me, who I was supposed to trust, and allow to trust me. I can't think of the words for them. Cat tells me to hurry. She says to say things to people when you can; her ma died before she had a chance to make amends over their falling out. She says you just never know what can happen. I know that she's right. I'll do it soon. I'll tell Sabrina soon.

22

POOL RULES

No Shouting

'Dad had a secret life,' I say, hearing my voice shake as the adrenaline continues to surge through me at the discovery. In the background I hear Alfie having a meltdown over baked beans; he doesn't want beans, he only wants marshmallows, or Peppa Pig shaped pasta. Aidan tries to calm him down while listening to me. I keep talking. 'He was an entire *other person. Hamish O'Neill,*' I say angrily. 'Did you ever hear him use that name?'

'Hamish O'What? No! Alfie, stop. No way, honey. Tell me more. Fine, you can have marshmallows for dinner.'

Confused by who Aidan is addressing at any time, I just keep talking. 'I met these men in the pub, they were on his marble team, they had never even heard of me. Said Dad was secretive, one of them thought he was a spy . . .' My voice breaks and I stop talking, concentrate on the road. I've taken two wrong turns and an illegal U-turn where everyone beeps me out of it.

'Sabrina,' Aidan says, worrying, 'do you want to wait until I'm home to look into this further?'

'No,' I snap. 'I think it's rather apt. Don't you? With everything you've been saying about me.'

He's quiet. 'Sabrina, you're not him, that's not what I was saying.'

'I'll call you later. There's somebody else I need to see.'

'Okay. Just . . .'

'Don't say *if I think it will help*, Aidan.'

He's silent.

Alfie suddenly roars down the phone, 'Beans make you fart, Mammeeee,' before we're cut off.

I never called Mattie Granddad because Dad never called him Dad. I must have questioned it at some stage as a child, but I don't ever remember the answer, I don't remember ever wondering why he wasn't Granddad, I just always knew he wasn't Dad's dad. I was told that my granddad died when Dad was young and Mattie married my grandma, who quite honestly scared me. They both did.

But it strikes me as odd now, at thirty-three years old, that despite the fact Mattie raised my dad from the age of six, I never considered him my granddad. Disrespectful.

Grandma Molly was tough, not soft like my Nana Mary and I felt she viewed me as though I never acted grateful enough, reminding me of my pleases and thank yous a thousand times a day and leaving me jumpy and never completely comfortable.

In later years Mum told me Grandma Molly always said to her, 'You give that child too much.' She also used to have a go at Mum about not having any more children, which for some reason wasn't happening for them. Now it could be treated, back then, Mum just kept trying. I think that had a huge part to do with how their relationship went sour, apart from the fact they were very different people who had different opinions on almost everything. Mum couldn't take the criticisms from her mother-in-law, who'd spent her entire life having and raising children, it was the entire point of her life.

'I wasn't used to someone not liking me,' Mum once told me. 'I tried really hard with her, but she still didn't like me. She didn't ever want to like me.'

The one thing they had in common was their love of Fergus.

When Dad visited Grandma Molly he did so mostly on his own. He called in on her from time to time, on the way home from work or on the way into town. Sometimes I was with him, sometimes not. We'd all meet at Christmas for an hour on Christmas morning. I'd sit quietly, overly thankful for my new set of pyjamas, while they all chatted. She died when I was fourteen and it felt like somebody I didn't know had died. Secretly I felt a bit relieved that I wouldn't have to visit her any more. Visiting her was a dreaded chore. Then at the funeral I saw my cousins, who I barely knew, all in tears and being consoled by my uncles over their loss, and I felt so guilty because I didn't care as much as they did. I didn't feel the loss like they did. And then I cried.

When I married Aidan I felt the right thing to do was invite Mattie to the ceremony and reception. Mattie didn't come.

I have rarely given Mattie much thought. My children don't know him, I never visit him. My mum abhors him, thinking him a vile old man who got even worse when Molly died. But again, I feel guilty about that. I thought Dad wanted nothing to do with his family, he certainly behaved that way, and I thought it was no big deal if we went along with that, if it was a relief to us. But now I wonder why I didn't probe, press, encourage, wonder. Why? And as his secrets come to the fore, I want to know these people. I want to know why Dad became the way he became.

Mattie is almost ninety years old and lives alone in a ground-floor one-bedroom flat in Islandbridge. I know his address because I send him an annual Christmas card. A photo of the kids every year. He's not expecting me to call.

'Who is it?' he yells.

'Sabrina,' I say, then add just in case: 'Sabrina Boggs.'

'Who?' he yells.

I hear the door being unlocked and we stand face to face. After squinting and glaring, looking me up and down, it is clear that a further explanation is required.

'I'm Fergus's daughter.'

He takes me in again, then turns and shuffles back to his armchair in front of the TV. He's wearing a short-sleeved shirt with a stained white vest beneath and he makes an effort to button it up with his gnarled fingers. He's older but pretty much exactly as I remember him during my childhood visits. In an armchair, distracted by the TV.

'Sorry I didn't go to your wedding,' he says straight away. 'I don't go out much to social things.'

I'm embarrassed. The wedding was in Spain and I knew he wouldn't make it. 'I know Spain wasn't easy for a lot of people, but I wanted you to know you were welcome.'

'Made a change for me to be invited somewhere instead of the Boggs,' he chuckles. He's missing some teeth.

'Oh, yes,' I redden again. 'It was a numbers issue, my family is so big that we just couldn't include everyone.'

His stare doesn't make it easier for me.

194

'You're not in touch with them.'

'With . . . my uncles? I wish that hadn't happened,' I say, genuinely meaning it, though I never realised it before. Sitting before me is the man who raised my dad and he's a stranger to me. 'Dad wasn't close with them, unfortunately, and I suppose that had an effect on me and them,' I explain.

'They were as thick as thieves,' he says, the thick sounding like 'tick'. 'They called him that. Tick. Did you know that?'

'They called Dad thick?'

'No. Tick. Because he was the smallest. The smallest Boggs.'

I have a feeling the house was split into Doyles and Boggs. I never asked Dad about whether it was an issue for them growing up. Why didn't I?

'But he held his own,' he says. 'He outsmarted them.'

I feel proud.

'Not that it was hard, with them pack of feckin' eejits,' he snorts.

'Does the name Hamish O'Neill mean anything to you?'

'Hamish O'Neill?' he asks, frowning, like it's a test and he's failed. 'No.'

I try not to express my disappointment.

'But there was a Hamish Boggs,' he says, trying to be helpful. 'The eldest Boggs boy.'

I nod, my mind whirring. I'd forgotten about Dad's eldest brother up until now, his name hardly mentioned. 'I've heard of Hamish. Were he and Dad close?'

'Hamish?' he says, surprised, as if he hasn't thought of him since he died. 'Him and Hamish were glued together. Your da would follow him around like a lapdog; Hamish would throw a stick and your dad would scramble to get it. Hamish was clever, you see. A dumb git, like I said, but he was clever. He'd find the smartest fella in the room and

195

he'd keep him under his thumb. Did that to your da. It worried his ma no end.'

This is new to me. I sit up.

He thinks for a while.

'Smartest thing to do was keep Hamish away from the lot of them. I kept telling Molly that.'

'And did she?'

'Well he died, didn't he?' he says, and laughs a cruel laugh. When I don't join in, he brings it to a slow end. 'That lad didn't get what wasn't deserved,' he says, finger wagging at me.

'How did Hamish die?'

'Drowned. London. Some fella punched him, he was worse for wear, fell into a river.'

I gasp. 'That's awful.' I'd known he'd died, but never knew the details. Never asked for them. Why hadn't I?

He looks at me, surprised that someone would think it so tragic after all these years, as though Hamish wasn't a real person. And now I can see he's wondering what my visit is about.

'Was my dad very upset when Hamish died?'

He thinks about it, shrugs a little. 'He had to view the body. Flew over on his own. Angus wanted to go, but sure I couldn't be sending all my staff away to London,' he raises his voice defensively, still fighting a forty-year-old argument over sending Dad over on his own. 'Ara' it was probably tough for him on his own over there. His ma was worried. First time away and all that, seeing his brother dead, but he had to go – the authorities thought it was him that was dead.'

'They thought my dad was dead?' I'm not sure I've heard correctly.

'Seems good ol' Hamish had been using Fergus's name

in London. God knows why, but if you piss off enough people like that boy did you'd have to change your name ten times over. He'd probably have worked his way through the entire family if he hadn't died.'

My heart pounds at that discovery, a clear link to Dad's alternate name.

'Come to think of it I remember hearing about a Hamish O'Neill,' he says suddenly. 'Funny, you've reminded me now. Knew it was familiar when you said it. Here's a funny story . . .' He shifts in his chair, livens up. 'I'd been hearing things about a lad, Hamish O'Neill, playing marbles locally. Didn't mean anything, but Hamish wasn't a common name around and when you'd hear it, a fella would listen out, and O'Neill, well, that was Molly's maiden name, before she became Boggs, and then Doyle. It didn't mean anything, but I told Molly. I was drunk, shouldn't have said it maybe, we were at the wedding – Fergus's wedding – and, no offence to your ma, but it was so hoity-toity the fuckin' thing drove me to the drink and gave me a loose tongue. So after I tell her, she chats to your da, him in his fancy blue suit and frilly shirt and looking like a poofter, and I see her slap him across the face. "You're not him," she says.'

He's laughing at this, laughing so hard, at the image of my dad being slapped by his mother on his wedding day. My eyes fill with tears and I try to blink them away.

'That put him in his place,' he says, wiping his eyes. 'Now I never knew if it was your da playing or if it was another fella, a coincidence as they say, but there weren't many who played marbles at that age, not around where we lived anyway. Ever since he was a mucker he'd be out on the road all day, playing, you'd have to bate him to get in for dinner. Every birthday and Christmas present, all he wanted for was feckin' marbles. All the lads were the same, but your da was the worst because he was the best. He even hung out in some dodgy places with Hamish, Hamish taking him under his wing thinking he's some bigshot agent making a few quid from his baby brother. I told your da when he was a teenager: "You'll never meet a wife if ye keeps playing those feckin' things." He gave up when Hamish died. At least it did him good that way.'

I came here looking for answers, for insight into Dad's life, though I wasn't sure if I'd get them. But if Hamish used Dad's name in London, it explains why Dad used Hamish's name for marble playing. As a sign of respect? Remembrance? To honour him? To bring him back to life? And no wonder Dad played marbles in secret, when everyone around him was telling him to stop. But why continue this into his adult life?

'How did Dad feel about Hamish having used his name?'

'Couldn't understand it myself, but your da took it as a compliment. Proud as punch that Hamish had stolen his name. Like he was something special. Puffed-out chest and all at the funeral. Silly boy didn't realise that Hamish was getting him in a world of trouble using his name. If Fergus had set foot in the wrong place at the wrong time, Hamish could have got his brother killed. But Hamish was like that, I told you: a leech. Sucking up everything in a person and moving on.'

There's a long silence.

'How did you and Grandma meet?' I ask suddenly, wondering what possessed her to marry this man after the death of her husband.

'Met her in the butcher's shop. She bought her meat from me.'

That was it.

'Must have been true love to marry a woman with four children,' I say, trying to bring positivity to it.

'Those four runts?' he asks. 'She's bloody lucky I married her at all.'

I take in the surroundings. It's simple and clean, he is keeping it well.

'Laura will be here soon,' he says, following my gaze. 'Tommy's daughter.'

'Oh, right. Of course.' I try to think of the last time I met my cousin.

'She comes on Fridays, Christina on Mondays, the lads every day in between, checking up on me to make sure I haven't keeled over and have maggots coming out of my eyes. That's why they moved me over here: Laura lives across the way, they can keep a better eye on me that way, stop me getting up to mischief,' he chuckles. '"Are ye all right, Grandda? Are ye still alive, Grandda?" Ah, they're a good lot, the Doyles. Tommy and Bobby's kids. Bobby's not with the ma any more, you hear that?'

I shake my head.

'Sad to hear that, I liked her. But Bobby can't get enough of the women, never could, and Joe can't stand them. He's a queer, you know that?'

'He's gay, yes, I know.'

'I blame his ma for that, always suffocating him – don't go here, don't go there – while the rest of them went out and about and raised themselves.'

'I'd say he was gay no matter how she was with him,' I say, having had enough of him now.

He laughs, 'That's what he says, but what do I know?'

Silence then. Uncomfortable. We've both reached the end of our chat.

'How's your da?'

'He's okay.'

'Still doesn't remember much?'

'Not everything.'

'No harm,' he says, almost sadly to himself. 'They wish he'd remember them though. Talk about it all the time.'

'Who?'

'The Boggs boys. The Doyle boys.'

'Of course Dad remembers them.'

'Not the recent years.'

'Well I suppose they weren't close in recent years,' I say.

'But they were,' he says, riled up like I've accused him of lying. 'These past few years they'd started meeting up again. They played marbles, would you believe. Them and his new woman. They all liked her. No offence to your ma, but they said this one was good for him. Kept them all together. He doesn't remember any of that?' He looks at me like he doesn't believe my dad's memory loss.

I shake my head, completely taken aback.

'Do you know her name?'

'Whose?'

'His . . . girlfriend. This woman.'

'Ah now,' he waves his hand dismissively. 'Never met her. But the boys know. They can tell you.'

With a weak, 'Tell your ma I was asking for her,' he closes the door and I just manage to avoid my cousin Laura, who's carrying a vacuum cleaner and a bucket and mop across from an opposite flat on the other side of the court-yard. I sit into my car feeling stunned by what I've learned.

I search through my phone for my Uncle Angus's number. He is my godfather, the one I have most contact with, which is limited to text messages on birthdays on the years that we remember.

I dial his number and hold it to my ear, my heart

pounding. Hello Uncle Angus, Sabrina here, you haven't heard from me in almost a year but I've just learned that you and Dad were pals again before his stroke and I've also just learned that you knew his girlfriend. Could you please tell me, who is she? Because I don't know. I seem to be the only one, apart from Dad, who doesn't know.

No answer. I hang up the phone, feeling angry and stupid once again. As the anger surges through me I turn the key in the ignition and pull out. As I drive towards the hospital I hear Mattie's words in my head, calling Hamish a leech.

At the time I felt Mattie was overly harsh. I could understand Dad feeling special and honoured by the fact Hamish hadn't forgotten him when he'd moved away. Dad obviously looked up to Hamish his whole life, thought the world of him, it was an honour for his brother to have taken his name. But as the anger seeps through me, I feel Mattie's words now.

Whether he planned to or not, Hamish did suck some of the life from Dad, and in doing so not only stole a part of Dad from me, but worse, Hamish stole a part of Dad from himself.

23

PLAYING WITH MARBLES

Aggravation

Cat leaves me after a dinner of salmon, garlic fondant potatoes and peas and green beans made by Mel, who's a marvel
in the kitchen and often cooks with produce from the small
allotment here on the yard, helped by a few of the inmates,
but not grumpy Max. He has nothing to do with anything
and complains about everything. Cat kisses me gently on the
forehead and I like it, it is so long since I've felt that kind
of intimacy. I now realise that visits from Gina are cordial
in comparison, not affectionate. Sabrina's boys shower me
with cuddles and hugs and thumps and clambering, and I
love that; Sabrina's hugs are maternal-like, always worried
about me; but Cat, I feel a connection with her, an intimacy.
I look up to her for more, but perhaps that is asking for too
much on what we jokingly call our first date. My great fear,
as Lea wheels me to my bedroom for the evening, is that I
won't remember Cat tomorrow. How many times did this
very event occur in the last year for me to forget it again
the next day or a few days later, maybe even a year?

'Penny for your thoughts, Fergus,' Lea says, picking up on my concerns as usual.

'I don't know.'

'You don't know?'

She helps me up out of my chair and I sit on the toilet. She leaves to give me privacy and returns to help when I'm finished.

Do I want Cat to have to do this for me? Is there a future for us? Am I going to improve? I was happy here, bumbling along, existing, living, being cared for, no pressures. But with her out there, knowing there is a life that I had but didn't know it until today, it makes me uneasy. I need to be there, I should be there. I need to get better, I need to wipe my own bloody arse.

'But,' Lea says, cutting into my thoughts, 'the other way of looking at it is that there's someone there for you, waiting for you, helping you. Someone who loves you. That should motivate you, Fergus.'

I'm confused. Have I said those thoughts aloud?

'And the other thing is, you've remembered quite a lot more today than usual. That's major progress. Remember when you couldn't move your right arm? And then all of a sudden you did? Knocked that glass of water right over on top of me, but I didn't care, I was jumping up and down like a happy lunatic, had to hold my boobs and everything, remember?'

I laugh along with her, remembering the moment.

'Glad that smile is back now, Fergus. I know it's scary, changes can be scary. But remember it's all good, you're getting better every single day.'

I nod, thankful.

'Have you had enough for the day?' she asks, standing at the end of my bed, holding my feet like she doesn't even realise it.

'Why?'

'Because you've a few visitors to see you. I thought I'd wait and see how you're doing before telling them if they can come in or not. Just maybe you've had enough today. I don't want to tire you out.'

'No, no, I'm not tired at all,' I lie. I do feel exhausted from the day, the places my mind has brought me, the day with Cat, but I'm curious. I look at the clock. It's eight p.m. 'Who's here?'

'Your brothers.'

'All of them?' I say, surprised. I've seen them of course over the past few years, but never all of us together.

'Well there's five of them, I don't know if that's all of them.'

Five. Is that all of them? No Hamish. There hasn't been a Hamish for forty years, but I've always felt that he's missing. No. Five is not all of them.

'Will I tell them to come in? It's okay if you don't want to,' she says, concerned.

'It's okay. Tell them I want to see them.'

'Okay. And Dr Loftus will probably call in to see you as well.'

Dr Loftus, the resident psychologist I have weekly sit-downs with, has obviously heard the news of my memory today.

'I'm off to the office to do some paperwork, but Grainne is here if you need her.'

Grainne. Who grunts when she lifts me from my chair to anywhere like I'm a sack of potatoes she wants to get rid of. 'Thanks, Lea.'

'You're welcome.' She winks, then she's gone.

I hear them before I see them and they have me smiling before they even arrive in the door, a bunch of teenagers pushing, shoving and bouncing off each other as they make their way in, though they don't look that way any more.

Angus, the oldest, is sixty-three and has practically lost all his hair, Duncan is sixty-one, I'm fifty-nine, Tommy is fifty-five, Bobby the charmer is fifty and Joe the baby is forty-six.

'Surprise!' they announce, ducking their heads in the door.

'Sssh,' someone says outside, probably Grainne, and they all grumble and give her abuse as they close the door on her.

'We heard you had a good day,' Angus says. 'So we thought we'd celebrate.' He takes out a bottle of whisky from his coat. 'I know you can't drink it, but we fucking can so not a word out of you.'

They laugh and try to find enough places in the small room to perch, settle and sit.

'Who told you I had a good day?'

'Cat,' Duncan says easily, to a few disgruntled stares from the others.

'You know Cat?'

'Who doesn't fucking know Cat? Oh, that's right, you didn't until today,' Tommy says, and that's the ice-breaker everyone needed. Tommy slides the chair over to Bobby for him to have. Bobby sits down despite his brother being older, but some things never change.

'She said you told her about the swear jar,' Bobby says. 'I did.'

'When did you remember that?'

'I'm surprised you even remember that,' Duncan says. 'You were always off stuffing worms up your hole.'

They explode with laughter while Bobby protests with, 'That was one time, all right!'

Dr Loftus enters. 'Do I hear a party in here?' he asks jovially, then fixes me with that intense look. There's barely room for all of us in here; it gets hot quickly, particularly under his gaze.

'So tell us, Fergus,' Angus says, pouring Dr Loftus some whisky. 'How did you remember the swear jar?'

I look out of the window, the moon high in the indigo sky, full and perfect, and I think of Sabrina. Lea's dimples, Sabrina's nose. That got it started.

'The moon,' I say.

'You don't believe in that voodoo stuff?' Angus says.

'I do,' Tommy says. 'I could tell you a thing or two.'

'I do too,' Duncan agrees.

'There could be something in it, all right,' Dr Loftus says, rubbing the stubble on his face. 'It's been an interesting day so far.'

'Sabrina could never sleep during a full moon,' I say, and they keep a respectful silence. They're a rowdy bunch but they know their place.

Joe hasn't said anything at all since he entered, the baby in the corner, observant and concerned. Self-contained. I'm surprised he's here at all, but appreciative.

'Which one of you stole the fucking marble swear jar?' I say suddenly, which sends them into a spin, laughing. Angus literally nearly pisses himself and launches into a spiel about his prostate, Tommy who smokes too much almost coughs to death. They argue and blame one another, voices raised over each other, fingers pointed, the banter flying.

I remember the moment. There were about fifty marbles in the jar, we'd had a busy swearing month that time. I'd made a new friend in secondary school, Larry 'Lampy' Brennan, who was big into swearing. He'd get himself into trouble and I'd get him out of it. My favourite rainbow cub scout had landed itself in the jar after I'd told Bobby he was a fat fuck and I desperately wanted it back. I'd been to the chemist every week, not caring what was in the brown paper bag, I'd helped peel potatoes, carrots, cleaned the toilet outside, I was the best boy that month.

'It was probably you and you can't remember,' Angus says as soon as he's gathered himself. 'You're not getting away with that.'

We all laugh.

'I don't think it was me,' I say, really believing it, feeling the wrench of finding it gone.

'To be honest, I always thought it was you,' Tommy says. 'You were always going on about the . . . what was it called, lads?'

'Rainbow cub scout,' they all say in unison, apart from Joe.

Dr Loftus laughs at them.

'You kept on at Ma about swapping it with another one, but she wouldn't let you,' Tommy recalls.

'She was a hard one,' Angus shakes his head, 'bless her soul. I thought it was you too, to be fair.'

'It was me,' Joe finally speaks up and everyone turns to stare at him in surprise. He laughs, guiltily, not sure whether he's about to be beaten up.

'It can't have been you,' I say. 'What were you – two? Three?'

'Three, one of my first memories. I remember pulling the kitchen chair over to the shelf, pulling it down. I put it in my cart – remember the wooden one with the blocks?'

Bobby nods.

'Just you two lads had that, we never had anything so

fancy,' Angus teases, but there's truth in it. Bobby and Joe always had more than we ever did, the last two babies while we were all out of the house working and giving Ma money that she poured into those babies, mostly Joe.

'I pulled it down the alley, behind the house, then threw it over the wall at the end. It smashed.'

'Where was Ma?' I ask, stunned. I never suspected Joe, not for a second, the rest of us fought for weeks about that.

'Chatting to Mrs Lynch about something, something important, heads together, smoking, you remember.'

We chuckle at the image.

'She noticed I was gone at one point. I remember her grabbing me in the alley and dragging me and the cart home. So it was me. Sorry, lads.'

'Jesus, good one, Joe. You got us.'

He's earned some respect in the room and we think about that revelation in a surprised silence.

'You could've caught a cold, I suppose,' I say, thinking of Ma's fear of losing Joe, and they all look at me in surprise and laugh their arses off again.

'We brought you something,' Angus says as the laughter dies down. 'One game and we're gone, if that's okay with Dr Loftus?'

'Perfectly fine with me.'

'Tada!' Duncan lifts up a game of Aggravation.

When a member of the family leaves or dies, it changes the dynamics of a family. People move and shift, take up places they either wanted to have or are forced into roles they never wanted. It happens without anybody noticing, but it's shifting all the time.

The week that we heard Hamish left Ireland for London,

and the week I'm in trouble with the gardai for being with
Hamish when he beat up those boys in school, Ma is like
a banshee. She won't let any of us leave the house, go
anywhere, do anything. Angus has a school dance she won't
let him go to, which is a big deal, so he's in a foul mood
especially as Siobhan was going to let him pop her cherry.
It's pissing rain outside and we're killing each other, testos-
terone levels high as we're all on top of each other in the
two-bed house. Mattie is close to beating the living daylights
out of all of us and he goes to the pub for the umpteenth
time that day.

I come up with an idea. I spend an hour in a corner of
our bedroom, the only space and peace that I can find,
and I work on it. Duncan accuses me of wanking and gets
a clatter over the head from Angus, which is surprising,
the first protective action from him. He's probably
surprised himself but he stands by it and for the first time
Ma doesn't punish him because he only did her job by
telling Duncan off, which makes Angus and Ma allies,
and Angus and me allies. The dynamics are shifting and
it's confusing.

I come into the living room with a handmade game of
Aggravation, a game I'd seen in my marble book. It's a
board game for up to six players and the object of the
game is to have all players' pieces reach the home section
of the board. The playing pieces are glass marbles, and we
can choose our own as long as we can tell them apart. The
game's name comes from the action of capturing an oppon-
ent's piece by landing on its space, which is known as
aggravating – something we'd been doing to each other all
week since Hamish left for good.

We play the game. We sit around the dining table, and
Ma and Mattie can't believe it as for one whole hour we

battle it out on the cardboard game. Bobby wins the first game. I am the best marble player, but this game has nothing to do with skill and everything to do with the roll of the dice. Bobby the charmer has always been the luckiest bastard of all of us.

We play that game all day, every day for a week until Ma is sick of us under her feet and says we can go out. In a way it teaches us about finding our place, our base, in the family and not just through the game, but from the sitting down and spending so much time together, quarantined together and learning to live without Hamish.

We play it again in my room forty years later; not the homemade version but a real game that Duncan has bought. Bobby wins again.

'You lucky bastard!' Angus says, disbelievingly. 'Every single time.'

I roll the marbles in my left hand, my right side was the paralysed side, the side that now has limited movement, so I couldn't knuckle down like I used to, even if I wanted to. But I like the feel of them in my hand, rolling them around, and I like the familiar clink as they tap against each other. It's rhythmic and it's relaxing. 'I'm sorry,' I say suddenly.

They stop bickering and look at me.

'For all those years. What I did. I'm sorry.'

'Ah would you stop it, you've nothing to be sorry for,' Angus says. 'We were all . . . we all had our own thing going on.'

I start to cry and I can't stop.

Dr Loftus politely tells them to leave, and I feel their supportive hands on my head and shoulders, patting me as they say their goodbyes. Angus stays with me, my protective big brother that stepped up to the plate when his nemesis had disappeared. He hugs me, holds me, rocks me, cries with me, until my tears finally subside and I fall asleep, utterly exhausted.

24

POOL RULES

No Littering

I'm driving and I can't breathe. My chest feels tight and my muscles are tense and I'm about to shout at anybody who so much as looks at me the wrong way, and whoever makes the slightest mistake on the road will get it. I'm racing to confront Dad and I know this is a bad idea. He remembers nothing, I know we are to be gentle with him, no aggressive pushing on matters he simply can't remember as it will upset him, but I am raging. It seems everybody knew about this woman and these marbles apart from me and Mum. His own family. It took the arrival of a box of marbles to learn this? What else is there about Dad, about everything in my life, that I don't know?

I park in the car park and clamber out. The car park is quiet, it's after nine p.m., not many visitors now that they've returned home for their Friday night out, or their Friday night in.

I race through the front doors, and as I wind my way through the corridors I slow down, my chest heaving with the effort of holding back an emotion I don't want to release. What am I doing? I can't go into Dad like this, it will worry him, upset him, set him back, stress him. I'm not even sure I can talk. I slow down to a stop. I smell chlorine. It's comforting. I have lived in the water since I was a child. I liked that it was my own world, I could float and drift and not have to speak to anybody, explain anything, just swim beneath the surface. It was always my escape. It still is now.

I've slowed down but my mind is still racing, it's getting darker and the moon is visible, perfectly round and full, keeping an eye on me as I've gone about my day, on this most peculiar day. And the biggest thought of all which occurs to me now is this: am I this closed, inside person that Aidan tells me I am because my dad was somehow shadowy and secretive? Did I get this trait from him? Though I never picked up on it when I was younger, never thought of Dad as shadowy and never considered myself as closed, until Aidan started mentioning it. Perhaps it's true that you never know yourself until someone else truly knows you. Today's mission stopped being about looking for missing marbles early on, it grew to become a quest to look for the man who owned them. I didn't know that it would mean eventually looking at myself. And I don't like what I've found. I don't like any of these discoveries. I can't breathe.

I stop walking altogether and instead turn and make my way towards the swimming pool. Through the viewing pane of glass I can see that it's empty; of course, nobody swimming at this time, and physio all finished for the day. It's 8.5 metres long, the tiles beneath are blue, the tiles on the wall are blue, with a wave effect in shades of blue mosaics. I pull the door open and the chlorine hits me.

214

I hear somebody call out. I'm not supposed to be in here. I can hear footsteps behind me. I speed up. They speed up. More footsteps. Then someone calls my name. I can't breathe, I can't breathe. My chest is tight. I think of Dad, I think of Hamish, I think of the marbles and the secret woman. I think of Aidan and me. I kick off my shoes. I rip off my cardigan. I dive in. I escape. And I breathe.

I don't want to ever come back up. I stay close to the floor of the pool, feeling weightless and free, the tension gone. I don't have to think, my body relaxes, my heart rate reduces. I see the legs and feet of others by the edge of the pool, shimmering like mirages, like I'm the only real thing here. I hear the water in my ears, smell the chlorine, love how my hair tickles my skin, feeling like velvet as it moves with me. I tumble and twirl around the pool floor, perhaps looking like a beached whale, but feeling like a ballerina, graceful as can be. I don't know how long I've been under. Over a minute, maybe two, but I'm feeling the need to go to the surface to get some air, just a quick gulp and then under again. This is what I love about being in a pool, this is my territory, I'm safe here.

I hear the sound of clapping or slapping and look around to see a hand slapping the water like they're calling a dolphin.

I whoosh to the surface.

Gerry, the kind porter, is looking at me with worry, concern, confusion, like I've completely freaked out and lost the plot. Mathew from security is halfway between amused and angry, but Nurse Lea is smiling.

I've attracted quite the crowd at the viewing pane. No sign of my dad, thankfully. I float on my back.

'Come on, Sabrina,' Lea says, reaching out her hand.

I'm tempted to pull her in with me.

215

The moon made me do it.
But I don't. Instead I climb out, a sopping mess.
'Feel better?' she asks, wrapping a towel around me.
'Much.'

25

PLAYING WITH MARBLES

Bottle Washers

The last time I saw Hamish before he was a corpse in London was when we parted ways in the alley after he beat up those two schoolboys. I was fifteen, he was twenty-one years old.

It was the last time I saw him.

But it wasn't the last time I heard from him.

I'm seventeen, I've finished school, the only one out of Hamish, Angus and Duncan who made it to the end. They're working with Mattie and I know that will be what I'll have to do too, there's nothing else I can think of that I want, but before that begins, I'm going to have an entire summer ahead of me to do whatever I want. Mattie can't give me a job until September because he has another young lad as an apprentice. Doesn't mean I get to sit on my arse though. I got a job working on the school grounds with the grounds-keeper, Rusty Balls. Not his real name but we nicknamed him that because he's so old he practically squeaks when he walks. I'm making my own money but I pay Ma every

217

penny I earn. She gives me back an allowance as she sees fit. It's always been that way with everyone. All the bills are in Mattie's name and Ma takes care of paying them all. It's unusual for me to get anything from the postman is what I'm saying.

I go home at lunchtime covered in muck, thorns and pine needles stuck in my skin, calluses on my hands, scratches on my face from clearing the bushes of beer bottles and rubbish. Bobby and Joe are playing outside on the road, down on all fours, dirty legs and hands as they concentrate on racing snails against each other. There hasn't been a marble played on the road since we all went to work. I always want to play but the lads are too lazy. They want to go out with their girlfriends or go to the pub with Mattie. No one ever wants to play marbles with me. Tommy's twelve and he's still as useless as a chocolate teapot. Neither Bobby nor Joe ever caught the marble bug, it seems to have been a solely Boggs trait. I know a few lads that still play but they're hard to find, seems as though everyone is outgrowing marbles except for me.

Bobby and Joe warn me about Ma's mood, so I kick off my dirty boots and leave them outside and intend on doing everything right from the get-go. I can't think of anything I've done wrong today.

'What's this?' she snaps at me when I walk in.

She's standing beside the table, knuckles resting on the plastic cover like she's an ape.

'What's what?'

'This.' She jerks her head at it like it can hear her.

I look at the table and see a parcel. 'I don't know.'

'Don't tell me you don't know, you do know,' she snaps at me.

I step closer and look at it. My name is written in capital

letters in black pen on the only piece of brown paper that hasn't been covered in brown sticky tape.

'I don't know, Ma, honest.'

She can tell I'm genuinely surprised. The ape knuckle goes from the table to the hip.

'Is it from Marian?' I ask. Ma brother's Paddy lives in Boston and his wife Marian is the only person who ever sends me anything. She's my godmother, I've only met her once and I don't really remember her but every birthday and Christmas card has some sort of miraculous medal inside. I don't believe in them but I stuff them in the bottom of my underwear drawer, because it would be bad luck to throw them out completely.

Ma shakes her head. She looks worried. The only reason she didn't open it is because she's afraid. Ma doesn't believe in privacy, what is in her house is hers, but she's looking at it like it's a bomb about to explode in her face. She's like that with new things, or if anything out of the ordinary happens. The same with new people in the house; she's quiet, looks at them like they're about to attack her, and she gets all defensive and snappy because she doesn't know how else to react.

I don't want her to watch me open it but I can't figure out how to say that to her.

'I'll get you a knife,' she says, going to the kitchen. At first I think it's so I can defend myself from whatever jumps out and then I realise it's to open it.

While she's in there we hear a blood-curdling scream coming from outside and Ma goes rushing outside to her baby Joe. While Bobby tells Ma about the bee that stung Joe, I grab the knife and slip upstairs to my room. The parcel has been badly wrapped, a lot of brown tape all over the place makes it a tough job to open, but I manage it finally and toss the paper aside. All I can see is a load of scrunched-up newspapers. Inside is a blue glass bottle. I'm confused. It takes me a while to see what I'm looking at but after some inspection I see that it's empty and on the top there's a rubber washer in the neck. Inside, there's a marble. My heart starts pounding and I know who it's from. Well, I don't know for sure, but I'm guessing it's from Hamish. It's been a year and a half since he left and I haven't heard a thing, but this feels like a message from him. I root through the crumpled-up newspaper pages on the ground, searching for a note, but there's nothing. My eyes finally fall upon a pair of tits. And then another pair of tits. I quickly uncrumple every single piece of paper to find it has been protected by two weeks' worth of the *Sun*'s page three. Loads and loads of tits. I laugh and hope Ma doesn't hear me. I quickly fold them up and stuff them under the carpet that comes away from the floorboards. I rush back to work, taking the bottle with me, before Ma finds me and demands answers that I don't have.

'Do you know what this is?' I ask Rusty.

Rusty, who always has a cigarette in his mouth, looks at it and smiles. He flicks his cigarette into the trees that I just spent the morning cleaning out.

'You find that in there?'

'No. It's mine.'

'It's mine if you found it here.'

'I didn't. It's from my brother. In England.'

'You don't even know what it is.' He gestures, 'Give it to me.'

I move away.

He grabs it from me, strong for an old man, and he studies it. 'Codd Neck bottle or marble-in-the-neck bottle. Haven't seen one of these for some years. My mother used to have them, all stored in the shed before the Black and Tans destroyed them all. She had poteen in the shed. Not what these bottles were supposed to be for, but that's why she put the poteen in them. It was designed for carbonated drinks, fizzy drinks,' he adds when I'm confused. 'Problem with glass bottles is that the pressure of the gas would force the cork stopper out, especially if the cork dried out. So a man named Codd came up with these marbles in the neck. The bottles were filled upside down, the pressure of the gas in the bottle forced the marble against the rubber washer, sealing it in.'

'How do you get the marble out?' It's all I want to know.

'You try to do that and I won't give you this back. You don't get the marble out. Some kids smashed them to get them out, but don't you go doing that. Some things are better left the way they are.'

The marble is plain and simple, just clear glass, no signs or markings that I can see that tells me it's a certain brand or make. There's nothing special about the marble at all, just that it is in the bottle.

'These bottles are rare. Blue was a colour for poisons so any smart mineral company wouldn't have used blue. I doubt there are many of these around.'

He looks at it closely, checking it for marks as I would a marble and my heart starts pounding, feeling possessive. I reach for it and he pulls it away.

He chuckles. 'What will you give me for it?' he asks, gripping it tight.

I could tell him what I think of him, put up a fight, but that won't get me the bottle back. Besides I've to spend every day for the rest of the summer with him. Reluctantly I reach into my pocket and give him a folded-up page three. I was planning on having a go in the bushes when I got time to myself; Beverly, nineteen, hot tits. Rusty looks at her and hands the bottle back instantly, and disappears into his woodshed with the page for twenty minutes.

I sit on the grass outside and stare at the blue bottle, wondering what it means. Does it mean anything? I know instinctively that it's from Hamish, it could only be from him. The fact that it's a marble and the page three girls make it obvious, his kind of humour. He was probably hoping Ma would open it, or that I'd open it in front of her. I can hear his chesty chuckle as he wraps it all up, probably wishing he could be there to see our reactions. Homebird Hamish, stuck away from us all. I search the bottle for answers; does it mean Hamish is working in a bottle factory? Does he want me to find him? Is he a bottle washer? I remember we called larger taws 'bottle washers' but never knew why; now I know it's because of the marble in the neck. Is the large taw a link to a big brother? Is he trying to tell me something? I look for hidden messages but then I realise that it's clear as day: there is a message in the bottle. Hamish didn't write it on a note and stuff it inside, but instead he found a bottle with a marble in it.

A message in the bottle.

It speaks loudly and clearly to me.

It says to me, *I'm still here, Fergus. I haven't forgotten you, I haven't forgotten the marbles like everyone else has, I know how important they are to you. Saw this, thought of you. Still thinking of you. Sorry for all that stuff that happened. Let's be pals.*

It says *Truce.*

26

POOL RULES

No Glass

I sit in the cafeteria with Lea, who has the ability to make you feel that the oddest thing you've ever done in your life is the most normal, like she sees it all the time, does it all the time, and maybe that's true. She emanates warmth and care and I can understand why she's Dad's favourite, and why he grumbles so much about the others.

It's evening now. The cafeteria is all closed up apart from the tea/coffee facilities, which we help ourselves with. Dad is asleep, he was asleep from the moment I parked and ran inside like I was hunting him down. I'm glad. Even though the swim calmed me down, it stops me from barging in there and asking him about everything that has come out today.

I don't have to say anything and Lea just knows, Dad has always said that about her. A skill we all wish we had, and wish the nearest and dearest to us had. Like Aidan, for example. I would just like him to know how I feel without having to ask, because he asks me all the time, convinced something is so wrong with me, with us, that he needs to fix it. Two months we've been going to a marriage counsellor yet there's nothing wrong with our marriage. It's me. I'm closed. I'm all inside. This is what he tells me. But I've always been like that, I don't know why it's bothering him now.

Yes, I do know; he said so at the last session: he feels like I'm not happy with him. But I am. There's nothing wrong with him.

Are you happy?

Yes I'm happy with you.

Are you happy with yourself?

Jesus, Aidan, you're starting to talk like one of those counsellors.

Yeah, I know, but are you happy with yourself?

Yeah. I am. I like my job, I love my kids, I love you.

Yeah, but that's not yourself.

What is it if my job, my kids and my husband aren't myself? I shout.

I don't know. Relax, I'm just asking, you're stressed.

I'm only bloody stressed because you keep asking. Okay, fine, you want to do this, let's do this. Am I happy with myself? Yes, I am mostly, but I'm tired, exhausted, up at seven, breakfast, school lunches, school drops, work, collection, lunch, activities, dinner, bath, bed, sleep. Do it again. Butter, ham, cheese, bread, slice. Raisins. Next.

But we can't really change that, can we? The kids have to get to school. You have to work.

Exactly, so stop asking.

But would you like to change your job?

No! I like my job.

Do you?

Do I? Yes, I do. But lately, no.

And another thing: I'd like to lose the weight I put on after Alfie. Seven pounds. My tits are full of fat, I want that gone. I want to be able to do the splits in a bikini on the beach while we're at it, while everyone's looking.

So work out.

I don't have time.

Yes you do, in the evening, I'll stay home, you go out. Go walking with the ladies around the block.

I don't want to fucking walk with the fucking ladies around the fucking block – all they do is gossip and ramble, I don't want a gossipy ramble. Stop laughing at me, Aidan.

Sorry. So join a gym. Go swimming for yourself, you never get to do that any more.

In the evenings, Aidan? When I'm so tired all I want to do is lie down or watch TV on the couch. Or be with you, because if I went out in the evening, when would I be with you?

Stay up an hour later.

But I'm already fucking wrecked.

Okay, okay, stop swearing so much.

Sorry. I just don't want to have to ask you a favour to mind the kids while I go to the gym of all places. I'd rather do something else, like go out. Feels like a wasted favour.

Is that it? You want to go out more? You always say you're too tired, that you don't want to go out.

I am too tired. And I'm tired of this conversation.

I just want to help you, Sabrina, I love you.

And I love you too. Really, it's not you, it's not anything, you're just making it something.

You're sure? It's not because of . . .

No. It's not because of that. I'm over that. I don't even want to talk about that. It's not that.

Okay. Okay – you're sure?

Am I sure?

Yeah. Yeah I am.

Do you want me to do more around the house? Help out more?

No, you're great, you do enough, remember we filled out that list of duties at the last session, you're great, you do way more than I thought, you're great, Aidan, it's not you.

But it's something?

Aidan, stop it. No it's nothing. There's nothing.

If there is, tell me, because it's hard to tell with you, Sabrina. I can't read you. You're quiet, you know. You keep it all inside.

Because I don't want to make a big deal of things, because there's nothing wrong, because you're making this all dramatic and really everything's fine. I'm just tired that's all, some day the kids will be older and I won't be tired.

Okay. And I'll take them camping on Friday and you can have a day to yourself, rest after work, don't lift a finger, don't do anything, okay?

Okay.

'Tell me, what did you discover?' Dr Loftus asks.

Dr Hotness, in Lea's words, was about to leave work when I dived into the pool, but word spread and he came to see me. And while I appreciate it, I hope I don't have to pay for this session. I tell Dr Loftus about everything I've learned today about Dad, about his double life, and I wonder how much of this Dr Loftus already knows, if he has been speaking with Cat and Dad's brothers for the past year, if everyone has known everything all along, apart from me. I now know how it feels to be Dad, for everyone around you to know things that you don't know, and it's upsetting. It has knocked me off my axis. And I think what hurts me the most is that in some version of his life, I didn't exist, that he chose for that to happen. I swallow the lump in my throat before continuing.

Dr Loftus is quiet.

'Did you know about this?' I ask.

He ponders this slowly. 'They came to me at various points during Fergus's rehabilition to try and help, offer information that they felt I should know about him that he no longer knows, and so yes I do know about some of what you say, but not its entirety, and certainly not that he had been using his brother's name. This is new.' He thinks. 'With a stroke there is often memory loss. You know this, we've discussed it before. Confusion or problems with short-term memory, wandering or getting lost in familiar places, difficulty following instructions – we've seen some of these with Fergus. The memory can improve over time, either spontaneously or through rehabilitation, and we've seen signs of both of these working using the brain retraining techniques. However . . .' He shifts in his seat and moves forward, elbows on the rickety table, shirtsleeves rolled up, the tired eyes of a man who's had a long day. 'Repression, or dissociative amnesia as it's sometimes referred to, is a different matter altogether. Repressed memories are hypothesised memories having been unconsciously blocked, due to the memory being associated with a high level of stress or trauma. Repressed memories are a controversial issue; some psychologists think it occurs in victims of trauma, some dispute that. Some think it can be recovered through therapy, again others dispute that.'

'You think my dad has deliberately repressed the marble memories?'

He takes his time. There are no yes/no answers with him, there never have been with Dad's condition, which is stressful and confusing. Why does he remember some things and not other things, why does he remember some things on certain days and not others? The stroke affected the memory, that's the only response that ever made sense to me.

'He remembers you and your mother and the life you've had together, he remembers his childhood and his relationship with his family, he doesn't recall his recent reunion with his brothers which preceded his stroke, this woman that he was in love with, and he doesn't remember the marbles at all.'

'But you said that people block out things that have been stressful and traumatic. Marbles made him happy. This woman and his brothers made him happy, by the sounds of it.'

'But by your telling, marbles forced him to separate his life into two. They forced him to become two different men, living two different lives. He was clearly under a lot of stress in his life before his stroke, his financial strains and losing his job, but this stress would have been heightened by the fact he was trying to live two separate lives. Now this is just a theory, Sabrina,' he says more casually, and I realise we're off the record here, this is not an official diagnosis. 'And it's late, and I'm tired and I'm just offering theories, but if he blames the marbles for bringing that stress on him, then it would offer some explanations as to why he has repressed the marble memories, despite the obvious joy they brought him before. They began as a kind of freedom to him, a place he could get lost in and then, as the years went by, they trapped him. He may not have seen a way out of it.'

'So forgetting them is a way out?' I have been so angry with him, so selfishly hurt about it all, that I didn't think of the pressure he must have been under, albeit self-imposed pressure.

'Again, repression is an unconscious thing. He wouldn't have consciously made the decision to block it out, but to survive . . .' He leaves it hanging in the air.

I think of Dad's expression when I showed him the bloodies. Recognition. Joy. Turmoil. Confusion. 'If I showed him the marbles, would it have a negative effect on him? Send him into . . . a stroke again?'

He's shaking his head before I've even finished. 'It wouldn't give him a stroke, Sabrina. It could upset him. But it could also bring him joy,' he says, with a shrug of the shoulders. No yes and no no.

I think of Dad's face when he saw the bloodies this morning, of how it changed from innocence to confusion, the other part of him caught between who he is now and who he has blocked out, both battling against each other. I don't want to cause him more stress.

'He had both reactions when his brothers showed him the marble game tonight. Delight at seeing them, followed by tears, but he seems to be working out something today, dealing with it all on an unconscious level.'

He's healing, I think to myself.

Lea had told me that my uncles had visited, I'd just missed them when I arrived and dived into the pool. Meanwhile Dad had fallen asleep, exhausted by his day.

'I discovered the marbles in the boxes that were delivered this morning,' I explain. 'Some are missing and I started out trying to find them. They're worth a lot of money. But then I found all of this out.'

He nods along encouragingly.

I cover my face in my hands. 'Or maybe it's me that's losing it.'

'You're not,' he laughs. 'Go on.'

'I thought if I could find all the marbles, and then show them to him, then they would magically unlock whatever is blocking his memories. I know you can't just fix a person like that, but . . . at least I'd be doing something to help.' My head pounds at the revelations the day has brought me, not just over Dad's secrets but, as the night draws in, my own intentions slowly surface, perhaps feeling safer under the cover of dark.

'Sabrina, just being here for him is helping. Talking to him. No one knows the triggers for the reoccurrence of memories; it can be sense, sound, or aided triggers like guided visualisation, trance writing, dream work, body work, hypnosis. And in my field, the existence of repressed memory recovery has not been accepted by mainstream psychology, nor proven to exist. Some of my fellow memory and cognitive experts tend to be sceptical.'

'And you?'

'I have a roomful of books on all of this stuff, what to say to Fergus, what to do with Fergus, but really,' he opens his arms, looking utterly exhausted and I feel so guilty for keeping him so long, 'really what matters is, whatever works.'

I'm thinking fast as I know he's about to leave any moment, return home to his real life with his own concerns. I've now decided that I don't want to upset Dad by showing him his marble collection; each will have a memory attached, it could be too much for him. But I want him to remember the joy of marbles. 'What if I buy him new ones, make new memories, make new joy?'

He smiles. 'I don't see what harm that could do.'

'What time is it?' I look at my watch. 'It's almost ten. Who sells marbles at ten at night?'

He laughs, 'Why does this have to be solved all in one day?'

230

Because it does. Because I can't tell him why, but I have a deadline. Fix things today or else. Or else what? Everything remains unfixed forever? Tomorrow I'm back on the hamster wheel.

As Dr Loftus bids me farewell, I take stock of myself. My jeans are still wet from the pool no matter how much I've tried to dry myself under the heater in the changing rooms, and I'm braless and T-shirtless beneath my hooded top, with the wet T-shirt and underwear in a plastic bag. Reality is setting in. I'm contemplating the fact that my mission to save my dad in one day is just not going to happen. Tomorrow I will wake up, Aidan and the children will come home and I will be all consumed by them, and this dream will have vanished, like so many other daily aims that never happen. I should go home, get some sleep, get the rest and recuperation I should have been getting while Aidan has the boys. That was the whole idea. But then Nurse Lea clears her throat from the doorway.

'Dr Hotness gone?'

I laugh.

'I wasn't eavesdropping . . . okay, I was, but don't ask any questions.' She hands me a folded piece of paper. 'I met a fella on Facebook, we were supposed to go out tonight to a party, meet in person for the first time – okay, it wasn't on Facebook, it was a dating site, but if by some divine miracle he looks anything like his profile then I'll marry him tomorrow.' Nervous laugh. 'Anyway. He's an artist. Does stuff with wood. And he has lots of artist friends. Here.'

She hands me a piece of paper with an address.

'What is this?'

'I'm mad about your dad, I've never seen anyone come on so much in one day. I want to help.'

231

27

PLAYING WITH MARBLES

Reproductions, Fakes and Fantasies

Cat is sitting at a table dressed in a white dress, white flowers pinned in her hair. She sips on a glass of white wine and throws her head back and laughs, a naughty dirty laugh which instantly makes the others laugh. That's the way with Cat, it's not always what she says that's funny, it's her reaction to it that is the hilarious part. It would be naïve to say she is always in flying form, she certainly is not, especially with her eldest daughter who gives her so much grief, a troubled young woman who is constantly problematic, not happy unless she is making her mam unhappy. Aside from that and almost in spite of that, Cat has the ability to put those things aside and enjoy life for what it is, or at least enjoy the other part of it. She never allows things to overlap, she separates her worries. Despite the way I have separated my life, I have never been able to do that. A problem in Hamish O'Neill's life is a problem in Fergus Boggs's life and vice versa. For example today, this beautiful day, she says, 'To hell with all of life's problems, let's just enjoy now, this moment, what we are doing now.'

I both admire it and am driven crazy by it. How can she ignore problems? But she doesn't, she puts them aside, chooses her moments to dwell on them. I have never been able to do that. I constantly dwell until they're gone away. And where are we ignoring our problems today? Five thousand miles away in the central coast of California's wine region at the wedding of Cat's dearest friend. At fifty years of age and the groom at sixty they're no spring chickens and it's not the first time for either of them, though they appear like two love-struck teenagers, as in love as I feel with Cat when I'm in her company. It seems to be the year of second marriages, this is my third wedding this year, and I remember the first on all three occasions, especially as one of them was mine. I wasn't invited to Gina's wedding but it was the one which affected me greatly. I wasn't expecting to be invited, Gina and I haven't had a pleasant word to say to each other since our separation over fifteen years ago but still, despite boyfriends after me, I considered her my wife. Now she's someone else's and I think of all the things that I did wrong. How good it was at the beginning, how I looked up to her, worshipped her, and only ever wanted to please her. It was that thinking that ruined our relationship, that ruined me. Why couldn't I just have seen her for what she is, known that she loved me for who I was? No matter how hard I tried to change myself, the roots of me were the same and she loved that. For a time at least. That sweet young woman with the freckle face is gone, now just a scornful woman who snaps at the slightest chance. Did I make her that way? Is it all my fault?

We are in Santa Barbara county, in July, in the sweltering heat. Cat, who is in her element, is bronzing herself in the full blaze of the sun, shoes off, manicured toes wiggling, cleavage big and tanned, jiggling when she laughs. She is the sunshine in my life and yet the greater she shines upon me the greater I feel the shadow cast behind me. Time is creeping up on me. I'm away from the sun, unable to take the heat. I have completely soaked my white shirt and because of that can't take off my jacket, which makes me all the warmer. I'm in the shade as much as I can be, drinking gallons of water, but at the heaviest weight I have been. Four stone above my usual weight, I'm feeling the heat, the discomfort, the heat of my balls, my thighs sticking together, my shirt too tight around my neck. The man who has plonked himself next to me in a white casual suit and a white hat tells me he's an art dealer, he talks of nothing but golf courses that he's played all around the world in such detail I want to tell him to shut the fuck up, shut the fuck up. But I hold back, for Cat's sake. I made the mistake of mentioning I played golf, which I once did, though it feels like many moons ago. I played mainly for work purposes, when I was a financial advisor and was keeping up with what was going on. I've had to sell my golf clubs, lose my membership as I couldn't keep up with paying the fees and I don't have the time for leisure any more. Anybody I played with has done the same and instead invested in Lycra and a bike and goes cycling on Sundays. Hearing about a game I had to give up does nothing to help my mood.

I didn't want to come away. As soon as Cat told me of the invitation I didn't want to come. I said as much, but she put her foot down. She insisted on paying. Whatever I felt when I was younger on honeymoon, I don't feel it now. I don't want anyone else paying my way. I want to pay my own way, but I couldn't afford the flight and now that I'm here I can't afford anything. Cat is covering it all. Every gesture, every kindness just makes me feel even worse, like my balls have been chopped off. And the company I've been in has been horrendous. I'm sure she's wishing she left me behind after all.

She looks over at me and I see the concern in her eyes. I put on a fake cheery grin, fan myself comically to let her know why I'm over here in the shade. She smiles and rejoins the conversation, I even keep up an extremely animated conversation with the art dealer beside me so she can see I'm enjoying myself in the moments that she sneaks a peek at me, thinking I don't notice.

Midway through talking about the par something on the eighth hole in Pebble Beach, my phone vibrates in my pocket. I'm happy to excuse myself and disappear inside to the air-conditioned reception of the vineyard. I take off my jacket, away from anyone's view and sit down. It's the text I was waiting for. Sonya Schiffer, a woman I contacted a few months ago as soon as I heard I was coming to Santa Barbara. Communicating with her behind Cat's back has stirred those old feelings inside me that I used to get when arranging nights out or nights away from Gina, but when I feel the feeling it is accompanied by guilt. My conscience has grown since meeting her, but it doesn't remove the need I have to get away and meet this other woman. I think hard about how to get away from here, I had a plan in action but now that I'm here I need to rethink it. Our hotel is further from the venue than I thought, it isn't easy for me to slip away, I must arrange a shuttle bus or get a lift from somebody, and if I feign sickness I'm sure Cat will want to come too. The music will start shortly and Cat loves to dance. She'll be up all night dancing non-stop with anyone and everyone, like she always does. She's a beautiful dancer and usually I watch her, but perhaps that's my time to escape. Wild horses couldn't drag her away from a dance floor. I can say I'm jetlagged or that I've a dodgy stomach. I had oysters for my starter.

Our inn is twenty minutes away from here, the hotel I've arranged to meet Sonya in Santa Barbara is forty minutes away. I need to get to our hotel to get the car and drive to the city. Can I make it? Meet Sonya, and be back in time before the wedding is over, before Cat finds me gone? I don't know, but the sooner I go the better the chances. When she sees me coming towards her she looks concerned. I rub my belly and explain to her, in a rush, that I must get back to our bedroom toilet. She knows I don't like to use the toilet when I'm out and about. I tell her I won't be long, I need to change my shirt too, I'm embarrassed; enjoy yourself, I'll be fine, I'll come back for the dancing. She wants to take care of me, of course. Cat is a nurturer but she also likes her space having lived alone for twenty years and is good at giving it to others and so I leave the party. I have a quick shower, change into a clean shirt and pants, take my overnight bag and drive to Santa Barbara.

The meeting place is a motel and I park in the car park and climb the stairs to the second floor. At the end of the corridor all the doors of the bedrooms have been left open as I was informed they would be for the room trading. I know Sonya straight away, I recognise her from her photograph and also because she's the only woman. At seventy-four years old she has published two books about marbles, playing and collecting, and is one of the leading experts in the marble world. I have asked her here to value my marbles, or rather Hamish O'Neill has, and after sharing photographs with her of my collection she was sufficiently intrigued to agree to come. At over three hundred pounds, and with arthritis in both knees, she is surrounded by fanatics eager to get a moment of her time. But as soon as I enter, it's just me and her. She, like me, wants to get straight down to business. The four rooms on this floor are all involved in the room trading, where people can discuss, swap, value their marbles. I've been to marble conventions before as Hamish O'Neill and have always thrived on the pure buzz of being surrounded by people as committed to marbles as I am. Seeing their eyes light up at the sight of a mint condition Guinea cobra or a striped transparent or an exotic swirl or even at a sample box they haven't seen before, or haven't seen in the flesh, reminds me that I'm not alone in being mesmerised by this world. Of course some of the people are even nuttier than me, spending their entire lives and savings on collecting without ever playing, but I always feel among friends at these meets, like I can truly be myself, though it's under my brother's name.

I owned both of Sonya's books before I contacted her. I had bought one in particular with the intention of trying to value my own collection but quickly realised I could be easily misled and tricked. I contacted her on the Internet, one of the most knowledgeable collectors there is. I haven't brought my entire collection, I couldn't have afforded the airline's weight charges nor could I have fitted any more in my bag without Cat suspecting. I've brought what I think are the most valuable. I haven't brought them to sell them – that I made abundantly clear to Sonya Schiffer. I don't know if I'll ever sell them or not; I always thought I never would, but the time is coming close. The banks are after me for an apartment I own in Roscommon, a stupid investment in an apartment block in the middle of nowhere that cost too much at the time and now is worth nothing. Because the school, shopping centre and anything else that was in the plans didn't go ahead, I can't let the apartment, never mind sell it, which leaves me in a difficult position of trying to pay the mortgage as well as my own.

I need to start gathering my pieces and seeing what I have in play.

Despite the fact that I have driven and need to drive back, Sonya insists that we drink whisky together. I have a feeling that my response has a great bearing on whether she values the pieces or not. She has come for a night out, not to be rushed. I can worry about the car tomorrow, give an excuse to Cat, I don't know what yet. I'll come up with something.

'My, my, you have quite the collection,' Sonya says as we sit down at a table in a bedroom. People swirl around us, talk, swap, play, even watch her at work, but they're not registering in my mind. I keep my eye on her. She's huge, so big her arse sticks out on both sides of the chair. She thinks I'm Hamish O'Neill, winner of the World Championship of 1994, individual best player in the same year. She wants to talk about that for a while and I don't mind reliving my glory days when there are very few people I can tell the story to. I tell her all about it in detail, how we beat the Germans' ten-in-a-row run and the bar fight that broke out afterwards between Spud on my team and one of the German teammates, and USA having to act as peacemakers. We laugh about it and I can tell that she's impressed and we return to the marbles.

'I bought your book to value them myself but I quickly learned there's an art to it, one that I couldn't master,' I say. 'I learned there are more reproductions out there than I thought.'

She looks at me intently. 'I wouldn't worry about reproductions as much as people want you to worry, Hamish.

When it comes to the collectable world, reproductions are not a new thing. Sparklers and sunbursts were an attempt to mimic onionskins, cat's eyes an attempt to mimic swirls. Bricks, slags, Akro and carnelian agates and 'ades were an attempt to mimic hand-cut stones, but despite this, all these marbles – except of course cat's eyes – are highly collectable today.'

I smile, thinking of my joke with Cat about her not being collectable at all, though she is the most valuable thing in my life, and Sonya looks at me over her glasses which are low on her nose. She watches me, as if evaluating me and not the marbles, twirls them around with the 10x loupe in her thick fat fingers, gold rings squished down on most fingers, with fat gathering around them. Those suckers are never coming off. 'But usually everyone and everything is mimicking something or other.'

I swallow, thinking it's a direct evaluation of me. As if she knows I'm not Hamish O'Neill, but she couldn't possibly.

After a time studying, during which I've downed too much whisky, she speaks, 'You've got some reproductions here and this, this has been repaired to fix a fracture, see the tiny creases and the cloudiness in the marble?'

I nod.

'That's from re-heating the glass. And you've a few fantasies,' she says, moving everything around. 'Items that never existed in original form. Polyvinyl bags with old labels,' she looks disgusted. 'But no, you're generally looking good here. You obviously have a good eye.'

'I hope so. We'll see, won't we?'

'Yes, we will.' She looks at the collection and laughs wheezily. 'Hope you've got time, because this will take all night.'

It is four a.m. when somebody called Bear drops me back at the inn in a pickup truck and speeds off. I can barely see straight after downing a bottle of whisky with Sonya. I try to concentrate on the path ahead of me and fall with my bag of marbles into the vines. Laughing, I pull myself out and stumble to the room.

As the pickup truck passed the vineyard I saw to my surprise that the wedding had wrapped up and there wasn't a guest in sight, not even my Cat. Unusual for an Irish wedding, though I suppose we aren't in Ireland and I should have known that it would be over early, with such a conservative bunch. I stumble into the inn, receiving angry glares from the owner who had to let me in at such an hour, and I bang into everything, door frames, furniture, on the way to the stairs. When I reach the bedroom, as if by magic Cat pulls the door open, hurt written all over her face.

'Where the hell have you been?'

I know I've done it again. No matter what I think about myself, how I think I can change, I always slip back into hurting people. The Hamish in me comes out, but I can't blame him any more, I never really could. It's me. It's always been me.

28

POOL RULES

No Alcohol

I wait in my car for Lea as she gets ready for the party. I blare the heating, trying to dry my jeans, which stick to my legs. I take the inventory out of my bag again and flick through it. Scanning his lifetime of memories, all catalogued in a neat script. I look through the photographs I took of the newspaper article on the Marble Cat wall. It's grainy and Dad is hiding in the back row, but it's him all right. For the first time I notice the date on the newspaper.

I call Mam, who answers quickly for so late at night.

'Mam, hi, I hope I didn't wake you.'

'Not at all, we're still up drinking wine – Robert is drunk-tweeting NASA,' she giggles as I hear Robert in the background shouting about aliens waving at him from the moon. 'We're out on the balcony watching the moon, isn't it marvellous? I should have known you'd be awake, you know you could never sleep as a little girl when there was a full moon? You used to sneak into our bed. I remember Fergus brought you downstairs for a hot chocolate one night, I found you both sitting in the dark at the kitchen table, him asleep, you looking outside.'

The moon made us do it.

I smile at the image. 'I haven't changed much.'

'Did the boys have a great day?' she asks.

'The best.'

She laughs. 'And I'm sure you have too. Nice to have the day to yourself. You don't get that much.'

Silence.

'Everything okay?'

'Do you remember my thirteenth birthday party? We had a marquee in the back garden, didn't we?'

'Yes, about thirty people, catering, the works.'

'Was Dad there? I can't really remember.'

'Yes, he was.'

'So he wasn't away that day?' The newspaper report is dated the day of my birthday, though it refers to the championships being held the day before.

She sighs. 'It was a long time ago, Sabrina.'

'I know, but can you remember?'

'Of course he was there, he was there in all the photographs, remember?'

I remember now. Me in my short skirt and high heels, looking like a tart. I can't believe Mum let me dress like that, though I know I didn't give her much choice.

'And what about the day before?'

'What did you find out, Sabrina? Just spit it out,' she snaps.

I'm taken aback by her coldness.

'I suspected,' she fills my silence, 'which is probably what you're about to tell me, that he was having an affair, away with somebody. He said he was in London for a conference, but when I called the hotel they had no record of him. I suspected something, he'd been doing his usual secretive thing leading up to that, heading off to places I knew he wasn't going to. He did that a lot. He came home the day of your birthday. I confronted him, I can't remember now, but he managed to weasel his way out of it as usual. Made me feel like I was going crazy, as usual. Why? What did you find out? Who was she? Was it that Regina woman? God knows there were many others, but he never admitted to her. I always thought they were together before we split.'

'I don't think he was with another woman, Mum. He was having a love affair all right, but not the one you think.' I take a deep breath. 'He was at the World Marble Championships in England. His team of six men, the Electric Slags, won. A newspaper published a photograph and an article about it on the day of my birthday. He's hiding in the back, but I know that it's him.'

'What! Marble championships? What on earth are you talking about?' She slurs as she talks and I don't think this is the best time to discuss it with her. I was wrong, I should have waited, but I couldn't.

'I told you about them, Mum, he's been playing marbles all his life, competitively. Secretly. He's been collecting them too.'

She's silent. So much to take in, I'm sure.

'It's him in the photograph, but he used a different name. Hamish O'Neill.'

I can hear her intake of breath. 'Sweet Jesus! Hamish was his brother, his older brother who died when Fergus was young. He wouldn't talk much about him, but I learned a few things about him over the years. Fergus thought the world of him. O'Neill was his mother's maiden name.'

So Mattie was right. This was all about Hamish. Hamish died using Dad's name, Dad in turn took Hamish's name.

I don't know if I'll ever truly know why. I don't know if I need to.

'There was a best individual player trophy for a Hamish O'Neill. I met with his team, they say that Dad is Hamish.'

Mum is quiet. Food for thought, I can't even imagine the memories she is accessing as she tries to understand it and piece it all together.

'Mum?'

'And he won this the day before your thirteenth birthday?'

'Yes.'

'But why didn't he tell me?'

'He didn't tell anyone,' I say. 'Not his family, not his friends.'

'But why?'

'I think he was trying to breathe life back into his brother. Honour him in some way. I think he didn't think anybody else would understand. That they'd think it was weird.'

'It is weird,' she snaps, then sighs and goes quiet. Then, as if she's feeling guilty, she adds, 'Nice though. To honour him.' Silence. 'Who on earth was I married to?' she asks quietly.

I don't know how to answer that, but I do know that I no longer want my husband asking the same thing of me.

Lea slowly lowers herself into the front seat wearing a neutral-coloured bandage dress, black leather jacket, smelling of perfume, caked in make-up and almost un-recognisable as the girl-next-door nurse I see most days.

'Too much?' she says anxiously.

The colour of the dress makes her look naked. 'No,' I say, starting up the engine. 'So tell me about where we're going.'

'You know just about as much as I do.'

I throw her a warning look. 'Lea.'

'What?' she giggles. 'I met him online. His name is Dara. He's delicious. We haven't met in person, but you know. . .' She shrugs.

'No, I don't know, tell me.'

'Well we met on an online dating site. We've Skyped a few times. You know,' she repeats, like I should know something.

'No, I don't know. What?'

She keeps on staring at me, jerking her head at me as if it will spark the answer, which it in fact does.

'Oh!' I say suddenly.

'Yes, now you've got it.' She faces front again. 'So we're pretty much well acquainted, but we haven't actually met yet.'

'You've had Skype sex and you're nervous about meeting him?' I laugh.

'My camera had a filter,' she explains. 'I don't.'

'And what does this mysterious Dara do that he knows where we can find marbles at eleven o'clock at night?'

'He does wood carvings. For chairs, tables, furniture. The party is at his office. I remember him saying there is a glass artist.'

I'm dubious.

We find the address of the full moon party that Dara gave her. We stare at it from across the river in silence, both deep in thought, probably thinking the same thing. We've been duped.

The address is a multistorey car park. It is on the grave-yard site of a ripped-down old shopping centre which was to make way for a new €70 million state-of-the-art shopping centre and cinema yet never was and so the multistorey car park stands alone in the wilderness far from any businesses which can utilise its parking. The moon sits above it, big and full, guiding us to it like the North Star, keeping a watchful maternal eye over our progress. But I can't help but think she's laughing at us now.

It's an enormous concrete monstrosity, but it's old school, ugly and red brick, tight and low ceilings, unlike the spacious light-filled car parks of today. It climbs eight levels high, not a car in sight on any floor. Halfway up, on the fourth floor, a glow appears from the mesh-gridded openings.

'Looks like he's home,' Lea says, trying to make light of it.

'Do you smell smoke?' I ask.

She sniffs and nods.

'Do you hear music?'

It is faint but it drifts from the fourth floor, a calm rhythmic bass.

Neither of us make a move.

'So maybe this is a party,' I say. 'Do you think this is dangerous?' We're in a neglected part of town that should have been developed but wasn't and then was left for dead, invited by a man who's good with tools, who Lea met on the Internet. I wonder if goodwill has run out for the day.

The site is completely surrounded by fencing, the wooden construction kind, and it is too high to climb with no gaps to pass through. We circle the entire thing and find that it has been opened at one section, inviting us in. We slowly walk through the fence, pass the barrier where ghost cars collect their parking tickets, and into the darkness of the multistorey. The ground level has been completely covered by graffiti, every single inch of the concrete walls and supporting pillars have been sprayed. I don't concentrate too much on the darkened corners, I don't want to linger, I need to keep moving. We follow the signs for the stairs, choose to ignore the lifts, which I guess aren't working anyway, and even if they are, I'm not interested.

Every scary movie I've ever seen has told me to be wary of car parks on my own late at night or even during the day, and yet here I am, going against every single instinct in my body. The sound of music and laughter gets increasingly loud as we tread lightly up the steps, not wanting to make a sound to alert them. There is a hum of conversation and that relaxing bass keeps us going, there is some kind of civilisation up there, one which doesn't sound like murderous screaming, gunshots and violent gang dance-offs. I expect to happen upon a homeless community, with laptops on Skype; I have prepared myself to run, to give them my money, my phone, whatever, just in case they get angry at my intrusion.

Lea readies herself, checks her reflection in her pocket mirror and reapplies her thick lipstick that makes her look like she's had collagen injections, then with a flick of her hair, she pushes open the door. I am stunned when we peek around at the inside. Everywhere I look I see trees, beautiful large greenery covering the grey concrete. They sit in stunning pots, Spanish and Mexican in style with beautiful mosaic tiles. Fairy lights run from tree to tree and candles light the meandering pathway through the trees. It feels like we're in this wonderland in the middle of a concrete car park. Grey and green, dark and light, man-made and natural.

'Hi, guys,' a young man says beside us and we turn to him in surprise. 'Can I see your invitation please?'

Our mouths open and shut, we are visibly shocked.

'She's a guest of Dara's,' I finally say, when Lea doesn't say a word.

'Oh, cool!' He stands up. 'Follow me. Sorry about the invitation thing, it's Evelyn, she's pretty insistent after last year. Apparently the party got crashed and it all got a little crazy.'

We follow him through the winding path, through the trees, and I feel like I'm in a dream.

'You guys did all this?' I ask.

'Yeah. Cool isn't it? Evelyn just got back from Thailand where she had full moon parties all the time. Doesn't exactly feel like Thailand, but concrete jungle was the theme.'

The path ends as it opens up to what looks like a living room. An enormous chandelier of beautiful twisted glass hangs low from the concrete ceiling, large pillar candles sit in the chandelier, the wax dripping down over the sides. Below it is a large Oriental rug and copious brown battered leather couches where a dozen or more guests gather and chat like they're at a house party. Music plays, not too loud chill-out music that we could hear from across the river, and a nymph-like girl in a sequined cat suit dances on her own with her eyes closed, fingers running through invisible harp strings in the air. Some look up to see us, most don't, they're a friendly bunch just checking us out and smiling their welcomes. A bunch of all ages, the artsy kind, very cool, very edgy, not at all like me and Lea, the mother of three and Nurse Kardashian.

'There he is,' she says, pointing quickly. Lea skitters over to Dara and they embrace. A moment later, out of their scrum, she shouts, 'Marlow,' to me.

I nod. Marlow. I'm here to see Marlow.

'Marlow,' Dara calls, then whistles and nods at me. A stunning man looks up from the group on the sofas. He's dressed in tight black jeans, a charcoal T-shirt, workman's boots, perfect physique, toned arms, long black hair, one side behind one ear, the other falling down over his face. Johnny Depp twenty years ago. He has one eye squinted as he inhales on a cigarette, and he holds a bottle of beer in the other hand. He looks at me, his eyes running over me. I shiver under his intense stare, don't know where to look. Lea laughs.

'Good luck!' She throws me a thumbs up and heads towards the barrel of beer in ice.

I swallow hard. Marlow smiles and leaves the company of a cool butterfly girl with body jewellery wrapped around her toned abs. He stops right in front of me, standing quite close for an absolute stranger.

'Hi.'

'Hi.' He smiles and sits down on the back of the couch so we're at the same eye level. He looks like I amuse him, but not in a teasing way.

'My name is Sabrina.'

I look around and see Lea settling down on a couch with a group of people, beer in hand, relaxed as anything. I try to relax too.

'I've lost my marbles,' I say with a smile.

'Well you've come to the right place,' he grins. 'Why don't we go into my studio.' He stands.

I laugh at that and he seems confused by my reaction, but walks away anyway. I look at Lea, who motions at me to follow Marlow. I follow him through the trees on the other side of the gathering and discover he hasn't been lying. Hugging the walls of the car park are offices and art studios.

'What is this place?'

'The art council let us work here. They came up with a great idea to utilise the space. The plan was to put something new on each floor, exhibitions on the third level, theatrical performances on the fifth floor . . . We've been here a year.'

He unlocks the door and steps inside.

There is glass everywhere, it glistens as the moonlight hits it.

'Wow, this is beautiful!' I look around, unable to stop as everywhere I turn is a glass masterpiece, either a jug, glasses, vases, panes, chandeliers – a myriad of gorgeous colours, some smashed and put back together again to make stunning creations.

He's sitting up on a counter, legs hanging, watching me.

'You make marbles,' I say, spotting a cabinet in the corner, little globes winking in the light, my heart suddenly pounding.

I remove my bag from my shoulder and take the inventory out, feeling on fire. I walk towards him, offering the folder. 'My dad was a marble collector. I found this inventory in his things, including the marbles, but there were two collections missing.' I try to rush to the exact pages that list the missing marbles but he stops me, a hand on my hand, which he keeps a hold of while reading at his own pace.

'This is incredible,' he says, after a while.

'I know,' I say proudly, and uncertainly, looking at his hand wrapped around mine like he doesn't notice it's happening, as though it's the most natural, normal thing in the world. He turns page after page, fingers running over my knuckles, which makes me nervous and thrilled at the same time. I'm a married woman, I shouldn't be standing here close to midnight holding hands with a handsome cool dude, but I am and I don't want to let go. He takes his time reading through the inventory, his fingers still slowly moving over mine.

The moon made me do it.

'This is quite the collection,' he says, finally looking up. 'So he was only a fan of glass.'

'What do you mean?'

'Marbles were also made from clay, steel, plastic. But he only collects glass.'

'Oh yes. I didn't realise.'

'Apart from steelies – he's got a few of them. But the most beautiful ones are handmade glass,' he says with a smile, 'then again, I'm biased. Which ones are missing?'

Tragically, I must let go of his hand to leaf through the pages and point them out. 'This. And this.'

He whistles when he sees the price. 'I can try to replicate them, but it's impossible for me to make them look exactly the same, and he'll notice the difference,' he says. 'A collector like him will know straight away.'

'He won't,' I swallow. 'He hasn't been well recently. Actually, I was hoping to find something new. I want him to make some new memories.' *Don't go back, Sabrina, move forward. Make new.*

'With pleasure.' He smiles, eyes playful, and I have to look away. 'So, Sabrina, I see here that the thing your dad was beginning to collect was contemporary marbles. He only has one, which is damaged – a heart, which is rather ironic, isn't it? This is where I feel I can come in. I can make you a contemporary art marble. See over there.'

He points to the display cabinet and I'm entranced by the variety he has. It's like a treasure trove of precious gems. So many intricate swirls and designs, colours and reflections bounce from the glass.

'You can touch them,' he says.

Opening the case, I'm drawn to a chocolate brown marble, like a snooker ball, and I'm surprised by the weight. They're larger than Dad's collection, not your usual playing marbles, but their colours and design are far more intense and intricate. Swirls and bubbles, they are hypnotising to look at and when I hold them up to the moonlight it seems they have even more depth, glowing from the inside.

'Interesting you picked that one,' he says. 'Is that your favourite?'

I nod, wrapping my fingers around it. It's almost as if I can feel the heat of the fire inside. 'But it's not for me.' I examine the collection again. 'He'd love any of these, I'm sure.'

It's not what I began the day searching for, but it feels right, like a better solution to driving myself insane looking for lost marbles that I probably will never find.

'No, no,' he takes the brown marble from me gently, and he places a hand on my waist as he examines it from behind me. 'I'll make you a new one now.'

'Now?'

'Sure. Have you somewhere else to be?'

I look out at Lea; she's lost in Dara's eyes, Dara running his fingers through her hair. It's almost midnight, I'm going home to an empty house anyway. I need to end my night with some kind of conclusion. Learning about Dad was satisfying, exhausting, draining, but I need to find a solution. I've opened a wound and I need to find something to help heal it. If I can't complete Dad's collection, then I must complete my own personal mission.

'How long will it take to make?'

He shrugs, coolly. 'Let's see.'

He doesn't walk around, he kind of glides, drags his feet but not noisily, like he's too relaxed to lift them. He turns on a gas canister, leaves me momentarily, disappearing behind the trees in the car park and returns with a six-pack of beer, a joint and a mischievous look in his eye.

I hear Aidan's voice in my head. *I just don't know if you're happy, Sabrina. You're distant. I love you. Do you hear me? Do you love me?*

Maybe I should leave, but if I haven't learned anything else from today, I've learned that I'm my father's daughter. I stay.

29

PLAYING WITH MARBLES

Increase Pound

I'm sitting before Larry Brennan, aka Lampy, known as such due to his teenage pastime of lamping animals late at night, usually rabbits, when we were teenagers. He had an uncle in Meath that he used to be sent to on weekends; his dad was an alcoholic and his ma had a nervous break-down and couldn't cope with much, so he was sent to his uncle, his sister sent to their aunt. His sister got the better deal. They were thinking he'd be in a better place than at home but they were wrong. His uncle wasn't much better than his da, he just seemed more responsible because he didn't have his own family to care for. He was functioning okay by himself. He was fond of the drink, too fond of Larry too, though I don't think I realised that until I was older and looked back on it. Larry always wanted me to go with him, I think his uncle didn't bother with him if he had a friend there, but I didn't like his uncle one bit. Tom was his name. I went once for the weekend and, despite the adventure, the misadventure, the freedom to do and eat and drink whatever we wished at whatever time of the day or night, I wouldn't go back whenever he asked. His uncle wasn't right. I should have known what was going on but I didn't.

The lamping was fun. Larry would take his uncle's air rifle and we'd go out to the fields in the pitch-black of night. It was my job to hold the light, one-million-candle strength, and stun the rabbits, then he'd shoot them. Half the time he didn't even get their bodies. I always remember thinking Ma would make a great stew with it, but I had no way of keeping it fresh and bringing it back, or I didn't ever ask anyone how. It wasn't about the food for Larry, it was about the kill, and I'm sure every rabbit he shot was really his uncle or his dad, or his ma or whoever else was letting him down in the world. Maybe even me for being right there and not doing anything about it.

Lamping was best done at the darkest hour; cloudy nights were good, but the best conditions were when the moon was new. I remember Larry checking the weather as it got close to the weekend, almost going mental and causing all kinds of hell in school when the weather wasn't good for lamping. I suppose he knew that he'd have to stay in the house all night and he knew what that meant. Hamish wasn't around then. I was sixteen and he'd headed off to Liverpool, but he would have loved it there, he would have come with me. And he would have sorted Larry's uncle out too.

I look at Larry 'Lampy' Brennan now, the same age as me, fifty-seven, but slim, trim, respectable. I'm sitting across from him at his desk, and I think of all of the things that I know about him. He's wearing a smart suit, employs a few dozen people, he's doing well for himself, dragged himself out of the shit and washed himself off. My heart

pounds as he smooths down his tie with manicured finger-
nails as he waits for my response, and I feel the tension in
my chest that just never goes away and I'm so heavy these
days I'm constantly wheezing, trying to catch my breath.

'I bet there's no one in your life now that knows where
we came from,' I say.

He pauses, unsure of what I mean.

'You know what I mean, Lampy.'

He freezes then and I know that I've brought him back
to being someone he's tried so hard to run away from in
an instant. He's sixteen again. He's Lampy Brennan and
it's mayhem in his head, the world is against him and he's
fighting for himself against everybody and everything.

'What are you saying, Fergus?' he asks quietly.

I feel the sweat trickle down my right temple and I want
to catch it but to do so would be to bring attention to it.
'I'm just saying that I'm sure a few people would be
surprised by the things I know about you. That's all.'

He leans forward slowly. 'Are you threatening me,
Fergus?'

I fix him with a stare, a long hard look, I don't need to
answer, let him take from it what he may. I need this to
work, I'm fifty-seven years old, I've cashed in every single
favour everyone ever owed me and more, now I owe more
favours than I'll ever have time to repay. I've hit a wall,
this is the last trick up my sleeve, reduced to threats like
the desperate lowlife I've become.

'Fergus,' he says quietly, looking down at his desk. 'This
decision isn't personal. These are difficult times. I took you
on because I wanted to help you out, out of loyalty.' He
seems shaken. 'We said we'd look at it after six months.
After six months I told you you had to up your game, you
were selling the least – and yes, I know it was early days.

But it's been nine months now, it's not good here, I have to start losing people. You were the last person in, which means you're the first person out. And frankly,' the anger seems to explode from nowhere as if he realises he should forget about being polite to me, 'threatening me isn't going to endear you to me, and it doesn't take away the fact that you are the worst salesman on the floor and you have earned the company the least amount of money.'

'You need to give me more time,' I say, feeling the panic rise, trying to sound cool, assured, like I'm someone he can trust. 'I'm still finding my feet. The first year is hard, but I'm getting there now. I have a real understanding of how things work around here.'

'I can't afford to give you more time,' he says. 'I just can't.'

I fight it out some more with him, but the more I push, the further he backs away, the tougher he becomes.

'When?' I ask quietly, feeling my entire world cave in on me.

'I was giving you one month's notice,' he says, and I think about one more month until it all falls apart. 'But in light of your threat, I am suggesting immediate termination.'

I have one more trick up my sleeve, the worst one of all, the one I have never wanted to resort to all of my life.

'Please,' I say and he looks at me in surprise, the anger evaporated, 'Larry please. I beg you.'

Favours, threats and, last but not least, begging.

'What on earth is going on here?' Cat yelps as she finds me on the floor of my apartment.

I've pushed all the furniture to one wall. The armchairs are piled up on the couch, the coffee table is filling the tiny cubby kitchen and the rug is rolled up and out on the balcony. A perfectly large space has been cleared before me on the floor and I have a Sharpie in hand and am about to deface the wooden floors.

I've drawn a small circle eight inches wide and am in the middle of drawing a larger circle around it eleven foot in diameter. I can't talk to her because I'm concentrating.

'Fergus!' she looks around, eyes wide, mouth open. 'We were supposed to have lunch with Joe and Finn, remember? We were all waiting for you at the restaurant. I called and called you. I ate with them alone. Fergus? Can you hear me? I went to your work, they said you'd gone home.'

I ignore her, working on the circle.

'Did you forget, Fergus?' her voice softer. 'Did you forget again? This has happened a few times now, are you well, my love? Something is not right.'

She is down on her knees beside me on the floor, but I can't look at her. I'm busy.

'Are you okay? Are you feeling well? You don't look . . . Fergus, you are dripping wet.'

'Right,' I say, putting the marker down and sitting back on my haunches as I feel another drip of sweat fall from my nose. 'This game is called Increase Pound, and that is exactly what it's going to help us do. The small circle is the pound, the large circle is the bar. You shoot the taw from—'

'Me?'

'Yes, you.' I hand her some marbles, which she takes as though they're hand grenades.

'Fergus, it's three p.m., shouldn't you be at work and not playing marbles? This is ridiculous, I have to get back to work myself. I don't understand, what's going on?'

'I was fired!' I shout suddenly, which silences her and makes her jump in fright. 'You're the bank,' I say, more

261

aggressively than I intend. 'You throw the marble and anything you hit in the pound becomes your property. If you don't hit anything your taw stays where it is and you go again. You have ten tries.'

I place my watch collection in the pound, the smaller inner circle. 'Throw the marble. Hit it.'

She looks at the watch collection and then at the items lining the circles which will follow and her eyes fill.

'Oh, Fergus, you don't have to do this. Joe can help you. You know that he's offered already.'

'I'm not taking handouts,' I say, feeling dizzy at the thought of baby Joe paying my way. Joe who was never really part of my family until Cat welcomed him in with open arms. It wouldn't be fair to him. 'I got myself into this mess, I'm going to get myself out of it.'

It was the marbles that got me into this situation in the first place. Getting rid of them will get me out of it. The lies, the deceit, the betrayal, me messing around, not focusing on the life I was living, splitting myself from myself and from my family. It's Alfie's birthday party and I can't bring Cat to visit, because Sabrina doesn't know Cat, she doesn't even know my great love, and I don't know where to start. To tell Sabrina about Cat would be to tell her about the marbles, and how can I do that? After a whole life of lying. Cat says she won't say a word until I find a way to tell Sabrina, but it will slip out, it's bound to, and then not to say it would be lying. Both of us lying to my daughter. Getting my marbles secretly valued in California was the real marker of how bad my financial situation had gotten. I was embarrassed, and that lie almost ended us, me showing up blind drunk back at the hotel. But she's sticking with me. She says she understands, but it's all a mess, it's all a mess. It's the marbles' fault.

Cat throws the marble. It's a crap throw, a deliberately bad one, and it misses. Cat and I have played marbles together on many occasions. As soon as I opened her up to my world I welcomed her into it; she has been to marble games with me, to marble conventions, she's not a great marble player, but she's not this bad.

'Do it properly!' I yell, and she starts to cry. 'Do it, do it!' I pick the marble up and force it into her hand. 'Throw it!'

She throws it and it hits the watch collection in the pound.

'Right, it's yours. It's the bank's.' I pick it up and toss it aside. 'Next!' I place down my ma's engagement ring.

She misses. I yell at her to try harder.

'Fergus, I can't. I can't, I can't, I won't, please stop.' Tears are streaming from her eyes and she collapses in a heap on the floor. I grab the marbles from her and I throw. I hit a ring box, that's it, Mammy's wedding ring: property of the bank. I throw it again and hit the Akro Agate Sample Box from 1930 valued between seven thousand and thirteen thousand. Of course I hit it, it is almost bigger than the pound.

Next are the World's Best Moons, in the original box, valued between four thousand and seven thousand. I hit it. My two most valuable collections. Them first, then everything else, everything must go.

'I've found a buyer for these,' I tell Cat a few days later, as I put the marble collections down in order for me to put on my coat. 'I'm meeting him in town later. At O'Donoghue's. He's flown in from London to buy them. Twenty thousand dollars' worth, we agreed fifteen thousand euro cash.'

263

'You don't look well, Fergus.' She runs her hand over my face, and I kiss her palm. 'You should lie down.'

'Didn't you hear me? I will, after I meet him.'

'You don't want to sell these. These are precious. All of your memories . . .'

'Memories last for ever. These . . .' I can barely look at them as I say it. 'These will pay the mortgages for a few months, give me time to sort something out.' What though? No job, no one hiring. Not at my age. Think, think, what, what. Sell the marbles.

'You're pale, you should lie down. Let me go for you.'

It's the best idea and we both know it. If I go I won't be able to part with them and I need to, or the bank will take my home from me.

She leaves with the marbles and I go to bed. She returns some time later, it's dark, I don't know what time it is and I feel like I haven't slept but I must have. She comes to my bedside and I smell wine on her breath.

'Did you sell them?' I ask.

'I got the money,' she replies, placing an envelope by the bedside.

'The marbles are gone?'

She hesitates. 'Yes, they're gone.'

She rubs my hair, my face, kisses me. At least I have her. I want to make a joke about her value but I can't figure it out.

'I'm going to take a shower,' she says, sliding away.

As soon as I hear the water start I do something I haven't done for a very long time, I cry. Deep and painful, like I'm a child again. I fall asleep before Cat is out of the shower. When I wake up I'm in hospital and the next time I see Cat is the first time I meet her, in a rehabilitation centre that I call home, where she is visiting a friend.

30

POOL RULES

No Lifeguard on Duty

Marlow hands me a pair of glasses, tinted pink so that the world is immediately rosy and helps my beer buzz. The glasses are to help my eyes when I'm looking directly at the flame.

'Cute!' He pinches my nose lightly and fires up the kiln. 'I love to work with glass because it's so easy to manipulate and shape,' he explains, moving around the studio with ease and comfort, knowing where absolutely everything is without looking; reaching, placing, like a dance. 'Do you bake?' he asks.

'Bake? Yes, sometimes.' With the kids, and thinking of them snaps me into gear. I have kids. I have a husband. A beautiful husband. A kind husband who wants me to be happy. Who tells me he loves me, who actually loves me. I take a step back.

'It's okay.' He pulls me closer again, hot hand on my waist. 'Glass reacts similarly to sugar when melted. You'll see. But first, here's one part I prepared earlier.'

I move closer and take a look at an image he lays out on the table.

'I've wanted to do this for a while but I was waiting for the right project to come along . . .' He looks at me through those long lashes again, marble blue eyes as though he's crafted them to perfection himself.

'You designed this?' I try not to look at his face. He's doing hypnotic things with his face. In fact with his entire body. Can't look, won't look, concentrate on the flame.

'Sure. It's made of finely ground glass powders. So there are two ways I could make your marble: here at the lamp, which creates the swirl effect you've already seen, but your dad has a lot of German swirls, not all handmade, so I think we should give him something different.'

He gathers a nucleus of opal glass on the end of a long stainless steel rod. He stands at the kiln, perfect posture, and slowly starts twirling the glass in the fire. The glass becomes illuminated, shiny and dripping like honey. He continues turning it to shape it into a sphere. Then he pulls it out of the kiln and I duck as the burning dripping glass is carried across the other side of the studio to an armchair. He sits on a wooden chair with high arms and he places the rod across the arms, and rolls it back and forth so that the glass at the end of the rod takes shape. The arms of the chair already have the indentations of the number of times he has done this. He's deep in concentration, no conversation now. In fact there's none for quite some time. He does this routine a few more times, moving back and forth from the kiln to the chair, beads of sweat on his forehead. He grabs hold of a newspaper in his palm and directly starts rolling the hot glass around in his hand to shape it.

At one stage during the process I remove my eyes from

him, feeling giddy and light-headed from the bottle of beer and an unusually emotional day, taken away by the chill-out music and the atmosphere, and I see Lea through the trees, dancing with Dara. There is a celebration in the air, things are great, life is great. Life is full of adventure. I can't remember the last time I felt like this. While I watch this all happen my body relaxes, I even sway a little to the music. I can't take my eyes off Marlow, and the beautiful honey-like syrupy glass.

I stand back as he pulls the rod from the kiln and instead of sitting in the chair, he carefully rolls it over the powdered glass drawing he has prepared earlier. Once the drawing is on the glass, he continues to shape it into a sphere, careful not to distort the intricate image inside. He plunges the glass into a pot of crystal glass for the final layer.

Marlow dips the shaped boiling-hot glass into a tin bucket of water, steam hissing and rising as it sizzles and hardens. He knocks it and it falls off the end of the rod, landing in the water and bobbing to the top.

'We'll leave it there to cool,' he says, mopping the sweat from his brow.

He must be able to see the way I've been looking at him because he finally looks up at me and smiles, that sweet amused look he's had since he saw me. He reaches for his bottle and slugs the entire thing down. It's after two a.m. and my head is spinning.

I remember the marble he's just created and make an effort to look in the bucket.

'No peeking until it has cooled,' he says, coming close to me. He pushes me up against the work surface, his hips against my ribs and he takes off my pink glasses. I try to adjust to the fact nothing is rosy any more, it's real, unfiltered, not just in my head. It sobers me quickly. He traces a line all around my face, over each of my features, taking all of them in, slowly and softly. My heart is pounding and I'm sure he can feel it through his thin T-shirt.

He kisses me, which begins slowly but very quickly becomes urgent. For someone who moved so rhythmically and slowly at work, there is something panicked and urgent about how he moves now.

'I'm married,' I murmur in his ear.

'Congratulations,' he continues, kissing my neck.

I laugh, nervously.

Five years ago, when I was pregnant with Fergus, a friend came to me and told me that Aidan had had an affair. I confronted him, we dealt with it. I made a decision. Stay or go, go or stay. He stayed. I stayed. We remained, but we didn't remain as we were. We got worse, and then we got better. We had Alfie since. In my angry moments, which come far less regularly than they did, I always felt that I would grab the closest opportunity I could get to getting him back, by having an affair too, to make sure he truly understood how I felt. I know it's childish but it was real. You hurt me, I'll hurt you. But years on and there has been no opportunity, not at the school run, not at the empty pool, not at the supermarket with the kids, or at karate, or at football, or at art class. No chance for an affair during the mum-related activities that fill my day. Butter, cheese, ham, bread, slice. Raisins. Next. And that made me even more depressed about it, because even if I wanted to get him back, I couldn't.

I know that Aidan loves me. He's not a perfect husband and not a perfect dad, but he's more than enough. I am not a perfect anything, though I try to be. Sometimes I wonder if love is enough, or if there are levels of love. And sometimes I wonder if he can see me, even when he's looking right at me. Last Sunday I went an entire day with green paint on my upper lip, from a morning of painting with the kids, and he never told me it was there. We went to the supermarket, we went to the playground, we walked around the park and not once did he say, 'Sabrina, you have green paint on your face.'

When I went home and looked in the mirror and saw it there, a big green gloop on my upper lip, I cried with frustration. Did nobody see me? Not even the boys? Am I this thing that is expected to be covered in dirt or food or green paint? Sabrina, the woman with paint on her face, the woman with the sticky stain on her trousers, the woman with the finger marks and food splashes on her T-shirt. Don't tell her it's there because it's always there, it's supposed to be there, it's part of who she is.

I asked Aidan about it, some high-pitched unhinged accusation about gloop on my face. He said that he just didn't see it there, which made me wonder, did he look at me and not see it or did he not look at me at all for the entire day. Which is worse? We spent an entire session at counselling talking about it, about this green gloop that he didn't see. Turns out I'm the green gloop.

The green gloop started it, the near-drowning tipped me over the edge. And then I went looking for lost marbles in an attempt to fix things, save things, complete things for Dad, when perhaps it is myself that I'm trying to figure out.

Aidan is afraid that I'll leave him. He has told me this, he has been afraid of this since his affair. But I have no intention of leaving him. It's nothing to do with him or what he did so long ago that I don't even feel the pain any more, just an echo of it. It's all to do with me. Lately I've been trapped, not myself, or being my real self and not liking it, whatever. Butter, cheese, ham, bread, slice. Raisins. Next. Watching an empty pool. Saving a man that doesn't want to be saved. Not being immersed in the thing I am most passionate about, but on the edges, on the outside looking in. Window-shopping with a full wallet. Shopping with an empty wallet. Whatever. Feeling outside, pacing the edges, feeling redundant.

I lived with a dad who I've just today learned was incredibly secretive, and despite never knowing this, I too became a secretive person, maybe unconsciously mimicking or shadowing him, not opening up to Aidan. It might have happened after his affair, maybe it was before. I don't know the psychological reasons for it and I don't even care. I'm not going to dwell, I'm just going to move on. The important thing is, now I have no secrets.

The past year I was feeling something. I was bored.

But I'm not bored any more.

I smile at the realisation.

Marlow is looking at me with a lazy grin. 'Don't you want to get him back?' he guesses. 'Tit for tat, tat for . . .' his hand travels up my top, '. . . tit.' We both laugh at that, and he removes his hand good-naturedly. 'I'm sensing no.'

'No,' I agree, finally.

He backs off then, respectfully, easily. 'It's cooled off now, if you want to take a look.' He scoops out the marble, polishes it and studies it before handing it to me.

'It's beautiful,' I say, transfixed. 'How much do I owe you?'

He gives me a final kiss. 'You're so sweet. This is for you –' He hands me a second marble. 'I have a theory that the marble is a reflection of its owner. Like with dogs,' he smiles. Then he picks up his beer and drags himself lazily back to the party that is still in full swing.

The marble he has given me is the brown one I was immediately drawn to when I first arrived. It looks like a plain brown marble when you see it first, but when I hold it up to the moonlight, it glows with orange and amber like it has a fire burning brightly inside. Just like its owner.

It is four a.m. when I finally drag myself and Lea from level four of the multistorey. The sun is rising over the city, my watchful moon no longer in sight; she has left me to my own devices now that my mission is complete. Lea collapses into the seat beside me, exhausted. For all her free love and serenity earlier, she now looks green in the face. She insists on coming to the home with me. She has an early shift, she'll sleep it off in the staff room. Besides, I know she cares enough about my dad to want to be with him first thing in the morning.

I don't intend on staying long. I just want to leave the marble by Dad's bed so that he sees it when he wakes. So that it's hopefully the first thing he sees when he wakes.

Of course the home is closed. I ring the doorbell and security recognises Lea and lets us inside.

'Jesus,' Grainne whispers, looking at her colleague. 'Look at the state of you.'

Lea giggles.

'Did you meet him?'

She nods.

'Well?'

'I'll tell you in the morning.'

'It is the morning,' Grainne laughs.

I tiptoe down the corridor, into Dad's room. He's lying on his back, looking old, but happy, snoring lightly. I balance the marble on his bedside locker, alongside a note, and kiss him on the forehead.

31

PLAYING WITH MARBLES

Heirloom

I wake up feeling like I've lived a thousand lives in my dreams. Fragmented memories linger in the moment I first open my eyes then delicately disintegrate like a morning frost in the sunrise. The ghosts of the past and present and their voices begin to diminish as I take in my surroundings. It's not Scotland where I have images of green and grass, lakes and rabbits, my da's hunched shoulders, sad eyes and the smell of pipe smoke; it's not St Benedict's Gardens where I woke up every morning as a child with another brother's feet pushed up against my face as we sleep top to toe in bunk beds. Not Aunty Sheila's bungalow on Synnott Row where we woke up on the floor of her house for the first year after arriving in Ireland, not Gina's ma's home in Iona where we slept for the first year of our marriage while we saved up enough money to buy our own, and not the home we lived in during our marriage. It is not the apartment that I lived in alone for so many years that for the first time in a long time is now so vivid to me and I can hear the calls and shouts from the football field beside me as I lie on on a Saturday and Sunday morning. Nor is it the bedroom I slept in with Cat, the one that feels orange and warm, sweet and glowing when I close my eyes. I'm here in the hospital, my home for the past year, the place where up until some time yesterday I was content to be in, to stay and call home. But I have a feeling now, no not a feeling, an urge, to leave. This is an empty place and outside is full, whereas before I felt the opposite. There has been a shift in my mind, something has moved ever so slightly, but that slight movement has had seismic implications. I feel hungry to know, where before I felt full. I want to hear now, where before I was deafened. In fact I had deafened myself. Self-imposed, for protection, I assume. Dr Loftus will tell me. We have a session this morning.

This change does two things to me. It makes me feel hope and it makes me feel hopeless. Hope that I'll get there, hopeless that I can't get there now.

My mouth is dry and I need water. I look around for my glass of water which is usually on my bedside locker, on the right side so that they make me practise moving my right arm. Where there is usually just my glass, I see a marble. A large, beautiful royal blue marble. It is lit up by the morning light coming through the window and it takes my breath away. It is a sight to behold, its beauty, its elegance, its perfection, such a rarity.

It is a sphere of the world. Within its royal blue ocean there lies a map of the earth, created to perfect proportions. The land, mountains, in browns, sandy and honey colours, every continent, country accounted for, every island. There are even wispy white clouds in the northern hemisphere. The entire world has been captured inside this marble. I reach over with my left hand to pick it up, I will not risk using my weakened right side, not at such a moment, for such a task. I turn it around, inspecting every inch. The islands intact, the ocean seems to glow from the inside. There is not a scratch, not a scuff. It is perfect. What a marvel, what a marble. Larger than usual, it is 3.5 inches in diameter, I let it sit in the palm of my hand, it's big and bold. I sit up, pull myself up, heart pounding at the discovery, I must get my glasses to see. They are on the bedside locker to my left, easier to reach for. I see, once they are on, that there is a note. I place the marble on my lap carefully and reach for the note with my left hand, a strain to reach so far and I must be careful not to knock the marble to the floor, which would be catastrophic.

I reach for it and settle back to read.

Dad,

You have the world in the palm of your hand.

Lots of love,
Sabrina
X

As the tears roll down my cheeks and I stare at it for what feels like an endless time, I believe her. I can do this. I can take my life back again. Sleep starts to call me again. Tired eyes, I take off my glasses and make sure the marble is safe. It reminds me of a marble I saw while on honeymoon, one I really wished to buy but couldn't afford. I suddenly have an image of Gina on honeymoon, of her face, young and innocent in a hotel room in Venice, freckles across her nose and cheeks, not a stitch of make-up, moments before we made love for the first time. That image of her is in my

275

mind forever, a look of love, of innocence. I have an over-whelming urge along with that memory to give her this marble, to give her the world. I should have done it then, but I will do it now, I will give her the part of me I held back for so long.

Sabrina will understand, as will Cat, as will Gina's husband Robert. In time Gina can pass it on to Sabrina or to the boys when they're older. It can be like an heirloom, passing the world on to the next generation.

And to Cat, I will give my full heart.

32

POOL RULES

Do Not Swim Alone

I arrive home at five a.m. It's been a long day and night. I yearn to fall into bed for at least a few hours before Aidan and the kids return.

I'm not sure about Amy's moon theories, but there's a comforting one that I heard while in the waiting room at Mickey's yesterday. A new moon is a symbolic portal for new beginnings, believed by some to be the time to set up intentions for things you'd like to create, develop and culti-vate. In other words, make new. Make new memories.

I think of myself as a little girl during the night of a full moon, wide awake, alert, head constantly thinking and planning, unable to rest, as though a beacon was sending messages. Was it the moon that made me do this? I don't know. I should probably not cancel my therapy sessions though. The real conversation has just begun.

It's bright as I walk up the path to my door, I see Mrs O'Grady my neighbour peeking out at me through lace curtains as I do the walk of shame. As I slide the key in the lock I don't feel like a different woman, but the same woman, slightly changed. For the better.

I dream of kicking off my shoes, stripping off my clothes and falling into bed, having a few hours until the kids come home, but the door opens before I have the chance to turn the key, and it is then I notice Aidan's car parked outside.

Aidan greets me, an exhausted handsome mess of a man whose expression makes me laugh instantly.

'Mummy!' the boys run to me, throwing themselves at me and grabbing a limb each. They squeeze me tight, as though they haven't seen me for a week instead of less than twenty-four hours.

I hug them tightly while Aidan looks at me, exhausted, but concerned.

'Where have you been?' he asks, when they give up on their cuddles and instead drag me down the hall to show me something so incredibly exciting that they have found. They bring me to the containers of marbles all laid out on the floor, I'd left them there before rushing out the door to Mickey's office yesterday morning.

'I was teaching them how to play,' Aidan says, guiding me away from them. 'I hope that's okay, they know to be careful with them. Although all I wanted to do is ram them down their throats – they've been a nightmare,' he groans, wrapping his arms around me, and pretends to cry. 'Alfie has not slept. At. All. Charlie pissed on the sleeping bags and Fergus wanted to eat a frog he caught for breakfast at four. We had to come home. Mind me,' he whimpers.

I laugh, hugging him tight. 'Aidan . . .' I say, a warning tone for what's about to come.

'Yes,' he replies, still in place, but his body stiffens.

'You know the way you said not to let *another* man kiss me . . .?'

'What?' he pulls back, his face contorted.
'Dad! Mum! Alfie swallowed a marble!'
We both run.

An hour later I kick off my shoes, peel off my clothes and
fall into bed. I feel Aidan's lips on my neck, and I've barely
closed my eyes when the doorbell rings.

'That's probably your lover,' he says grumpily, turning
over and leaving me to answer it.

I groan, pull on my dressing gown and drag myself to
the door. A blonde woman smiles nervously at me. I recognise her and try to place her. I recognise her from the
hospital. I speak to her in the canteen, in the halls, in the
garden, when we're waiting for our loved ones. And then
it all falls into place. Our loved one was the same person
all along. I smile, feeling a major weight lift from my
shoulders. I hadn't been completely in the dark. *I know
her.*

'I'm so sorry,' she says, apologetic. 'I know it's a Saturday
morning and I didn't want to disturb you and the children.
I've been awake most of the night waiting for day to come,
this was as long as I could wait. I just have to give you
this.'

I turn my attention to the large bag she's holding out
with two hands. She hands it to me and I take it. It's heavy.

'It's part of your dad's marble collection,' she says, and
I stop breathing. 'I took them from him before he had his
stroke, before he sold the apartment, for safekeeping. He
sent me out to sell them. I pretended to him that I did. The
money I gave him was a loan from his brother Joe.' She
looks haunted by that admission. 'I felt it was important
to keep them safe, they are so precious to him.' She looks
at them as though she's unsure of letting them go. 'But you

should have them. The collection should be complete, just in case he asks for them again.'

I look at the bag in total surprise that they're here, in my arms.

'I haven't even told you who I am,' she says shakily.

'Are you Cat?' I ask, and her face freezes in shock. 'Please, come in,' I say, grinning and opening the door wide.

We sit up at the breakfast counter as I carefully open the bag. I want to cry with happiness. An Akro Agate Company, Original Salesman's Sample Case from 1930 and the World's Best Moons original box of twenty-five marbles. I run my hands over them, unable to believe that they are here, that after a day of searching for them, they eventually found their own way home.

33

PLAYING WITH MARBLES

Bloodies

I'm lying on the floor of Aunty Sheila's living room. Around me, Hamish, Angus and Duncan are in sleeping bags, fast asleep. My hand throbs from where Father Murphy walloped me today and I can't help it, I start to cry. I miss Daddy, I miss the farm in Scotland, I miss my friend Freddy, I miss the way Mammy used to be, I don't like these new smells, I don't like sleeping on the floor, I don't like Aunty Sheila's food, I don't like school, and I particularly don't like Father Fuckface. My right hand is so swollen I can barely close it and every time I close my eyes I see the cold dark room he locked me in today and I feel panic, like I can't breathe.

'Hey!' I hear someone whisper and I freeze and stop crying immediately, afraid that one of my brothers has heard and will tease me.

'Psst!'

I look around and see Hamish sitting up.

'Are you crying?' he whispers.

'No,' I sniffle, but it's obvious.

He shuffles over on his bum, moving his sleeping bag closer to mine so that we are side by side. He gives Angus's head a kick and Angus groans and rolls over to make room for his feet. At eleven years old Hamish always gets what he wants from us and he always does it so easily. He's my hero and when I grow up I want to be just like him.

He puts his finger on my cheek and wipes my skin. Then he tastes his finger. 'You are fuckin' crying.'

'Sorry,' I whimper.

'You miss Da?' he asks, lying down beside me.

I nod. That's not all of the reason, but it's part of it.

'Me too.'

He's quiet for a while and I don't know if he's fallen back asleep.

'Remember the way he used to do the longest burp?' he whispers suddenly.

I smile. 'Yeah.'

'And he belched the entire happy birthday song on Duncan's birthday?'

I laugh this time.

'See? That's better. We can't forget things like that, Fergus, okay?' he says, full of intensity like he really means it, and I nod, very serious indeed. 'We have to remember Da the way he was, when he was happy, the good things he did, and not . . . not anything else.'

Hamish was the one who found Da hanging from a beam in our barn. He wouldn't tell us exactly what he saw, none of the gory details, and when Angus tried to make him, he punched him in the face and almost broke his nose, so none of us asked again.

'Me and you, we'll remind each other of stuff like that. I don't sleep either most nights, so you and me can talk.'

I like the sound of that, just me and Hamish, having him all to myself.

'It's a deal,' he says. 'Shake on it.' He grabs my hand, my sore one, and I whine and cry out like Aunty Sheila's dog when you step on its paw. 'What the fuck happened?'

I tell him about Father Murphy and the dark room and I cry again. He's angry about it and puts his arm around my shoulders. I know I won't tell the others this, he would flush my head down the bog if I did that and I like him holding me this way. I don't tell him about me pissing myself though. When I came home, I didn't tell anyone about what Father Murphy had done to me. I would have, but Aunty Sheila noticed it and helped clean my hand and bandage it up, and she said not to bother Mammy with it because she's upset enough. Everyone's upset, so I didn't tell anyone else.

'What have you got there?' he asks, as my marbles clink in my other hand.

'They're bloodies,' I say proudly, showing him. I sleep with them that night because I like the feel of them in my hand. 'A nice priest gave them to me when I was in the dark room.'

'For keeps?' Hamish asks, studying them.

'I think so.'

'Bloodies?' he asks.

'Yeah, they're red, like blood,' I explain. I don't know much more about them, but I want to.

'Like you and me,' he says, clinking them around in his hand. 'Blood brothers, bloodies.'

'Yeah.' I grin in the dark.

'You bring them into school with you tomorrow,' he says, giving them back to me and settling down in his sleeping bag again.

Angus tells us to shut the fuck up and Hamish kicks him

in the head, but we're silent until his breathing tells us he's fallen asleep again.

Hamish whispers in my ear: 'Put them bloodies in your pocket tomorrow. Keep them there, don't tell anyone else, none of the lads, or the Brothers will hear and they'll take them from you. And if he locks you in that room again, you'll have them. While everyone's working and getting their heads slapped off them, you'll be in there, playing. Do you hear?'

I nod.

'That thought will help me tomorrow, thinking you're in there having a blast, pulling the wool over their eyes. You can't cross a Boggs,' he says.

I smile.

'And the more they put you in there, the greater you'll be. Fergus Boggs, the best marble player in Ireland, maybe even the whole world. And I'll be your agent. The Boggs Brothers, partners in marble crime.'

I giggle. He does too.

'Sounds good, doesn't it?'

I can tell even he's excited by it.

'Yeah.'

'It'll just be our secret, okay?'

'Okay.'

'Every night you can tell me what you learned.'

'Okay.'

'Promise?'

'I promise, Hamish.'

'Good lad.' He ruffles my hair. 'We'll be okay here,' he says to me. 'Won't we?'

'Yeah, Hamish,' I reply.

He holds my sore hand, gentler this time, and we fall asleep together.

Partners in marble crime. Bloodies forever.

EPILOGUE

On Monday morning I return to work.

'Good weekend?' Eric asks, studying me, and I know he's assessing my mental stability after the mug-throwing incident.

'Great, thanks.' I smile. 'Everything is fine.'

'Good,' he says, studying me, blue eyes luminous from his orange fake tan. 'You know I checked that phrase for you. The one about feeling antsy.'

'Oh yeah?'

'It can also mean sexually aroused.'

I laugh and shake my head as he chuckles his way back into the office.

'Eric,' I call. 'I'm going to start teaching my dad how to swim next week. And I was thinking of trying something different here. Aqua aerobics classes. Once a week. What do you think?'

He grins. 'I think that's a great idea, Sabrina. Can't wait to see Mary Kelly and Mr Daly do the samba in the water.'

He gives a sexy little hip roll, which makes me laugh.

Grinning happily, I sit on the stool and watch the empty pool, the pool rules sign glaring down on us all like a crucifix in a church. A reminder. A warning. A symbol. Don't do this, don't do that. No this, no that. So negative on the surface, and yet, a guide. Take heed and you'll be grand. Everything will be fine.

Mary Kelly is in hospital recovering from her heart attack, in a stable condition thankfully. I'm feeling anything but empty though, I feel rejuvenated, with fire inside, like I could look at nothing all day and still be okay, which is what will happen.

Mr Daly arrives in his tight green swim shorts, like an extra layer of skin, tucking tiny wisps of hair he has left into his too tight rubber hat.

'Good morning, Mr Daly,' I say.

He shuffles by me grumpily, ignoring me. He grips the rail and slowly descends into the water. He steals a glimpse at me to see if I'm looking. I look away, wanting this to happen straight away. He lowers his goggles over his eyes, grips the metal bars of the ladder and goes under.

I walk over to the ladder, reach into the water and pull him up.

'You're okay,' I say to him, lifting him out of the water, helping him up the ladder and sitting him on the edge of the pool. 'Here,' I hand him a cup of water which he downs, with trembling hands, his eyes red, his body shaking. He sits for a while, staring into space, in silence, me beside him, arm around him rubbing his back, while he calms. He's not used to me sitting with him after. I gave up on that some time last year when I could tell it wasn't going to stop him. All I had to do was save him and take my seat again. He gives me a sidelong look, checking me out suspiciously. I continue rubbing his back, comfortingly, feeling skin and bone, and a beating heart.

'You left early on Friday,' he says suddenly.

'Yes,' I say gently, touched that he noticed. 'I did.'

'Thought you mightn't be coming back.'

'What? And miss all this?'

He bites the inside of his mouth to stop himself from smiling. He hands the cup back to me, gets back into the pool and he swims a length.

ACKNOWLEDGEMENTS

I'd like to thank all the people who shared their marble memories with me: in all of my twelve novels, I don't think I've ever received quite the reaction when I've shared the topic I'm writing about. Personal stories just tumbled out of people, and whether those stories were big or small, each of them reinforced my belief that marble memories go hand in hand with key moments in adolescence. All of these shared memories encouraged me along the way.

Thank you Killian Schurman, glass artist and sculptor, who spent many hours showing me the process of marble making. Anything incorrect in the marble making scene is entirely my doing. Thanks Orla de Brí for connecting us and for inspiring me through your own work. Thank you to Lundberg Studios for sharing your expertise, and inspiring 'Marlow's' universe marble. Two books in particular were constantly in use; *Marbles Identification and Price Guide* by Robert Block, and *Collecting Marbles; A Beginners Guide* by Richard Maxwell. Thanks to Dylan

Bradshaw for answering my odd questions about the silent hairdryer that I'm sorry never made it to the final edit!

As ever, all my love to David, Robin and Sonny. Mimmie, Dad, Georgina, Nicky and the gang. Fairy godmother Sarah Kelly, Marianne Gunn O'Connor, Vicki Satlow and Pat Lynch.

Thank you Lynne Drew and Martha Ashby for the epic edit. The ever joyful Louise Swannell, Kate Elton, Charlie Redmayne and all of the HarperCollins team. Thanks to the booksellers, big and small, independent and chain, physical and electronic. And most important of all, thank you readers.

Praise for *The Mythological Dimensions of Doctor Who...*

"In a television show fandom that hoards its myths and canon tight to its chest, *The Mythological Dimensions of Doctor Who* is a welcome inhalation of air; examining many of the very 'set in stone' beliefs that we hold true, while examining the etheric connections between a television series and some of the greatest mythological traditions of all time. A solid read."
—Tony Lee, writer of IDW Publishing's *Doctor Who Ongoing*

"*The Mythological Dimensions of Doctor Who* offers fascinating perspectives on that iconic time traveler of contemporary popular culture. The articles in this new collection successfully join Doctor Who's fan-based cultural history to well-accepted academic scholarship on mythology. From Arthurian legend and Batman to medieval Scandinavian Valkyries and modern wartime morality, the diversity of subjects and themes explored in this collection offer compelling insights on the roles mythologies, both past and present, play in contemporary consciousness. By addressing newcomers to the Doctor Who series as well as those who have followed the Doctor's multiple incarnations since the 1960s, this volume is likely to become one of those classic works that raises the bar for future study in this field."
—Leslie A. Donovan, Tolkien Studies scholar and Associate Professor at the University of New Mexico, author of "The Valkyrie Reflex in J. R. R. Tolkien's *The Lord of the Rings*: Galadriel, Shelob, Éowyn, and Arwen."

"A collection of excellent essays that is engaging for the serious fan and will deepen the interest of the new viewer. Every generation has a method of storytelling to pass its collected wisdom to the next. This book helps us connect the themes of a modern television legend to the timeless myths of the past."
—Ken Deep, Co-host of *Doctor Who Podshock*

"Doctor Who has evolved into a mythological system, with all the use of archetypes and self-contradictory variation that implies. This collection addresses that fact, and both examines the mythology of the show, and seeks to make connections to other mythologies, both ancient and more recent, offering new perspectives on a familiar show."
—Tony Keen, British Science Fiction Association

"This book assembles essays which are both valuable 'eyewitness accounts' of Doctor Who's mythic status in television culture at the close of the first decade of the twenty-first century, and applications of methods used across disciplines to assess Doctor Who's debt to legend, particularly the Nordic and classical traditions, as well as modern and postmodern anxieties concerning gender and power. Its authors display awareness of the importance of Doctor Who's longevity in shaping its multi-authored identity since 1963; they are drawn from inside and outside academic life and so offer a rich diversity of voices for the consideration for students, critics and historians of contemporary media."

—Matthew Kilburn, Oxford Doctor Who Society

"This collection of fascinating essays dissecting Doctor Who as mythological construct could not be timelier as the new series approaches with promises of being more like a fairy tale. *The Mythological Dimensions of Doctor Who* offers a range of new perspectives on the show, not only in it's own internal mythology built up over four decades but through its use of classic folklore and legend as inspiration for a myriad of stories as filtered through the sci-fi/fantasy lens.

Drawing on such diverse sources, from the Middle Earth of Tolkien to the streets of Gotham city in the *Batman* comics, the Doctor's adventures are looked at for their treatise on morality and the human condition. The Time Lord reflects all aspects of our humanity and it is through that mirror that we come to appreciate the importance of our own values in the universe."

—Jamie Beckwith, Lead Writer of *The Terrible Zodin*, www.doctorwhottz.blogspot.com

The

Mythological Dimensions
of
DOCTOR WHO

The

Mythological Dimensions
of
DOCTOR WHO

Edited by

Anthony Burdge
Jessica Burke
Kristine Larsen

The Mythological Dimensions of Doctor Who

Printed in USA.   First printing 2010, Kitsune Books.
Second printing, 2013, CreateSpace.

Cover art by Andy Lambert

Contents

Acknowledgments

The editors are grateful to everyone who has helped bring this volume to fruition. A work of this nature does not become manifest without a combined effort of people of varying talents and knowledge.

Anthony would like to dedicate this volume to his parents Anthony and Diane, who infused in him a joy, and love, of reading and writing. None of Anthony's published essays or contributions to academia would not have been possible without their encouragement.

Jessica would like to thank her parents, Charles and Geraldine, for their continued support and love, to Russell T. Davies for having the immense brilliance to bring *Doctor Who* back into our universe, and to Luna Lovegood Burke-Burdge for reviewing the manuscript in her own faithful feline fashion.

Kristine would like to thank Anthony and Jessica for their valued fellowship, and her favorite "Doctor," her thesis advisor, Ronald Mallett, for teaching her everything she knows about the physics of time travel.

From the start, and hopefully in chronological order through the production stages of this book, we are indebted to: (1) Mike Foster, the North American representative of the Tolkien Society, who was instrumental in getting Anthony and Jessica their first published essay seven years ago. His sage advice has been fundamental in their lives; (2) to The Mythopoeic Society and Lynn Maudlin for encouraging Anthony, Jessica, and Kristine to work together on MythCon 39. It is from this conference, and the work of guest speaker Leslie Donovan, that Kristine and Jessica's essays were inspired, which in turn gave birth to this volume.

As the ideas for this volume took shape, we are equally indebted to Tolkien scholar and author Anne Petty who brought the idea to Lynn Holschuh and Kitsune Books, and has graciously written our Afterword.

While Anthony and Jessica were writing their contributions and compiling the volume, they were absorbed in an abundant amount of 4th Doctor stories, supplied by friend Robert J. Fass, for which we are very thankful.

Throughout the entire process, Barnaby Edwards of the Doctor Who New York (DWNY) fan group (www.dwny.org) has been our stalwart companion and at times our own Cloister Bell—our fact-checker and friend who went above and beyond the call of duty. Without Barnaby's work on editing, proofreading, and checking commentary on every contribution, and again for the final manuscript, this volume might not have happened. We are equally grateful for Barnaby's exceptional preface, which is a testament to his leadership in the Doctor Who community.

As the contributions took shape and were finalized, we all owe an immense debt to Laurie Greenwold Campos who increased Anthony's MS Word expertise and vastly improved his manuscript-building skill set. Laurie's advice, tools, and reading of the manuscript significantly sped up the process of compiling and bringing the manuscript into a good enough form for submission to Kitsune.

Our readers were very much key in shaping the final manuscript. For that, we are grateful to Jason Fisher whose advice on the Tolkien material, linguistic matters, and overall structure are very much appreciated. We are very grateful to Matthew Kilburn for his advice and thoughts, alongside contributors Colin Harvey and Leslie McMurtry, whose careful reading assisted the editors enormously. Thanks also to Simon Guerrier, both for our Foreword and his advice early on that gave shape to the manuscript.

Lastly, thanks to Dr. Matt Hills for his dedication, support, and acceptance to write a very last-minute contribution. This has truly earned him the title of "Time Lord."

Foreword

Dream the Myth Onwards

Simon Guerrier

Do stories matter if we know they're not true?

That seems to be central to the idea of myth. They are stories that matter. Ken Dowden, in his book *The Uses of Greek Mythology*, argues that "myths are believed, but not in the same way that history is."[1] If they were true they would be history. But stories still illuminate the truth. The father of psychoanalysis certainly thought so. Sigmund Freud used the stories of ancient mythology to illuminate aspects of the human condition. Most famously, he named a group of unconscious and repressed desires after the mythical king of Thebes, Oedipus. The story of Oedipus has been retold since at least the fifth century BCE. By linking to it, Freud suggested that the desires he'd uncovered were not new or localized. They were universal.

Freud was clearly fascinated by myth. His former home in London – now a museum – contains nearly 2,000 antiquities illustrating myths from the Near East, Egypt, Greece, Rome and China, many lined up on the desk where he worked. He argued that psychoanalysis could be applied to more than just a patient's dreams, but to "products of ethnic imagination such as myths and fairy tales."[2] But, as Dowden points out, you can only psychoanalyze where there is a psyche. Who are we analyzing when we probe ancient myths – which have been retold for thousands of years? Do we examine a myth as the dream of an original, single author, or of the culture that author belonged to? Dowden argues that "psychoanalytic interpretation of myth can only work if it reveals prevalent, or even universal, deep concerns of a larger cultural group."[3]

He also quotes Carl Jung, who developed the idea of the "collective unconscious," a series of archetypal images that we all share in the preconscious psyche and which, as a result, appear regularly in our myths. Jung warned against efforts to interpret the meanings of these images: "the most we can do is *dream the myth onwards* and give it a modern dress."[4] That seems to me what Doctor Who does, retelling old stories in new ways, surprising us with the familiar. The archetypes of *Doctor Who* – the invasion, the base under siege, the person taken over by an alien force, regeneration – have been embedded for decades. Yet the series keeps finding new ways to present them, and new perspectives and insights along the way.

That's also true of this book, probing the Doctor's adventures for new perspectives and insights. The essays contained here don't take Doctor Who as the dream of one single author whose unconscious desires can now be exposed. Instead, it probes our shared mythology as *Doctor Who* fans – of which the TV show is just a part – to explore our own cultural unconscious.

"Myth" means many things in this book. It's any fiction with a ring of truth. It's any story with cultural, psychological value. It's any work with staying power, whose themes and ideas are still relevant generations after the first telling. It's the established, fictional history of characters and worlds, the "continuity" so often complex and contradictory. It's the moment at which a character becomes a hero or even a god. It's anything we want it to be.

And that is why it's so revealing.

---

1 Ken Dowden, *The Uses of Greek Mythology* (London: Routledge, 2000 [1992]), 3.

2 Sigmund Freud, *Totem and Tabo.* (Leipzig and Vienna: 1913. English translation ed. J Strachey, London 1955). Cited in Dowden, 30.

3 Dowden, 31.

4 Carl Jung and C. Kerényi, *Science of Mythology: Essays on the Myth of the Divine Child and the Mysteries of Eleusis* (1949, English translation). In Dowden, 32.

Preface

The Mythology of a Legend

Barnaby Edwards

Myth and *Doctor Who*—two things that have gone hand in hand since the show's very first episode on November 23, 1963. From the mysterious old man in the junkyard with almost no background to the god-like race he hails from that is depicted in "The War Games" and "The Three Doctors"; from the myth-inspired space opera of "Underworld," "Pyramids of Mars," and "The Time Monster," to the Doctor perhaps being, in some future incarnation, one of the greatest mythical figures of all time: Merlin. *Doctor Who* has never shied away from using the classical myths of the British, the Greeks, the Romans, the Egyptians, and many others to invent great stories. At the same time, it has created its own legends and myths along the way, for other times and other civilizations.

Whether or not it was a specific intention of that first production team, led by Verity Lambert and Sydney Newman, we shall never completely know, but their creation of a old man and a young girl who are "wanderers in the fourth dimension" and about whom almost nothing else is known, save their non-human state, is surely as definitively myth-creating as it gets. This is reflected in the opening moments of the very first episode, "An Unearthly Child," showing a policeman patrolling by a fog-shrouded junkyard in present day (at the time of broadcast) London. Something strange and mysterious is starting here. The Doctor and Susan are deliberately vague about their origins, and it takes time to develop their characters and motivations, but even in these very earliest stories the Doctor and his companion(s) make an impact wherever they land. It's not a stretch to imagine that their exploits and accomplishments will be passed down the generations among the people they meet on their adventures and that those stories will be told forever. A legend was born.

Being a time travel show, *Doctor Who* has demonstrated the unique ability to not only build on myths of times long past, but to build myths around the time yet to come. The Doctor has shown up at the tail end of the Trojan War, where he provided the impetus for the wooden horse that brought the conflict to an end; has visited the mythical city of Atlantis at least twice, helping to destroy it both times; and has entered the mythology of a great many other worlds on his travels through time and space, from Draconia to Karfel, from Peladon to the Ood Sphere. Along the way, he has even become a legendary figure to the Daleks themselves, who after being thwarted by him so many times bestow on him a mythical name: the *Ka Faraq Gatri* ("the Destroyer of Worlds"), first used in the novelization of "Remembrance of the Daleks."

Sometimes these interactions on other worlds seem to bear more than a passing resemblance to many traditional myths and legends of Earth, as the Doctor encounters aliens resembling bulls living in a maze, and travelers who have voyaged around space for an eternity seeking the long lost source of their civilization that they eventually find under "the tree at the end of the world, guarded by two dragons."[1] The mythical counterparts to these adventures seem clear, and lead the Doctor to ponder whether "myths are not just old stories of the past, but also prophecies of the future."[2]

The modern incarnation of the series has taken this concept of mythmaking to new levels, and in the process has inspired this current volume. The legendary nature of the Doctor across time and space has been used to great effect, illustrated on an earthbound level by the character of Clive and, specifically, his website and research, as featured in the very first episode of the reincarnated series, "Rose." Since then the stories that have been told about the last of the Time Lords have been used to frighten the otherwise invincible-seeming Vashta Narada into seeking a 24-hour truce, after they have acquainted themselves with his legend in the books of the library from which they spawn.

The reason for the fear and respect that stories of the Doctor instill in the Vashta Narada is powerfully demonstrated in the manner of the punishments he deals out to the Family of Blood. Following the failure of their attempt to steal the Doctor's life-force, the members of the Family are, variously, trapped inside every mirror, only to be glimpsed from the corner of your eye, wrapped in unbreakable chains formed in the heart of a dwarf star, tipped into the event horizon of a collapsing galaxy as an eternal prison, and frozen in time as an ever-living scarecrow in a field watching over England.

These are not the actions of the adventuring scientist and explorer with which we typically associate the character of the Doctor. Rather, these are the actions of a mythological god-like figure, who, in the words of Tim Latimer, the schoolboy who becomes connected to the Chameleon Arch fob-watch, "is like fire, and ice and rage," "the storm in the heart of the sun," and who "burns at the center of time and can see the turn of the universe."[3] That the description of the punishments meted out by the Doctor to the Family is narrated by a third person—the character of "Son of Mine"—only goes to illustrate what tales might have been told of the Doctor across all of time and space. These are tales that have passed into mythology on a thousand worlds.

Perhaps the Doctor's actions have been exaggerated in the story that Son of Mine tells, and perhaps many of the other stories told by other people who have encountered the Doctor exaggerate and distort his actions. But no matter how accurate, these are the tales that so frighten the Vashta Narada when they read them in the Library that they offer the aforementioned truce. These are the tales told by River Song of the Doctor and the TARDIS—"I've seen whole armies just turn and run away, and he'd just swagger off back to his TARDIS and open the doors with a snap of his fingers. The Doctor, in the TARDIS. Next stop everywhere."[4] And these are the tales that cause her to describe him to her colleagues as "the only story you will ever tell—if you get out of here."[5] These are stories about a Legend.

The mythmaking aspect of *Doctor Who* reached perhaps its greatest heights when dealing with the Doctor's own people, the Time Lords of the planet Gallifrey. They are not named until the show is at the end of its sixth year in "The War Games," and in that story they are portrayed as an almost god-like people with immense power, and their home planet is not even named. Nor are any of the representatives of the race that we meet in that epic story named, other than the Doctor and the War Chief. They can almost immediately be considered the Gods of the *Doctor Who* universe.

In "The Deadly Assassin," when we are given our deepest glimpse into the lives and history of this legendary race, they are seen to be so old that even their own rituals and the roots of their technologies have become myths to them. They no longer have knowledge of the purpose of the Rod, Sash, and Key of their mythical founder—Rassilon. As the series has developed, these myths about the past of the Time Lords have taken on ever greater significance and been the source of an ever-increasing number of stories —from the tales of the "great vampires" and the great battles the two races fought across this universe, and others, to the games in the Death Zone that the early Time Lords indulged in, reflecting the similarities between the Time Lords and the pantheon of Greek and Roman Gods who used humans as their pawns in the games they played against each other.

While the representation of the Time Lords in the television series has not always lived up to this connection that can be made between the Time Lords and the Gods of our Earthly mythologies, often as a result of budgetary constraints, this has not stopped the idea from taking root with numerous writers. In the television stories featuring Time Lord society, and the later stories told within the Virgin Publishing New and Missing Adventures, the BBC Books Eighth Doctor Adventures, and the range of Telos Novellas, these creators have provided a great pantheon of powerful men and women: Rassilon, Omega, the Pythia, and the mysterious Other, to name just a few. These beings use the lesser peoples and races as their playthings and to provide amusement, and the world that they inhabit is a world of gods, demi-gods, and creatures of immense power, such as the Black and White Guardians, the Celestial Toymaker, the Chronovores, the Gods of Ragnarök, and the Eternals. Some of these figures send the Doctor on quests for the Key to Time and for Enlightenment, and some just challenge him to win his freedom. But whatever the level of interaction these challenges appear to be as much about distraction and amusement, as about saving the universe. The parallels with the gods of our ancient Earth mythologies are clear.

When the series was relaunched in 2005, the new production team examined all this accumulated mythmaking and added their own twist. They threw it all away. There are likely many reasons for this, not least of which would be increasing the appeal of the show to a general public that has little idea of the previous forty-two years of continuity, beyond the icons of the TARDIS, the Daleks, and the 4th Doctor's scarf. The results of this decision speak for themselves, and it has had an unexpected benefit. It has turned the Doctor into even more of a legendary figure than he had been before. And along the way, the Time Lords have regained the mystique that was lost in their previous television appearances, and have again become the god-like figures that caused the War Chief, way back in "The War Games," to quake in his boots at the very mention of their name. They are again a race we can imagine waging the war across time and space that devastated other races, such as the Gelth and the Nestene Consciousness, and eventually almost destroyed themselves in the process. Such is the scale of that destruction that by the year 5 billion they are not believed to ever have existed, and the name Time Lord is spoken in hushed, respectful, and disbelieving tones. All of this has been echoed in the portrayal of the Doctor himself and in the characters with whom he has been associated, and with whom he has traveled.

The essays in this volume cover many aspects of the myth of *Doctor Who*. From the way memory plays a part in how the characters the Doctor encounters on his travels view him, to its effect on those of us who have followed him through television, books, and audios, from explorations of the Doctor's morality to in-depth analyses of how Valkyries, Gandalf, and Batman have accompanied him on his travels, unbidden, and perhaps unseen. There is something for every taste here, whether you are a student of mythology or simply want to look at how storytelling has evolved in

Doctor Who through the years, and see how, even when the television series was not on our screens, the myth of *Doctor Who* and his world kept changing and evolving. It is indomitable, unstoppable, unassailable, and unending, like all the best legends. Long may it continue!

---

1 "Underworld," 4th Doctor, Classic Series 1963-1989.
2 *Ibid.*
3 "The Family of Blood," 10th Doctor, Russell T. Davies (New) Series 2005-ongoing.
4 "The Forest of the Dead," 10th Doctor, Russell T. Davies (New) Series 2005-ongoing.
5 *Ibid.*

Introduction

"Steve Glosecki sees our culture as 'technologically advanced, but mythologically depleted.'" (*Shamanism and Old English Poetry*)

Humans are, by our very nature, mythmakers, largely because we are innately curious about the world around us. This curiosity drives us to ask questions and seek answers, even when answers are not swift in coming. In the past this was largely the case, either due to a lack of technology or a given question being beyond the scope of science (such as questions concerning an afterlife or the nature of good and evil). Myth readily filled in the gaps of our knowledge, and indeed formed the fundamental basis of science, in the form of creation myths. Therefore, since the dawn of time, humanity has had mythological intentions. Whether conscious or unconscious, labels and explanations were created, and although relevant to a given culture in a given time, unifying strands can be easily ascertained. Fast forward to the twenty-first century, and the need to know still exists, reflected in the popularity of Google and Wikipedia, and numerous documentaries on cable television channels.

However, in modern times, many of our cosmological connections have been lost, due in part to the insidious light pollution that robs us of our view of the stars, as well as the modern convenience of standardized and automated timekeeping. The average person might be able to point out the Big Dipper and the Belt of Orion, but how many know the legends behind these constellations? Precious few. We teach bowdlerized versions of Greek myths to ten-year-olds and then act surprised when we have to painstakingly point out the classical references in Shakespeare, Pope, and Dickinson to these same students five years later. Many adults do not recall sufficient mythology to complete the average crossword puzzle. In most cases the "modern mind" no longer is able to process unnamed phenomena and filter the energies of the earth or cosmic anomalies as archaic people once did. It therefore may appear that mythology has lost its relevance to our modern world. Or has it?

As modern technology increasingly allows us to probe the depths of the universe, simultaneously looking further outward in space and backward in time, we find ourselves face to face with those very same questions our ancestors pondered—where did it all come from, where is it all going, and most importantly, what does it all mean? Science cannot replace myth; it merely causes it to shape-shift. While photons from across the universe and earliest moments of creation travel into the view of the Hubble Space Telescope, humans as physical beings are frustratingly unable to join in the great cosmic journey through space and time. Our bodies are trapped in the here and now, but our minds are free to wander, as authors such as H.G. Wells well knew.

Enter our intrepid Time Lord, the Doctor, who has broken the shackles of temporal and space travel limitations and been our celestial avatar, as transmitted to our television for the last forty-six years. The amassed mythology woven around the Doctor, his companions, his home planet, and his adventures, have not only entertained fans since 1963, but reintroduced them to their own mythological legacy by re-visioning these classical tales through a technological lens. As Joseph Campbell notes, the journey of the hero resonates with the human spirit at its very core, and transcends any specific culture or century. Like the mythic tales of long-dead civilizations, the journeys of the Doctor form a mythos of their own, with all the typical issues of internal continuity common to what J.R.R. Tolkien would term a "Primary World" mythological structure. Yet as these essays will demonstrate, the "Secondary World" of the Doctor is in no way inferior or less relevant to our own, especially in the questions it explores and the lessons it teaches. The Doctor's encounters and narratives have presented and reinterpreted Earth's mythical past on numerous occasions, as a number of contributions within this volume will discuss. These threads of story exist within the larger tapestry of the Doctor's own Gallifreyan, Time Lord, pattern. However, in many ways these "alien" encounters act as a mirror that forces us to examine our own human condition and our part in defining what it means to be human.

Already possessing an enormous intellect, and mental prowess beyond the greatest of Earth's own minds, the Doctor's ability to time travel and cross dimensions comes from technology, in the form of the TARDIS. For fans, the Doctor's vehicle provides a portal, an alien technology that can be used to cross into the world of myth and legend. As fans, we become fully immersed into this Secondary World, as the character and narrative resonate with our own experiences, insecurities, hopes, and fears. Regardless of the fan's knowledge of mythology or interest in the subject, *Doctor Who* not only opens a vast gateway to explore fictional worlds, but also has the power to awaken our interest in its source material, including mythology, socio-political policies, cultural beliefs, and historical events.

Fans of *Doctor Who* have created a culture of their own, in which creativity, intelligent analysis and discourse, and occasionally heated discussion and disagreement are celebrated. Whether constructing a police box, knitting scarves, hosting a podcast, or running and organizing a community dedicated to honor its spirit, the *Doctor Who* fans are encouraged to explore the deeper meaning of the series and what it means to them personally. It can be argued that in these and many other ways the Doctor and his adventures are now a part of our cultural and mythological heritage.

The title of this volume pays tribute to our own planet within the *Doctor Who* Universe, and the volume contributors have sought to engage, inform, and challenge readers to consider the mythological aspects and meanings of the series from a variety of viewpoints. In these pages, the reader will find the *Doctor Who* canon related to myth and memory, thoughts on death and wartime morality, and crossing into other mythological landscapes such as Middle-earth, Gotham City, and Frankenstein's laboratory, using specific lenses to focus on various facets of the mythology surrounding the Doctor. Our hope is that readers will finish this volume with more questions than answers, and will be motivated to ponder the answers to these questions for themselves. After all, the journeys of the Doctor are nowhere near completion, and like the universe in which he travels, the human imagination and creative spirit are infinite.

—*The Editors*

A Note on Conventions Used

Being very aware that the Doctor can be cited in a variety of ways per his incarnation, e.g., Tenth, first, 1st, in many different media, in this volume we chose the numerical representation: 1st, 2nd, etc.

Series numbers are likewise styled: 1st series, 2nd series; Series 1, Series 2; but season 1, season 2, etc.

Each chapter also cites numerous episodes that range across all ten Doctors. The entire episode title is used at first mention, then shortened upon subsequent mention, e.g., "Pyramids of Mars"/"Pyramids"; "The Edge of Destruction"/"Edge"; and so on.

Frequently used acronyms:

NA – New Adventures
BBC – British Broadcasting Company
BF – Big Finish
LOTR – *The Lord of the Rings*
OFS – *On Fairy-Stories*

Canon, Myth, and Memory in *Doctor Who*

C. B. Harvey

For *Doctor Who*, issues of canonicity are more ambiguous than for other long-running science fiction series such as *Star Trek* and *Star Wars*: unlike the producers of the two American franchises, the BBC has never offered an official edict as to what constitutes canon in relation to *Doctor Who*. In this chapter, I explore the complex interrelationship between constructions of canon as determined by both the creators and consumers of various *Doctor Who* media. I examine the extent to which these attempts at imposing a single, definitive truth upon the often disparate iterations of the *Doctor Who* franchise draw heavily upon conceptions of myth prevalent within the wider culture. I explore the ways in which *Doctor Who*, its producers, and its fanbase utilize existing mythological structures and in turn use these as a method for configuring *Doctor Who* itself as mythology.

Central to my approach is the concept of memory and how it informs ideas of both mythology and canon. I explore the ways in which communal and subjective remembering plays a part in the construction of the mythological and canon. In examining these multiple processes I draw upon my own biographical experience as a viewer of the *Doctor Who* television program as both a child and an adult, my identity as a fan of the show who consumes myriad kinds of spin-off material, and more lately my identity as a writer commissioned to produce *Doctor Who* prose material officially sanctioned by the BBC and published under license by the British company Big Finish.

I argue that memory understood as something that is both embodied and emplaced can help explain the ways in which the producers and consumers of *Doctor Who* media use multiple approaches drawn from mythology in their efforts to imprint a single, definitive canon on *Doctor Who* in all its manifold guises.

Regenerations

The longevity of the *Doctor Who* television program means that, much like its eponymous hero, it has frequently "regenerated". The black-and-white studio-bound 1960s version of the program feels very different to the color adventures of the 1970s, which in turn differ markedly from the program as it existed in the video-effects-heavy 1980s, and is in turn very different again from the cinematic sweep of the current iteration of the series, which began in 2005.

In the days before an avid fan base was able to purchase commercially available video tapes and DVDs, the pressures of week by week production meant that ongoing continuity across the series was not always afforded a great deal of attention by the various production teams, at least in terms of the show's longer, more established history—although continuity *between* stories in a specific season was not always guaranteed either. This is not to suggest that long-term continuity was entirely absent, but that sometimes it amounted only to broad adherence to the rules of the series: the Doctor is an alien, he travels through time and space in a machine that is larger on the inside than on the out, this machine is called the TARDIS, and so forth.

Arguably the most drastic change to this approach came with the advent of John Nathan-Turner as the show's producer—from 1980 until the original series' effective cancellation in 1989—who constantly reintroduced older aspects of continuity into the show in an attempt to impose a greater sense of unity onto the program. In fact it's ironic that, as John Tulloch and Manuel Alvarado observe, fans saw Nathan-Turner's emphasis upon continuity as the characteristic that made him stand out as different from his predecessors in the role.[1]

Related to these issues of continuity is the concept of canon, since contradictions arising from a lack of continuity can raise questions about the "authenticity" of events within the diegesis or narrative level of the program. For example, upon meeting the 10th Doctor in the new series episode "School Reunion," the character of Sarah Jane Smith remarks, "You've regenerated," to which the Doctor replies, "Half a dozen times since we last met." Since Sarah Jane Smith had in fact met a later incarnation of the Doctor in the1983 20th anniversary special, "The Five Doctors," this raised questions for some fans about whether showrunner Russell T. Davies had effectively "de-canonized" the earlier serial, which, in common with other issues of canonicity, provoked various ripostes from fans explaining as to why this wasn't the case.

Without an official edict on the subject, ideas of what constitutes canon have proliferated amongst *Doctor Who*'s ardent fan base, evident in fanzines and more latterly on Internet forums such as the now defunct *Outpost Gallifrey* and *GallifreyBase*. The issue is complicated not only by the inconsistency of the various televisual incarnations of the program but by the multitudes of spin-off media. In the 1960s and 1970s this extended to *Doctor Who* annuals and comics, as well as other merchandise such as ice lollies, chocolates, and toys;[2] and in 1979 Marvel's *Doctor Who Weekly* appeared,[3] featuring a critically well-regarded comic strip and offering official-sounding verdicts on issues of canonicity and continuity.

The program's long hiatus from television from 1989 until 2005 was interrupted by the charity-inspired "Dimensions in Time" in 1993 and the BBC/Fox television movie in 1996 (both of which occupy positions of contentious canonicity with the fan base, although the latter now seems to be generally accepted as genuine). The void, meanwhile, was filled by the Virgin novel range that sought to build upon and expand the *Doctor Who* mythos, by the BBC's own range of tie-in novels,[4] and by numerous fan-developed video and audio productions. In 1999 Big Finish was granted the license to produce *Doctor Who* audio productions.[5] Over the following years these plays would see Peter Davison, Colin Baker, Sylvester McCoy, and Paul McGann each reprise the role of the Doctor.

The interrelationship between the creators of *Doctor Who* media and an active and vocal fan base adds a further level of complexity. A number of the individuals involved in various *Doctor Who* spin-off media have since gone on to work on the rejuvenated version of the television program. These include Russell T. Davies, who penned the 1996 Virgin novel *Damaged Goods* and was showrunner since the program's resurrection in 2005 up until the final episode of the 10th Doctor David Tennant's tenure; Paul Cornell, whose 1995 Virgin novel *Human Nature*[6] formed the basis of the 2007 television episodes "Human Nature" and "The Family of Blood" and who has worked extensively for Big Finish; Robert Shearman, whose Big Finish script *Jubilee* was adapted (with significant changes) to become the 2005 television episode "Dalek"; and Gareth Roberts, who wrote *Doctor Who* novels, co-wrote Big Finish audio plays, wrote comic strips for *Doctor Who Magazine*, and authored the 2005 interactive episode *Attack of the Graske* before going on to write the *Doctor Who* television episodes "The Shakespeare Code" and "The Unicorn and the Wasp," as well as contributing to spin-off program *The Sarah Jane Adventures*.

Me and Doctor Who

I am a long-term *Doctor Who* fan. I was born in 1971 and watched the show avidly throughout the latter years of Tom Baker's reign as the Doctor, throughout the Peter Davison epoch, and, albeit with declining enthusiasm, into the eras of Colin Baker and Sylvester McCoy. I collected *Doctor Who Weekly* from its first edition in 1979 through its transformation to *Monthly* and then *Magazine*. Each Christmas I received a *Doctor Who Annual*, cherishing the battered Patrick Troughton annual

I inherited from my older brother. My room was bedecked with posters of the various Doctors and copies of Target novelizations. My passion for the show was only rivaled by my simultaneous love of *Star Wars* and my occasional forays into the *Star Trek* and *Blake's Seven* universes, though such trysts were inevitably tinged with guilt at betraying my first love.

The academic Henry Jenkins identifies *The Simpsons* as an example of "transmedia" storytelling, because of the multiplicity of media forms through which *The Simpsons* franchise is delivered.[7] *Doctor Who* has existed in transmedial form since its success first became apparent: notably in terms of the so-called "Dalekmania" that led to the merchandising of the 1960s and very nearly resulted in a US-made Dalek spin-off show, as well as the aforementioned Annuals produced by World Distributors under various company names.[8]

Marsha Kinder suggests that children's consumption of media is interpolated by a "fairly consistent form of transmedia intertextuality."[9] Consistent with this, my earliest memory of *Doctor Who* derived not from its televisual incarnation, but from the spin-off media. During a class at school when I was six years old, I drew a picture of mummies menacing the Doctor and Sarah Jane Smith inspired not by the show itself but by the WH Allen and Co. hardback novelization of the 1975 story "Pyramids of Mars", adapted by Terrance Dicks from the original script by Robert Holmes and originally published in 1976. In point of fact, I have no recollection of having watched the television version of "Pyramids," and I didn't see this particular serial in its entirety until its release on DVD in 2004. However, the iconography of this particular story played (indeed still plays) an influential role in my wider conception of *Doctor Who*.

Genre Trouble

By the wider public, *Doctor Who* is almost certainly viewed as a science fiction series. However, in their book *About Time: The Unauthorized Guide to Doctor Who 1975-1979*, Tat Wood and Lawrence Miles explore the vexed issue of whether *Doctor Who* can actually be characterized as science fiction, concluding that the show is sometimes science fiction but that the format is loose enough to enable some stories to be classed as horror and others as fantasy.[10] Yet, according to Darko Suvin, central to the idea of science fiction is the concept of "cognitive estrangement," which refers to the way in which the genre not only recasts aspects of the everyday world in new ways, but overtly draws our attention to these differences.[11] According to this definition, those *Doctor Who* stories that feature iconography more readily associated with fantasy or horror could easily be framed as science fiction.

However, such an overtly rationalist idea as cognitive estrangement seems to me problematic, since it explicitly ignores the embodied and emplaced aspects of media consumption, and by extension our emotional engagement with such media. Any purely "rationalist" approach is untenable, as it smacks of a Cartesian separation of mind and body.

For the cultural studies critic Chris Rojek, embodiment and emplacement are contingent upon one another: embodiment refers to the viewer's somatic or physical engagement with media, constantly affected by ongoing physiological processes, and emplacement alludes to the individual's relationship to physical and cultural resources.[12] How an individual is "emplaced" with regard to resources—be they economic or cultural—will have a bearing on aspects such as diet, which in turn affects physiology. Furthermore, I would contend that the interactions between embodiment and emplacement and the media artifact are what produce our emotional responses to the program, which in turn feed into our continuing appreciation of the program.

Allowing for the role of emotion in the consumption of *Doctor Who* material necessarily suggests a highly subjective approach. However, that "Pyramids" should have been voted the story fans most desired to see released on DVD suggests that I am not alone in viewing the story as hugely significant, and in some sense emblematic of the best *Doctor Who* can offer.[13] Certainly *Doctor Who Magazine* (in its various iterations) played a role in reinforcing the totemic significance of this particular story, although it seems likely that the semiotics of the story—that is to say, the language of audiovisual signs via which meaning is conveyed—are themselves central in ensuring its longevity in the popular memory, when other stories are much harder to recall.

That "Pyramids" should prove able to carry its mythic status over into supporting spin-off materials suggests a potency rooted in its narrative and iconography. Understanding how such potency operates might prove illuminating in understanding the interrelationship of affect and semiotics in the generation and regeneration of mythic structures. Indeed, Henry Jenkins, in conversation with Matt Hills, has suggested the need to establish an "affective semiotics" capable of accounting for the role of the physiological, emotion, and feeling in the consumption of media.[14] Central to this is surely the concept of memory, in terms of how the individual recalls material, how the creators of the material themselves remember and invoke memory, and how wider communities—fans but also everyone else—remember.

Remember, Remember

Lance Parkin initially identifies two versions of the term "canon," one descended from the biblical conception of canon and one derived from F.R. Leavis' idea of the Great Tradition,[15] before going on to identify a third variation derived from fan appreciation of Sherlock Holmes.[16] Parkin talks about the "consensus" by which *Doctor Who* fans agree what constitutes canon. This necessarily suggests a collective understanding of a body of work that constitutes that canon, a kind of collective memory. Clearly, the mythological must similarly be understood as the product of collective memory, if the term is to have any meaning.

However, Parkin also highlights the oxymoronic concept of "personal canon"[17] by which individual fans determine which stories are—or are not—authentic: to underline the point, the *Doctor Who Tardis Index File* suggests in its definition of "Canon" that it "differs from fan to fan."[18]

The sociologist Barbara A. Misztal argues that it is important to understand the nature of the interrelationship between the various kinds of individual memory and "social" or "collective" memory.[19] In fact, she suggests that collective memory is subjective because in different individuals it evokes different associations and feelings, so in that sense it is simultaneously collective and subjective.

Again, memory needs to be understood as embodied as well as emplaced: as the neuroscientist Steven Rose observes, memory is the product of multiple bodily states, comprising "circulating hormones, physiological processes, the immune system."[20] Gillian Cohen cites the psychologist Endel Tulving's view that human memory is constituted by a variety of interacting behavioral, cognitive and brain systems, and processes.[21]

Ideas of mythology and canon therefore need to be understood as the product of a dynamic interrelationship through which audiovisual material is subjectively understood via both embodiment and emplacement. That "Pyramids" possesses a greater resonance with a wider body of people perhaps obtains in the particular ways in which the story—and the spin-off material associated with it such as the novelization—produces specific emotional responses in its audience.

The Mythmakers

For Laurence Coupe, myth is characterized by an ongoing dialectic between, among other aspects, "memory" and "desire."[22] As participatory consumers of all kinds of stories, we necessarily engage with narrative bringing to bear memories derived from our own experiences more generally, but specifically our experience of other stories: the aforementioned transmedial intertextuality that Kinder identifies as representative of children's consumption of media.

These memories engender expectations, perhaps the desire to see the Doctor triumph and the foe defeated, or a subjugated population liberated, or loved ones rescued, or the planet Earth saved from oblivion: or, in the case of the 2008 Series 4 finale, "Journey's End," all of these things.

Unsurprising, then, that various *Doctor Who* production teams have sought to use mythic undercurrents in more or less explicit fashion since the program's inception in 1963. As well as using enduring mythic structures from the wider culture—which may themselves have already been mediated by other creative practitioners—this might also apply to the ways in which the iconography of the *Doctor Who* franchise itself is redeployed to enhance the program's own standing as a mythic structure. Such a process is characterized by J. David Bolter and Richard A. Grusin as "remediation."[23]

Throughout the series' history, both in its classic and more contemporary incarnations, *Doctor Who* has remediated existing mythic structures in a variety of fashions. Older television stories from the classic run of the original series such as the 1978 story "Underworld" and the 1979/1980 story "The Horns of Nimon" recast the Greek myths of Jason and the Argonauts and Theseus and the Minotaur, respectively.

Frequently, though, the Classic series remediated much more recent narratives. "Pyramids," the story that had such an effect on me (at least by proxy), heralds from an epoch of the program often described as its gothic period, in which the Producer Philip Hinchcliffe and Script Editor Robert Holmes consciously sought to push the series in a more adult direction. Often this took the form of remediating iconography and narrative tropes and techniques familiar from the Hammer films, which had in turn reinvented the 1930s Universal horror movies for a 1960s and 1970s audience. While "The Brain of Morbius" most obviously draws upon the *Frankenstein* myth—itself remediating aspects of the Greek myth of Prometheus—it also recasts Robert Louis Stevenson's *Strange Case of Dr Jekyll and Mr Hyde* in *Doctor Who* terms. The 1977 story "The Talons of Weng-Chiang" (written by Robert Holmes) draws heavily on various aspects of actual Victoriana as well as ideas of Victoriana. These range from Sherlock Holmes to Fu Manchu, the latter being a pulp character that while not strictly Victorian or even Edwardian is often erroneously associated with this era. In terms of "Pyramids," the influence of the Universal and Hammer versions of *The Mummy* and its sequels are obvious to see.

So far, the contemporary television version of *Doctor Who* has proven less willing to adapt classical myth to its format, though when dealing with literary subjects such as Charles Dickens, William Shakespeare, and Agatha Christie it has proven willing to deploy narrative techniques familiar to these writers as part of the plot in each instance. However, the contemporary *Doctor Who* has taken the familiar iconography of the *Doctor Who* series and frequently subverted it.

When Christopher Eccleston's 9th Doctor memorably stumbles into his TARDIS in the 2005 episode "Father's Day" (written by Paul Cornell), only to find it has transmuted into an actual police telephone box, the effect is shocking because it subverts our prior knowledge of the television show. The TARDIS itself carries mythic status within the wider culture. Again, this is not a new technique: the explosion of the TARDIS in the 1968 story "The Mind Robber" might have had a similar effect upon its contemporary audience, since five years into the show's run the TARDIS had already become a kind of national icon.

In each case, memory is implicated in how the mythic structure is employed. Certainly a prior understanding of Greek mythology is not a prerequisite for understanding the unfolding of the plot of either "Underworld" or "The Horns of Nimon." Intimate awareness of gothic literature or the films it influenced is similarly unnecessary for an understanding of "Talons," "The Brain," or "Pyramids." Similarly, the viewer of "Father's Day" only needs to remember that the Doctor's TARDIS is bigger on the inside and contains lots of "alien tech," information that is contained within the episode. In each case, though, the emotional intensity of the episode is likely to be different if the viewer does have prior knowledge of the mythic structures informing the program: though neither "Underworld" nor "Horns" are critically well-regarded, the program-makers clearly felt there to be a potential pleasure in seeing Greek myth rearticulated in the context of the *Doctor Who* program. Understanding the intertextual influence on the various stories of the gothic era of *Doctor Who* might have supplied an additional ironic charge to the viewing experience.

In the case of "Father's Day," the twist of seeing the TARDIS rendered into a simple wooden police box is all the greater if the viewer possesses awareness of the TARDIS's pivotal and iconic role in the history of the program, and its curious empathetic relationship with its owner, an idea that has been variously hinted at since the era of the 1st Doctor, William Hartnell. Rafer identifies Tulloch and Alvarado's observation that *Doctor Who* plays upon its own history to reach "...an ever denser mythic reality": for Rafer, the "programme's mythic reality [...] is reinforced with Christopher Eccleston's Doctor confronting Autons and Daleks."[24]

Spin-Offs, Canonicity, and Consistency

"I'm a Time Lord... I'm not a human being; I walk in eternity..."
(4th Doctor to Sarah Jane Smith, "Pyramids," 1976)

"The Doctor is half-human."
(The Master to Chang Lee, *Doctor Who—The TV Movie*, 1996)

The revelation of the "half-human" nature of the 8th Doctor in the 1996 television movie co-produced by the BBC and Fox Television caused—continues to cause—much vexation amongst the fan base, since it seems to overturn a central shibboleth of the series, apparently ignoring the preceding thirty-three years of continuity, in which the Doctor is portrayed as wholly alien, despite his peculiarly British mannerisms. For many fans this constitutes a betrayal of the mythology of the series, to the extent that there has been some contention regarding whether the 8th Doctor counts as an official Doctor, despite the BBC's presentation of him as such in publicity and marketing material at the time of the television movie's premiere. That officially sanctioned spin-off material should try to correct the "fact" of the mythology is perhaps unsurprising. Throughout the 8th Doctor series of books (published by BBC Books) attempts are made to clarify this particular Doctor's heritage, even to the extent of employing the concept of a "bottle universe" by way of explanation (recalling similar strategies in the *Superman* comics).

The instance of the 8th Doctor is illustrative because of the way in which it highlights the interrelationship of canonicity and spin-off media. At the time of writing, the new series of the television program produced by BBC Cardiff and generally regarded by the fan base as canon has included two references to the 8th Doctor: (1) glimpsed as a drawing in the episode "Human Nature," alongside illustrations of the Doctor's other incarnations; and (2) again alongside his other incarnations in the 2008 Christmas special "The Next Doctor," portrayed via info-stamps, portable databases of information used by the Cybermen.

In both cases, interestingly, the 8th Doctor is portrayed via representative modes within the diegesis, that is to say, the fictional world of the program: in other words, as memories, which we might read and accept as liable to being misremembered, as opposed to flashbacks in which diegetic truth is portrayed. In fact, both "Human Nature" and "The Next Doctor" concern themselves with the problems of memory as a central theme, and problems of remembering and misremembering can be perceived as a recurring concern for the Cardiff-produced series.

For some fans, these references serve to canonize the McGann Doctor, but they also seem to lend legitimacy to the audio stories produced by Big Finish under license from the BBC in which McGann continues to appear as the 8th Doctor (that some of Big Finish's 8th Doctor stories have also been broadcast on the BBC Radio 7 digital radio channel further reinforces the official stamp of the Corporation).

Additionally, the framing of the references to the 8th Doctor in "Human Nature" and "The Next Doctor" through a further level of representation—the drawing, the info-stamp—gives official sanction to the idea of a "fuzzy" incarnation of the Doctor. This is an idea further reinforced by the BBC's official *Doctor Who* website, intoned by an authoritative but otherwise unidentified female voice-over: "The 8th Doctor's first adventure was to save Earth at the end of the twentieth century. There are many stories told about what happened next, but due to the Time Wars we don't know how many are true."[25] Indeed, the Time Wars serve an important role for many fan commentators in helping explain away inconsistencies through the series, and offer a potential loophole for more problematic works that might otherwise prove too contradictory to include.

Ironically, the linked television episodes "Human Nature" and "The Family of Blood" proved controversial for other reasons of canonicity because they were derived from Paul Cornell's Virgin novel *Human Nature*, in which similar events occurred to the 7th Doctor. Some fans worried that the television series effectively overwrote the novel, decanonizing it. Cornell felt compelled to write a piece on his own website ridiculing the idea of canonicity in a show that is fundamentally about time travel, and the contradictions that this necessarily implies.[26]

Do I Count?

In 2006, my gothic-themed horror story won the first *Pulp Idol* award, an annual competition operated by the British science fiction, fantasy, and horror magazine *SFX* (Future Publishing). This brought me to the attention of Joseph Lidster, a prolific contributor to Big Finish's range of *Doctor Who* audios, and at that stage editor of one of their BBC-licensed *Short Trips* anthologies, subtitled *Snapshots*. Lidster invited me to pitch an idea, which was looked at by the BBC and subsequently commissioned.

While the BBC have not issued a proclamation on the subject of canon, other strictures are in operation for those working on licensed material, as is the case with Big Finish's *Doctor Who* output. As well as operating within the specific terms of Big Finish's license with the BBC with regard to the *Short Trips* books, as a writer of *Doctor Who* spin-off material I had to obey the established rules of the franchise.

In pitching my first *Doctor Who* short story for Big Finish, I elected to use the 6th Doctor and his assistant Mel: their actions within the story clearly had to retain fidelity with the characterizations portrayed on screen (and subsequently on Big Finish audio) respectively by Colin Baker and Bonnie Langford. While I was allowed to use certain aspects of the mythology (chiefly the TARDIS) many other aspects were off limits, particularly reusing established characters or monsters, the copyright of which might be owned by someone other than the BBC.

There was a sense in which I was able to play with certain of the *Doctor Who* toys but that I had to return them to the toy box undamaged once I had finished. Not to say that this wasn't profoundly enjoyable: I found as a writer of licensed material the pleasure derived from placing existing familiar characters in new contexts and enabling them to interact with my own invented characters.

Each of the *Short Trips* collections offers a particular slant. In the case of *Snapshots*, the slant was that of the effect the Doctor has any other people's lives. The story in question, "The Eyes Have It," revolves around a bug exterminator called Lionel Tooley coming to visit a blind elderly woman after complaints from the neighbors about strange goings-on. Lionel encounters the 6th Doctor and his companion Mel who are investigating a distress signal. The trio make their way into the elderly woman's loft, where she then locks them in. Here in the darkness of the attic they find the originator of the distress call, a gigantic crablike creature who has apparently stolen the old woman's eyes. Taking his cue from the Doctor, Lionel finds within himself the inner strength that is key to defeating the alien.

The story draws upon iconic *Doctor Who* mythology: the distress call, the stranded alien, the interplay between the regular *Doctor Who* characters and the characters specific to the story are all borrowed in some sense from the landscape of television *Doctor Who*. Other aspects, such as Mel being unable to scream, are played for laughs as well as serving the plot, since this was one of the aspects the character was renowned for in the series: and indeed Bonnie Langford is probably still best known in Britain for her childhood role as Violet Elizabeth Bott in the BBC's 1977 television adaptation of the *Just William* novels, in which her catchphrase was "I'll scream and scream until I'm sick, sick, sick!" Additionally, the story uses generic traits familiar from both horror and fantasy, and which I hoped retained a mythic charge: the secluded mansion, the elderly woman's collection of disturbing china dolls. The visiting bug exterminator is an idea familiar from much filmic and televisual fantasy: *The Twilight Zone* and *Buffy the Vampire Slayer* both employed similar techniques, amongst many others.

I was subsequently asked by Cavan Scott and Mark Wright to pitch a larger, Victorian-themed short story for the *Short Trips* anthology they were editing, entitled "Ghosts of Christmas." This time I chose the 7th Doctor and Ace, and started from the idea of *The French Lieutenant's Woman*: unfortunately I found that while the Victorian theme worked, setting events around a cobb was too far removed from the Christmas theme, so in the eventual story—entitled "But Once A Year"—the inheritance from John Fowles' novel is the idea of an alien intelligence residing in a mysterious fossil. I combined this with biographical information I remembered reading about Robert Louis Stevenson's childhood (confined to bed), and a poorly child became the central character in the narrative.

Again my approach echoes some of the mythic devices employed by the original television series: mysterious fossils have featured in several stories, notably "The Stones of Blood," and Victoriana was explored to critically lauded effect in the story "Ghost Light." In fact, the well-documented legacy of H.G. Wells to *Doctor Who* means that writing a story in a Victorian setting feels like an easy fit.

But can either of my stories be said to be canon? Clearly only a tiny proportion of the television audience for *Doctor Who* would necessarily even be aware of such spin-off literature, even if they considered themselves fans. Even amongst those fans who might seek out such literature and despite the deployment of tropes and techniques familiar from the classic *Doctor Who* series, a lot of fans would almost certainly not class the prose stories as official in the same way one of the television stories would be considered canon.

This is clearly different from the normal state of affairs, where screen-based narratives are invariably classed as inferior to prose narratives: in the *Bizarro World* of science fiction canon there is a curious reversal, whereby audiovisual narratives are accorded greater precedence than prose, or indeed audio material featuring the same cast as the original television incarnation. Wood and Miles describe such material as "secondary sources," whereas the television series is presented as "the 'truth' about the *Doctor Who* universe."[27]

As a general rule, screen-based *Doctor Who* counts as more authentic than versions in other media. Even this, though, is not entirely a hard and fast rule: the two *Doctor Who* feature films, *Doctor Who and the Daleks* (1965) and *Dalek Invasion Earth 2150 AD* (1966), in which Peter Cushing starred as Dr. Who, an Earthman scientist in the H.G. Wells mould, are not generally regarded as canon. As Wood and Miles observe, however, they are fondly remembered by the fan base, partly because of constant repetition on terrestrial television, and almost certainly better remembered by casual viewers than the television versions they were adapted from.[28]

Intriguingly, the short story "The Five O'Clock Shadow" by Nev Fountain, which appears in *Short Trips: A Day in the Life*, attempts to incorporate the Cushing films into the official continuity by suggesting that the characters from the movies are figments of the real Doctor's imagination, brought about as a means of defeating a foe. This is a further role of spin-off media: the ability to seal up holes in continuity, to effectively shore up the overarching mythology.

Again this is perhaps most evident in the case of the 8th Doctor, whereby various spin-off media have attempted to account for this Doctor's description of himself as "half-human." The Big Finish audio *Zagreus* (2003) even attempts to account for the multiple versions of the 8th Doctor, an example of a piece of spin-off media evidently attempting to knit together potentially mutually contradictory stories told by other pieces of spin-off media.

Conclusion

In the course of this essay I have outlined some of the ways in which canon, myth, and memory interact in the ongoing invention and reinvention of *Doctor Who* in its multiple forms. I have suggested that communal ideas of canon and myth need to be understood as emplaced and embodied, both in terms of the active consumer of the material, and with regard to the originators of such material. These are far from being mutually exclusive groups: as well as those working on the television versions of *Doctor Who*, there are the individuals involved in the energetic spin-off industry, some of whom have crossed over into the contemporary television *Doctor Who*, not to mention producers of fan fiction.

Additionally, there are the children like me who played Daleks in the playground, or drew pictures of the Doctor and Sarah Jane Smith being menaced by terrifying mummies. In the past, producers of *Doctor Who* television serials have drawn upon the mythical in a fairly explicit fashion, for instance, in terms of "Underworld" and "Horns," where myths are recalibrated to work in a *Doctor Who* context. Other *Doctor Who* television serials take mythologies that have already been mediated by other creative forces, such as "The Brain of Morbius." Still other television stories play with and reinforce *Doctor Who*'s own mythology, such as "The Mind Robber" and "Father's Day."

But the process of mythologizing extends too into wider debates about canon and continuity as they relate to spin-off media. In my own tiny contribution to the *Doctor Who* universe I not only sought to play upon the mythology of the series, but also to bring to bear other intertextual references from outside the series derived from my own experience. Many creators of *Doctor Who* licensed material use their work as an opportunity to correct problems, and help connect together the sometimes disparate aspects of *Doctor Who* into one coherent whole. The Cardiff-produced television series and BBC more widely, while apparently eager to side-step contentious issues of canon, offer methods by which fans and producers of spin-off material can construct an over-arching mythology.

In each of these cases, communal and subjective memory interact in a dynamic and reciprocal fashion: *Doctor Who* is simultaneously a collective yet very personal experience, and its enduring appeal lies in the ongoing interactions between these two kinds of embodied and emplaced remembering, and the emotions such interactions provoke.

1 Tulloch and Alvarado, 216.
2 Richards, 282.
3 Richards, 422.
4 Richards, 379.
5 Cook, *Doctor Who: The New Audio Adventures – The Inside Story*, 13.
6 Cornell, *Human Nature*, 1995.
7 Jenkins, 147.
8 Richards, 379.
9 Kinder, 47.
10 Miles and Wood. *About Time, The Unauthorized Guide to Doctor Who, 1975 – 1979, Seasons 12 – 17*, 129, 131, 133.
11 Alkon, 10-11.
12 Rojek, 85.
13 "DVD Poll Results" in *Doctor Who Magazine*, no. 332 (July 2003).
14 Jenkins, 26-27.
15 Parkin, "Canonicity Matters: Defining the *Doctor Who* Canon," 246-247.
16 Parkin, 260-61.
17 Parkin, 259.
18 "Canon" at http://tardis.wikia.com/wiki/Canon. accessed June 29, 2009.
19 Misztal, 9-11.
20 Rose, 7.
21 Cohen, 307.
22 Coupe. *Myth*, 1st edition, 1997, 197.
23 Bolter and Grusin, 273.
24 Rafer, 127-28.

25 Unidentified female voice-over, *The Beginner's Guide to Doctor Who* at http://www.bbc.co.uk/doctorwho/classic/guide.shtml

26 Paul Cornell, *Canonicity in Doctor Who* at http://www.paulcornell.com, published February 10, 2007.

27 Miles and Wood, *About Time, The Unauthorized Guide to Doctor Who, Volumes 1-6,* various.

28 Miles and Wood, *About Time, The Unauthorized Guide to Doctor Who, 1985 – 1989, Seasons 22 – 26, The TV Movie,* 390, 395.

Holy Terror and Fallen Demigod:
The Doctor as Myth

Neil Clarke

In his introduction to the subject, Robert A. Segal suggests that there have been theories surrounding myth for as long as there have been myths. Consequentially, it is a concept riddled with ambiguities, and any definition must be framed in the broadest of terms. He therefore proposes defining myth as a story (rather than a doctrine or principle) "about something significant."[1]

Rather than rigidly proposing that the protagonists must be god-like, he suggests "only that the main figures be personalities—divine, human, or even animal,"[2] who are either the cause or the recipient of given occurrences. His final caveat is that "to qualify as a myth, a story ... be held tenaciously by adherents."[3]

On these terms, *Doctor Who*, based as it is around concepts of good versus evil—a topic of not inconsiderable "significance"—can undoubtedly be located within this idiom. However, the broadness of a definition designed to encompass numerous thinkers' interpretations of myth means that a very wide range of stories could be similarly located under its auspices. Perhaps what particularly defines *Doctor Who* is its awareness of its relationship to myth, though this appreciation did not arise within the production until recently, certainly in terms of the Doctor himself having more to do with locating the character within grand terms popularly seen as representative of myth. That is to say, within popular culture, myth is considered synonymous with the gods and monsters and earth-shaking conflicts of classical or ancient legend, rather than the definitions of thinkers like Jung or Lévi-Strauss, which are not specific to a given type of narrative.

Throughout the various incarnations of *Doctor Who* as a show, the production teams' approaches to presenting the character of the Doctor have understandably changed and progressed. Therefore, sometimes the Doctor has been presented as a literal figure, an alien traveler, while at other times in terms redolent of figures from legend and fairytale, as a lonely god or lost prince.

This conception of legend or fairytale as synonymous with myth does become notable in relation to a discussion of *Doctor Who*'s relationship to the form. The lack of detail renders the 1st Doctor, particularly, unknowable and magical in a way gradually lessened by the introduction of his race, planet, and a certain amount of backstory. This initial portrayal of the Doctor as an otherworldly, enigmatic figure arises by means of distancing the viewer. While this effect may be seen to elevate the character from normality and by extension into otherworldly and legendary terms, it does not necessarily take the series into the realm of myth. This tension between fairytale and myth demonstrates the more problematic elements of reading *Doctor Who* within the elements of myth, especially when dealing with more specific theories than the aforementioned definition. Northrop Frye, for instance, offered a heroic pattern applicable to myth that comprised birth, triumph, isolation, and the defeat of the hero.[4]

Though *Doctor Who* employs a cyclical, endlessly renewable structure, it is possible to discern these phases within its cycle of regeneration and individual incarnations of the title character. Using the run of Tom Baker's Doctor as a template—for many the definitive incarnation—"Robot" would represent birth and "Logopolis" (or even the entirety of the somber season 18) defeat and isolation from long-standing friends Romana and K9. This is a simplistic application of Frye's pattern, though, with triumph comprising the entirety of the intervening stories.

Broadly speaking then, each Doctor is equally adherent to the concept of the mythic hero, whether this was a conscious decision of the production team in question or not. It was not, though, until the end of the series' original run that the Doctor, in the form of Sylvester McCoy's 7th Doctor, was most willfully identified as such purely on the basis of what is seen on screen. There are as many interpretations and definitions of the mythic hero as there are of myth itself, but the Jungian writer Joseph Campbell's particular theory of heroism demonstrates how much the concept is linked to ideas of classical mythological figures. Campbell's hero goes through a journey comprising separation, initiation, and return, experiencing a "fateful region of both treasure and danger ... variously represented: as a distant land, a forest, a kingdom underground, beneath the waves, or above the sky, a secret island, lofty mountaintop, or profound dream state."[5]

A better evocation of the Doctor's varied travels can scarcely be imagined. The 7th Doctor saw a readdressing of the character in less literal terms, where he was suddenly "far more than just another Time Lord,"[6] and aspersions were cast on his place in the Time Lord hierarchy, alluding if not to the specifics of theories like Campbell's, then at least to the suggestion that myth is inextricably linked with magic and fantasy.

In *Doctor Who*'s return in 2005, the opportunity was taken to strip back the Doctor's past, withholding key details and not overloading the audience with continuity. While turning expectations of the Doctor on their head made sense at the end of the eighties, reacting against decades of a staid approach to the Doctor's past and origins, there was no need to destabilize the basics for an unfamiliar generation in 2005. However, showrunner Russell T. Davies did introduce large changes, namely Gallifrey's destruction through its involvement in a Time War with the Daleks, wherein the Doctor destroyed both races and became a battle-scarred survivor. This effectively new backstory, covering the off-screen years, injected a tragic element of loneliness into the character, a key trait of classical heroes.

More than Just a Time Lord: "Remembrance of the Daleks" and "Battlefield"

It was in season 25, following the light, whimsical approach of season 24 that 7th Doctor script editor Andrew Cartmel consciously instigated a new approach to *Doctor Who*. By looking beyond its trappings, he attempted to pare back the series to its essentials, coming to the conclusion that the character of the Doctor had been eroded by years of over familiarity. Inspired by the darker approach of violent, uncompromising stories like "The Seeds of Doom," "The Talons of Weng-Chiang," and "The Caves of Androzani," Cartmel came to see that the Doctor "could be a much bigger, less human and less predictable character."[7] That is to say, as Gary Gillatt puts it in his collection of essays, *From A to Z*, "a man on a noble voyage of discovery into unknown lands and shadowy places rather than simply an excitable tourist on a cheap package tour around the universe,"[8] as he had perhaps been in danger of becoming in season 24. This noble voyage is also a defining part of the archetypal hero as defined by Joseph Campbell.

However, Cartmel was aware that to create an enigmatic figure in the series' initial run, then-editor David Whitaker had to do little more than withhold information. By comparison, to restate a comparable sense of mystery, Cartmel had to be more proactive, and "briefed the writers of the twenty-fifth season to include in their stories some elements casting doubt on aspects of the Doctor's established history and on the true nature of the character."[9] Season 25 introduced a Doctor who knew exactly what was going on, or was actively orchestrating events. Cartmel "always hated it when [the Doctor] was zapped on the head, or knocked unconscious and tied up," things he saw as symptoms of an opposingly literal approach to the character. "I always thought that was demeaning to him. If he does get tied up, it should have been part of his plan all along... In one sense, it's the cheapest, most crass device possible. In another, it's a piece of characterization that gives you chills down the spine."[10]

Cartmel's vision would see its fullest expression on screen in the two televised stories by Ben Aaronovitch: season 25's "Remembrance of the Daleks" and the following season's "Battlefield." Grounded in a recognizable setting, a realistic world of cafés, schools, and B&Bs, populated by housewives and vicars and undertakers, a more domestic setting than typical of earlier near-modern/contemporary settings, "Remembrance" retained the previous season's breeziness and energy, but coupled with a welcome complexity. In this story the Doctor exercises power of life over death, of creation and destruction; he can destroy solar systems, talk Daleks to death, and contact spaceships with a vintage camera and some fairylights, all in time for tea. Though not explicitly representative of myth theories in an academic sense, this level of power is suggestive of classical creationist myth and godhood. A Doctor who preemptively knows what's going on is quite a radical break with the past, while the destruction of Skaro's system in this story is specifically indicative of the new magnitude of the character, equitable to the "significance" of the earlier definition of myth. This more dangerous portrayal of the character is a far cry from the vulnerable and all-too-often ineffectual cricketer, or even, despite his edginess, Tom Baker's bohemian, who, while mysterious and (mainly) non-violent, was essentially a slightly more eccentric than average action hero.

Though operating under the auspices of myth, these Doctors did not have a persona cultivated with the magical heroism in mind that arises from the connotations of Campbell's hero and the "exotic, supernatural world"[11] he encounters. In this sense, the portrayal of the Doctor in this story was unprecedented; in the words of Doctor Who Magazine's Time Team (four fans' ongoing odyssey through every TV episode): "He's no longer just a traveler in space and time—he's a ruthless, genocidal warrior, one who seems totally in control of the situation every step of the way."[12] In the café scene of "Remembrance," during which the Doctor debates the possible consequences of his actions, this story allows us the novelty of being allowed to see beyond the surface of the Doctor's character, into his uncertainty, and displaying an intimate introspection also unexplored over the majority of the previous run. This element would continue to be explored in both the New Adventures and the new series, for example, in encounters with different companions' long-lost fathers in Kate Orman's New Adventure Return of the Living Dad, or Series 1's "Father's Day."

In "Remembrance," the return to the Totters Lane setting from "An Unearthly Child" could even be seen as the action of returning home, one of the nodes of Joseph Campbell's definition of heroism.

The following season's story by Aaronovitch, "Battlefield," though not critically acclaimed or a prime example of its era, nevertheless portrays an even greater preoccupation with and awareness of the series' past. It is in this ambitious approach, more so than ordinarily shown, that the series engages with concepts demonstrative of the significance integral to myth. "Battlefield" is supported by themes like nuclear Armageddon, and though a less than successful story, it's noticeably sophisticated and experimental in a way *Doctor Who* hadn't been since, say, season 18.

There's a complex, adult awareness of the Doctor as a legendary figure, and, as in "Remembrance," he is explicitly presented in a mythologized way, in this case because the story deals with the repercussions of the actions of a future Doctor who will become Merlin. (As an aside, the UNIT sergeant, Zbigniew, must be one of the first characters in televised *Doctor Who* to acknowledge the concept of the Doctor being legendary on earth in a way similar to mythical heroes of antiquity.) Similarly, UNIT and the Brigadier are further elements of the past reimagined in line with the current production team's approach, rather than being rehashed verbatim; UNIT is international and hardware-oriented, while the Brigadier is given a domestic life.

However, though a conscious decision to inject mystery back into the Doctor and make him a more impressive figure, the so-called "masterplan" of script editor Andrew Cartmel was nevertheless unfocused. Adversaries from the Gods of Ragnarök to Fenric and Light are of a more supernatural bent than previously typical, in line with the "vengeful superhero"[13] the Doctor had become, but Cartmel's seasons contained no ultimate goal or revelation, in the sense of the thematic story arcs of Russell T. Davies' Bad Wolf or Medusa Cascade. While it is true that the series' unforeseen cancellation curtailed any further intended developments, and the seeds for interlinking stories within seasons were only just being sewn, with long-reaching arcs not having gained prevalence by the eighties, in retrospect the lack of any definitive conclusion is all too noticeable.

Destroyer of Worlds: New Adventures/New Series

Following the conclusion of the 1963 to 1989 run on television, Virgin Publishing picked up the 7th Doctor's story where "Survival" left off, in their series of New Adventures. Aimed at a more adult audience, these books featured not only increased sexuality and violence, but a sophistication of themes developed directly from season 26's run. Consequentially, the portrayal of the Doctor developed there continued to be expanded, creating a figure a far cry from the more straightforward portrayal of the television series. Perhaps the most explicit continuation of the 7th Doctor came from former script editor Andrew Cartmel himself. In his *War* trilogy, the Doctor's all-knowing, underlying control and manipulation of events is increased to such an extent that, though he barely plays any active role, his presence is felt throughout. That the Doctor here can control a situation with the appearance of only the barest effort renders him a supremely powerful, awe-inspiring figure. This portrayal of the Doctor as too vast a character to be comfortable with is exaggerated even more by author Dave Stone.

In his unhinged NA *Sky Pirates!*, the Doctor is presented as extremely alien, to the extent of being unaffected by trivialities like local gravity; there is a deliberate acknowledgement that his hat mysteriously never blows off, and his suit remains preternaturally clean; food and objects appear around him at will; and he can secrete electrostatically active substances from his pores. It is even suggested that he is something monstrous crammed down into human form, while anyone who notices these things is likely to lose their train of thought.[14] These attributes emphasize a gulf between the Doctor and more mundane characters, comparable to supernatural classical heroes.

Russell T. Davies' conception of *Doctor Who* owes various debts to the New Adventures' analytic approach to the tenets of the series, and led to the creation of a pool of writers Davies would later draw on to develop a version of the show both aware of its past and capable of pushing its format without losing sight of its fundamental appeal. Though the new series gives us a Doctor with his backstory painted in grand, sweeping strokes (not least the Time Lords' destruction), he is also more grounded by increased emotional involvement with his companions and the people they encounter than was often true in the past. The series also tries to have its cake and eat it by enhancing the down-to-earth moral choices he must make, and the effects of his lifestyle, as demonstrated by the montage of those who have sacrificed themselves on the Doctor's behalf in "Journey's End:" "The Doctor: the man who keeps running, never looking back, because he dare not."[15] The repeated loss of the people the 10th Doctor holds dear (Reinette, Rose (twice), Astrid, Jenny, River Song, Donna, and even the Master) straddles both these approaches: the immediacy of the emotional and the classically tragic grief and isolation of the epic. This layer of tragedy and loss creates the distancing effect that helps to suggest the larger than life nature of the character, while his portrayal as "lost prince"[16] allows a romanticizing to sweeten the pill for general viewers— distancing, but not to the extent of inaccessibility.

Demigod and Courtesan: The Adventuress of Henrietta Street

Lawrence Miles' work is characterized by ambitious concepts exhibiting large amounts of creativity, detail, and imagination, making him a particularly influential author within *Doctor Who* novels. His *Alien Bodies* established various concepts that would become mainstays of the BBC's 8th Doctor range of novels, namely a future war involving Gallifrey and an unspecified Enemy (a possible precursor of Russell T. Davies' Time War, though this Enemy is explicitly far worse than the Daleks), as well as tangential factions including the non-corporeal Celestis, and the bat skull-wearing time-traveling voodoo cult Faction Paradox.

The Adventuress of Henrietta Street constitutes a prolonged portrayal of the Doctor from an entirely mythologized perspective, written almost entirely without conventional dialogue, except as occasional snippets presented as scripts. In its unconventional format, the novel is capable of being more extreme in its divergence from a typical presentation of the Doctor than would be viable in a mainstream format like the televised series. Styled as a faux-historical text, *Henrietta Street* draws on various sources including characters' diaries and letters. While the epistolary style is an established literary device, here the fictional source material is presented as having been co-opted into a coherent whole, rather than being set down as complete documents. This technique, then, is employed as the distancing technique that allows the portrayal of the Doctor as an "elemental" figure. Explicitly of dubious accuracy, the novel strips the Doctor of the specifics of his planet and race; instead, we see him as the eighteenth century characters do. Where, in general terms, the Doctor is perhaps most accurately described as an ageless, changeable alien adventurer, Miles presents him as nothing less than an elemental, and a "fallen demigod."[17]

During the period the novel spans, the Doctor is living among the prostitutes of a Covent Garden bordello—the House of Scarlette on Henrietta Street, which acts as his base of operations. The contrast of the largely asexual Doctor with the rich, heady decadence of the eighteenth century, with its *bagnios*, courtesans, ritualists, *demi-rep* (women of doubtful reputation), and *tantrists* seems calculated to present him as an intriguingly iconoclastic figure, while even basic details about his circumstances are withheld. It is never even specified how he came to arrive in this century without the TARDIS: "'He walked here' … is all Scarlette would ever say, when anybody asked her how the Doctor came to be staying at Henrietta Street."[18]

A similar iconoclasm is present in Miles' decision to have the Doctor marry—an unprecedented event for an almost reverentially static character. Miles not only has the character married off, but has it occur as a symbolic ritual binding the Doctor to the earth (following the inadvertent destruction of Gallifrey as part of the War in Heaven arc implemented in the earlier *Alien Bodies*). The transgressive shock of any sort of wedding for the Doctor is further compounded by his bride being the owner of the House, "half-sorceress and half-prostitute"[19] Scarlette—the titular adventuress—wearing a blood red wedding dress, in a ceremony taking place in the crypt of a Caribbean church, attended by ritualists, tantrists, cabalists, and representatives of various arcane witch-cults and secret societies. Through the ceremony, "the alchemical wedding of the Doctor (representing the elemental) and Juliette (representing the earth), the Doctor hoped to bring a new security to the troubled world and, perhaps, to give *himself* roots in a universe where he no longer truly belonged."[20] The ceremony epitomizes the symbolic, fairytale-like approach of the novel, reflecting Miles' view that *Doctor Who* has "more in common with folklore than with science fiction."[21]

Though the extent of this portrayal might be unprecedented, even more so is the way the Doctor's initiation of a war with the House on Henrietta Street as his base of operations brings prostitution, tantra, and, by extension, sex to the fore. In fact, the foe against which he is fighting—*babewyn* apes, manifestations of the limits of human knowledge—are themselves, at least initially, manifested by attainment of a certain plane through tantric sex acts. This alone can be seen as a statement of intent from Miles; he is not concerned with treating the *Doctor Who* toy box ordinarily. From the sexual elements of *Henrietta Street*—this is a novel that opens with an extended sex scene between one of the Henrietta Street House prostitutes and a huffing MP, leading to the summoning of a *babewyn*—Miles segues into a similarly uncompromising attitude to the Doctor's form and function as a character. He is overtly compared to "godlike, elemental creatures called *Vidyeshwaras*" (Lords of Wisdom), held by *tantrist* lore to inhabit the state of *Shaktyanda*; "perhaps Scarlette saw the Doctor as such a being."[22] Similarly, he is also cast in a typically tragic role, akin to that afforded by the loss of his people to the Time War in the 2005 series: "Many of the women ... came to think of the Doctor as a tragic figure: an elemental cast out of his own world, trapped at the House perhaps as a kind of penance."[23]

The whole novel is suffused with ideas that relate more to the fantastical level Campbell's theories seem to suggest, rather than typically science fiction concepts broadly rooted in real—if speculative—science. For example, the Doctor effects the arrival in the House of his companions Fitz and Anji. While unspecified within the dubiously-accurate narrative, it is suggested this is produced at least in part by a harnessing of the power of the synchronized menstruation of the House's women, taking place on "one of the House's 'bleeding days'"; "A lot of the women later described the experience in surprisingly biological terms, as if the energy came from within their own bodies."[24] Similarly, the Doctor uses a séance to ascertain where to place a wedding invitation marked "Family" in order to "deliver" it; it is placed within the structure of the gallows at Tyburn, where it remains several months later, even though by then the Doctor is claiming it has been received.

More broadly, the Doctor is presented in enigmatic terms inductive through the simple expedient of withholding discussion of any details about him in any detailed terms (also, this was during a period of amnesia in the novels, an attempt to jettison all past continuity). The distancing returns the Doctor to the enigmatic state of the very earliest stories.

As part of his attempt to find his place in the universe following Gallifrey's destruction in *The Ancestor Cell*, the Doctor writes a book entitled *The Ruminations of a Foreign Traveler in His Element*, which continues the reduction of his entire lifestyle to fairytale terms: "much of his *Ruminations* takes the form of a catalogue, an assemblage of demons fought, people encountered and dream-worlds visited"[25] —once again, a less literal interpretation of past adventures by comparison to straight referencing, fully compatible with Campbell. The presentation of the Doctor's *Ruminations* is reflective of Miles' broader approach; established tropes of the series' mythology like Gallifrey, Kasterborous, Omega, Rassilon, while in some cases alluded to, are never explicitly mentioned, allowing for a broader, more sweeping picture of the *Doctor Who* universe's workings. "I've always seen the Time Lords as being elementals rather than aliens anyway,"[26] says Miles.

Everything in this novel is disrupted or limited in this way; facts and details are either incomplete, missing, or only alluded to, with even the often ubiquitous sonic screwdriver only mentioned as a totemic object in the Doctor's will.[27] Equally, the TARDIS is not described as anything as literal as a "time machine," or as specific as a Gallifreyan Type 40 TARDIS, rather as "a lodestone of the highest elemental power. ... Its weight was such that when activated by correct ritual it would bend and warp the world, in a manner familiar to Sanskrit-speaking peoples, til every *babewyn* in its realm would scream in fury."[28]

Perhaps the ultimate example of Miles' worldview comes at the novel's conclusion, when the diseased second heart that has been killing the Doctor is removed by the novel's villain, Sabbath, cabalistic ex-secret service operative and all-purpose mastermind, who transplants it into his own chest. This event is rendered in entirely fairytale terms similar to the non-literality of myths like that of, for example, Daedalus. The fictional narrator, supposedly collating the available records and evidence, even freely acknowledges that the records of these events only exist in the form of the wildly spurious testimony of an uneducated Maroon (escaped slave) guerrilla who is present.

However, despite Miles effectively enabling the reader to see his techniques in action, this in no way lessens this scene's impact, and, in fact, epitomizes the prevailing approach of the entire novel. Almost any *Doctor Who* story could be reduced to myth, or portrayed in a style conducive to the form to similar effect as in this story, by being presented in similar manner. The reader is left in no doubt that the approach here is very much deliberate, deriving from the style in which it is approached. However, it is possible to find examples of stories in which not only the events in question are subject to a similar effect, but where the Doctor himself is openly acknowledged, even by other characters, as myth-figure.

The Engine of History: The Cabinet of Light

Daniel O'Mahony's novella for Telos Publishing, *The Cabinet of Light,* expresses the Doctor not even as a character per se, but as the type of archetypal hero Campbell and Frye deal in. Unlike *Henrietta Street*, the events of this story are presented in conventional prose, and though O'Mahony shares with Miles a portrayal of the Doctor as more than a purely corporeal alien, here it is in the way characters perceive and interact with the Doctor that this is expressed.

The unspecified Doctor of *Cabinet* is barely present in the events of the novella and is divorced from the specific traits of his on-screen incarnations, becoming a larger, ever-present force infusing the entire narrative. The removal of the Doctor from the narrative leaves the surrounding characters—and reader—grappling with him as something less specific and human than is ordinary. *Cabinet* is a conscious, explicit attempt to portray the Doctor himself as myth. "He's a mischief, a leprechaun, a boojum," says one character, bookseller and collector of incunabula, Syme. "The Doctor is a myth. He's straight out of Old English folklore, typical trickster figure really."[29] Neither part of an ongoing narrative, nor specifically located within the series' past, *Cabinet* is in a position to challenge the portrayal of the Doctor. Here, the Doctor is throughout linked to concepts of light, which becomes a metaphor for progress and enlightenment—itself related to the journeys of the hero-archetype. This is most explicitly illustrated when the protagonist, time-sensitive American ex-solider and would-be investigator Honoré Lechasseur, visits Syme for possible leads. Syme relates a narrative interpretation of a series of prehistoric cave-paintings apparently showing the overthrowing of a cave-dwelling matriarchal system by the Doctor, initiating the patriarchal system through the bestowal of the gift of fire. In a gender-inversed variation of "An Unearthly Child" (another return to the hero's beginnings), "The old man-messenger brings fire and also reason," by exposing a stranger to the tribe as a killer and liar. "Dissemblance, such a radical concept for these people! The old man brings not just fire but new ideas. Fire and these new ideas change the way society operates, the power of the cave-mothers is eroded ... the men become powerful. ... He introduces the male principle. The matriarchy is overthrown. History begins."[30]

Aside from linking the Doctor with a mythological figure like Prometheus, this retelling of the very first *Doctor Who* implicates him in no less an event than the beginning of (male-dominated) civilization. The Doctor could scarcely be presented in more fundamental terms than as the instigator of human society as we understand it, once again taking the Doctor back to the significance of myth. The Doctor himself inhabits only the fringes of the story, appearing in only one scene. Ensconced in a bombed-out, moldering bookshop we meet an imperturbable, Holmesian Doctor. "I'm a Holy Terror," he declares. "I am what fear itself is frightened of. I'm the sleep of reason. So I'm told, but I can't keep up with what I am most of the time."[31] The Doctor is of course a character who lends himself to reimagining and varied interpretations, beyond (at the time of writing) the ten actors to have portrayed him on screen, as well as numerous apocryphal versions like Aaru Production's Peter Cushing films, stage plays, spoofs, and Big Finish's *Doctor Who Unbound* audio adventures. This propensity for variation is the Doctor's defining feature, perhaps along with the relative morality he exhibits in comparison to other broadly similar action-adventure figures. In this case, it is the capability of the character to appear familiar and at the same time unique, which makes the alignment of the character with heroic blueprints so effective.

The very idea that the Doctor can be painted in such broad strokes demonstrates his uniqueness as a character, even more so than cultural figures like Sherlock Holmes, James Bond, or even Robin Hood. While definable as heroes in the theoretical sense, the Doctor nevertheless has the advantage, in that the concept of an ever-changing, near-immortal, time traveler lends itself to this kind of scope in a way that Sherlock Holmes' grounding in a specific milieu cannot compare to. *The Cabinet of Light* demonstrates perhaps the boldest realization of this scale and potential in its description of the Doctor as "the personification of the engine of history."[32]

Conclusion

The portrayal of the Doctor and his adventures in line with myth-archetypes has been closely associated with the increase in input from figures from a fan background, beginning with the likes of Andrew Cartmel and Ben Aaronovitch in the late eighties, reaching a peak with the almost exclusively fan-oriented (and -driven) novels of the nineties, and continuing into the current series. Despite having originated at the very beginning of the show, this approach derived at that time from reluctance to state details about the character's background. While having broadly the same effect on the character as Cartmel's introduction of deliberate nods to the idea of the details revealed in the intervening years not being definitive, the lack of self-awareness of this property in the sixties gives a notably different tone to this approach to the Doctor. In that period, the absence of details spoke for itself, without its effect being spelled out in explicit celebrations like the consciously stirring, "He's like fire and ice and rage ... He's ancient and forever"[33] speech from "The Family of Blood."

It's notable too that the presentation of the Doctor in a mythic idiom seems synonymous with the dark elements of his character—the 1st Doctor is openly unpleasant to his unwilling companions, especially up to the end of "The Edge of Destruction" and notoriously appears on the verge of murdering an injured cavemen to preserve his own life. While the 7th Doctor is not as ambiguous on such an immediate level, in his manipulation and game playing, he can certainly be ruthless—companion Ace bearing the brunt of much of this trait. His line, "You're no use to me like this,"[34] spoken of her anger in "The Happiness Patrol" makes clear his perception of her as an attribute he can use to his own ends, and makes his understandable but breathtakingly cold dismissal of her in "The Curse of Fenric" all too believable ("...unless I had to use her somehow"[35]).

Similarly, in the new series, it is often in the darkest stories that the Doctor is most explored—habitually the second two-parter of the season, as the story arc for that year comes together and the tone becomes more serious. In Steven Moffat's "Silence in the Library"/"Forest of the Dead," the character is developed not by plumbing the depths of his past (as in "Remembrance of the Daleks," "Silver Nemesis," and "The Curse of Fenric"), but by suggesting a possible future, through the eyes of Professor River Song. As such, even a misleadingly minor moment, when the Doctor opens the TARDIS' doors with a snap of his fingers—something he has previously denied that he is able to do—becomes a consciously "epic" moment.

This kind of approach to the Doctor can be seen as an attempt to portray the Doctor as something bigger and deeper than "just a kids' hero," and is perhaps best characterized as an attempt to elevate and expand the character in a way general audiences would probably see no need for, as evidenced by its prevalence in the areas where fan influence was on the rise.

The Doctor arguably could not survive as the one-level character of the seventies and eighties. Fascinating though the character of an eccentric alien traveler may be, he could not have remained this alone indefinitely.

Arguably, by the time Cartmel came along, the character was overdue for some sort of rejuvenation. While all the Doctors are, in their ways, brilliant—especially when viewed in isolation—the cumulative effect of the eighties' Peter Davison and Colin Baker, albeit with their very different approaches, were not afforded much opportunity for variety or depth within their characterization, or through the type of stories offered. Cartmel's radical rethinking of the character rejuvenated it enough to support numerous books, and arguably largely underpinned the returned series, with a sense of scale, albeit coupled with a very contemporary awareness of real emotion.

The 3rd and 4th Doctors had strong enough personalities and enough stories effective on their own terms to not need great depth. Crucially, their stories were broad enough to have populist, mainstream appeal. The early to mid-eighties, by contrast, presents a period when *Doctor Who* was apparently made for anoraks, in its reliance on so-called "hard science" and mathematics (CVEs, etc.), and, despite the soap opera bickering of the regulars, a lack of credible human interaction. Thus, all too often the stories of this era are flat and lacking in real danger, intelligence, or humor (think "Four to Doomsday" or "Terminus"). Despite superficial changes of tone—like the gloriously ultraviolent nihilism of season 22 (by BBC standards: cannibalism, gassing, stabbing, rat-eating, blood-licking, dismemberment, and that's just "The Two Doctors"!)—regardless of the quality of stories like "Vengeance on Varos" or "Revelation of the Daleks," the series didn't deliver anything fundamentally new.

In fact, somewhat bizarrely, given how logically the new series locates the contemporary/future/historical settings at its heart, seasons 22 and 23 especially eschewed this variety for a surfeit of futuristic stories. Intrinsically the least interesting, being the hardest setting to ground in realism or emotion, and with an attendant lack of predefined detail that comes as standard with a historical period (and especially given the apparent inability of then script editor Eric Saward to square the 5th Doctor's vulnerability and pacifism with the violent universe he encounters, and the 6th's giving in to it), these stories effectively demonstrated that this was not a viable approach in the long run. The time was ripe for a change. The more magical 7th Doctor, and his equivalently more experimental stories—genteel (cannibal) old ladies, a hippie circus turned evil, a time-travelling seventeenth-century witch— came at just the right time. While hardly bothering the mainstream viewing public, the increasing development of both the character and his stories came to create something with far more scope than the series had seen for several seasons. However, it is perhaps Russell T. Davies and his canny production team who have created the most effective synthesis of different elements of the show, rebuilding it from the ground up, jettisoning unnecessary elements, and using a combination of returning foes and new monsters. The mythic undercurrents to the Doctor most specifically addressed by Andrew Cartmel are still present, but combined with domesticity, and real, human traits like jealousy and lust and sex, and—vitally—the popularism that previously ensured the show's accessibility. On these terms, the relationship of the character to myth continues to provide a multilayered depth for the character, arguably essential to his longevity.

---

1 Segel, 5.
2 *Ibid.*
3 Segel, 6.
4 Segel, 81.
5 Campbell, 58.
6 "Remembrance of the Daleks," 7th Doctor, Classic Series 1963-1989.
7 Gillatt, 151.
8 *Ibid.*
9 Howe, Stammers, and Walker, 113-114.
10 Cook, 47.
11 Segel, 105.
12 Pritchard, 45.
13 Stone, various.
14 *Ibid.*
15 "The Stolen Earth"/"Journey's End," 10th Doctor, Russell T. Davies (New) Series 2005-ongoing.
16 "Human Nature"/"The Family of Blood," 10th Doctor, Russell T. Davies (New) Series 2005-ongoing.
17 Miles, *Henrietta Street*, 148.
18 Miles, *Henrietta Street*, 27.

19 Miles, *Henrietta Street*, 18.
20 Miles, *Henrietta Street*, 173.
21 BBC Online, "Interview: Lawrence Miles."
22 Miles, *Henrietta Street*, 30.
23 Miles, *Henrietta Street*, 56.
24 Miles, *Henrietta Street*, 61.
25 Miles, *Henrietta Street*, 102.
26 Outpost Gallifrey, "The Outpost Interview: Lawrence Miles."
27 Miles, *Henrietta Street*, 194.
28 Miles, *Henrietta Street*, 196.
29 O'Mahony, 25.
30 O'Mahony, 25-26.
31 O'Mahony, 78.
32 O'Mahony, 26.
33 "Human Nature"/"The Family of Blood," 10th Doctor, Russell T. Davies (New) Series 2005-ongoing.
34 "The Happiness Patrol," 7th Doctor, Classic Series 1963-1989.
35 "The Curse of Fenric," 7th Doctor, Classic Series 1963-1989.

I Am Vengeance, I Am the Night, I Am . . . the Doctor?

Leslie McMurtry

"I am vengeance, I am the night, I am Batman . . ." —Batman in "Nothing to Fear" by Henry T Gilroy /Sean Catherine Derek, *Batman: The Animated Series*

"I'm the Doctor. I'm a Time Lord. I'm from the planet Gallifrey in the Constellation of Kasterborous. I'm 903 years old and I'm the man who is gonna save your lives and all 6 billion people on the planet below." —The 10th Doctor in "Voyage of the Damned," by Russell T. Davies, *Doctor Who*

A venture into the local Forbidden Planet retailer of merchandise from films, TV, and comics reveals that, due to the prevalence of the new series and the popularity of the recent films, respectively, *Doctor Who* and *Batman* are trendy and popular. You can find the Doctor in all kinds of media, including books, magazines, TV, comics, and audio, and Batman in comics, TV, film, and video games. The two properties of phenomenon share 115 years of existence between them, an impressive statistic in the short-term world of pop culture. The key to both *Doctor Who* and *Batman's* longevity is the adaptability of both series, their abilities to rewrite their own mythologies while still using revolving characters and roles, keeping a malleable format with recognizable tenets. While these fictional universes share many qualities, the characters of Batman and the Doctor (especially as written in the new series) show many similarities as well. These include shared characteristics of "cosmic angst," a notion of interminable loneliness, and a purported nonviolent/nonlethal approach. This paper looks at the similarities of the fictional worlds of the *Doctor Who /Batman* franchises, the characters of the Doctor/Batman, and what this might reflect on pop cultural trends.

> *"But when he brushes up against a screen,*
> *We are afraid of what our eyes have seen:*
> *For something is amiss or out of place*
> *When mice with wings can wear a human face."*
> —Theodore Roethke, "The Bat"

If you're reading this book, you're familiar with the story of how *Doctor Who* was brought to British television screens on 23 November 1963. However, it may not follow that you're an expert on all things comic book, so a short introduction to *Batman* now commences. Who created *Batman* and how it was done has been controversial, with Bob Kane receiving the bulk of the credit and Bill Finger and Jerry Robinson also declaring their contributions. In late 1938, Kane was twenty-four years old and asked by National Publications (later DC Comics) to create a hero "as powerful and appealing as Superman."[1] His influences ranged from The Scarlet Pimpernel[2] to the Birdmen in *Flash Gordon*[3] to Zorro and the Shadow, though bats were a common pulp image. Finger claims Batman's alter ego, Bruce Wayne, was his idea: "Bruce Wayne's first name came from Robert Bruce, the Scottish patriot. Bruce, being a playboy, was a man of gentry. I searched for a name that would suggest colonialism. I tried Adams, Hancock... then I thought of Mad Anthony Wayne."[4] Batman made his debut in *Detective Comics* #27 and went to his eponymous title in 1940. Finger continued to write and Kane to draw, with seventeen-year-old student Jerry Robinson brought in to ink panels in the third *Batman* story.[5]

"Just a twinge of cosmic angst..."
—The 5th Doctor in "The Five Doctors" (Terrance Dicks)

In 1963, when William Hartnell played the Doctor for the first time and stepped out of a then-functional police box, *Batman* had been running in comic form for over twenty-five years, already an iconic superhero. The Doctor gave little indication of ever being something similar. But the seeds for similarities were already sown.

Both the Doctor, at least as reimagined by Russell T. Davies in stories from "Rose" onward, and Batman have a direct relationship to cosmic angst that is central to the power and appeal of their characters. Bruce Wayne's past, which has remained largely the same in all of *Batman*'s myriad adaptations and universes, pins the origin of Batman squarely in his childhood. After witnessing the murder of his parents (the philanthropic Waynes) in a back alley in the corrupt Gotham streets, the child Bruce Wayne grows into adulthood seeking vengeance and then justice. The traditional version is that he put himself through the finest academic and fighting schools that money could buy (and as the Wayne fortune was considerable, those were substantial).

To fight crime, though, Bruce eventually realized, he would have to inspire fear. Fear manifested itself to him in the form of a bat, which, depending on the version, flew by his window, broke his window, or swarmed around him. This motivated him to don a cowl and cape and prowl Gotham's streets as its dark avenger. It is also the first indicator in Bruce Wayne's/Batman's existence that his life (and career as a fictional being) would be forever tinged by cosmic angst. Looking forward to an era of psychology rather than ethics and allegory, Batman's origin proved him more complex, fighting crime not "simply because his father told him to or because he was inherently good."[6] Batman's tragic past has primed him to take heroic action; it has also set him apart from other heroes made in his same mold. To be fair, Bob Kane created Batman months before he created a back story for his hero, which was actually co-authored with Bill Finger in December 1939[7]—before then, the two had referred to him as a "bored young socialite."[8] In this, to a degree, Batman shares his character beginnings and their vagueness with the Doctor. Because *Doctor Who* is "made over a long period of time" like *Batman* "by all sorts of different people ... they made it up as they went along."[9] After all, it wasn't until 1969 and "The War Games" that the Doctor's race of Time Lords was even mentioned, and his home planet was not named until 1973's "The Time Warrior." Not until "The Tenth Planet," did we learn the Doctor could regenerate, and we did not even know that term existed until "Planet of the Spiders"!

Though the Doctor mentioned almost from the beginning that he was an outcast amongst his people, "a wanderer in the fourth dimension . . . [an] exile,"[10] the exact nature of what sent the Doctor from Gallifrey was vague at best. When Rose Tyler meets the 9th Doctor, she finds out that he is an alien who can travel in space and time and goes around saving people's lives from other, hostile aliens like the Nestene Consciousness and its plastic-grubbing Autons—in person she finds him energetic, enigmatic, animated, mercurial, and what she is told by Clive clearly shows him to be mysterious. However, it isn't until "The End of the World," that Rose (and the audience, if they are new viewers) finds out the Doctor is a Time Lord—the *last* of the Time Lords:

> The Doctor: My planet's gone. It's dead. It burned like the Earth. It's rocks and dust before its time.
>
> Rose: What happened?
>
> The Doctor: There was a war, and we lost.
>
> Rose: A war with who? . . . What about your people?
>
> The Doctor: I'm a Time Lord. I'm the last of the Time Lords. They're all gone. I'm the only survivor. I'm left traveling on my own because there's no one else.

Always an exile, the post-2005 Doctor now heaps on the survivor's guilt, a trait he shares with Batman. It was unclear at the time of "An Unearthly Child" why the Doctor and his granddaughter Susan were exiles from their home planet and time, but the idea has been noticeably milked for more emotion post-2005, and the Doctor feels a range of emotions about this, none of them particularly comfortable. Rage, loneliness, guilt, despair, nostalgia and a certain coldness are some of the traits the 9th and 10th Doctors exhibit in relation to being the last of the Time Lords.

From such an inauspicious beginning, it's no wonder Bruce Wayne epitomizes the troubled, tortured superhero, which, in turn, has caught the imagination of so many for so long—in a modern age of complicated emotional lives, characters very often must be unsettled to be empathetic. One of the ways this is most clearly manifested is Bruce's inability to form lasting relationships.

Throughout various interpretations, Bruce Wayne/Batman has had short-lived relationships with women from many milieux: society women like Julie Madison, Vicki Vale, and Silver St Cloud, heroines from Batwoman, Wonder Woman to Sasha Bordeaux, and even villains like Catwoman and Talia al Ghul. In fact, it is intriguing that Batman's most long-lived and turbulent on-again, off-again relationship is with Catwoman/Selina Kyle. Part of the inherent problem with Batman's relationships is the risk factor—any emotional attachment could be used to his enemies' advantage. For example, Christopher Nolan's reincarnation of Batman for the noughties[11] in *Batman Begins* and *The Dark Knight* creates the character of Rachel Dawes, an assistant district attorney for Gotham and a childhood friend of Bruce Wayne's. Rachel's disgust with the young Bruce's attempt to take justice into his own hands is part of what spurs him into reform as a justice figure that eventually takes shape as Batman; at the end of *Batman Begins* when a relationship just seems possible, Rachel spurns Bruce's attempts until he has given up his quest. A romance between them is irrevocably negated when Rachel is killed by the Joker in *The Dark Knight*. With such emotional baggage, it's no wonder that Batman might manifest extreme angst.

Though the Doctor's status as extraterrestrial for many years made him more of a friendly or avuncular figure to the show's audience and the Doctor's various companions, recently his (and the show's) thoughts have turned to romance. While it's true the 8th Doctor's kiss in the TV movie was a shocking harbinger of things to come, it wasn't until Rose Tyler's unspoken attraction to the Doctor that the subtext (some would say very-visible-text!) to seasons 1 and 2 of the new series was formed. The Doctor's reciprocation of her affections was sensed but very literally unspoken in "Doomsday"; it remained officially pooh-poohed by him (but not his Meta-Crisis clone) in "Journey's End." The 9th and 10th Doctors' (would be) romances have assured a complexity factor as they have ranged from the tragic (Jabe, Madame de Pompadour) to the unrequited (Martha), all of them hammering home a central message that was elaborated upon in "School Reunion": the Doctor never stays with any of his companions indefinitely. "I don't age. I regenerate. But humans decay. You wither and you die. Imagine watching that happen to someone you … You can spend the rest of your life with me, but I can't spend the rest of mine with you."[12] This has obviously caused much pain on the part of some of the companions left behind (Sarah Jane Smith, for example) but, if we are to believe the Doctor, it's caused him anguish and loneliness, too. According to Christopher Eccleston, "[The Doctor's got] a sadness, that he's got no home … 'I'm lonely, I want somebody to come with me.'"[13] In both "The Runaway Bride" and "The Next Doctor," the 10th Doctor alludes to his loneliness and feeling of loss for companions. Telling Jackson Lake about his companions, he says that they all leave him, "I suppose, in the end, they break my heart" (which is a curious thing to say when he has two hearts!).

There's another way that the Doctor and Batman are social outsiders, and this is their working outside the norms of socio-cultural normality. Batman is considered by many in Gotham to be an undisciplined vigilante and leaves the long arm of the law to Commissioner Gordon and his associates. The Doctor refuses to do paperwork—"The Brigadier wants me to address the Cabinet, have lunch at Downing Street, dinner at the Palace, and write seventeen reports in triplicate. Well, I won't do it. I won't, I won't, I won't! Why should I?"[14] In a broader sense, perhaps both heroes can have the accusation leveled against them that Davros sends to the Doctor in "Journey's End": "The Doctor, the man who keeps on running, never looking back because he dare not, out of shame"— they don't pay enough attention to the consequences of their heroics. Harvey Dent in *The Dark Knight*, having survived when Rachel Dawes, the woman both he and Bruce Wayne love, has died, could level the same charge at Batman and indeed, most of Gotham City spends the timeline of the film trying to understand Batman's motives and the consequences of his actions.

The success of Batman as a brand is down to many factors, but some of the most salient are the character's distinctive look, his angst-ridden backstory (which we've already discussed), and his purported nonviolent approach. It was in 1939 "newly appointed DC editorial director Whit Ellsworth [wanted] to keep the actual violence in Batman stories to a minimum."[15] Early stories in the *Detective Comics* range had Batman using a gun, but executives quickly concluded that too much violence would alienate readers. This conceit that Batman should capture rather than kill criminals and avoid brutal violence whenever possible, seemingly at odds with an action comic, has been one that has stayed with the character consistently since then. It is certainly a directive that has caused narrative tension, sometimes to an almost unbelievable degree. Many of Batman's recurring villains have often mocked this prime directive and have returned to haunt him once they have escaped Arkham Asylum, jail, or other temporary solutions to their problematic, bad-to-the-core psyches.

The Joker marvels at Batman's commitment to nonlethal action in *The Dark Knight:* "You are truly incorruptible, aren't you? You won't kill me out of some misplaced sense of self-righteousness."

Likewise, the Doctor has a longstanding, highly documented nonviolent approach. "Never cruel, never cowardly" is the famous phrase from script editor Terrance Dicks. All of the actors who have played the Doctor and many of the writers have cited this characteristic as one of the Doctor's best qualities; Tom Baker memorably said, "The Doctor doesn't shoot anybody, drink, beat up women, but somehow he has a heroic appeal to children."[16] Batman has his utility belt and the Doctor has his sonic screwdriver, both high-tech solutions for achieving nonlethal results. According to a list compiled in the *Giant Batman Annual* of 1961,[17] the items in the Caped Crusader's utility belt were futuristic at the time of writing but achievable by today's standards, demonstrating a link to real science. No one has yet come up with a sonic screwdriver like the Doctor's (or been bored enough to want to put up a lot of cabinets), but it, too, is an important device, not only in furthering the story, but as a nonviolent means to defeating adversaries. In "Utopia" the Doctor scolds Captain Jack for bringing out a pistol, even to shoot the ravaging Futurekind; "Army of Ghosts," "The Sontaran Stratagem," and "Face of Evil" are just a few examples of when the Doctor is annoyed or enraged at other characters wielding guns.

By contrast, the Doctor has used everything from jelly babies to water pistols to persuade his adversaries to think twice about their evil deeds, but even he must admit to some inconsistencies. The 3rd Doctor famously used his Venusian aikido in hand-to-hand combat, the 5th and 6th Doctors have been known to pick up and wield a gun if not actually shoot someone with it, and a scene in "Seeds of Doom" had the 4th Doctor disarming and kicking down hired goons. In "Mindwarp," the Doctor is accused by the Valeyard of shooting Crozier's beast—"the struggle discharged the gun accidentally!" the Doctor insists, though the courtroom presiding over his trial is not altogether in agreement with him. (While this "evidence" could have been fabricated like much of it was during the Doctor's trial, we assume because of its early use in the story that it was "real.") Like Batman's enemies, the Doctor's serial adversaries also seem to take advantage of his rule against killing. This is explored many times, but perhaps most memorably in "Genesis of the Daleks" where the Doctor has the option of destroying the Daleks for all time. It's an option he doesn't take, making him a nonviolent catalyst for good, but a decision that will continue to plague him. Having been through the Time War, the 9th Doctor can shout in rage at (he thinks) the last surviving Dalek, "Why don't you just die?!" Perhaps what makes both Batman and the Doctor so heroic is that they're aware of the limitations of their nonviolent / nonlethal approach and yet continue because they see it as the morally right way of proceeding.

"The children of time are moving against us . . ."
—Davros in "The Stolen Earth" (Russell T. Davies)

The two heroes are also similar in that, though they stand on their own as characters (as we have discussed, they are characters of solitude and loneliness), they are surrounded by "the gang." Indeed, in most storytelling of a serial kind, it is difficult not to have a gang. It is interesting to note, however, how much the two gangs share in common and how they differ. Batman did not actually pick up a gang until April 1940, when Bob Kane created Robin, the Boy Wonder, reportedly so Batman had someone to talk to and give the comic book readers someone of their own age with whom to identify.[18] Because of the introduction of Robin, the comic's circulation nearly doubled. Robin was swiftly joined by more of Batman's cohorts, many of them short-lived, such as Batwoman, Batgirl (*Prisoners of Three Worlds*, 1963), Batman Jones (*The Career of Batman Jones,* 1957)[19], Nightwing, and Huntress, to name a few. Batman's long-time ally in the Gotham City Police Department, Captain then Commissioner Jim Gordon, has survived in almost every version of *Batman* since, from the Tim Burton films to *Batman: The Animated Series* (*B:TAS),* to the Christopher Nolan films, and throughout the comics into the twenty-first century.

Batman's lack of lasting romantic relationships notwithstanding, the series has a recurring subgenre in femme fatales, many of them supervillains like Catwoman and Poison Ivy but also characters such as Janice Porter in *Dark Victory* and the Sarah Essen presented in *Batman: Year One.* Unlike Superman, who required enemies with incredible powers in order to create compelling stories,[20] most of Batman's supervillains were criminals with a good gimmick. The classic rogues gallery includes such nemeses as the Joker, Catwoman, Two-Face, Mr. Freeze, the Riddler, Poison Ivy,

Ras al Ghul, and the Scarecrow. Their motives range from insanity to greed to revenge to misplaced environmental fanaticism. Not to be underestimated is the role of the ordinary citizen in *Batman*. Shifting the POV from the heroes to the ordinary citizens of Gotham is a device used frequently in post-1999 comics as well as in the Nolan films.

Where the writers of *Batman* originally came up with Robin for the purposes of their solitary hero needing someone to talk to, it is long-held wisdom that the Doctor requires his companions (or assistants) so that he can explain the plot to them. Also both roles (Robin and the companion) provide a place for the viewer (originally children) to have some identification. Batman has had many crime-fighting protégés, but the Doctor has, in forty-six years, had many more companions. Their backgrounds and characteristics have changed considerably over the years, from the alien schoolgirl Susan to the quipping journalist Sarah Jane Smith to the omnisexual buccaneer Captain Jack Harkness. If there is one companion who has lasted the test of time best, it's probably Alistair Gordon Lethbridge-Stewart, originally a Colonel when the Doctor met him in 1968's "The Web of Fear" and since then the famous Brigadier who has been brought out of retirement more than once. Throughout the 1970s he and the 3rd and 4th Doctor worked closely together with UNIT during many of the Earth-bound adventures of the era. However, as UNIT faded into the background with occasional returns, the Brigadier never seemed to stay out of the series for long, appearing in "Mawdryn Undead," "The Five Doctors," "Battlefield," in a 2008 episode of *The Sarah Jane Adventures* ("Enemy of the Bane"), and mentioned in various comics and books and audios up to and after the 2005 TV series. The TARDIS herself could be dismissed as a bit of the Doctor's kit, much like Batman's costume, utility belt, or Batmobile—yet she is more of a character than a mere assemblage of parts, and has followed the Doctor on his adventures since 1963—perhaps his most enduring companion.

By contrast, there are few significant femme fatales (until, perhaps, recently) in *Doctor Who*. Organizations like the Celestial Intervention Agency could possibly mirror the mob in *Batman,* but in general the Doctor's gang is much smaller in type and size than Batman's. In rare cases like "Journey's End," where many of the Doctor's companions and friends are stuffed in the TARDIS, we get to see the Doctor's gang at work in a similar fashion to assemblages of comic book teams or leagues. Though sometimes Batman fights organized groups (gangland warfare was addressed in *No Man's Land,*[21] among others), these are not organized into races or families as much as with the Daleks, Cybermen, and other alien/hybrid races trying to destroy Earth. While in the *Batman* universe there is not much distinction between monsters and villains, most of the

Doctor's adversaries can be split into either category. Recurring villains such as Davros and the Master are flanked by favorite monsters like the Daleks and the Cybermen, who make their way into almost every era of broadcast *Who*.

> *"There have been many companions—but only one me!"*
> —The 6th Doctor in "The Twin Dilemma" (Anthony Steven)

If you feel nothing else between *Doctor Who* and *Batman* is comparable, the series' success must be noted. Their longevity is due certainly to their ability to adapt, and that recipe for adaptation seems to come down to three components: changing the format with the audience, proliferation in media, and a willingness to rewrite its own mythology. *Doctor Who* is a wonderful example of a TV show changing its format in order to continue producing: the departure of William Hartnell and the decision for the Doctor to change body, form, and personality but still be the same (alien) man is still a stunning creative innovation on the part of Innes Lloyd: "an opportunity to tweak the show's format whilst at the same time maintaining the integrity of its fictional universe."[22] This, of course, has enabled the show to run much longer than the producers could then imagine: now to include eleven recognized canon Doctors, and a superb capacity for changing the tone every few years.

While Batman is himself a human (a superhero without the superpowers) and can't regenerate physically the way the Doctor can, the franchise itself is enabled to dip in and out of Batman's timeline. Frank Miller's influential *The Dark Knight Strikes Again* reimagines Batman somewhere in the future, still fighting crime at the age of 50, and nearing the end of his era. Miller also went back to the beginning of Batman in *Batman: Year One,* a tack taken up by Jeph Loeb and Tim Sale in *The Long Halloween* and *Dark Victory.* Without running into huge continuity issues, anyone wishing to write a *Batman* comic could set it anywhere between the two extremes and find ample material.

Doctor Who, of course, began life as a TV show and has, despite the long absence from TV screens (1989-2005, with brief appearances in between), remained a TV show. Almost immediately after its success in 1963 it dispersed into other media: comics, followed by the Target novelizations, then later the Virgin New Adventures range, then the BBC books in 8th Doctor and Past Doctor ranges, and the current range that corresponds to the TV broadcast team. This is not to mention the Big Finish audio stories, which not only detail the exploits of past Doctors but also past companions and all combinations thereof. With the success of the new series, merchandising has mushroomed into every possible corner of the market. From toys, to stationery, calendars, all the way from bubble bath to socks, are an unqualified success and a good spread over media. Meanwhile, Batman began in *Detective Comics* in 1939 and has survived a World War. Like *Doctor Who,* it still manages to thrive in its original format, and there hasn't been a week since 1940 that hasn't seen a new *Batman* comic published.[23] Over the years, *Batman* jumped first from comic to TV screens (the live action 1960s series and the 1992 *Batman: The Animated Series* and further spin-offs) and eventually to films. It is interesting to note that while its presence on comics pages continues undaunted, *Batman* has conquered the film industry, from the 1989 seminal film by Tim Burton, its sequels, the Joel Schumacher films, and the reimaginings by Christopher Nolan—most of these commercial successes.

The real key to both series' adaptability is the willingness of both productions to reinvent, rewrite, and otherwise augment its mythology. This makes an introduction for the new fan to either fandom both accessible and daunting: starting with new *Who* is enjoyable and cheerfully easy but the forty-year mythology looms large, and the cultural iconography of Batman is so ingrained one could start anywhere in *Batman* comics, yet again, backstory might make things confusing. The example of Harley Quinn is one where a character invented in 1992 for *B:TAS* proved so popular she moved from that realm into mainstream comics. A henchwoman of the Joker's, her creators on the TV show further developed her character in the graphic novel *Mad Love* in 1994, which was adapted into an episode for *The New Batman Adventures* (1999). Further live action and animated series appearances followed, and a series of mainstream comics ran from 2001–2003. Concurrent with Harley Quinn in the *Doctor Who* universe is probably the example of Sally Sparrow, who was created by Steven Moffat originally for the 2006 *Doctor Who Annual.* She then became the heroine of his popular episode "Blink."

Though Batman himself is reinvented to an extent with every incarnation, it's his arch-villain the Joker who perhaps has the highest degree of flexibility, managing to remain scary and relevant in each new incarnation while incorporating most of the traits that heralded his introduction in 1940.[24] As each of the Doctors has had his own "look," each artist from every decade since the 1940s has placed his personal stamp on the character. He has gone from an outrageous lunatic funny man with no backstory ("The Joker's Comedy of Errors," 1951) to Cesar Romero's wacky and mostly harmless version from the 1960s TV show to the increasingly more violent version from the mainstream comics and the films, with a brief stop off in a more lighthearted, less brutally violent Joker in *B:TAS,* as voiced by Mark Hamill. His backstory, when it is given, has revolved around an accidental fall into a vat of chemicals that has permanently disfigured him and (probably) driven him insane. However, working within the mythos but creating something relevant for the reenvisioned, ultra-realistic Gotham of *The Dark Knight,* the film's Joker reclaims some of the mystery surrounding the character's backstory. Though the Master, the Doctor's arch-nemesis, has always been portrayed as an evil and rogue Time Lord, he too has been able to regenerate and change facets of his personality. The most recent incarnation, seen in "Sound of Drums" and "Last of the Time Lords," was given a sympathetic backstory by the Doctor, who hints they knew each other as children (though previous audio stories, preceded by David A. McIntee's Missing Adventure *The Dark Path,* were the first to posit this idea).

Nowhere, however, is there a more tangled web in *Doctor Who* continuity (except for the UNIT years!) than in deciding canon for the Daleks. As presented in the second story ever made, "The Daleks," they were once a race of Dals who, unlike their related species the Thals, retreated into metal cities on the planet Skaro and in order to survive radiation, encased themselves in metal symbiotic casing machines. During this process their emotional base was so altered that they only had concern for the propagation of their own species. The 1st Doctor was able to escape from this first meeting with the Daleks only to meet them many more times (as the commercial popularity of the Daleks was almost instantaneous). However, in the story "Genesis of the Daleks," the 4th Doctor on the planet Skaro meets Davros, who apparently creates Daleks from Kaled mutation encased in Mark II Traveling Machines. As Davros proved almost as popular as the Daleks, he appeared many more times throughout the series, lending credence to the rewriting of that particularly continuity.

After mentioning the Daleks, it's impossible not to add the example of the Time War as a huge new development in terms of continuity in the *Doctor Who* universe. Described in "The End of the World," and mentioned in a mysterious way in several stories after that, the show's creators have been deliberately coy about citing concrete information. Certainly before 2005 and Russell T. Davies' tortured, battle-weary 9th Doctor, the Doctor's home planet of Gallifrey has suffered many contradictory fates on paper. Post-Time War, however, it has apparently ceased to exist in any time or place, leaving the Doctor, somehow, as the only survivor of his race (until the Master's return in 2007). The fan response has always been equivocal: wanting to know more about the Doctor's past yet wishing to preserve the enigma that is at the heart of the character. Will the Time War ever be fully explained? If so, there is huge scope for recreating and augmenting the series yet again.

As stated at the very beginning of this essay, Forbidden Planet (and many other retailers) are filled to the brim with *Doctor Who* merchandise and *Batman* merchandise. One good reason for this is the timing is right. In an attempt to look at the series from an objective point of view, Graham Kibble-Smith wrote ". . . But Is It Art?" for *Doctor Who Magazine*, a valiant effort to place the series of *Doctor Who* within the context of the other top shows on British TV at the time.[25] While ultimately it was decided that comparing Pertwee's *Doctor Who* to *Monty Python's Flying Circus,* Patrick Troughton's *Doctor Who* to *Cathy Come Home,* and Tom Baker's *Doctor Who* to *Fawlty Towers* was like comparing apples and oranges, many of the TV critics quoted in the article still held many eras of *Doctor Who* in high regard, as good or better than the "best" TV on British screens at the time. These days, it's much easier to find magazine and newspaper articles lauding the show in general and certain episodes in particular. Similarly, graphic novels and comics have been, in the past five years or so, reclaimed as literature in their own right. Before then, the comic book fan was a stereotype—"for many people fandom carries with it the connotation of mania."[26] However, just as by the noughties fans of *Doctor Who* in the seventies, eighties, and nineties were becoming writers of the show in their own right, "The architect of the so-called "Silver Age" of superhero comic books, Julius Schwartz, began his career as a fan."[27] Put another way, comic books and graphic novels have not only become cool, they've become literature to be appreciated and studied.

Superficially, Batman and the Doctor could not be more different. The Doctor mentions Batman in "Inferno" and a plastic Batmobile is among the ephemera in his pockets in "Talons of Weng Chiang," but one suspects Batman's violent attacks on Gotham City's criminal underclass would send the Doctor into a rage, or at least tongue-clucking disapproval. In the world of Batman as the detective, especially in the truly gritty reimaginings by Frank Miller, Christopher Nolan, and the like, an alien being like the Doctor in his whimsical TARDIS would be laughed at. Batman is clearly a product of his environment: Gotham City has always clearly been identified with New York City, and Batman has often teamed with patriotic superheroes, making him steadfastly American; the Doctor has always been played by a British actor, always manifested an interest in British culture, and rarely visits other countries—a British institution. Yet, the two might find each other remarkably similar if they got to know each other. They are heroes to children whom adults are more than happy to follow, too. Both have the weight of angst driving them on to do their heroics, and both are committed to taking the moral high ground (nonviolent/nonlethal behavior).

Both have difficulty forming lasting relationships, particularly of the romantic variety. Both have approached their long character lives with the backing of a gang, supported by companions and sidekicks, thwarted by recurring villains and monsters. Both *Doctor Who* and *Batman* are superb at altering scope, theme, and origin in order to appeal to new audiences. A recipe for 115 combined years of success, and hopefully much longer than that.

---

1 Simpson, 58.
2 Duncan and Smith , 223.
3 Jones, 149.
4 Scott Beatty, 2008.
5 Jones, 152.
6 Jones, 155.
7 Gresh and Weinberg, 34.
8 Jones, 150.
9 The Watcher, "The Watcher's Guide to the Eighth Doctor," 50.
10 "An Unearthly Child," 1st Doctor, Classic Series 1963-1989.
11 Shorthand for the decade 2000-2009, online entry.
12 "School Reunion," 10th Doctor, Russell T. Davies (New) Series 2005-ongoing.
13 Christopher Eccleston, interview on *Doctor Who Confidential* as part of the Season 1 DVD set.
14 "Robot," 4th Doctor, Classic Series 1963-1989.
15 Gresh and Weinberg, 34.
16 Tom Baker, "I Liked Doctor Who Because It Was Fun, Fun, Fun," http://www.textfiles.com/sf/whob4.txt
17 Gresh and Weinberg, 39.
18 *Ibid.*
19 *Bendis, Kane, and Finger, various.*
20 Gresh and Weinberg, 35.
21 Gresh and Weinberg, 44.
22 Morris, 17.
23 Simpson, 58.
24 Finger, *The Joker: Greatest Stories Ever Told*, various.
25 Kibble-White, 24-33.
26 Duncan and Smith, 173.
27 Duncan and Smith, 171.

Grateful thanks to Jamie Beckwith, Carol Renfro, and Steven Sautter for their help with this essay.

The Professor's Lessons for the Doctor:
The Doctor's Sub-creative Journey Toward Middle-earth

Anthony S. Burdge

Introduction: The Merging of Worlds

In the final episode of the revived *Doctor Who* Series 3, entitled "Last of the Time Lords," the Master states to the Doctor, "Say hello Gandalf; except, he's not that old." The Doctor, captive of the Master, does not reply, only stares out the window while sitting in a wheelchair, his body having been altered by the Master to show his true age. After my post to the Russell T. Davies message board, I was met with arguing members who insisted that this line was nothing more than a pop culture reference bowing to the popularity of the Peter Jackson *Lord of the Rings* films, or homage to Tolkien. Yet the line is coupled with imagery of Gollum and an almost angelic Gandalf the White, both linked to the Doctor himself. By the writers of *Doctor Who* incorporating Gandalf and the related *Lord of the Rings* imagery into this episode, there now exists a connection between Tolkien's epic tales of Middle-earth to the equally immense, mythological framework of the *Doctor Who* universe. Both *Who* and Tolkien have enormous, comparable followings, and it makes perfect sense for past and current *Who* writers to draw upon Tolkien's work as they have with other mythological cycles. It also shows that like Gandalf, the Doctor has had other names. It is not therefore beyond the scope of reason if we look back at Classic and New *Who* stories and reflect how the Doctor has interacted with "fictional" characters alongside historical and mythological elements from our "primary" world.

Most readers know the character of Gandalf primarily from J.R.R. Tolkien's own ring cycle, *The Lord of the Rings (LotR)*. Further reading of the *LotR* reveals that Gandalf has had a different name for each of the races of Arda he interacted with,[1] Tharkun, Olorin, and Mithrandir, to name a few.

Beyond the stories, Tolkien's letters and essays, as well as the critical analysis surrounding his work all expose Tolkien's very particular methodology of creating a believable secondary world for humanity to explore.[2] The landscape of Middle-earth, and the world of Arda in which it exists, is contained in numerous other volumes beyond *LotR* that Tolkien created. The writers of *Doctor Who* in their own process[3] are not as overtly concerned as Tolkien was with how creative writing could be a divine process, which may be due to the use of different media within which the *Doctor Who* team writes. Tolkien, unlike Davies, didn't have concerns about special effects, costume costs, or television production budgets.[4] What is evident, and more readily important in discussion of the *Doctor Who* universe and world-building within it, is that the writers of *Doctor Who* have made for us, the observer, a fully believable world in which we are absorbed and emotionally invested.

Readers have been equally invested emotionally in the land of Middle-earth and have felt as if they are no longer a part of the primary world or what humanity knows as mundane reality, thereby creating an alternate reality. By acknowledging Middle-earth as a part of a world to traverse, as envisioned, constructed, and manifested upon the page by Tolkien, with its own landscape, people, history, and mythology, it is entirely possible for the Doctor, a being of supernatural ability, great age, and a personal story well beyond what we know, to have visited it. Tolkien often spoke of these methods of secondary creation as that of sub-creation (a term coined in his essay *On Fairy-Stories*).

Sub-creation refers to the act of poet, artist, and creative being using the methods of the Creator in the act of creation. Tolkien was the sole creator of the world of Arda, its people, landscapes, and events. According to Diana Pavlac Glyer in her work, *The Company They Keep: C.S. Lewis and J.R.R. Tolkien as Writers in Community*, Tolkien stated that his plan was to "leave scope for other minds and hands wielding paint, and music, and drama emphasizing that each individual creative act is a participation in something large, complex and beautiful, as party to a creative continuity."[5] The mythology of *Doctor Who* has built into it the continuation, evolution, and longevity of the character's mythical qualities through his regenerative process. I have to agree with Lou Anders, when he states: "*Doctor Who* is the truest expression of Joseph Campbell's *Hero with a Thousand Faces* ever conceived. The idea of an alien, come down to earth, repeatedly dying and resurrecting for the salvation of others is as close to the perpetual reenactment of the eternal Hero's Journey as you can hope to find."[6] There has also been abundant scholarship written applying Joseph Campbell's analysis of the Hero's Journey to Tolkien's characters such as Frodo, Gandalf, and Aragorn.

Yet, as Anders points out in *The Discontinuity Guide*, "since no one single person built the ship or manned the tiller as [the *Doctor Who* series] voyaged across three decades , *Doctor Who* tended to stray all over the map. Its *continuity*, the agreed upon collective mythology of consistent details that paint the reality of a fictional world, is a hodgepodge of factoids, histories and asides that are often inconsistent, illogical and flat-out contradictory.[7] Tolkien's work is not entirely free of this either, for as Verlyn Flieger warns us, "the published *Silmarillion* gives a misleading impression of coherence and finality, as if it were a canonical text, whereas the mass of material from which that volume was taken is a jumble of overlapping and often competing stories, annals, and lexicons."[8] But *Doctor Who* was born in a day, eight years after *LotR* was published, when story mattered more and special effects less.[9] The reader and viewer then digest and interpret the world of Tolkien and *Doctor Who* subjectively, as brilliantly discussed, in particular regard to *Doctor Who* exclusively, by Colin Harvey in this present volume.

The process of Tolkien's methodology is his own subjective experience, which his readers then collectively experience through his letters and literature. Every student of Tolkien's work can adapt their own creative structure from his literary and linguistic techniques. For my purposes, this essay will examine Tolkien's "sub-creative" methodology of world-building, supplemented by thoughts from Russell T. Davies on writing for the revived *Doctor Who* program. To speak of all writers of *Doctor Who* would be a worthy investigation but for the course of this chapter it is only necessary to focus on Davies, because it is from a line from his 2005 revived *Doctor Who* program that this paper was first spun. Additionally, this framework of thought will in turn illuminate how characters such as The Celestial Toymaker (via the 1st Doctor televised serial of the same name, and subsequent encounters in the book series) and The Master of the Land of Fiction in "The Mind Robber" create "fictional" realities to challenge the Doctor.

Therefore, Tolkien's universal process becomes evidently applicable to non-humans. The discussion will also highlight the Doctor as Merlin, as shown in the 7th Doctor's story "Battlefield" and his eventual 10th incarnation, alongside Martha Jones and Shakespeare, battling witchcraft-wielding Carrionites, who may have been the inspiration for the witches in Macbeth, in the context of "The Shakespeare Code." Each case will give evidence to the concluding discussion whether the Doctor could have indeed been Gandalf.

Considering J.R.R. Tolkien, Russell T. Davies, and Sub-creation

Does Tolkien need a lengthy introduction? Modern audiences know him for *The Hobbit, The Lord of the Rings*, and *The Silmarillion,* plus his other volumes concerning the Middle-earth *legendarium*, which were published posthumously by his son Christopher. Of particular note for our current discourse is his 1947 essay, based on his March 8, 1939 presentation, delivered at the University of St. Andrews, *On Fairy-Stories (OFS)*. Tolkien's main thrust of the essay considered that for fantasy to be true, the sub-creator's intent must be to manifest a believable secondary world consistent with the mechanics of the primary world. Throughout *OFS*, Tolkien attributes aspects of his own faith and idea of the Singular divine light, or Creator, to the sub-creative process, where Man, Sub-Creator, is refracted or splintered from that whole.[10]

Tolkien's illustrative metaphor, seen through the lens of his faith, begins to chain together the sub-creative act to the fantastic. In this, it is hinted that the experience of sub-creation, through a connection with divinity, is fantastical in its expression of strange and wondrous notions.[11] Further reading suggests Tolkien's need to categorize the forms of the sub-creative act, which now becomes fantasy, or that of Faërie.[12] The fantasy here is formed through an attachment to humanity's realization, and awareness of internally subjective tools. For Tolkien, fantasy is a subjective human right, as shown in his later contribution, an essay discussing *Smith of Wootton Major* asserting the operation of fantasy and Faërie as a necessary part of human life:[13] "...health and complete functioning of the human as is sunlight for physical life: sunlight as distinguished from the soil, say, though it in fact permeates and modifies even that."[14] For Tolkien's detractors, his "fantasy" has been called escapist in more the derogatory sense than its function for humanity, which also has been the case for Davies who feels associating escapism with fiction and writing is condescending.[15] The modes both Tolkien and Davies write in are not entirely dissimilar as they are both writing as a way of engaging with the world.[16] On one hand, the essential power of fantasy is the control to make a world immediately effective through the sub-creator's intent of the will. The "magic" of the world is not an end in itself; its operations are its virtue, among which are the satisfaction of certain primordial human desires, the survey of the depths of space and time, and closely held association with other living things.[17] The sub-creative, fantastical process, Tolkien argues, is an entry into Faërie, the Perilous Realm, which is the essence of fantasy. Fantasy does not exclude Gallifreyan Time Lords, whose own *Grimm Reality*[18] has indeed shown that the Doctor has journeyed into, and is not completely unfamiliar with, Faërie. Tolkien had a complete grasp of how humans relate with each other and our inherent tie to the landscapes we live within, which Davies cites, with regard to his own process, is a demonstration of good writing. Basically, good writing is having a fundamental understanding of psychology, not in a degree sort of way, nor a purely academic sense, but in a realistic, human perspective.[19] The world of Arda began life as a repository for Tolkien's own linguistic explorations. At the heart of Tolkien's love of story is his equal if not higher love of language. Linguistic patterns affected him emotionally, like color or music.[20] Davies' process is quite similar in the crafting of words to present the world he creates and explores.

Yet, is the world presented on the pages of Tolkien, or in an episode of *Doctor Who,* a fiction? The term fiction for most implies fake, which both Tolkien's work and the worlds of *Doctor Who* have been labeled. For Davies, the very word "fiction" implies another world, literally a different place.[21] By considering this and the Tolkienian methodology discussed, these worlds then must be tangible places, parallel to and within our primary world, which likewise suggests that hobbits, wizards, Time Lords, Gandalf, and the Doctor exist as we do, and it is up to readers and viewers to access these tangible worlds via the creative, imaginative mind. By placing his tales as a history prior to our own, Tolkien's sub-creation becomes manifest within the chronological timeline of the primary world. The Doctor who travels freely to the past, present, and future Earth, can then easily access the Ages of Middle-earth. The timeline Tolkien presents for Middle-earth is separated into Ages, each a history set in an older period of our planet. If each sub-created story keys certain emotional levels, allows us to feel and care for the characters, then are these worlds any less real than you are? Tolkien and Davies have provided the necessary means for humanity to realize their potential as mythmakers, which is why the terms of sub-creation set a foundation that awakens and crystallizes our experiences through the fantastical process.

Fantasy can, of course, be carried to excess or madness, deluding the minds out of which it came.[22] What happens when the ability to create a world, whether by human or non-human entity, is taken to extremes to the detriment of others?

Fantasy Gone Mad: The Celestial Toymaker

In April of 1966, "The Celestial Toymaker" aired, starring William Hartnell as the 1st Doctor. It was the ambition of the late *Doctor Who* producer John Wiles to create a story that would exploit the miraculous in the Universe in which the TARDIS would come to a halt right up against a gigantic face, the very face of God.[23]

The intent of the writers of the program was to place the protagonists, and the TARDIS, against completely unusual backgrounds, with the challenge of plunging them into a completely different environment outside the "known" universe. Unfortunately, much of what is left of the original broadcast "The Celestial Toymaker," written by Brian Hayles and Donald Tosh, are reconstructed stills with the original audio and amongst the 'lost' episodes of the Classic series. But, was the Toymaker a god? He is the first of many beings with god-like forces at his command to menace the Doctor, which are of importance to this discussion as are the Toymaker's abilities to create alternate realities.

The role of the Toymaker is said to be the Guardian of Dreams, one of the six Guardians, as related to the six pieces of the Key to Time, which have been depicted in Gary Russell's 1999 novel *Divided Loyalties*. Preceding the Russell tale was *The Nightmare Fair (1989)* by former series producer Graham Williams. In *The Nightmare Fair* we find a Toymaker who took to games as a distraction from being the destroyer of the worlds he had come to create, essentially throwing off any "pretense of purpose and meaning."[24] In the opinion of Tat Wood and Lawrence Miles, "to the Victorian mind, 'Celestial,' was a euphemism for 'Chinese,' often with connotations of drug use." This notion may only be applicable when studying the origin of the Toymaker's Tri-logic game,[25] or his choice of dress. The term, and definition of "Celestial," with greater applicability to the Toymaker, is in relation to the visible heavens, sky, or of realms of divinity. A definition such as this is explored and illuminated in the Davis novel, which adds more foundation to the character's name through the detail of his study:

> ...The Toymaker's study appeared at first like a room. Then, as you became accustomed to its dimensions, you realized that instead of a roof there was a black immensity of outer space and the twinkling stars of the galaxies. The walls stretched up towards the blackness until they became indistinguishable from space and merged with it.[26]

The Toymaker's realm is outside what the Doctor knows as normal time and space. In the Williams treatment, we are told that the Toymaker carries his own matter with him, which has allowed him to create and destroy worlds and give life to his testing ground known as the Toyroom. The TARDIS, and its crew, have been drawn to the Toyroom, and their "safety barrier" has been penetrated by a "great power" according to the Doctor, which alludes to an ability of the Toymaker's to reach beyond his realm. In speaking of the Toymaker's realm, the Doctor tells Steven and Dodo:

> "We are in the world of the Celestial Toymaker... He has created a universe entirely in his own vision, where he manipulates people and turns them into his playthings. He gains control of your mind

through these screens. Be careful; it's a trap."[27]

The toys, as seen in his study, and later the dolls present at the various games Steven and Dodo must play, may indeed be those who have become trapped within the Toymaker's realm after losing to his games. Some of the participants within the games are constructs of the Toymaker, yet some like the King, Queen, and Joker, appear to be in the same position as the Doctor, Steven, and Dodo—there to challenge yet find their way out as well. Yet, to whose time is the author referring?

If Steven and Dodo allowed themselves to believe what they are subjected to, then the projections on the screen and the varied elements become a manifested reality for them, which would further solidify them into the universe of the Toymaker. This is clarified when the Doctor warns Steven, "He is trying to get us in his power and make us a permanent fixture in his universe."[28] But the argument of belief versus sentience of the dolls and beings in the Toymaker's realm is explored in the argument between Steven and Dodo:

"I wonder if we'll ever see the sergeant and the cook again," said Dodo.

Steven shook his head in disbelief. "You still believe in these creations of the Toymaker, don't you?" he said. "You can't see that they are just phantoms – things created in his mind."[29]

Once Steven and Dodo leave from the company of the Sergeant and the Cook, they are not aware that the Toymaker appears and speaks to the Sergeant and the Cook, which indicates to the reader that Steven and Dodo are trapped there just as the others are. They are just as trapped as dolls within the Toyroom but still have a chance to win their freedom, yet must first succeed at the task set before them.[30]

A moment's reflection upon the Doctor's analysis allows the audience in on the fact that the Toymaker is the ruler of a separate universe of entirely his own devising and only his rules apply. The universe of the Toymaker responds only to his voice, but once the Toymaker is engaged in a challenge of games with his opponents—in this instance the Doctor, Steven, and Dodo—he is then bound by the rules of the test. Does the Toymaker, out of ego, arrogance, or assumption bind himself to the rules as he believes he will not lose? Or, once the realm, like the Toyroom, is created by him, is he bound by its rules? Or is it the nature of the realm that lures him in so that he is unable to break the rules once the game is engaged? In the end of the serial, the Toyroom is destroyed when the Doctor outwits the Toymaker by mimicking the Toymaker's voice in order to make the last move of the trilogic game from within the TARDIS. This had to be done in order for the TARDIS to dematerialize at the same time the realm was destroyed so players were not drawn into the destruction. The Toymaker and the Doctor have met previously as the opening of the 1st Doctor story indicates, and is expanded upon in *Divided Loyalties*. With the ability to create and destroy worlds, to affect, limit, or change the nature of a player in his games (i.e., control of the Doctor's voice and appearance) the Toymaker is of limitless power.

What we know of the Toymaker in the 1st Doctor's encounter, the televised serial, is further clarified by the 6th Doctor in *The Nightmare Fair*: "You're not from this Universe," he repeated, "that's why there's no trace. That's why the Laws of this Universe don't concern you. You're from another Time and Space!"[31] In reviewing the Toymaker's ability to create and destroy worlds through his celestial abilities we can see that he would then qualify under the framework of Tolkien's sub-creator methodology, allowing him to be within Davies' own definition of fiction. The example of the Toymaker illustrates that there are beings encountered by the Doctor who are able to create a "fictional" world, which means that such worlds are manifested constructs, secondary worlds, that corporeal beings like the Doctor and his companions are able to interact with. What happens when the beings within the realm are known characters from literature?

"...in a place where nothing is impossible": Exploring the Land of Fiction

"The Mind Robber," a five-part serial, was the only *Doctor Who* story written by Peter Ling. Ling later published *The Mind Robber* a 1986 novel, through Target Books. In writing the story, Ling was told not to think of traditional sci-fi and the result became a world where fictitious characters and mythical creatures traverse the same landscape, though are not entirely aware of one another. "The Mind Robber" story arc has been cited as being "clever and original," and "enjoyable fantasy," or perhaps the result of a stoned, hallucinogenic trip.[32] Ling's story veered from the usual format of invasion stories and into an exploration of The Land of Fiction, as it has come to be known by the Doctor and his companions. At the end of the previous story, "The Dominators," the TARDIS and crew were faced with having to escape from a volcanic eruption. "The Mind Robber" opens with the Doctor, faced with the TARDIS' imminent destruction, who reluctantly presses an emergency button that takes the TARDIS out of his time and space dimensional reality into an unknown, unexplored domain. "We are nowhere," states the Doctor. There are a few notable elemental similarities to "The Celestial Toymaker"; "The Mind Robber" appears to take those ideas and flesh them out more.

When the TARDIS lands in the Toyroom, Steven and Dodo, upon exiting momentarily each view different things they both are emotionally invested in, on the Toymaker's "memory window," which the Doctor warns them not to get trapped by. Similarly, Zoe and Jamie, in "The Mind Robber," view their individual homelands from within the TARDIS on its scanner. This causes Zoe to rush out of the TARDIS to explore, Jamie chasing after her. Outside the TARDIS they both end up in a white, misty, nothingness inhabited by white robots. In accordance to the rules of the realm, whether it is the Land of Fiction or the Toyroom, both stories parallel one another in the similarity of the companions' struggle with the amount of belief they invest in the reality of the inhabitants of these realms, which are either toys or literary creations. The Doctor's encounter with the Toymaker in the Hartnell episode failed to truly explore a battle of the mind and wits as I had hoped to see. Instead, I believe the Troughton/Ling treatment is a better fulfillment of those expectations.

The Master of the Land of Fiction (not to be confused with The Master as portrayed by Roger Delgado, Anthony Ainley, or John Simm, to name a few) seeks to test Jamie, Zoe, and the Doctor throughout their journey in his realm. They encounter Gulliver, a Minotaur, Medusa, Rapunzel, toy soldiers, white robots, and a comic book hero named Karkus.

The Land not only gives life to fictional, mythical characters; it also has the power to manifest the imaginative faculties of those who become trapped within it: for example, Jamie, wishing he had a rope with which to climb, sees Rapunzel's long braid as it appears. The forest where the Doctor seeks Zoe and Jamie is made up of tall trees that are actually letters, which, upon climbing to the top, Jamie finds that they comprise a long series of phrases. Ultimately the Master seeks to find his replacement in the Doctor, which is hinted at by the title of this particular story. This is accomplished by testing the strength of his mental faculties in believing what is real or what is not. The Master is revealed to have been from the Earth year 1926. He was a writer of fiction, has been trapped by and hooked up to the Master Brain, where his imaginative faculties were used with the goal of ultimately overpowering all of humanity.

In the later *Doctor Who* New Adventure novel, *Conundrum*, it is revealed that the Gods of Ragnarök[33] created the Land of Fiction and later abandoned it. The Master is needed by the Master Brain in order to keep the characters alive, which is part of the law of the participant and reader.[34] The Master, as a writer, who imagines and writes into "reality" the events and characters within the Land of Fiction, is essentially a sub-creator, in very much the Tolkien sense. It is in this mode, sub-creators manifesting their imaginative constructs, tied into the Master Brain, that the Doctor and the Master have their final battle.

There has been much analysis as to whether this entire episode is a dreamscape because "The Invasion" opens with the Doctor in the same position and the same chair he had occupied before his mind was first invaded in "The Mind Robber." I agree that all of these events indeed do take place in a realm not of our tangible mundane reality (as most may believe is the only reality), but on a level of worlds accessed via the mind and not necessarily the body. When we read, for instance, *The Lord of the Rings,* or view an episode of *Doctor Who,* we are participants supporting in the belief, consciously or unconsciously, of sub-created worlds by becoming emotionally and mentally absorbed into them. These worlds in particular contain mechanics and aspects of the primary world. When the Doctor and the Master call upon the variety of characters to do battle, they are seeking to force the belief of one reality over another through the amplification of their own individual mind with the Master Brain. It can now be said that aside from the realm of the Toyroom, which the Doctor can interact with, he to some degree creates fictional characters and events, which are the product of an Earth-bound writer.

Overall, I do agree with the observations of Ken Deep and Louis Trapani[35] that "The Mind Robber" has the ability to introduce to children, through fictional characters like Gulliver, children to a variety of stories they may not have previously known. While Whovians may have more enjoyment from stories of invasion, Gallifreyan political dramas, mythological treatments like "Underworld" and "The Horns of Nimon," or pure science fiction. But this trip through the proverbial rabbit hole greatly adds to the Doctor, and TARDIS', ability to cross the dimensional barriers of time and space. If a writer has the intent, such as Tolkien and the Master, whether by self will or dominance of an outside intelligence, to create a secondary world with words then would such a creation be imprinted upon the fabric of time itself?

The Craft of Ancient Harm, Time Approaches for Our Charm

The use of words to produce a desired result has been used to create worlds, as seen in the previous discussion, but they have also been used in charm and ritual to open a portal for alien invasion as seen with the Carrionites, the antagonists of "The Shakespeare Code." The story, written by Gareth Roberts, takes place in sixteenth century London, where the Doctor and Martha meet the Bard himself, William Shakespeare. Practitioners of a word-based science, the Carrionites must meticulously combine words, phrases, and setting into a mathematical, technological word craft, what the Doctor refers to as old magic. Unfortunately Roberts did not avoid the rather tired and even offensive[36] stereotypical use of witches, or the parallel of witches and carrion in the very name of his alien species.[37] The Carrionites' word science, with their use of poppets[38] and cauldrons, is thought of as witchcraft, which suggests that witchcraft, as it is known in our world, is the science of an ancient species of space-faring creatures. As noted in *Doctor Who Magazine #382,* the Carrionites, or witches, hearken to the inspiration for the witches in *Macbeth.* This is a science not entirely unfamiliar to esoteric practitioners of ritual magick, rune singers, shamanic healers, and other ritualized spiritual beliefs.

The power of the word, whether the intent is for good or ill, can produce a desired result if the energy and focus is precise. The tantamount charm for the Carrionites spoken in the Globe Theater by the Shakespearean players will release the remaining imprisoned Carrionites from the Deep Darkness. Similar to the events of "The Mind Robber," the Master brought to life via his imagination and writing mythical and fictional characters, whereas the Carrionites are able to also produce a manifested, tangible effect through the use of words, albeit temporarily: the release of their race. In addition to the Doctor actually mentioning the 7th book of Rowling's Harry Potter series, an extra highlight for Harry Potter fans, was a triumphant "Expelliarmus! Good ol' J.K." Fans familiar with Hogwarts School of Witchcraft and Wizardry would be proud that this spell, another crossing of worlds if you will, helped to destabilize the Carrionites' desired tangible outcome and ultimately confine the entire Carrionite race to the Deep Darkness.

As shown in the previous example of "The Mind Robber," this is not the Doctor's first experience with words utilized in a manner where a corporeal effect is preferred. The Carrionites sought not to create a fully functional world such as the Master or the Toymaker had, but they are sub-creators nonetheless since a formulaic use of words is their tool. Whether magic is an alien science or an occult, esoteric practice, the 10th Doctor is not entirely unfamiliar with conjuration and sorcery since he has encountered spell casting as a form of power before. For example, previous Doctors such as the 3rd and 4th encountered spellcraft in stories such as "The Daemons" and "The Image of the Fendahl."

Sideways in Time: The Many Faces of the Doctor

At the top of this discussion we noted two occasions when the TARDIS was lured outside time and space, the first being the 1st Doctor's trip to the Toyroom, the realm of the Celestial Toymaker, and the second being the 2nd Doctor's travels "sideways in time," to the Land of Fiction. Between the 10th Doctor's Shakespearean excursion and the Land of Fiction was the 7th Doctor's Arthurian exploits in the four-part story arc, "Battlefield." In "Battlefield," the Doctor receives a signal, directed at Merlin specifically, from "sideways in time," a parallel dimension, which he explains to Ace: the TARDIS travels forward, backward, and occasionally from one universe to another. This is the first of clues that the course of the tale will not be very linear. In examining "Battlefield" and seeking to unravel the very involved storyline, I found that a 10th Doctor term seems applicable here: "wibbly-wobbly, timey-wimey." The critique of Tat Wood and Lawrence Miles regarding "Battlefield"—"Oh, well it was worth a try"[39]—does a disservice to this wonderful facet, an evolution of the character of the Doctor. Miles and Wood's critique sounds tired and overdrawn as their analysis tends to focus more on fault of the story than its charm and fun. A preferred and prophetic statement by the authors of *The Discontinuity Guide* is applicable here: "The Doctor has always been Merlin, symbolically speaking, so it's good to know that he finally gets to play the part."[40] This heartwarming sentiment illustrates not only Cornell, Topping, and Day's shared love for "Battlefield," but also the dimensional implications of the Doctor's mythos..

The Doctor states, "Well, if my hunch is right, the Earth could be at the center of a war that doesn't even belong to this dimension!" And, nothing could be truer. By ritual and incantation, Mordred and Morgaine rip open the fabric of space and time, allowing armies of good and evil knights from another dimension to continue their battle on Earth. When the revived Ancelyn, a knight who fell out of the sky in a very Python-esque moment, calls the Doctor "Merlin," Ancelyn cites knowledge from evidence of the Doctor's mannerisms. Ancelyn acknowledges that the Doctor, or Merlin, possesses many faces and many names. Ancelyn's knowledge may stem from the future Doctor having imparted secrets of his regenerative process or a reference to Merlin having changed guises to Britaelis in the service of Uther Pendragon.[41]

As the Doctor and Ace leave, the Doctor tells Ace that he has not previously met Ancelyn or Mordred. These points are later elaborated upon when Ace asks the Doctor, when they are entering a chamber within the underwater spacecraft, if he is indeed Merlin. The Doctor's immediate answer is, "No, but I could be," adding that the claims of Ancelyn and Mordred are of his future self, which are events from his future, or even his personal past. According to Morgaine, Merlin had been trapped in an ice cave, but Morgaine is told that as a master of time Merlin is not bound so easily. Depending upon the literature sourced for Merlin, he is either trapped within a tree or an ice cave by Morgaine, Morgan Le

Fey or Viviane, Nimue or any number of other magical fey women in the Arthurian legendarium. Immediately, for those who know the T.H. White and Disney-fied *Sword in the Stone* versions of the Arthurian tale, the character of Merlin lives backward in time. The unfolding evidence and revelation of the Doctor as Merlin also works backward in time as well.

Morgaine using energy bolts to disable helicopters, magical rituals opening and joining dimensions, and the Doctor, showing knowledge of these acts and warning Ace that they should worry about sorcery, stem from the work of T.H. White and Disney versions that depict Merlin as a wizard. Prior to White, we have Tennyson, quoted by the archeologist Warmsly, and further back *Le Morte D'Artur* by Sir Thomas Malory, which was the primary source for White and Tennyson. Though the comic book Camelot 3000 inspired the futuristic beam weapons, an intercepted energy burst, and nuclear weapons for "Battlefield," the Arthurian material is primarily drawn from Tennyson (nineteenth century), Malory (fifteenth century) and Geoffrey of Monmouth (twelfth century). In the Platt *Battlefield*[42] novel, it is Malory's text that the Doctor arms himself with prior to the TARDIS materializing.

"It's all a matter of timing," the Doctor exclaims to Ace, referring to her finding the silver bullets and the trap that shuts them both in the tunnel where the Doctor has the foresight of both events. These are gifts of prophecy and dreaming better related to Merlin as depicted in the *History of the Kings of Britain* by Geoffrey of Monmouth. For instance, the green, ecto-plasmic dragons that the 7th Doctor encounters can be sourced to Monmouth's chapter detailing the "Prophecies of Merlin."[43] One of his prophecies spoke of two dragons, one Red and one White. The dragons lay sleeping below a pool that he had ordered to be drained while he denounced the lies of Vortigern's magicians.[44] The dragons also are seen in other references as fighting each other beneath the stones of a castle, or streaming in the air sending prophecy to Arthur prior to his kingship

I am of the opinion that the 7th Doctor does begin to display Merlin-esque qualities, recollection of future knowledge and events, when Morgaine communicates with him telepathically, though it is a future Doctor incarnation that is actually, or implied to be, Merlin. The mental prowess of the Doctor has long been established since the 2nd Doctor and the Cartmel "Dark Doctor" plan beginning in Series 25. It is in "Battlefield" that the Doctor makes varied use of his mental powers, such as the suggestion for Warmsly and his friend to stay behind at the bar. The Doctor's evolving gifts of prophecy and mental prowess continue to bring awareness to the actions of his future self. In using these abilities he is able to manifest subtle actions he predicts his future self would do based on the surrounding events, such as the voice pattern recognition key and the runes that signify the entrance to the tunnel. "Dig Hole Here," is how the Doctor translates the Norse runes, but the runes are an odd choice as they are not found, nor were used, in Wales or Cornwall, a critique overlooked by Miles and Wood.

The abilities of the mind are not entirely unknown to the 4th Doctor as we have seen in "Terror of the Zygons" where he conducts a "spell" taught to him by a Tibetan monk when he hypnotizes Sarah Jane. Yet, we know that the powers of telepathy were taught to the Doctor by his mentor Borusa. The knights of "Battlefield" reference the "mighty arts" of Merlin and Morgaine, and these arts were used by Merlin to cast down Morgaine at Baden. The use of spells, conjuration, and magic the 7th Doctor attributes to Clarke's Law; any advanced form of technology is indistinguishable from magic.[45] The Doctor also tells Ace that the reverse can also be true, which loosely preserves his notion that magic doesn't exist. The era of the 10th Doctor demonstrates more Spock-like mental powers and still maintains the questionable attitude toward the Carrionites' word science as magic found in "Shakespeare." When the 10th Doctor uses these abilities he seeks to heal, read, or wipe a mind, which unfortunately becomes the fate of Donna Noble.

The role Merlin has played throughout history and literature has evolved, whether as a seer, prophetic dreamer, wizard, conjurer, magician, or mentalist. The Doctor has had a few of these attributes, prior to and after his association with the guise of Merlin. With regard to the thesis of the Doctor and fictional characters (outside of the assumption of Merlin's historical implications) we can see a further elaboration upon this point in "Battlefield." Aaronovitch's version of Merlin is drawn together from numerous narrative threads into a unique version that embodies all of the previous powers and abilities. Similarly, these elements characteristic of wizards and the mechanics of mentally constructed landscapes can set coordinates for Middle-earth.

Becoming Mithrandir: Where the Doctor Meets the Professor

This discussion sought to demonstrate several points from two intertwining perspectives. First, the mechanics of sub-creation were examined from the Tolkien and Davies methodologies of world building. The focus was then shifted toward world builders within the *Doctor Who* Universe and the use of word crafting fictional elements, of which the Toymaker, the Master, and Carrionites were examples. These mechanics, events, characters, and landscapes are all imagined, mentally constructed worlds made tangible for the Doctor to interact with. Therefore, we have sub-creation within our primary world, as well as secondary worlds of *Doctor Who.*

The proverbial door is opened for a Middle-earth/or Whovian crossover when the Master (the renegade Time Lord, not the one from the Land of Fiction) states: "Say Hello Gandalf, except he's is not that old." The implication of this statement is two-fold. First, the latter part, "except he is not that old," indicates, equates, and places Gandalf within time and space—but clarifies the Doctor is not as old as Gandalf, which does not deny the existence of Gandalf within the *Doctor Who* Universe. The acceptance of the age of Gandalf via the Master may be true as Tolkien's archaic world of Middle-earth is said to come from an ancient document, the Red Book of Westmarch recorded by Bilbo and passed down to Frodo, and the events depicted within are prior to the primary world's known recorded history. Yet, how would the Master know for sure whether the Doctor indeed visited Middle-earth? Gallifrey is gone, so there are no current records of the Doctor's whereabouts.

The use of sub-creation within the Doctor Who Universe, where antagonists willingly create realms and worlds within or outside known time and space, or are able to manifest already established literary characters, illustrates the potential for the Doctor to visit Middle-earth. In the case of "Battlefield," the Doctor is paralleled with and established as having been, or going to be, Merlin. Regardless of the Doctor's opinion of magic and sorcery, the conduction of energy for a desired result (magic), in addition to having divine or otherworldly prowess, being a kingly advisor, as well as guide of a fellowship are all elements also attributed to Gandalf. The origin of the name of Tolkien's wandering wizard is from the Old Norse *Gandalfr* incorporating the words *gandr* meaning both "wand" and (particularly in compounding words) "magic" and *alfr* meaning "elf" or in a wider sense "mythological being." Hence *Gandalf* means roughly "magic–elf/being," or wizard.[46] For those unfamiliar with Tolkien's epic, Gandalf is an Istar, a member of the Istari, or, Heren Istarion[47], translated as "Order of Wizards," who have the same outward appearance as Men, but possess greater mental and physical powers. Tolkien refers to Gandalf in a 1954 letter as an angel incarnate, but his earthly guise limits his powers.[48]

The naming of the Doctor as Gandalf foreshadows events to come within the episode. The placement of Tolkien's tales within the context of the history of the primary world can be seen by the anglicized term Middle-earth, which originates with the Old Norse word *miðgarðr,* later translated from the Old English form *middangeard.* This refers to a time prior to modern history, middle or early history prior to recorded history.

Therefore, it is not a far stretch, accepting of course that Tolkien's ring cycle and events of Middle-earth are a historical series of events from an ancient time on our planet, which then makes the old cliché, history repeats itself, abundantly clear and applicable within the context of "Journey's End."

The Doctor is aged and imprisoned by the Master upon his airship, the commandeered Valiant, not dissimilar to the heights of the Tower of Orthanc, the home of Saruman where Gandalf had been trapped. The Doctor takes advantage of the Archangel Network, a matrix of psychic energy created by the Master, and has Martha travel the world telling the Doctor's story.[49]

After Gandalf's escape and eventual fall in Moria during battle with a Balrog we do not see him again until his return in *The Two Towers,* resurrected by his own Maian (Tolkien's term for "lesser" angels) regenerative abilities, and assistance from the elves.

Upon entering the wooded realm of Fangorn, the Elf, Man, and Dwarf spot an old man who has been tracking their movements. He confronts the trio of Aragorn, Legolas and Gimli, apparently aware of their mission to find Merry and Pippin. When the old man's grey rags are thrown off his gleaming white robes shine with an otherworldly radiance. The 2002 film version of *The Two Towers* illustrates where each of the three hunters, as they become known, are blinded by Gandalf's radiance as Gandalf the White. With a wave of his staff he is able to cast away the axe of Gimli, cause Aragorn's sword to blaze with fire, and then cause the arrow of Legolas to disappear in flight with a flash of flame. Yet, it is not until they call him by name, either Gandalf or Mithrandir, that the White wizard recalls who he was to them. Gandalf informs them that he has become what Saruman should have been[50].

The state of affairs created by the Master on planet Earth has similarities to the Scouring of the Shire. The Shire, turned into an industrial nightmare orchestrated by Saruman, was an additional challenge for the hobbits upon their return home after the events of the Ring. Similarly, Aragorn believes Gandalf has returned beyond all hope in their need, but Gandalf does tell them they do not have any weapon that could hurt him.

The Doctor's emergence from his cage, at a moment prescribed by Martha to humanity, as he channels the fuel of psychic energy, is similar to Gandalf's own return described above. All of humanity is chanting "Doctor, Doctor..." in hope that he will restore their lives to the normality and peace they once had prior to the Master. To further this parallel, the Doctor casts aside, with a wave of his hand, the Master's laser screwdriver, the source of the Master's hold over the Doctor, which is akin to Gandalf snapping the staff of Saruman or casting aside the weapons of Aragorn, Gimli, and Legolas.

One finds other parallels to Tolkien's work in the *Doctor Who* Universe, one being "The Five Doctors," with *The Lord of the Rings,* but, hopefully, the evidence I have discussed illustrates the statement made by the Master as the first direct relation to the mythological dimensions of *Doctor Who* and Tolkien. The mechanics of the Doctor interacting with "fictional" worlds and literary characters have been in place since the early days of the show. The additional insight from Tolkien and Davies adds to how world-building is possible within the primary world and is achieved by the Doctor's antagonists. This all opens the potential of the Doctor having traveled to the age of Middle-earth, which on a linear timeline this could have been the precursor to his role as Merlin, or possibly hasn't been done –yet.[51]

---

1 For those unfamiliar with Tolkien's tales of Middle-earth, Arda is Tolkien's term for the Earth as it was known in his prehistory. Originally a flat world until the fall of Númenor, Arda then was reshaped and became round, the lands reforming, and was where the later tales and Ages of Middle-earth took place. Tolkien explains in his *Letters* that he constructed a historical time, keeping the tales upon mother-earth for a setting. For instance, Tolkien expressly states that the Shire was once in the region that is now Europe (Carpenter, 283).

2 For further discussion on this topic see "The Maker's Will....Fulfilled?" by my wife Jessica Burke and me, *Tolkien and Modernity Volume 1*, Cormare Series 9 (Switzerland: Walking Tree Press, 2006).

3 Christopher Tolkien, JRRT's son and literary heir, posthumously published his father's notes for *The Lord of the Rings* and *The Silmarillion*, which become the 12-volume *History of Middle-earth* series. Plus *Unfinished Tales, The Silmarillion, The Children of Húrin,* all were posthumously published.

4 Tolkien thought the *LotR* "unsuitable for dramatization" (*Letters,* 228), and was very critical of subsequent film treatments he reviewed (*Letters* 270-7).

5 Diana Pavlac Glyer. *The Company They Keep: C.S. Lewis and J.R.R. Tolkien as Writers in Community.* Ohio: Kent State University Press, 2007, 222. Tolkien states he has left room for other artists to explore and write tales of Middle-earth, but his estate will not allow authorized, copyrighted versions to be produced. Aside from the successful Peter Jackson films, licensed not by the estate or by Tolkien Enterprises, there have been many independent films and fan fiction within the structure of Tolkien's Middle-earth.

6 Cornell, Topping, and Day, 10. Lou Anders is an American writer, editor, and author of "Square Pegs Into Round Holes," which is the introduction to

The Discontinuity Guide from which this quote is derived. This version has been cited as being a scanned unofficial reprint but provides a great introduction, which I drew mostly upon for my discussion.

7 *Ibid.* It should also be noted that according to Paul Cornell (http://www. paulcornell.com/2007/02/canonicity-in-doctor-who.html) and new series writers Russell T. Davies and Steven Moffat, there is no official "series bible" nor official canon. But for the purposes of this paper the cited quotes are made applicable for the course of discussion. For a further discussion of what constitutes canon see "Canon, Myth and Memory," by Colin Harvey in this volume.

8 Flieger, Verlyn, *Interrupted Music*, 63.

9 Cornell, Topping, and Day, 10.

10 Tolkien, *The Monsters and the Critics*, 144.

11 Tolkien, *The Monsters and the Critics*, 139.

12 Tolkien, *The Monsters and the Critics*, 122.

13 Flieger, Verlyn, *Smith of Wootton Major*, 101.

14 Tolkien, *The Monsters and the Critics*, 145.

15 Davies and Cook, *Doctor Who: The Writer's Tale: The Untold Story*, 250.

16 *Ibid.*

17 Tolkien, *The Monsters and the Critics*, 122.

18 Bucher-Jones and Hale, *Grimm Reality*.

19 Davies and Cook, *Doctor Who: The Writer's Tale: The Untold Story*, 71.

20 Carpenter, 212.

21 Davies and Cook, *Doctor Who: The Writer's Tale: The Untold Story*, 250.

22 Tolkien, *The Monsters and the Critics*, 144.

23 Barnes, 46.

24 Miles and Wood, 112.

25 The term "trilogic" was originated by the scriptwriters of 'The Celestial Toymaker' as the name of the game the Toymaker challenged the Doctor with, which he was busy solving throughout the episode. The origin and basis of this game is from a Chinese game called "Tower of Hanoi." Two immediate references to the Trilogic game, its Chinese origins, and its relation to the "Tower of Hanoi" are: http://en.wikipedia.org/wiki/Tower_of_Hanoi, and http://www.shannonsullivan.com/drwho/serials/y.html

26 Davis and Bingeman, 9.

27 Davis and Bingeman, 12.

28 Davis and Bingeman, 13.

29 Davis and Bingeman, 65.

30 Davis and Bingeman, 60.

31 Williams, 119.

32 Chapman, 70.

33 See "The Greatest Show in the Galaxy (7J)."

34 Miles and Wood, *About Time, Volume 3,* 216.

35 *Doctor Who: Podshock* Episode 7 (NY: Broadcast 9/21/2005) Internationally renown, #1 Doctor Who Podcast.

36 For further clarity on why this appears offensive to certain communities refer to an expanded discussion of this topic in "Doctor Who and the Valkyrie Tradition, Part 2: Goddesses, Battle Demons, Wives and Daughters,"endnote #41, by Jessica Burke in this volume.

37 For a greatly expanded, far more eloquent discussion on the Carrionites/ Witch image see "Doctor Who and the Valkyrie Tradition, Part 2" by Jessica Burke in this volume.

38 The word "poppet" is an older spelling of "puppet," from the Middle English *popet,* meaning a small child or doll. In British Dialect it continues to hold this meaning. Poppet is also a chiefly English term of endearment.

In folk-magic and witchcraft, a poppet is a doll made to represent a person, for casting spells on that person. These dolls may be fashioned from such materials as a carved root, grain or corn shafts, a fruit, paper, wax, a potato, clay, branches, or cloth stuffed with herbs. The intention is that whatever actions are performed upon the effigy will be transferred to the subject based in sympathetic magic. It was from these dolls that the myth of Voodoo dolls arose.

39 Miles and Wood, *About Time,* Volume 6, 302.

40 Cornell, Topping, and Day, 340.

41 Geoffrey of Monmouth, 207.

42 Platt, *Battlefield,* 52.

43 Geoffrey of Monmouth, 170.

44 Geoffrey of Monmouth, 171.

45 Clarke's Law, a reference, not elaborated by Wood and Miles, which refers to "Hazards of Prophecy: The Failure of Imagination", in the collection "Profiles of the Future."

46 Shippey, 16, 17.

47 Also the chosen name of the society I founded: Heren Istarion: The Northeast Tolkien Society.

48 Carpenter, 156.

49 These events are told in the novel *The Story of Martha* by Dan Abnett.

50 Saruman was the head of the Istari (wizard) Council, but shed the White robes for his more prismatic, many-colored robes when Gandalf confronted him and became a prisoner in the Tower of Saruman. Saruman did this when he turned to his darker ways of serving Sauron and creating armies of Uruk-Hai. By "regenerating" into this role, Gandalf now assumes control of the Council and has greater ability to further the cause of the people of Middle-earth against the will of Sauron.

51 The author would like to thank Dr. Kristine Larsen for her collaboration on Mythcon 2008, and her dedication, support, advice, guidance, and companionship as this project came to fruition.

.

Life During Wartime: An Analysis of Wartime Morality in Doctor Who

Melissa Beattie

Introduction

One of the greatest differences between the classic *Doctor Who* and the revival is that the new series takes place during and after the last great Time War.[1] Though we know only a few of the events of this war, we can see the toll taken on the 9th Doctor by them, specifically the clear evidence of severe emotional trauma that can be seen to impact his interactions and reactions, a trait that continues after his regeneration into the 10th Doctor.

But this trauma has had another effect. It is my opinion that the Doctor is operating under what can be thought of as a "wartime morality." This means that his definition of what is moral or just is based on combat conditions. Thus there should be specific rules defining what can and cannot legally and morally be done, and at what times and under what circumstances those rules apply. To determine this, a textual analysis of the series, treating it as a coherent narrative, shall be done. This will involve an extrapolation of first general Gallifreyan morality and then more specific views of morality in warfare, especially moral relativism. By then analyzing instances of conflict, predominantly within the revival, where the Doctor is variously prisoner, captor, aggressor, and victim, this paper will discuss whether his actions, as governed by both Gallifreyan and human (predominantly Western) morality, are morally right or wrong. In those instances where he seems in breach of his own moral code, and/ or rules of engagement, (e.g., "Dalek,") there will be a discussion of why this change may be, thus moving toward a more psychological analysis of character. Ultimately, this analysis will be used to support both that the Doctor is a moral relativist, and that this relativism combined with a mentality at war and/or in its immediate aftermath create fluctuations in his ability to abide by this moral code, as well as in its expression.

Time and Relative Morality in Space

The overall narrative analysis would, at first, seem to be a very simple juxtaposition, much in the style of Lévi-Strauss.[2]

Hero: Villain
Moral: Immoral

This breaks down when the topics themselves are so subjective. The Doctor as a character has never been an archetypal "hero" in the Hollywood sense;[3] his incarnations have always had a depth of character that has prevented such simple classifications. Thus, we must combine this reading with a more psychoanalytical approach.

As Barthes reminds us, there is a strong cultural component to any interpretation. This extends beyond mythic structures and into any sort of analysis. The sociological "symbolic-interactionist" paradigm, wherein one creates one's own, individual reality, is the culmination of this concept. Thus, to begin, we must first ask, what is morality? For the sake of clarity, we can use the following definitions.

Morality

The definition of morality changes from culture to culture. Perhaps the most useful definition is that morality is a societal code of acceptable conduct.[4] This, however, reveals the major problem in moral discussion, which is that what culture 'A' sees as being a moral code may be vastly different from culture 'B.' Because the series is primarily Western in focus and attitude, the basic, familiar meanings of fairness, being good, avoidance of causing intentional harm, and the like can be used. But morality, as the pre-Socratics and later philosophers have stated, is subjective.[5]

That is to say that morality varies not just from culture to culture, but from person to person and even within the same person at various points in his or her life. Thus the Doctor's morality may not reflect the common morality of the Time Lords; indeed, we do know that they often disagreed on many points. Conversely, however, the Time Lords did often use the Doctor on what could be considered black ops, or operations that would be "officially unofficial," because they would require the Doctor to get his hands dirty.[6] Though the Time Lords are virtually extinct, this culture is the one in which the Doctor grew up. Therefore, according to what Barthes would term "cultural training," the morality the Time Lords ingrained into him should still be visible, despite his being a somewhat atypical member of his species. This is best shown by "Terror of the Autons," in which a Time Lord comes to warn the Doctor about the Master. The unnamed Time Lord points out that he believes that Doctor's hearts are in the right place, with the implication that the Master's are not. Thus, while the Doctor is a rebel against Time Lord society, he does not appear to be considered actively immoral.

Gallifreyan Morality

Though much about Time Lord society is unclear, including issues of class and hierarchy, some general statements can be made. Based upon evidence from the Classic series, the Time Lords were once a cruel people, who would, for example, kidnap other beings and force them to fight in the Death Zone. This was (supposedly) ended by Rassilon, who forced the Time Lords to mend their ways. The Time Lords, having embraced these reforms, no matter their source, subsequently developed a policy of non-interference and pledged to uphold the laws of Time, so that major changes to history did not occur. Presumably, keeping dangerous technology out of the hands of other races would also have contributed to this decision. (cf. "Underworld," "Mawdryn Undead").

Though routinely interfering to the point of having been exiled because of it (cf. "The War Games," and "Spearhead From Space"), the Doctor seems to go to great lengths to uphold the rule of adherence to the course of history, even into his tenth incarnation. Like the Stoics, the Time Lords seem to believe that, on the whole, history is immutable, with a defined track;[7] similarly, they seem to prize thought over emotion, holding themselves at a remove and not engaging emotionally with other races.[8] This preference to avoid engagement is not restricted to dealings with other races, however. The traditional statement by Gallifreyan judges at sentencing as stated in "Shada," was "We but administer; you are imprisoned by the power of the law."

This suggests a habitual rejection of responsibility in the culture as this statement takes responsibility from the judge to the law as an independent entity and gives it to the law-breaker. Thus the Doctor's own preference of avoiding the consequences of his actions may be culturally founded, as well as his own ever-present personality trait.

While the Time Lords seemed to accept death as being perfectly natural and necessary, a fact underscored by the Doctor's uncomfortable reaction to immortality,[9] killing seems to be something they are very strongly against. They did have a termination chamber for the most dire crimes and/or emergencies, but it was virtually never used. We can thus assume that killing would be considered immoral by Gallifreyan standards as well.[10]

That being said, we have seen the Doctor, in various incarnations, come across the problem of killing on both a small and large scale. His reactions vary somewhat, even within the same incarnation. The 4th Doctor first asked if he had the right to destroy the Daleks, though, admittedly, this was in a time zone before they had become a menace, and the threat was based predominantly upon the Doctor's own foreknowledge in "Genesis of the Daleks." Yet in the later "Destiny of the Daleks," the 4th Doctor not only killed many Daleks, but used Davros' own hand to do so, taking what was clearly a dark glee in forcing the Daleks' creator to be their destroyer. While the Daleks are certainly a special case, as will be discussed below, that the Doctor leaves a trail of bodies in his wake is clear to even the casual observer.

In all cases, however, there was always the implication that killing was never the desired outcome. This is best seen in "Warriors of the Deep," when, while surrounded by corpses, the 5th Doctor says that there should have been another way, and again when he asks Tegan in "Resurrection of the Daleks" if she thought he wanted such carnage. In "Boom Town," Blon Fel Fotch points out that only a killer would understand that sometimes a captive is spared on a whim. The Doctor's reaction to her accurate statement and subsequent awareness of the death and destruction that follows what she terms his "happy little life" proves that, in this at least, the Doctor and the Time Lords were and are in full agreement about the innate immorality of killing, even if necessary.

Wartime Morality

By both human and Gallifreyan standards, killing, and thus warfare, should be immoral. And yet, killing was sometimes seen as being necessary and the Time Lords fought a war to the death. How did they reconcile their own moral standards with unalterable necessity?

We know some of these answers. The government of Gallifrey often turned to the Doctor for their dirty work, in order to keep their own hands clean. We can even speculate that the Doctor was chosen to be the one to destroy Gallifrey, the Time Lords, and the Daleks for the same reason—he was the only one who could handle the moral conflict. He understood pragmatism and necessity, and yet was still moral enough to do as he was told by Gallifrey. Whether the Doctor was intended to survive the subsequent holocaust is an open question; he has already stated in "Dalek" that his survival was "not by choice."

Perhaps an even stronger piece of evidence for the Time Lords' desperation for soldiers who could reject their own ingrained morality was in the resurrection of the Master. While in "The Five Doctors" the Time Lords had called in the Master before—to save the Doctor, no less—in the final Time War, they felt they needed someone who was completely *immoral*. They felt a psychopath who liked to hurt and kill would be a perfect soldier. If nothing else, this shows how anathema war and killing were to the Time Lords; they apparently did not realize that someone who harms for pleasure would flee from any potential harm to themselves. Homer gave a perfect example of this in *The Iliad*, when Ares, who made war for pleasure, flees at the first wound, whereas Athene, goddess of rational war, stayed on the battlefield and aided the soldiers on her side.[11]

This contradiction of rational war, irrational war, and the moral implications of both are problems that all cultures struggle with. But what is it that makes a war rational or just? How can we apply morality to an immoral act? The answer lies not in subjective morality per se, but in *changeable* morality. One of the major obstacles to training soldiers is just this; most human religions and cultures have as a basic tenet that murder is an abomination, a sin against whatever one holds sacred. And yet, in war, soldiers must be taught to kill the enemy, or they will die: "kill or be killed." Therefore, soldiers must be trained out of their ingrained, peacetime morality into wartime morality.[12] One of these methods is the use of articles of war.

This paper defines "articles of war" as a code stating such things as how and when an enemy can be attacked, how prisoners are treated, and how noncombatants are dealt with in combat areas.[13] If one follows these rules, and has a reason for their own actions, then they can consider themselves to be, if not exactly moral, at least justified. It is these articles we hope to define for the Doctor, based on examples seen predominantly in the series revival. Once we have defined these articles or rules of war, we can observe whether he himself follows them.

At the "Whoniversal" Appeal conference held at Cardiff University in 2009, it was put both to a discussion panel and the audience in general whether or not human morality was applicable to the Doctor, who is, after all, a Time Lord. The consensus was that, as the Doctor is written, directed, and performed by humans, specifically Westerners, then the associated morality can be applied to him based upon the Barthesian concepts discussed above.[14] Therefore, contemporary Western/human moral ideals can be used as a basis to understand the Doctor's morality, despite his genesis elsewhere. There are, of course, differences between the Doctor's moral stance and that of the contemporary humans with whom he interacts, which shall now be discussed.

To begin, the only way to understand the Doctor's moral stance in any incarnation, but the 9th and 10th especially, is to consider him a moral relativist, or someone who determines that course of action A is more "right" (morally correct) than action B under certain circumstances.

This is in opposition to a moral absolutist, who believes that action A is always correct, no matter what.

This does not, however, necessarily correlate to the morality or immorality of the enemy. For example, in "The Sound of Drums" and "Last of the Time Lords," the Master destroyed Earth and imprisoned and tortured the 10th Doctor himself and his Companions, yet the Doctor still treated his adversary with mercy. Conversely, earlier in Series 3 episode "The Runaway Bride" the Empress of the Racnoss and her children were killed unmercifully. Though the Empress was an active threat, her children were a danger only because of their appetites—a natural trait. The Doctor still killed them in front of the Empress, without mercy. The moral relativism relates to the Doctor's view of what is morally better in a given situation. This view, of course, varies from time to time as discussed above.

Relativism can also be understood as making the best, or most morally correct, of bad choices, or the one that will cause the least harm. This is apparent in two main examples: Series 1's "The Unquiet Dead," and Series 4's "Planet of the Ood," both of which have at their heart a discussion about what is "right" and "wrong" in context.

Let us begin with "The Unquiet Dead." The crux of the moral debate was whether or not the Gelth should be allowed to use human corpses to escape the gaseous form in which they had become trapped by the events of the Time War. Rose argues against this plan, saying it is different from the organ donation analogy the Doctor draws. "Yeah, it is different," the Doctor replies. "It's a different morality. Get used to it, or go home." Thus the Doctor acknowledges here that someone with an absolute or inflexible morality cannot function in so fluid a context as travel in both time and space.

The second example, "Planet of the Ood," makes this point even more strongly. Questions of morality abound, most notably in this exchange: "It's weird," Donna says. "Being with you, I can't tell what's right and what's wrong anymore." The Doctor replies, "It's better that way. People who know for certain tend to be like Mr Halpin." Even more than this rather blatant statement of moral relativism being the best way to cope with life on the TARDIS are the events of the episode itself and the hanging threads from "The Impossible Planet" and "The Satan Pit," which "Planet" explores. In the earlier two-part episode, the Doctor was forced to let the Satan-possessed Ood die, but did not at any time over the course of the two episodes question their position of servitude. Though, as he says to Donna in this episode, he was rather busy at the time;[15] as will be discussed more below, slavery and unlawful captivity do seem to be concepts he believes to be always immoral.

That being said, however, what the Doctor does not consider when freeing the Ood in "Planet" is the effect it will have upon the Second Great and Bountiful Human Empire of the late forty-second century. If the empire is, as Donna suggests, run on the backs of slave labor, then the Doctor has just removed the economic foundation of the whole civilization. Though we do not know for certain what the effects of that were,[16] this lack of consideration of long-term consequences is one of the effects of a combination of moral relativism and the type of snap decision-making required in any emergency, most notably in combat. This is a very common state of affairs for the Doctor, perhaps best seen in "The Long Game," where the Doctor frees Satellite Five from the Jagrafess and leaves immediately thereafter. He does not consider what would happen to the 4th Great and Bountiful Human Empire if its news and other information services were suddenly destroyed, however, and finds in "Bad Wolf" that the Earth has entered into "one hundred years of Hell."

While this is not meant to pass judgment on the innate morality of the Doctor's actions in either "The Long Game" or "Planet," it does point out that, even if the Doctor does choose what seems, at the time, to be the best course of action based upon his own morality, the ultimate consequences of his decision may not be positive for all concerned, including innocent bystanders.

Definite Articles

So, what, then, are the rules of war under which the Doctor is operating? We can break them down into three main categories.

Rules of Combat: When faced with open conflict, such as in "Rose," "World War Three," "The Christmas Invasion," "The Runaway Bride," and "The Sontaran Stratagem," the Doctor generally offers one warning, or one chance for the enemy to surrender or otherwise leave peacefully. It is only when this offer is rejected that the Doctor will let loose a generally devastating attack. This is a logical rule of engagement—it allows the opposing forces a chance to let reason hold sway, and to neither kill nor be killed. This has also been adopted by Martha in "Journey's End," and by Jack in some instances.[17] The Doctor shows this approach most clearly, however, in "The Poison Sky," when he teleports to the Sontaran fleet in order to give them a chance to surrender. He tells Martha and Donna that he has to do this, despite the fact that he would be killed by the atmospheric converter. This strongly supports the notion that a warning is a requirement, as does the Doctor's rejection of Jack's very pragmatic suggestion of killing the Master while they were (they thought) protected by a perception filter in "The Sound of Drums." This can also be considered another expression of the cultural inability of the Time Lords to take full responsibility for their actions, as discussed above in regard to "Shada;" a warning allows the enemy to choose its fate of its own free will.

This, in theory, would remove responsibility for the death of this enemy from the Doctor, though in practice we do see the Doctor react to being forced to kill. This system does not always work, however.

In "Rose" the Doctor attempts to peaceably speak with the Nestene Consciousness and get them to leave the planet. A peaceful solution is rendered impossible, however, when the Nestene realize that the Doctor has anti-plastic concealed upon his person. Despite his insistence that he was not going to use the liquid, it is the act of carrying this weapon that leads to the assault, rather than the Doctor offering a warning and then, when it is refused, striking. He also does not offer the Lady Cassandra a warning in "The End of the World," though her teleportation from Platform One immediately upon her revealing and implementing her plan does allow one to argue that the Doctor did not have an opportunity to do so.

In most cases, however, enemies on *Doctor Who* do not accept the Doctor's offer of a last chance. There was one instance where they did, however. In "The Christmas Invasion," the Sycorax commander accepts the Doctor's challenge of single combat for the Earth. This was a way for both humans and Sycorax to survive, and was done in all good faith. The commander's attempted treachery aside, the Doctor essentially offers a peace treaty to the Sycorax; they leave the Earth forever and go on about their lives. The Sycorax accept this bargain, and begin to leave. The rules of war have been followed by all, more or less: single combat decided the outcome, not requiring a war or a high body count. A peace accord is struck, and the conflict ends.

This honorable ending is scuttled by Harriet Jones, who orders the retreating spaceship blown out of the sky. Her action leads to another rule of combat: accepting an enemy's surrender. The Doctor very clearly believes that a defeated and retreating enemy must not be killed. To do so is a violation of the articles or rules of war. That, I believe, is why he reacted so very badly to Harriet Jones' order; to him, she just committed a war crime.[18] Given that genocide, which the Doctor has committed against the Daleks, is a war crime by any standard, the fact that this trusted ally has herself committed a war crime must be even more painful for him.

The incident can, however, also be considered a shattering of a quasi "mirror self" for the Doctor. This suggests that the Doctor saw Harriet Jones as an honorable war leader in the same way as he must have been for

Gallifrey. Therefore, when she commits a war crime as he did, the image he had of her, as a reflection of himself but without his flaws, would be a highly traumatic experience for him. This, then, explains his reaction. It would also be a forerunner to the mirror self created from the Doctor's severed hand in "The Stolen Earth" and "Journey's End," which featured both Harriet Jones' demise and the regenerated clone (here denoted Doctor #2) destroying the Dalek fleet.[19]

On a smaller, more personal scale, this same sense is seen in Series 4's "The Doctor's Daughter." In this episode, which features a (seemingly) ages-old war between humans and Hath, the Doctor has managed to broker a peace. This is threatened when Cobb, head of the human faction, attempts to murder the Doctor. Jenny, the Time Lord's engineered daughter, takes the bullet instead, leading the Doctor to hold a revolver to Cobb's head. Instead of eliminating the threat to future peace, however, he vehemently states that he never would kill out of anger.

The Doctor's offer of a chance to stop or surrender can also be seen in extraordinary circumstances such as at the end of "Evolution of the Daleks." Over the course of that episode, the 10th Doctor witnesses the genocide of human/Dalek/Time Lord hybrids by the Daleks. This includes the leader of the Cult of Skaro, Sec, who has both become a human/Dalek hybrid and has shown a willingness to change and grow. By the end, three of the four remaining Daleks have also been killed. The Doctor's response to the last, Dalek Caan, is to offer it mercy. He says that he is the one being in the universe who could offer the Dalek compassion, and further states that he will not be responsible for the death of the species. This could be interpreted as being a chance for Dalek Caan to surrender and thus live. If it were to reject the offer and subsequently attack, then it would conceivably be taking responsibility for its own death.

Alternatively, the offer could also be interpreted as an inducement to or even offer of assistance with suicide for the Dalek. One can argue the intent of this interpretation two ways. The first, a simple elimination of the threat, has antecedents in the actions of the 7th Doctor in "Remembrance of the Daleks." In that instance, he induces the last remaining Dalek in the assault party to self-destruction after the 7th Doctor has caused the destruction of the Dalek fleet, including (he believes) Davros, and the destruction of Skaro and its sun. He tells the Dalek that it is the last of its kind, and that even its home-world is a burnt cinder orbiting a dead sun. The parallels to what would later happen to both the Doctor and Gallifrey in the Time War are obvious. Because of the context in "Evolution of the Daleks," however, and the reawakening of the 10th Doctor's morality through the influence of Donna and Martha both, I would support a second interpretation. If the Doctor was offering Dalek Caan death, that could still be seen as an act of mercy. This has its antecedents in "Dalek" when, instead of continuing to exist as an anomaly, the Dalek begs to be ordered to self-destruct. Rose accommodates this request, both eliminating the threat and, potentially, allowing the Dalek an end to its torment. The Doctor does tell the Dalek that he is the only one who can offer it compassion; if we take him at his word, then this interpretation does seem more likely.[20] As Dalek Caan escapes via an emergency temporal shift, however, this point is rendered moot.[21]

The treatment of noncombatants in war is another moral issue. We see the Doctor deal with this most in "The Parting of the Ways," as he must decide whether or not to kill everyone on Earth and on Satellite Five in order to kill the Daleks. As in this situation, we must assume that most of the Time Lords were similarly "collateral damage." Unlike the destruction of Gallifrey, the Doctor chooses the high moral ground and opts to not commit mass murder again.

This can be contrasted to "The Age of Steel," where the Doctor is again faced with the problem of humans having been twisted against their will into Cybermen. The Doctor does ask if he can destroy the Cybermen by removing their emotional inhibitors, and, as in "The Parting of the Ways," is given "permission." This time, however, the Doctor does in fact carry out his plan, and does not appear to have any moral compunction about sending the Daleks and Cybermen into the Void in "Doomsday."[22]

In "Runaway," the children of the Empress of the Racnoss can also be seen to have been noncombatants, though by their nature they were considered a threat to the Earth. The Doctor offers his one warning to the Empress, then destroys her children ruthlessly. The Toclafane, which the Master calls his children, were destroyed in much the same way. Although the Master had been given many chances to cease his actions, and it was actually Jack who destroyed the paradox machine, it seems to have been the Doctor who devised the plan.

Finally, Series 4's "The Fires of Pompeii" addresses this issue when the Doctor is forced to choose between allowing the Pyroviles to invade the Earth, sparing Pompeii, Herculaneum, and the other nearby towns destroyed by Vesuvius, or by triggering the eruption himself, saving history and dooming thousands. The Doctor, though fully aware that this is one point in history that cannot be changed, still hesitates to engage the mechanism, just as he did in "The Parting of the Ways." Donna covers his hands and engages the device with him, tacitly giving her approval for his actions in much the same way as Mrs. Moore did in "The Age of Steel."

We can thus see a progression from a general care for noncombatants to an acceptance of their loss at his hands. While an argument can be made that the Cybermen and Toclafane were no longer human and were, in fact, already dead, this cannot be said about the children of the Racnoss. That line of reasoning also implies that human life is worth more than alien life, which is debatable. The Doctor seems also to require support or even permission for his actions which would kill noncombatant humans from a human in order for him to enact his plan: Jack fulfilled this function in "Parting," Mrs. Moore in "Age," and Donna in "The Fires of Pompeii." Even then, however, if the human is not present at the critical time, then the Doctor may not enact his plan. The 9th Doctor had gained support from Jack when the Delta Wave emitter was still under construction, but Jack was killed by the Daleks just before the Doctor was ready to pull the lever, which the Doctor was ultimately unable to do. A human is also sometimes required to stop him, as in "Dalek" and "Runaway," when Rose and Donna respectively prevent the Doctor from killing the Dalek in cold blood and from spending too much time under the Thames flood barrier, watching the Empress of the Racnoss' children die.

Treatment of Prisoners: The Doctor and his companions occasionally capture and are often captured. We see definite signs of what, in his mind, is the proper treatment of prisoners. In "Rise of the Cybermen," the Doctor surrenders himself and the Tylers in order to save their lives, and is completely taken aback when the Cybermen move in for the kill. He even says, completely uncomprehendingly, "But we've surrendered!" That suggests that it is completely ingrained for him to not kill prisoners. His discomfort in "Boom Town," with bringing Blon Fel Fotch back to her home-world to face a death sentence supports this as well, and his reactions to the captive patients in being used for medical experiments in "New Earth" and captives being tortured or killed for the amusement of others as in the reality shows in "Bad Wolf;" even the mentally ill patients in Bedlam in "The Shakespeare Code" strongly suggest that he would consider any sort of harm done to a prisoner to be morally wrong. Though the 10th Doctor does not explicitly express an opinion on the Master's use of pain, suffering, and death as amusement in "Journey's End," we can extrapolate from the Doctor's reactions in this episode and elsewhere that he would not approve, forgiveness of the Master or no.

The Doctor also is seen taking exception to imprisoning or killing sentient beings either for personal gain or out of a fear that they might be harmful, just because the beings are different. This is the case in "Army of Ghosts," when he is repulsed by Yvonne Hartman's belief that it is acceptable to shoot down any passing alien craft in order to obtain technology, and in "Midnight," where he adamantly opposes casting out Sky and whatever lifeform was possessing her to die when they were unsure of its motivations.[23]

There is, however, one major divergence from this moral code. In the episode "Dalek," the Doctor tries to kill the captive Dalek, while it is still restrained, and without any provocation beyond its presence. The Dalek does, admittedly, move its weapon about when it learns who the Doctor is, but there is no power; the Doctor knows this before he attempts to destroy it. While we can understand his reaction as being based on centuries of conflict capped by the trauma of the loss of his people, we can only call this an immoral act, contrary to the above-established rules of war.

General Morality Relating to War: As stated above, war requires killing. We have numerous examples listed of the Doctor's abject abhorrence of that act, either by his own hand or through indirect means. He will kill if need be, but we have seen him routinely object strongly to mistreatment and/or murder of noncombatants/innocents as discussed elsewhere. By the 3rd series, especially over the last nine episodes, he seems to be trying to be more moral and compassionate, to the point of severely inconveniencing himself and others.[24] Series 4, despite its more militaristic theme, continues this to the point of confronting the Doctor with the darker side of empowering his companions, as will be discussed below.

This does not mean that the Doctor acts in accordance with his moral code at all times. He allows Lady Cassandra to dry out and, as they thought, die after she was responsible for deaths on Platform One in "The End of the World." This is a far harsher penalty than would have been the case later in the same incarnation (cf. his ambivalent response to Blon Fel Fotch in "Boom Town"). He is extremely cruel to the Family of Blood, most likely as a response to the severe emotional trauma he suffered through being human and returning to being a Time Lord. Once again, while his response is understandable—and, from a certain point of view, in accordance with the rule requiring the enemy to have one chance before the Doctor attacks—it is more eternal torment than death. And, as stated above, harming prisoners seems to be extraordinarily immoral to him.

These three categories make up the main rules of combat under which the Doctor seems to operate under most circumstances. There is, however, one major divergence from this code of conduct.

The Exception that Proves the Rule—Daleks

What is, perhaps, most clear about the Doctor in all of his incarnations is that the Daleks are a special case for him. It was he who first encountered them, in the Hartnell-era serial "The Daleks" and it was in this early adventure that the Doctor and his companions incited a conflict between the Thals and Daleks for the travelers' own needs. In addition, the Doctor also tells the dying, genocidal Daleks that, even if he could help them, he would not do so. Over the course of the series, the Doctor would encounter them again and again, with escalating stakes.

In their paper "The Human Factor: Daleks, the Evil Human and Faustian Legend in Doctor Who," Moore and Stevens point out that in most of the Classic series' Dalek stories, there was an amoral human who had made an almost Faustian deal with the Daleks. This bargain generally led to the amoral human's death.[25] They state that this was the case in every story except "Planet of the Daleks," and "Resurrection of the Daleks," but what Moore and Stevens do not discuss is that, in those serials, the amorality they see as being given to a human is in fact transposed onto the Doctor himself and is expressed by his own actions. In the former case, after destroying a Dalek, the 3rd Doctor states "You know, for a man who abhors violence, I took great satisfaction in doing that." While this is minor to be sure, it does suggest a slightly darker side to the Doctor.

The more obvious moral ambiguity comes in "Resurrection." Though one can argue that mercenary Lytton is the Faustian amoral human, it is this episode where the 5th Doctor moves past one who kills clear and present threats in combat situations, to someone who attempts murder. The Doctor decides that Davros must die, and enters the disabled scientist's lab with the intent of shooting him in cold blood.[26] The Doctor is ultimately unable to do this, due both to his own delay and outside events, but it is worthy of note that it was at the end of this serial, which also featured his willingness to use a bioweapon on the Daleks as well as his destruction of a great many Daleks in combat, that Tegan decides that she has had enough of death and violence and leaves.

As though this were not enough, the progression of the 7th Doctor into moral ambiguity was also begun in "Remembrance." Though the white supremacists of the serial fulfill the Faustian role as described by Moore and Stevens, the Doctor still not only arranges for the destruction of the Dalek home-world of Skaro, but does so as the President-elect of the High Council. Whether the Doctor actually had this authority or not is unclear,[27] but, if the Daleks believed this to be the case then, to them, this was a clear act of aggression by the leader of Gallifrey, and could certainly be seen as an act of war. Russell T. Davies has called "Genesis of the Daleks" the first strike of the Time War;[28] "Genesis" could thus be seen as either the formal opening of hostilities between the two powers, or a progression into "total war."

Whatever the case, by the beginning of Series 1 of the revival, the 9th Doctor has become one of only a handful of survivors from either side of the Time War, and suffers an almost knee-jerk reaction to seeing what is believed to be the last Dalek in the universe. He first tries to run, but, upon seeing that the Dalek is a helpless captive, he violates his own apparent code of conduct for prisoners and attempts to destroy the creature. At the end of the episode, he tries again, despite the Dalek clearly having been rendered no threat. Although he does keep more to his established moral compass in subsequent episodes involving the Daleks, as discussed above, the militaristic theme continues through them. Most notably he tells Martha "that's an order!" when trying to get her to leave him in "Evolution of the Daleks"; she refuses, asking if the Doctor is "some sort of Dalek." While it is true that the revival's connection between the Doctor and the Daleks appears first in "Dalek," it continues into "The Parting of the Ways," and culminates in the Doctor drawing the connection himself in the final scene with Dalek Caan in "Evolution." I would argue it is more the Doctor unconsciously slipping back into a military mode ordering his troops in battle.

The military theme, continued in Series 4, begins to appear in "The Sontaran Stratagem," when Donna asks if the Doctor turns all of his companions into soldiers, and culminates in a confrontation between the Doctor and Davros in "Journey's End." In this, the Doctor is confronted by a communications screen in the Crucible's Vault, which shows Martha, Jack, Sarah Jane, Jackie Tyler, and Mickey, all of whom are warning Davros that they are engaged in some plan that will lead to Davros' destruction, as well as that of the Earth, if not even more carnage. Instead of being presented as saviors making impossible decisions to defend others, however, Davros tells the Time Lord that all of his "children of time" have been taught by the Doctor to be violent killers. This can be easily refuted, however.

Though the Doctor does enable all of his Companions to stand up for and defend themselves, many of them had some form of military or similar training long before they met him. Ian (1st Doctor) would have had to have done National Service and was an able fighter. Steven (1st Doctor) was an astronaut, which, at the time in which he was written, would have meant a military background. Sara Kingdom (1st Doctor) who appeared in "The Daleks' Master Plan," was a member of the Space Security Service. Ben (1st Doctor) was in the Royal Navy. Jamie (2nd Doctor) was a Jacobite soldier. Zoe (2nd Doctor) was a martial artist ("The Mind Robber"). Everyone from UNIT, including Harry Sullivan were military (3rd and 4th Doctors). Leela (4th Doctor) was a warrior. Turlough (5th Doctor) was in the Trion military before his exile. Ace (7th

Doctor) was an explosives expert. Jack (9th and 10th Doctors) had gone to war "as a boy" (cf. *Torchwood* "Captain Jack Harkness," "Rose"2) as well as being an ex-Time Agent, implying law enforcement and/or military-style training. Only Martha joined UNIT after leaving the TARDIS, and it was implied that she was placed there by the Doctor (cf. *Torchwood* "Reset," "The Age of Steel," "The Sontaran Stratagem").

Despite this information, of which the Doctor is aware, Davros's accusation clearly takes him aback, and informs such subsequent decisions as essentially fostering his cloned self with Rose in order to teach Doctor #2 restraint and control, much as she did with his 9th incarnation. It also causes him to refuse Lady Christina DeSouza when she asks to travel with him in "Planet of the Dead." How this will continue throughout the rest of the Doctor's 10th incarnation and into his 11th remains to be seen.

As discussed above, there was one major incident where the Doctor seems to have severely violated his code of morality; the climax of "The End of the World." I would argue, however, that the decision to allow Lady Cassandra to dry out and (presumably) die can be understood as a function of this wartime morality, specifically that of his responses to the Daleks. This can be understood if one recalls the context. The episode features the Doctor taking Rose to the destruction of the Earth in fire, just as Gallifrey was destroyed; this in itself can almost been seen as analogous to a flashback brought about by Post Traumatic Stress Disorder. Cassandra also, uncaringly, allows innocents to die both so that she may prosper financially but also because she believes herself to be above other species as a "pure human." Her racism mimics that of the Daleks, who forced the Doctor to destroy his own home-world and badly affect others such as the Nestene and the Gelth. He sees in her someone who should die, and refuses to show her mercy, because she is guilty of similar crimes to both the Daleks generally and himself.

Conclusion

Morality is in the eye of the beholder. It is not only subjective, but changeable based on the circumstances, which is why a simple Lévi-Straussian analysis fails. Rules of war define how one acts morally during what is an intrinsically immoral situation, with the intention of minimizing the very basic moral conflict with regard to killing. This is true for humans and Time Lords alike, and, as is the case with many human codes of morality, it is relative both to personal and situational circumstances. Though the Doctor is, to a degree, an atypical member of his species, as with any other being he still reflects the morality with which he was raised, despite rebelling against Gallifreyan indolence and non-interference.

Based upon the evidence available, however, the Doctor seems to be operating under the following rules of engagement that determine his actions in any instance of conflict or crisis:

- A warning and a chance to surrender must be given before the Doctor attacks.
- A surrendered enemy must not be harmed. Prisoners likewise must not be harmed.
- Noncombatants should be spared when possible. When impossible, permission or support must be given for the plan by a representative of those to suffer as collateral damage.
- Killing is immoral, but sometimes necessary as a last resort. Murder out of anger or fear is never permissible.

As discussed above, however, both personal and cultural moral codes can vary over the course of a lifetime. The Doctor's own moral code is no exception. The 9th Doctor initially attempts to be fair to his enemies, offering them a warning and only killing if absolutely necessary, though his emotions briefly get in the way of his morals in "The End of the World," and "Dalek," thus continuing the tradition of the Daleks as a "special case" in which the Doctor's morality can be unclear. It also shows how badly this tendency has been exacerbated by the Time War. Yet by "Boom Town," he is again questioning himself over the appropriateness of death as a punishment for killing, a penalty he himself escaped.

Ultimately, in "The Parting of the Ways," he chooses not to commit genocide against the Daleks— and, incidentally, mass murder of all humans on Earth—even though this decision would have led to his own death, if not for Rose's intervention.

After the regeneration, the 10th Doctor begins to suffer a decline in his morality. Though his reaction to what he sees as Harriet Jones' war crime is somewhat out of proportion, we can see him taking the moral high ground, offering idealism about the Sycorax being fair to Jones's pragmatism. Later that series, however, he does choose to kill the formerly-human Cybermen by driving them mad, and eventually sends them and the Daleks out into the Void.

By the beginning of Series 3, however, the Doctor has lost Rose, who had acted as his moral compass, and has fallen further into immorality. He kills the Empress of the Racnoss' children in front of her, then allows her to be killed. But, with Martha's influence, and after his encounter with the Dalek/Human hybrid and the subsequent creation and loss of

Human/Time Lord hybrids, a change begins to progress. He tries to be more compassionate, more moral and just. This does not mean that he cannot be cruel, as with the Family of Blood, merely that he is trying to mend his ways. This is never clearer than in "Last of the Time Lords," when he not only forgives the Master for all of his crimes, but expresses a desire to help, and even rehabilitate, his nemesis.

When the Master chooses death rather than regeneration, and the Doctor's companions both choose to remain on Earth in large part due to their experiences with him, the Doctor finds himself not only alone but once again reminded that, because he is so powerful, his actions can have severe consequences. This is underscored by the line in "Voyage of the Damned," saying that anyone who could do anything would be a monster, and again by his response to Donna in "Partners in Crime," when he tells her that traveling with him can be "complicated." Still, the increasingly moral trend from the end of Series 3 continues, as Donna notes that the Doctor lets the Adipose children go free, as they are just children and could not help where they came from. "That Martha must've done you good," Donna opines. These two moral implications, responsibility for his actions and a return to his moral code, both culminate in "Journey's End," where he faces both his effect on his companions (that is, a purported militarization) and a version of himself willing to destroy the Dalek fleet. Though the former is debatable, the Doctor is badly affected by seeing the violence he can bring about, and takes steps to remain within his moral bounds. These include fostering his other self with Rose, trying to save Davros, and, by "Planet of the Dead," deciding to refuse anyone who desires to travel with him.[29]

What can be said about this progression? Perhaps only that Series 1 through 4 represent a healing process, complete with backsliding and missteps, such as the regression into solitude to protect others suggesting a re-entry into a state of emotional lockdown much as was seen in Series 1 of the revival. This is perhaps not surprising, given that "Journey's End" was, in large part, the Doctor being forced to confront the Time War and all that it entailed, especially his own actions. We can but hope that we will see in later episodes the Doctor once again easing out of the mindset, and the attendant morality, of life during wartime. Time will, as always, tell.

---

1 Rose, after having absorbed the Time Vortex, states that the Time War ends with her actions in "The Parting of the Ways." This is further supported by the series 3 episode "Utopia," where the Doctor states that the last act of the Time

War was the resurrection of Captain Jack Harkness, also in the series 1 episode "The Parting of the Ways." Thus, the entirety of series 1 of the revival can be classified as having occurred during wartime, relatively speaking, though we do not necessarily see warfare in every episode.

2 For discussion of Lévi-Strauss, see J. Fiske. Television Culture. London: Routledge, 1987. 131-135; for Barthes, see *Ibid*. 303-35.

3 D. Rafer, 123-137, for a deeper discussion of this topic.

4 "Morality," Stanford Encyclopedia of Philosophy, http://plato.stanford.edu/entries/morality-definition/ accessed 11/06/09.

5 For pre-Socratic morality, see Barnes, 214-215, inter alia. For moral relativism, see, for example, Moser and Carson, *Moral Relativism,* and Cook, *Morality and Cultural Differences*. For morality generally, see, for example, Scheffler, *Human Morality*, as well as the various primary sources such as Spinoza, Kant, Nietzsche, and others.

6 cf. "Genesis of the Daleks," 4th Doctor, Classic Series 1963-1989.

7 Certain major points in history are immutable, though there is flexibility in some instances; cf. ,"The Fires of Pompeii." Adding in these fixed points is considered wrong; cf. "Utopia."

8 "The Invasion of Time," "The Five Doctors," and "The Trial of a Time Lord." For a good introduction to Stoic thought, see Long, *Hellenistic Philosophy*. The Doctor also now considers himself the highest authority on these matters, cf. "School Reunion."

9 Immortality, of course, being something that is considered not only a curse but also unnatural in Time Lord culture; cf. "The Five Doctors" and "Utopia."

10 As is the case with modern human cultures, the fact that war and murder are immoral does not necessarily prevent such acts from occurring.

11 Homer, *Iliad*, V. 859-906. Athene is often considered a goddess of war in the context of the restoration of peace; that is to say, she would fight if threatened, but not if unprovoked.

12 J Wallace Sr., USN (ret), Pers. Comm., 2002.

13 The Shadow Proclamation seems to have some sort of authority in negotiation between potentially hostile parties; in "Rose," the 9th Doctor approaches the Nestene Consciousness under "article thirteen of the Shadow Proclamation." In "The Stolen Earth," they are described as "police," though a peacekeeping body like the United Nations might be the best analogy.

14 M. Beattie (moderator), et al., "Who's Morality?" Panel at "Whoniversal" Appeal: An Interdisciplinary Postgraduate Conference on Doctor Who and All of its Spin-Offs, 2008.

15 Not only were the Doctor and Rose on a planet that was orbiting a black hole, but he had lost the TARDIS in addition to having the possessed Ood and the possessed Toby Zed committing murder.

16 One is tempted to speculate, however, that the troubles of the fifty-first

century (cf. "The Talons of Weng-Chiang," Torchwood's "Adam") may reflect the fallout from the eventual fall of the Second Great and Bountiful Human Empire, though there is no direct evidence. Humanity was apparently only just reaching back out over half the galaxy (cf. "The Invisible Enemy," "The Doctor Dances") and was clearly weakened; there is historical precedent for economic collapse leading to political instability (e.g., the Roman *latifundia* system and the American South during Reconstruction). Without more data, however, this must remain speculative, though Russell T. Davies has implied a long-term fallout from saving Caecilius and his family in "The Fires of Pompeii." The Doctor's changing of history led to Caecilius having as a descendant John Frobisher "Children of Earth: Day Five" (Torchwood). That episode saw the end of the familial line, and given Frobisher's key role in the miniseries, one could argue that the Doctor' saving "just one" family had a great effect 1,930 years down the line: Torchwood Declassified (3). That realization of the "ripple effect" does support the first speculation.

17 In Torchwood's "Countrycide," Jack states that the cannibal villagers "don't deserve warnings," implying that he normally considered a warning to be required. "Children of Earth: Day Five" would be an exception, though one can make the same argument as was made for the Doctor in the beginning of series 1 and 3: severe emotional trauma and the loss of a moral compass.

18 This statement should not be interpreted to attack or defend either Harriet Jones or the Doctor's actions.

19 For discussion of Lacan, see Fiske, *Television Culture*.

20 We can also recall that this episode featured the Doctor demanding that the Daleks kill him; though I do not intend to suggest that the Doctor has a death wish of any kind, the parallels are telling.

21 It is possible that these events play into Caan's decisions in "Journey's End," when he rejects the Dalek worldview embracing hatred and denying compassion and mercy.

22 These events can be further contrasted with the 4th Doctor's refusal to destroy the Daleks, though because that attempt at genocide was based upon foreknowledge of the Daleks' future actions the analogy is not exact.

23 This has Classic Series parallels as well, most notably "The Invisible Enemy" where the 4th Doctor returns a virus to its natural habitat as it has a right to exist, just not as so great a threat.

24 cf. He is becoming human in "Human Nature/The Family of Blood" and especially being a captive for a year in "Last of the Time Lords" along with the Jones family and Jack. In "Family of Blood" it is explicitly stated that the reason the Doctor went to all the trouble of hiding as a human was in order to be kind. Had the Doctor taken a harsh approach in any of the referenced episodes, none of these traumas need have taken place.

25 Moore and Stevens, 138-158.

26 cf. "The Doctor's Daughter," when the 10th Doctor states he never could shoot an unarmed man in anger.

27 The Doctor had been appointed President first in "The Deadly Assassin" and then again after Borusa was petrified in "The Five Doctors." He was stripped of the title in "The Trial of a Time Lord," and declined to regain the position at that time.

28 "Rose," *Doctor Who Confidential.*

29 It is true that the Doctor seems to reject Lady Christina because of her seeking only adventure. But the Doctor specifies that he travels alone now, because of what has happened before to his companions.

"It Turns Out they Died for Nothing": Doctor Who and the Idea of Sacrificial Death

Melody Green

From the very first storyline "An Unearthly Child," in which a group of cavemen believe that sacrificing the Doctor and his companions would buy fire from the sun, the BBC series *Doctor Who* has frequently relied on the motif of sacrificial death in order to create suspense, solve problems, and develop storylines. Early storylines, such as "The Myth Makers" and "The Aztecs" include this image, as do more recent episodes such as "Tooth and Claw" and "The Doctor's Daughter." While sacrifice is a common motif that Western fantasy and science fiction have inherited from their roots in mythology, this series does more than simply repeat the same old patterns. Instead, it provides a complex exploration of the meanings and values of sacrificial death, reinforcing its place in popular culture while, at the same time, drawing into question certain attitudes and assumptions about such extreme behavior. An understanding of exactly how the *Doctor Who* series both supports and challenges the idea of sacrificial death needs to begin in the work of two theorists who focus on the concept of sacrifice: Dennis Keenan and René Girard. In *The Question of Sacrifice,* a study of the various roles that sacrifice plays in the work of several philosophers and theorists, Dennis Keenan explains that in popular thought sacrificial death is considered "a necessary passage through suffering and/or death (of either oneself or of someone else) on the way to a supreme moment of transcendent truth."[1]

Keenan later expands the definition, explaining that a sacrificial death is a death that buys something that could not be gained any other way. For example, in "Father's Day," Rose's father dies to save the world. Because of Rose's earlier attempts to save him from becoming the victim of a meaningless tragedy, his death is the only thing that can buy this salvation.[2] Throughout the *Doctor Who* series, various sacrifices are brought into being by situations in which someone perceives a need, and the only way that this person or these people can see that need being met is through a sacrificial death. These can be based in ritual or ancient mythologies—which occur in "The Aztecs," "The Myth Makers," and "The Stones of Blood"—or may be motivated by life-threatening emergencies, such as in "42" when Captain Kath McDonnell takes hold of her possessed husband and deliberately steps out of a spaceship with him.

Throughout *The Question of Sacrifice*, Keenan's main argument is that while exchange is at the heart of all sacrifice, in contemporary Western culture this intrinsic connection is often viewed as potentially self-serving and therefore dubious at best. An example of how this works would be the prevailing attitude about the sacrifice of soldiers for the purpose of gaining land, oil, or even security. In the same light, while viewers may admire the multitude of characters in the *Doctor Who* series who have died to save others, even these are sacrifices that Keenan would argue are selfishly motivated. One example that demonstrates Keenan's claim occurs in "Tooth," when Sir Robert Macleish, the owner of Torchwood estate, gives his life to buy a potential escape for the others. His death purchases not one, but two things: the lives of the people he loves, and his lost honor. This purchase of the lives of others certainly appears disinterested, but buying back the honor he lost when he betrayed Queen Victoria to potential assassins is not. This, according to Keenan, would be viewed by many as a tainted sacrifice, because the person who chose to do so gained something by it.

The true sacrifices, or the best sacrifices, according to Keenan, are the ones that occur under circumstances in which the individual who makes the sacrifice expects nothing in exchange. As Keenan explains, in order to be viewed as a real sacrifice the event "must necessarily be a sacrifice for nothing, a sacrifice for no reason, no goal."[3] This is, of course, a paradox: the language of sacrifice is the language of exchange. Therefore there must be a motivation of some sort behind any sacrificial act or it is not sacrificial. Keenan introduces the terms "economical" and "aneconomical" in order to describe these two different attitudes about sacrifice: the economical sacrifice is undertaken to buy something specific, while the aneconomical sacrifice buys nothing, but is instead an act of extravagance or profligacy.[4] While this may be viewed by some as the only pure sacrifice, it cannot exist. For a sacrifice to be a sacrifice, something must motivate it. As soon as that motivation exists, however, the sacrifice has a purpose, thus it cannot possibly be aneconomical. An awareness of this tension between the myth of an ideal, unselfish sacrifice and the reality that sacrifices exist to buy things of value to the one making the sacrifice is one of the marks of contemporary Western society. Because of recent historical events, including wars and acts of terrorism, we live at a potentially ephemeral moment in which the very definition of sacrifice is brought into question.

Before examining this questioning of sacrifice in *Doctor Who*, however, René Girard's concept of the scapegoat needs to be added to the conversation. According to Girard, violence, particularly the types of violence found in religion, mythology, and active communities, is based in mimesis, or imitation. In *Violence and the Sacred*, Girard explains that everything humans learn, including desire, is based in mimesis. Learning in early childhood happens through imitating others in the way they walk, talk, and act. In the same manner, the child learns to desire the same objects that are desired by the person or people the child imitates in other ways. Girard explains it thus: "Desire itself is essentially mimetic, directed toward an object desired by the model."[5] Unfortunately, when two people desire the same thing, a conflict ensues. In *Things Hidden Since the Foundation of the World,* Girard explains that this imitative desire, or "acquisitive mimesis," quickly escalates into something else. The rivals move their focus off of the object and onto each other. Eventually, the desired object or ideal that caused the rivalry in the first place is completely forgotten in their fascination, albeit a horrified or horrifying fascination, with each other.[6]

A good example of how acquisitive mimesis works can be seen in the episode "Last of the Time Lords." The Doctor and The Master both desire the planet Earth. The Doctor wishes to see it grow and thrive as he believes it should, while the Master plans to use it for his own nefarious ends. When the Master captures the Doctor, he does not destroy his long-time enemy, but keeps the Doctor imprisoned in his headquarters. The Master appears to be enthralled by the very existence of his captive, and plays with the Doctor as a cat does with a mouse. When the Doctor, through the faith of those who believe in him, is finally empowered to defeat the Master, he plans to imprison his enemy—with himself as the jailer. The rivals will, as the Doctor describes it, never again be apart, but he looks forward to settling down with the enemy he knows he can never trust. Planet Earth is no longer an issue in their conflict; instead, as has happened before in their mimetic cycle of rivalry, they are only concerned with each other.

This, of course, is also a common theme in the superhero story. The evil villain is the one who wants to control the world; the hero is the one who wants to keep the world the way it is. Both desire the same object: the world. But as they cross paths, the two characters become fascinated with each other, learning their strengths and weaknesses, looking for their Kryptonite. Girard explains: "Each rival becomes for his counterpart the worshipped and despised model and obstacle, the one who must be at once beaten and assimilated."[7] This is acquisitive mimesis; this is also the relationship between The Doctor and The Master.

Another, closely related form of violence that Girard explores is what he labels "conflictual" mimesis. This begins in imitative desire as well, but it occurs when two or more individuals agree that they have the same adversary.[8] Acquisitive mimesis becomes conflictual mimesis when the desires of a community are involved, but the initial object of desire, whether it is for peace, or food, or comfort, or whatever, are forgotten. In this circumstance, the community converges in an allegiance against one chosen enemy. This conflict is then resolved in the kind of sacrifice that Girard explores in multiple texts including *The Scapegoat* and *Violence and the Sacred*. He calls this mode of sacrifice the "scapegoat function."

Essentially, the scapegoat function looks like this: when, in a community, there is a mimetic crisis, a crisis of desires that seem to be threatened, collective violence occurs. The group chooses a victim and, when that victim dies, the crisis is believed to be over. An excellent example of this at work in *Doctor Who* is in the episode "Midnight."

In the first stage of the scapegoat function, as explained by Girard in *The Scapegoat*, a great social crisis occurs. When this happens, members of a community feel that the fabric of their culture is being destroyed, which, in turn, they fear will lead to their own destruction.[9] "Midnight" began with the formation of a small, temporary community when a group of strangers meet each other on a sightseeing tour of an apparently uninhabited planet. The Doctor encourages the individuals on this trip to begin to talk to each other, sharing stories that reflect who they are, while at the same time pulling them closer together in a spirit of conviviality. When the shuttle breaks down, however, fear of the unknown and of death causes the members of this temporary community to change their attitudes. Their short-lived culture based on shared experience is threatened, but so are their very lives.

The next thing that happens in Girard's scapegoat model is that, because of the developing fear, the members of a community begin to direct accusations of violence against one person or one group of people. These accusations are generally of crimes that, if they had been performed, would destroy the very fabric of society as the accusers see it. The accused are not chosen randomly, but are people who "stand out." At different times in history, this scapegoating occurred because of differences in culture, background, religion, disability, degrees of wealth, or even levels of authority. Whatever it is that makes this one person stand out also makes him or her the ideal victim. Girard argues that the victim of collective violence is not chosen because he is different; he is chosen because he is not different enough: "in all the vocabularies of tribal or national prejudices, hatred is expressed not for difference, but for its absence."[10] The crimes that the scapegoat is accused of are crimes that remove difference and therefore eliminate the current social order.[11]

In "Midnight," this stage of Girard's scapegoating function begins after the people on the shuttle encounter something that knocks on the outside of the small ship that is keeping them alive. It appears that somehow the creature has entered the shuttle and has taken over the body of one person who had been, until this moment, just another member of the community. The woman named Sky is now marked as being different from the others, and so she, or the creature that is possessing her, is blamed for the deaths of the driver and the mechanic as well as damage to the shuttle. The crime that this creature, and/or Sky herself, is accused of is more than mere murder; it is a double murder that tears apart their community because without a mechanic, a driver, and a working shuttle, this crime could lead to the total destruction of their own community.

In all actuality, there is no evidence that the creature killed the two men at all—it is just as probable that the creature that appears to have possessed Sky was running from whatever killed the captain and the mechanic. At the same time, the knocking on the side of the shuttle could have been caused by another creature that had been chased away. But this accusation of a hideous crime focuses the small community's fear onto one scapegoat, while at the same time justifying the group's desire to cast Sky out of the shuttle into the light of a sun that would quickly kill her.

At this point, it is important to be aware that the desired object that initially lead to the fear and stress, which in this case is personal safety and the ability to go home again, is so far out of view that it no longer matters. Instead, the victim takes the blame for something more immediate: it could be something in the physical world, such as a lack of rain, or something in the supernatural world, such as sin, or the anger of the gods. No matter what the accusation, however, the community believes that in the death of that person their problems are solved. Members of a society engaged in working out this function believe that their immediate problem is solvable through the death of the scapegoat.

Generally, the next stage in the scapegoat function works this way: having chosen their scapegoat, a society focuses all of their mimetic violence on him and kills him. Frequently, but not always, surrounded by the trappings of ritual, the mimetic crisis is solved by this death because the community has projected all of its violent tendencies onto this scapegoat. The communal stress is thus temporarily relieved. In "Midnight," however, the Doctor complicates this stage because he sees it for what it is: mass hysteria. He argues with the others, trying to stop the group murder that is coming. Unfortunately, instead of listening, the other travelers transfer their fear onto this stranger who quickly proves himself to be a much better victim. He is accused of being "like an immigrant" and of "wanting this to happen." His "immigrant" status marks him as different; his apparent desire for this event is the horrific, community-destroying crime he has committed. The community continues to find things that are "different" about him: he is accused of not holding an advanced ticket like everyone else. Under any other circumstances this might appear unfair, but would hardly be considered a valid reason for demanding that person's death. Most importantly, the Doctor himself has claimed to be "clever" and let it slip that he is not human. He is different, but not nearly different enough. The crimes he has committed—enjoying himself, getting on without a ticket, and admitting that he is not human—mark him as a better scapegoat than the creature that has possessed Sky. At this point, being alien and looking human are far more disturbing than being alien and looking alien should be.

This reflects another aspect of the scapegoat model: transference of guilt. In being a scapegoat, the sacrificial victim symbolically takes on the guilt of the other members of the community. In this case, however, there is a literal transference: as the other people on the shuttle begin to focus their accusations on the Doctor, the creature possessing Sky stops the Doctor's ability to move or speak, presenting the appearance of passing from Sky to him. The creature in the woman's body can now speak like one of them, and joins the others in demanding that the Doctor be killed so that everyone else has a better chance of survival.

This working out of the scapegoat model takes a third turn. The creature in Sky's body uses a phrase that the Doctor is known to use, thus giving away the fact that it has not let go of the woman at all but is instead working on a second victim. At this point, the hostess on the shuttle realizes that the Doctor is not the one at fault. However, she still agrees with everyone else that someone must die for the good of the community. Only one person in the shuttle can see this desire for violence for what it is, but at this moment he has no ability to speak for himself. So, while the rest of the community is in the process of dragging the Doctor to the door in order to throw him into a light that will kill him, the hostess grabs the possessed Sky and jumps with her out of the shuttle. This nameless hostess willingly sacrifices herself to save the others, and immediately after this act of self-immolation, the whole shuttle falls silent.

The act of self-sacrifice moves this scapegoat mechanism into a new stage: according to Girard, the scapegoat function occurs over and over again within a community, and only ends when that people group witnesses the death of a victim they know to be innocent. When the hostess willingly sacrifices herself to destroy the creature possessing Sky, the communal crisis ends. Emotionally drained, each person stops his or her behavior. Even more importantly, the people still alive on the shuttle realize that the hostess and the Doctor, and even Sky herself, were all innocent. This realization only occurred, however, because the hostess willingly chose her own death. She has not for a moment been considered part of the problem, but she has taken onto herself the responsibility of saving the others. This self-chosen responsibility, along with her innocence, Girard argues, causes each individual to face the violent tendencies in him or herself and see them for what they are, thus ending that community's desire to scapegoat. In this case, each individual is left to reflect not on the crime that they have committed, which they would have justified to themselves in a sense of self-righteousness, but on the crime that they almost committed. If whatever has taken over the body of Sky is the real problem, then not only are Sky and the hostess who chose to die with her innocent, but so is the Doctor that they almost killed for no reason. [12]

Another example of the innocent sacrifice that ends a cycle of violence can be seen in the episode "The Doctor's Daughter." In this episode, two communities have been engaged in a violent battle for generations. Neither side knows what the original fight was about; the mimetic conflict that began this battle has disappeared as each "child of the machine" focuses his or her attention on their enemy and the war itself. This conflict appears to end, except for that single rogue general, not when the two sides find the "source," which they believe to be a weapon, but when Jenny, the cloned child of the Doctor, throws herself between her father and the gun that is aimed at him. The Doctor, in being the only person present who clearly speaks out against violence, is once again marked as a scapegoat. Jenny's death, however, is something different. A child of the machine herself, her innocent death again reveals the violence in the two conflicting communities for what it is.

The complete story arc of *Doctor Who* that began in 1963 and is still going includes many sacrificial deaths of both varieties: economic exchange and the sacrifice that is part of Girard's scapegoat model. With the introduction of the 9th Doctor, the questioning of sacrifice begins. While individual episodes still frequently include apparently noble sacrifices that occur in order to save others, a new storyline is introduced. This meta-narrative, or over-arching storyline that shapes the background of the shorter stories, focuses on an individual scapegoat from a cosmic mimetic conflict involving the fate of the entire universe. This storyline, however, does more than just repeat the scapegoat model as outlined by Girard and so fully demonstrated in "Midnight;" instead, it reveals the futility of the scapegoat model not by sacrificing an innocent victim, but by reversing roles.

The self-chosen sacrifice to buy an immediate need is still upheld within this meta-narrative, and is undertaken by such characters as an extremely wealthy and powerful woman whose ancestors were trees, a soldier on a planet that impossibly orbits a black hole, and a crooked

TV salesman who restores his good name by dying in an attempt to kill the creature planning to take over England during the coronation of Elizabeth II.[13] Sometimes the Doctor himself risks his life to save others, only to survive at the last possible moment, as occurs in "Evolution of the Daleks" when the Doctor tells the Daleks they can kill him if it will stop them from slaughtering the people who live in Hooverville.[14] These episodes support the idea of a willing sacrifice: in each case, the sacrifice or the willingness to be a sacrifice buys something critical to the story and is therefore rewarded.

The large number of personal sacrifices in individual episodes are, however, set against the larger story of the Doctor himself, who has become the scapegoat for the mimetic rivalry between two groups of people who have conflicting philosophies and motivations regarding time and their relationship to the rest of the universe: the Time Lords and the Daleks. The Time Lords uphold the belief that the universe should be allowed to run on its own; the Daleks wish to rule it. Intriguingly, this rivalry does not culminate in the ritualized or emotionally-heightened immolation of a victim. Instead, in this particular mimetic conflict it is not the scapegoat who dies, but the rivals. The two communities in conflict are destroyed, while their scapegoat continues to live as the last of his kind.

The Doctor has been coded as a potential scapegoat from the beginning. John Tulloch and Manuel Alvarado hint at this when, in *Doctor Who: The Unfolding Text*, they explain that every single thing that happens in the first episode, "An Unearthly Child," deliberately marks The Doctor as "other".[15] From his clothes to his behavior, the Doctor is defined as intrinsically different from and therefore suspected by the other characters, including his granddaughter and traveling companion, Susan. Tulloch and Alvarado continue to explain that throughout the series, the Doctor is defined not as a presence, but as "absence" and "mystery".[16] For the first several years on the air, he had no home, no name, and no identity. The only clue given is in the first episode when he explains to two British schoolteachers the predicament he and his granddaughter are in: "Susan and I are cut off from our own planet, without friends or protection. But one day we shall get back, yes, one day."[17] As the first couple of seasons progress, the Doctor's own granddaughter identifies more with the science and history teachers who join them on their travels than she does with him, and even she cannot explain why her grandfather remains nameless.

Even when, years later, the Doctor is finally given a home planet, Gallifrey, and a race, Time Lord, he is still marked as separate from the other Gallifreyans. He is of a different class than many; he has been exiled to earth. He has been accused more than once of being a criminal, has been put on trial for his life, been given a job as a special agent working for their government, been made president of Gallifrey and in "The Mysterious Planet" finds himself removed from office.[18] Later, in "Remembrance of the Daleks," he claims to still hold this title, and adds to it "Defender of the Laws of Time" and "Protector of Gallifrey."[19] Equally important, he is one of a few Time Lords who, for reasons not explained, is known by a title instead of a name. It is not accidental that the other frequently appearing Time Lord who goes by a title instead of a name, the Master, has also at different times throughout the series been placed in the role of a scapegoat. Both titles suggest the scapegoat nature of these two characters. "Doctor" is the title given to people who work to heal others, and the victim's death supposedly heals the community. A "Master" is a person separated out from others as a person with authority. In *The Scapegoat*, Girard points out that one of the things that leads a person to be marked as a potential victim of mimetic violence is the position of power they hold over others.[20] There is, however, a marked difference between the two Gallifreyan scapegoats: the Doctor tends to become complicit in his own victimization while the Master always rejects it. For example, in "Arc of Infinity," the 5th Doctor at least appears to agree that he must die to save his people, but in "The Deadly Assassin," the Master refuses to accept his own death.[21] One thing that they both have in common, however, is the Time Lord's potential for regeneration: as such, both nameless Time Lords can serve as scapegoats more than once.

While the two potential scapegoats prove to be handy for the Time Lords to keep around, this structure of sacrifice is brought into question several times in the series. For example, in "Arc," the Gallifreyan high council believes that they must sacrifice the Doctor in order to save the universe, but they are being manipulated in ways that they do not understand.

The most direct and effective challenge to the scapegoat model occurs in the storyline that begins with the 9th Doctor. It quickly becomes clear that a tragedy has occurred between the last story, a rather dubious account of the 8th Doctor saving the Earth at the turn of the current millennium, and the moment that the 9th Doctor is introduced. The 9th Doctor's second episode reveals that he is the last Time Lord left alive; the next several episodes slowly reveal that this is because of a battle involving the Time Lords and the Doctor's arch-enemies, the Daleks. While the Time Lords present themselves as generally peaceful beings who want to preserve the universe in its current state, the Daleks believe that the Dalek is the highest form of life and everything inferior must be exterminated, first on their own planet, then in the whole universe. In the earlier series, the Doctor is the Time Lord who first discovers these creatures, and he is the one who has been given the job of eliminating them.[22] At one point, the High Council of Gallifrey sends the Doctor back in time in order to attempt to destroy the Daleks at the time they are first created. There is one flaw in this plan: whatever his relationship is to the other Gallifreyans, as a Time Lord, the Doctor cannot bring himself to destroy even the most evil life forms imaginable.

The 9th Doctor, however, has changed his attitude about this enemy. In "Dalek," the Doctor is captured by a man who collects aliens and introduces his new find to the crown jewel of the collection: the last Dalek. The conversation between these two enemies is the biggest clue the audience has been yet given of the pieces missing from the Doctor's story:

> DOCTOR. Your race is dead. You all burned. All of you. Ten million ships on fire. The entire Dalek race wiped out in one second.
>
> DALEK. You lie.
>
> DOCTOR. I watched it happen. I made it happen.
>
> DALEK. You destroyed us?
>
> DOCTOR. I had no choice.
>
> DALEK. And what of the Time Lords?
>
> DOCTOR. Dead. They burnt with you. The end of the last great Time War. Everyone lost. [23]

Two important details are revealed here. The first is that, apparently, all but one of the Daleks and one of the Time Lords are dead. The Doctor, who has always stood against the Daleks even when he chose not to destroy them so long ago, is now responsible for the death of their entire species. This discovery of one last live Dalek clearly has a strong impact on the Doctor. The man who steadily refuses to carry a weapon suddenly begins a frenzied search for the most powerful thing he can find in order to do what he is supposed to: kill the last Dalek and end the Time War. This is reflected in the second important point that is revealed in this dialog: the Doctor is the one responsible for the deaths of all of the Daleks. He was not just present when it happened—he boasts that he made it happen.

This revelation of the Doctor's involvement is reinforced when this

Doctor and his companions face not one Dalek, but a whole fleet of them. In "The Parting of the Ways," Rose, who was present at the death of what the Doctor had previously believed to be the last Dalek, begins an important conversation:

> ROSE. You said they were extinct. How come they're still alive?
>
> JACK. One minute they're the greatest threat in the universe, the next they vanished out of time and space.
>
> DOCTOR. They went off to fight a bigger war. The Time War.
>
> JACK. I thought that was just a legend.
>
> DOCTOR. I was there. The war between the Daleks and the Time Lords, with the whole of creation at stake. My people were destroyed, but they took the Daleks with them. I almost thought it was worth it. And now it turns out they died for nothing.[24]

At this point the Doctor distances himself from any responsibility, but he links the deaths of his own people with those of the Daleks more closely. While he does not yet claim any responsibility in the statement "my people were destroyed," this exchange makes clear that he feels himself to be in a position to judge the value of the sacrifice that was made. The Doctor here points out the mimetic rivalry between the Time Lords and the Daleks. They are two different people groups who both want the same thing: the whole universe existing by their rules. The Time Lords lead by non-interference, in such a way that only creatures such as Daleks or planets that have gone extremely wrong even know of the Time Lords' existence. The Daleks would rule by destroying everything that is not Dalek. The Time Lords are saviors while the Daleks are destroyers, and, with his long history of standing out as a scapegoat for his own people, as well as for the Daleks, the Doctor is in the perfect position for the usual culmination of the conflict. But a strange thing happens. In this case, the mimetic rivals die together while the scapegoat lives.

The Doctor's role in the end of the mimetic rivalry is hinted at in other episodes and at other times, one of the clearest occurring in "The Satan Pit," when the Doctor meets a creature who has been bound in chains since before the universe began. Among his current companions, the question arises whether or not the creature is actually Satan, so, when the Doctor addresses this enemy, he asks: "What, then, you are the truth behind the myth?"[25] He does not receive an answer, but the creature addresses another issue: "This one knows me, as I know him. The killer of his own kind."[26] This creature who claims to be the ultimate evil recognizes the Doctor. The Doctor, the one who risks everything with the same level of commitment whether he is saving a whole planet or one small child, is, according to this ancient, malevolent creature, a murderer—more specifically, the murderer of the Time Lords. Other hints are dropped throughout the series, such as the way the Daleks continually refer to the Doctor as "our greatest enemy" and "the destroyer of our people." It is even occasionally pointed out that in ancient Dalek legend, there is a name for the Doctor: "The Oncoming Storm."[27]

More is explained when the Doctor learns that not only did the Daleks survive the destruction of their people, but so did one other Time Lord. This other survivor is not just any Time Lord, but the other supposed nameless one who has been used by the Gallifreyan High Council for their own ends and has been accused of crimes, tried for his life, and been found guilty. The Master has also been a scapegoat, but while the Doctor chooses to uphold the laws and beliefs of Gallifrey, The Master rebels against them, acting more like a Dalek than a Time Lord in his desire to control others. This man, the Doctor learns, only survived the Time War because, at the moment when all of the Time Lords were destroyed, The Master had already turned himself into a human in order to hide. Unfortunately for him, he had to turn himself so completely human that for many years he could not remember his own history. But after regaining his memory, he goes to Earth, the place that the Doctor has grown to love so much. While there, he contacts the only other Time Lord through a cell phone:

MASTER. Back home. Where is it, Doctor?

DOCTOR. Gone.

MASTER. How could it be gone?

DOCTOR. It burned.

MASTER. And the Time Lords?

DOCTOR. Dead. And the Daleks, more or less.

MASTER. The Time Lords only resurrected me because they
    knew I would be the perfect warrior for a Time War. I
    was there when the Dalek Emperor took control of the
    cruciform. I saw it. I ran. I ran so far. I made myself human
    so they wouldn't find me. Because... I was so scared.

DOCTOR. I know.

MASTER. All of them? But not you. Which must mean—

DOCTOR. I was the only one who could end it. And I tried; I did. I tried everything.

MASTER. What did it feel like, though? Two almighty civilizations burning. Oh, tell me; how did that feel? You must have been like God.[28]

The moment the Master learns that The Doctor was the only survivor of the war, he is immediately aware of how the Doctor must have survived. He is aware that the Doctor obtained the power to destroy not one, but two worlds. Knowledge of the earlier series suggests that, like other unusual abilities the Doctor received in unusual circumstances, this power was given to him by the Gallifreyan High Council, the people who have previously used him to achieve their own ends. In this case, however, their scapegoat does not die to buy a limited peace, but the two rival communities die while the scapegoat lives. Like all scapegoats, the Doctor is separated from the rest of his people by death, only this time it is theirs, not his. The idea is that this mimetic conflict is so huge that it cannot end in a mutual sacrifice, but can only end when both communities are dead. Even this grand gesture, however, does not end the cyclical system; the mimetic rivalry continues every time the Doctor meets more surviving Daleks, and now it begins again, this time between the Doctor and the Master, both Gallifreyan scapegoats interested in the Earth.

Because it becomes increasingly clear that many Daleks survived the Time War, generally by falling through time, the Doctor's action that was supposed to have ended the conflict was little more than a grand, but devastating gesture. Even when the Doctor believed that all of the Daleks were dead and the Time War was over, he describes the sacrifice he was required to make as "almost worth it."[29] In other words, at that point he had his doubts about the value of the sacrifice, but as more Daleks and Dalek war ships appear, the Doctor becomes increasingly aware that the holocaust he brought upon his own people bought nothing. Just as it turns out that not all Daleks died, with the reintroduction of the Master, it becomes clear that even the aspect of the sacrifice that included Time Lords was not quite as all-consuming as the Doctor had believed. The mimetic rivalry continues. The sacrifice meant nothing, because it did not stop the Daleks, it did not completely wipe out the Time Lords, and it did not even end the war itself. The pain and loss of the sacrificial victim remains and the cycle continues: the enemy always survives the sacrificial gesture, and so the sacrifice must occur again and again with the same outcome every time. The Doctor sums up the conflict between himself and the Daleks in "Daleks in Manhattan:" "They survived. They always survive when I lose everything."[30]

Doctor Who is complex in its relationship to and presentation of sacrifice. The series supports the self-sacrifice of a willing victim, condemns the sacrifice of the unwilling scapegoat, and casts doubt on the idea that mimetic rivalry and sacrificial systems can ever really be brought to an end. While occasionally the Doctor exhibits Messianic qualities, his sacrifice is never once for all, but must be repeated again and again. At the same time, the character who shows the most kindness and compassion in the whole series is the very character who is guilty of the mass destruction of two civilizations. He is not only accused of horrific crimes that eliminate difference between the two people groups, he has committed an unthinkable crime in the name of ending a war. The good Doctor is guilty of murder and is trapped in a never-ending scapegoat mechanism that cannot be escaped, if for no other reason than the simple fact that he now believes he must justify the deaths of his people.

Doctor Who thus differentiates between types of sacrifices; while the scapegoating mechanism, which involves placing the blame and responsibility for a societal ill on one person, is presented as futile destruction, the self-sacrifices chosen by individuals to save the lives of friends or companions are presented in a positive light. Ultimately, the *Doctor Who* series asks its audience to witness and understand the working out of mimetic rivalry. In other words, the Doctor at times called the "lonely angel" and the "lonely god" becomes the scapegoat causing not the rivals themselves but the viewer to see the scapegoating mechanism at work in him- or herself, with the potential of ending sacrificial systems not inside the text, but outside of it.

---

1 Keenan, 1.

2 It is worth noticing that while the Doctor could not save Rose's father from dying, he could change the sad death of a rather hopeless individual into something his daughter Rose perceives as much better—a self-sacrificial act that turns a man who was nothing in life into a hero in death.

3 Keenan, 2.

4 Keenan, 2-3.

5 Girard, *Violence and the Sacred*, 146.

6 Girard, *Things Hidden Since the Foundation of the World*, 26.

7 Girard, *Violence and the Sacred*, 36.

8 Girard, *Violence and the Sacred*, 26.

9 Girard, *The Scapegoat*, 14.
10 Girard, *The Scapegoat*, 22.
11 Girard, *The Scapegoat*, 21.
12 Girard, *The Scapegoat*, 100-111.
13 "The End of the World," "The Impossible Planet," "The Idiot's Lantern," 9th and 10th Doctors, Russell T. Davies (New) Series 2005-ongoing.
14 "Evolution of the Daleks," 10th Doctor, Russell T. Davies (New) Series 2005-ongoing.
15 Tulloch and Alvarado, 27.
16 Tulloch and Alvarado, 29.
17 "An Unearthly Child," 1st Doctor, Classic Series 1963-1989.
18 "The Mysterious Planet," 6th Doctor, Classic Series 1963-1989.
19 "Remembrance of the Daleks," 7th Doctor, Classic Series 1963-1989.
20 Girard, *The Scapegoat*, 18-19.
21 "Arc of Infinity," "The Deadly Assassin," 4th and 5th Doctors, Classic Series 1963-1989.
22 "The Daleks," "Genesis of the Daleks," 1st and 4th Doctors, Classic Series 1963-1989.
23 "Dalek," 9th Doctor, Russell T. Davies (New) Series 2005-ongoing.
24 "Parting of the Ways," 9th Doctor, Russell T. Davies (New) Series 2005-ongoing.
25 "The Satan Pit," 10th Doctor, Russell T. Davies (New) Series 2005-ongoing.
26 "The Satan Pit," 10th Doctor, Russell T. Davies (New) Series 2005-ongoing.
27 "Dalek," "The Girl in the Fireplace," 9th and 10th Doctors, Russell T. Davies (New) Series 2005-ongoing.
28 "The Sound of Drums," 10th Doctor, Russell T. Davies (New) Series 2005-ongoing.
29 "Dalek," 9th Doctor, Russell T. Davies (New) Series 2005-ongoing.
30 "Daleks in Manhattan," 10th Doctor, Russell T. Davies (New) Series 2005-ongoing.

Doctor Who and the Valkyrie Tradition Part 1:
The Valiant Child and the Bad Wolf

Kristine Larsen

Over the decades-long run of the *Doctor Who* television series, its titular character has been accompanied by an eclectic pantheon of companions, most of whom have been female. These women are generally strong, active characters who aid the Doctor in his ongoing mission to save the universe (and its inhabitants) from itself. Strong female characters abound in the mythological traditions of cultures worldwide, ranging from fertility goddesses to sorceresses and every conceivable manifestation of the feminine in between. For example, one of the enduring (and curious) feminine archetypes found in Northern European/Germanic literature is that of the valkyrie. In her review of the valkyrie tradition, Damico traces the roots of the famed female warrior (most widely known in modern culture through Wagner's *Ring* cycle) through numerous Indo-European cultures, illuminating the archetype's connection with "Irish war-goddesses, the Vedic *Divo duhita*, the Teutonic *idisi*, and certain twin sky-goddesses of ancient Greek lore."[1] As with most mythic archetypes, the character of the valkyrie has evolved over the centuries within the Northern European/Germanic tradition, leading to a schizophrenic dichotomy by the tenth century.

The valkyries apparently began as ferocious goddesses of slaughter who roamed the battlefield for victims. Davidson notes that the Anglo-Saxon "*waelcyrge*, 'choosers of the slain' in Anglo-Saxon glosses, is equated with the Latin word for Fury."[2] In Old Norse literature there also appears a valkyrie tradition (apparently more recent in origin) in which the female warriors are "benevolent guardians" who identified heroes and pledged their undying support to them. Damico argues that these two seemingly contradictory traditions actually reflect twin traditions in Oðin-worship and beliefs in the afterlife.[3] Jochens argues that there is another division in the tradition of what is included under the blanket term valkyrie, namely truly mythical creatures properly named *valkyrjur* in Old Norse (who are counted among the gods and demigods) and legendary heroines who embody some of the properties of the *valkyrjur*, but who form meaningful (and often romantic) relationships with the heroes. These valkyrie-like heroines Jochens terms *skjaldmeyjar,* or shield-maidens, a term familiar to readers of J.R.R. Tolkien's *The Lord of the Rings,* and most obviously represented in that work in Éowyn, Lady of Rohan. However, Jochens also notes that the terms valkyrie and shield-maiden are frequently used interchangeably in both Norse literature and scholarly research on that subject, and that convention will be continued here.[4]

In her seminal work, "The Valkyrie Reflex in J.R.R. Tolkien's *The Lord of the Rings,"*[5] Leslie Donovan identifies a number of characteristics that are both associated with the valkyrie tradition and applied to an analysis of female characters in Tolkien's trilogy. Four of these traits are common to multiple feminine archetypes:

- Divine or semi-divine origin
- Nobility (high social status)
- Supreme beauty
- Superior reasoning skills, intelligence, and insight[6]

Donovan next lists six traits specific to the Valkyrie Reflex:

- "Otherworldly radiance," sometimes linked to "battle fires"
- Masculine strength and physical prowess
- The fulfillment of ritual and ceremonial functions, including the bestowing of gifts
- The possession of prophetic insight and the utterance of prophetic remarks
- Freely choosing to act of her own (strong) will
- The ultimate loss of an important and beloved object, person, or skill[7]

Donovan also notes that the relationships between some heroes and valkyries found in Germanic heroic poetry "alter the course of events in the human world."[8] In her more general survey of valkyric traits and powers, Damico identifies several other characteristics common in this tradition:

- An erotic relationship between the "valkyrie-bride" and the hero[9]
- Grief on the part of both parties resulting from said relationship[10]
- The ability of the valkyrie to both spur the hero into action and bring about his destruction through that action[11]
- Supernatural powers that result in the valkyries not being limited in time and space[12]

These traits, as well as the juxtaposition of mercy and mercilessness, savior and slaughter, define a rubric against which we can measure any female character in the *Doctor Who* Universe. This essay and its companion piece by Jessica Burke will apply the valkyrie template to certain of the companions of the 9th and 10th Doctors, with the remainder of the current work focusing on she who is alternately referred to in the series as "the valiant child" and the "Bad Wolf," Rose Tyler.

As Donovan argued in her work on the Valkyrie Reflex in *The Lord of the Rings*, Tolkien did not simply use the valkyrie archetype as written in medieval texts, but adapted and reenvisioned the valkyries in light of the cultures of Middle-earth.[13] Likewise, we should not expect the women of *Doctor Who* to be cookie-cutter valkyries, but instead reflect recognizable attributes of this archetype as applied to the twenty-first century. In addition, although fourteen attributes were listed above, it can be argued that they can be easily intertwined into several sets of attribute clusters that are more sensibly discussed in these groupings. An example that highlights both these caveats is the combination of divine/semi-divine origin and noble social status. Since the main female companions of the 9th and 10th Doctors are human, the definition of a "divine" origin must be taken as metaphorical or symbolic. As will be argued later in this essay, in the case of Rose, it is more proper to say that she was "reborn" into semi-divine status as the Bad Wolf in the story arc of the same name. Rose's transition into the Bad Wolf and beyond also parallels her transition from ordinary working-class girl to true companion of a Time Lord and Defender of the Earth.

Although her titular episode makes it painfully clear that Rose Tyler was not born into a life of luxury or status, from the beginning it is evident that she transcends her humble official social status, especially as compared to those around her (most notably her mother and boyfriend). For example, from the beginning of "Rose," she demonstrates curiosity, grace under pressure, logical and intelligent thought processes, and bravery. Rose investigates strange sounds while in the basement of Henrik's department store, and when faced with the unworldly specter of animated mannequins, she calmly explains it as an elaborate prank executed by students. After meeting the Doctor, Rose searches the Internet for information on the mysterious stranger, coming across Clive's website. While she is successful in convincing Mickey Smith (her ordinary boyfriend with a rather ordinary last name) to drive her to Clive's house, Mickey does not share in Rose's sense of adventure and drive to solve the mystery, instead fearing that Clive is some sort of pervert or mass murderer who lures his victims to his lair through his website. Several episodes later, in "World War Three," Mickey declines an invitation to join Rose and the Doctor in their space-time travels, admitting to the Doctor that the idea is "too much." Similarly, Rose's mother, Jackie Tyler, is painted as a stereotypical working class house frau, more concerned with local gossip and sexual conquests than the apparent crash landing of an alien ship in the Thames.[14]

Rose also distinguishes herself from her human peers and aligns herself more closely with the Doctor in her ability to see through his bravado and blustering egotism. In "Rose," she refuses to accept the simple explanation that he's "the Doctor" and is not convinced that it sounds "impressive." Instead, she demands a logical, detailed explanation of who the Doctor really is and what his role is in the events unfolding around her. Likewise, at the beginning of her second episode,[15] the Doctor attempts to impress her by taking her further and further into the future. She playfully deflates his ego by claiming that he's not as impressive as he believes himself to be. By the middle of her second season,[16] Rose comes to accept danger as her constant companion. When the Doctor notes that the TARDIS has a queasy feeling about their latest landing point, Rose jokes that they can just get back into the craft and take off if there's a chance of trouble, to both of their immediate amusement.

There are two additional ways in which Rose is elevated from the humble social status of her human birth. In "Rise of the Cybermen," Rose and the Doctor disguise themselves as serving staff to infiltrate alternate-world-Jackie's birthday party, and in "School Reunion," Rose infiltrates the school's alien staff in the guise of a cafeteria server. In both cases, Rose is clear to differentiate between the disguises and how she sees herself, largely in the form of vociferous complaints to the Doctor. In three episodes Rose has encounters with servants and slaves, and although she is compassionate and empathetic in all cases, those of low social status are careful to recognize Rose's superior status, setting her apart from themselves. For example, in "The End of the World," Raffalo the blue repairwoman is openly thankful that Rose gives her permission to speak, but is clearly deferential to Rose. In "The Unquiet Dead" and "The Impossible Planet," Rose strikes up conversations with Gwyneth the servant girl and the Ood slave race respectively, and demonstrates palpable concern for their working conditions. If these examples appear too subtle, the writers hammer home the point in "Tooth and Claw," when Queen Victoria bestows the title of Dame Rose of the Powell Estate upon Miss Tyler. Therefore, although Rose was not born to high social status, through her interactions with the Doctor and her own personal traits, those around Rose clearly acknowledge she is no ordinary Londoner. As Captain Jack Harkness notes in "The Parting of the Ways," Rose is "worth fighting for."

The next two attributes that frame Rose as a valkyrie are beauty and "otherworldly radiance." Our first vision of Rose is as a young, tousle-haired blonde beauty getting out of bed to begin her day. We soon learn that she is nineteen years old and unmarried, further connecting her to the valkyrie tradition. Jochens explains that because a woman's strength was believed to peak around this age, prior to her marriage, it was only in this stage of life that a young Norse woman could be seen in the role of warrior.[17] Due to her natural beauty, Rose does not require the trappings of high fashion to paint her as a woman, and she often dresses rather plainly, in jeans, sneakers, and a t-shirt or sweatshirt. Despite this fact, the men around her often make a point to comment on her looks. In "Dalek," Henry van Statten describes Rose as a "rather pretty" piece in the Doctor's personal collection. While observing Rose through his binoculars in "The Empty Child," Jack Harkness comments "excellent bottom," and to Rose's horror, her own father comments on her beauty in ways that a father probably should not in "Father's Day." After taking over Rose's body in "New Earth," Cassandra admired her new physical form in a mirror, commenting on its curves and "nice rear bumper."

On those occasions when Rose does dress more formally, the Doctor (and the audience) certainly take note. For example, in "The Unquiet Dead," Rose picks out a formal Victorian dress and head piece in order to blend in with the England of Dickens. The Doctor's heartfelt response— "Blimey, you look beautiful"—is quickly qualified with the caveat that she looks beautiful for a human. "The Idiot's Lantern" opens with a view of Rose from the knees-down, exiting the TARDIS in pink high heels and black stockings. The camera pans up to show us she is dressed in an exceptionally feminine outfit from the 1950s, including a pink dress with crinolines.

Although her blonde hair stereotypically adds to her beauty, it also accentuates her luminous nature. When she is beamed into the Sycorax spacecraft, Rose is referred to as "the yellow girl" by the aliens.[18] On occasions when she is backlit (such as the scene in "Dalek" when she and the Dalek are walking out to the upper level), her blonde hair appears to glow like a halo. The same is true whenever she wears white, such as the white shirt in "Dalek," white jacket in "The Aliens of London," and white lab coat in "Army of Ghosts." Rose's connection with golden sunlight is highlighted in "Tooth" when the werewolf notes that she "burns like the sun," and most especially in "Dalek."

After becoming contaminated by Rose's DNA, the Dalek shoots a hole into the roof of van Statten's facility in order to let a beam of sunlight fall upon his now-exposed flesh. Rose protects the vulnerable creature from the Doctor's rage, explaining that the Dalek just wants to feel the sunlight. Like the valkyrie of old, Rose is also associated with numerous battle fires (such as the Nazi-set fires Rose flies over in "The Empty Child"), explosions (e.g., the exploding school in "School Reunion," the exploding mortuary in "Unquiet"), and even a cylinder of blue light marking a tractor beam in "Empty."

Closely aligned with Rose's physical beauty is her sexuality, another important trait of a valkyrie. For example, one of the first scenes of "Rose" shows her sharing public displays of affection with her boyfriend Mickey over a lunch date. Rose is also pursued romantically, albeit briefly, by both Adam and Jack Harkness. She is a beautiful woman who is naturally desired by men, although there is only one who holds the key to her heart (and not coincidentally the TARDIS as well). Her desirability and sexuality are highlighted on many occasions through comments by numerous characters. Cassandra describes her newly borrowed body as "a bouncy castle"[19] and purposefully unbuttons Rose's shirt further to expose her cleavage. When Rose asks Mickey to use his computer to research the Doctor, Mickey jokes that it is a ploy to get into his bedroom ("Rose"). When Rose and Mickey are briefly reunited in "Boom Town," they make plans to spend part of the night in a hotel, plans that never come to fruition because Mickey sagely surmises that he cannot compete with the Doctor for Rose's affection.

Rose's own words and actions also bring attention to her sexual nature. When the Doctor gives a partial list of plastic items that will come to life thanks to the Nestene Consciousness, Rose adds breast implants to the collection (leading the viewer to a rather interesting mental image). In "Unquiet," Rose and Gwyneth discuss their various troubles with men, with Rose's conversation quickly turning earthy. Gwyneth comments that Rose is a curious mixture of superficial high status and internal wildness, which Rose takes ownership of, retorting that perhaps it is good to be a "wild thing." At the end of the same episode, Charles Dickens is flustered by a kiss on the cheek bestowed by Rose, and the Doctor is quick to discourage the author from pursuing it further. Rose flirts shamelessly with Jack Harkness in "The Doctor Dances" and afterwards accuses a visibly jealous Doctor of "captain envy." When the Doctor retorts that he's not even a real captain (having been "defrocked"), Rose bemoans the fact that she was not able to witness that event in person.

In the valkyrie tradition, the relationship between the hero and the valkyrie is an erotic one, hence the term "valkyrie-bride." However, despite the great love between these two pivotal characters, their relationship is a troubled one, and often leads to the death of one or both partners, or some other kind of eternal separation. A similar situation is central to the relationship between Rose and the Doctor, as will be explored later in this essay. Throughout Rose's first two seasons, the air is thick with repressed love and unresolved sexual tension between Rose and the Doctor. On brief occasions, one or the other character will lower their defenses, such as Rose cajoling the Doctor into an awkward slow dance in "The Doctor Dances." Other characters, such as Pete Tyler, Jabe the Tree, Mickey, and even a constable in "The Aliens of London" are quick to pick up on what Rose and the Doctor deny is the true nature of their relationship, even to themselves, until it is too late.

Another of the characteristics of the valkyrie is her ceremonial role in the court, for example, as a giver of gifts. Rose gives a number of meaningful and symbolic gifts to those around her over the course of her first two seasons, ranging greatly in tangibility. Just as Galadriel kisses Frodo on the head before sending him off on his impossible Ring quest into the heart of Mordor in the film version of *The Lord of the Rings*, Rose ceremonially kisses the forehead of the Doctor's space helmet before he descends into the mine shaft and the company of the great demon in "The Impossible Planet." When the Sycorax's leader chops off the Doctor's hand (taking his sword with it), Rose tosses the Doctor a new weapon as soon as his hand regenerates.[20] In "The Long Game," Rose innocently gives Adam a TARDIS key in case he needs a safe and quiet place to rest. She also unknowingly gives him the key to his own downfall, namely her "superphone," which Adam keeps after borrowing and uses for his personal gain. Some of Rose's greatest gifts cannot be quantified. Although in the end she was unable to prevent her father's inevitable death in "Father's Day," Rose is heartened by Pete's thankful explanation that she was able to gift upon him extra hours of life and knowledge of his daughter as an adult. In addition, Rose gives her father the comfort of not dying alone, and closure on the part of the young driver, who stops and takes responsibility for the accident in this new reality.

Perhaps the greatest gift Rose bestows upon another (besides the love and support given to those close to her, especially the Doctor), can be found in "Dalek." Rose gives the creature renewed life (through her DNA) as well as the freedom of death, which the Dalek begs for at the conclusion of the episode after contemplating its new "contaminated" state of being. In ordering the Dalek to destroy itself, she gives the creature the suicidal end it cannot bring about otherwise, and an alternative to the emptiness of an eternity of exterminating.

One of the supernatural traits Damico attributes to the valkyrie is the ability to supersede limitations in time and space.[21] Since the fundamental basis of the entire series is that the Doctor and his companions travel across time and space, it may appear that this trait is applied equally to all of the Doctor's companions and does not truly contribute to Rose's valkyric traits. On the contrary, Rose travels farther than most of the Doctor's companions, both in time and space. In "The End of the World," Rose and the Doctor travel five billion years into the future to witness the end of the Earth, and exactly one season later in "New Earth," they make the same temporal transition to witness how the human race prospered despite the death of their planet. In "Impossible," the Doctor notes that they are on a sanctuary base, meaning that they have traveled to the "edge of the universe." As described later in this paper, in her Bad Wolf persona Rose briefly masters time and space. But among the greatest evidence of Rose's superior mastery over space-time is seen in her travels between different dimensions—different universes—in the 10th Doctor arcs of "Army of Ghosts"/"Doomsday," and "Partners in Crime" through "Journey's End." Despite her ability to traverse these dimensions, her control over them (and her role in them) is painfully limited (as seen in "Journey's End"). By the time of "Turn Left," Rose cannot divulge her true name, for fear of destroying that which she seeks to save. She can only explain that she has "crossed too many different realities" and her actions can endanger causality itself.

After space-time facileness, the valkyric trait that most easily befits one of the Doctor's female companions is their nearly unanimous call to decisive actions of their own free will. Rose is certainly no exception to this rule. In her first episode, when the Doctor invites her to become his traveling companion, Rose inquires about the danger, which the Doctor freely admits to. After initially begging off under the excuse that she is responsible for her mother and "this stupid lump" (aka Mickey), Rose makes the admittedly impetuous decision to join the Doctor since he can also travel in time. After witnessing the end of the Earth, and additional examples of the danger the Doctor attracts, Rose is given the opportunity to return to her old safe life. There is a moment of hesitation, but she affirms her desire to face the unknown and continue traveling with the Doctor—after he buys her some traditional London chips, of course.[22] Among Rose's other demonstrations of free will are her determination to not allow her father to die alone[23] and her conscious decision to "sign up" for an official tour of duty with the Doctor at the end of "World War Three." Of course a further inventory could be made of occasions when Rose makes decisions to put herself in danger in order to save others (most especially the Doctor), but that would result in a list of most of the episodes in which she appears.

Traveling with the Doctor requires not only determination and bravery, but the ability to defend oneself as well. While Rose is not the only one of the Doctor's female companions who can be said to exhibit masculine physical strength and warfare skills on occasion (e.g., Martha

Jones), as with others of the traits listed above, Rose appears to exceed many of the previous companions. In her very first episode, Rose saves both the Doctor and a whimpering Mickey from the hands of the Nestene Consciousness by using her gymnastic ability (for which she had earned a bronze medal in school) to knock over the Doctor's captors.[24] Several episodes later in "The Long Game," when chaos ensues on Floor 500 Rose is able to free herself from her manacles before the Doctor and aid in his rescue. Rose's gymnastic skills are also on display in "The Empty Child," when she climbs a rope with the intention to reach a troubled child. Unknown to her, it is the mooring rope for a dirigible, and she flies over London during a Nazi bombing, clinging to her lifeline for an unbelievably long period of time before finally losing her grasp. In "Fear Her," Rose easily wields a pick axe and breaks the Isolus pod free from its asphalt prison, then turns the ax on Chloe's barricaded bedroom door while the girl's impotent mother watches.

It is in her apparent ease with weapons that Rose cements her role as a woman warrior. When she and the Doctor are apparently menaced by the Ood at the start of "Impossible," Rose instinctively grabs the nearest possible weapon to her, in this case a stool, and takes up a defensive stance. Rose and Mickey roam the S.S. Madame de Pompadour comfortably bearing equally large guns,[25] presaging Rose as grim weapons-bearing interdimensional warrior in "Stolen Earth" and "Journey's End." Rose was truly speaking the truth in "Fear Her" when she explained "I'm tougher than I look."

Not only is the valkyrie a mixture of beauty and strength, she also uneasily combines benevolence and destruction, salvation and the slaughter. She is both a giver of gifts and a potential taker of lives. In the case of *Doctor Who*, this precarious balance lies at the very heart of the series itself. In at least four episodes in Rose's first two series, characters make a point to remind the audience that death and destruction are the Doctor's constant companions.[26] As one of the Doctor's closest companions, Rose not only shares in his adventures, but also in the danger and moral dilemmas his adventures entail. However, Rose brings her own potential for slaughter to the table, separate from the Doctor's vengeance. In "World War Three," Rose suggests to Harriet Jones that a nuclear bomb could be launched at the Slitheen. Harriet responds with a disapproving scold: "You're a very violent young woman." Rose acts as the bringer of death to Daleks on several occasions. For example, in "Dalek," Rose not only gives life to the "last" Dalek through her DNA, but brings about the death of his pure "Dalek-ness," and at the end of the episode, she brings about his ultimate demise through ordering him to commit suicide.

Among the valkyrie's other weapons are her superior wisdom,

reasoning power, and intelligence. On a number of occasions, Rose is seen using her intelligence to solve problems, and on others she directs those around her to think logically to find a solution to the problem at hand. Several examples are found in Rose's eponymous first episode. As previously noted, Rose attempts to make sense of an illogical situation when faced with animated mannequins in the basement of Henrik's department store. She reasons that the most logical explanation is students, who would have the time and temperament to take part in what we in America would call Rose being Punk'd. Even the Doctor compliments her on her reasoning skills (which are unfortunately off track at that moment). In the restaurant, when faux-Mickey attacks, endangering all the patrons, Rose hits the fire alarm and directs everyone to leave immediately. When the Doctor describes the Nestene Consciousness's transmitter, Rose immediately identifies it as the famous ferris wheel (conveniently placed behind the Doctor). Rose demonstrates similar puzzle-solving skills in "The Satan Pit," when she figures out the demon's plan (shown as parallel to the Doctor's epiphany), and in "Fear Her," when she identifies Chloe Webber as the cause of the children's disappearance.

Rose uses her intelligence as an effective weapon in order to save the lives of herself and others on several other occasions. In "World War Three," Rose saves herself, Harriet Jones, and the Doctor when the Doctor cannot assure their safety. Knowing that a conventional missile is headed towards their location, Rose reasons that an internal closet will provide them additional safety from the blast, similar to riding out an earthquake. The trio survives the blast thanks to Rose's ingenuity. Similarly, when Rose, Jack Harkness, and the Doctor find themselves surrounded by gas-mask people in "The Empty Child," Rose realizes that firing the sonic blaster *at* the approaching menace will not save them, and instead points the weapon at the floor, allowing them to fall down to the next level and to safety. As a final example, in "Tooth and Claw," Rose directs Sir Robert's family and household staff to save themselves from the werewolf by acting together as a team to pull at their chain's attachment point to the wall, which succeeds in breaking them free.

Rose's intelligence is not limited to practical problem-solving, but also waxes philosophical at the appropriate times. On her first real adventure in the TARDIS, Rose visits Earth five billion years into the future, at its demise, and ponders for herself—and the audience—the sheer magnitude of witnessing the death of one's world billions of years after everyone she has loved is dead and turned to dust. Perhaps it is this first experience with the fragility of life that instills in Rose an ability to see beyond the exterior of a person, into their soul and motivation. This is perhaps best seen in "Dalek," when she protects the revitalized Dalek from being killed by the

Doctor. As she sagely explains to the Time Lord, the Dalek is changing, but so is the Doctor. Which of the two was currently the most monstrous was clearly open to interpretation, although as the Doctor realizes, the answer was probably easily seen with a look into the mirror.

Along with a natural human intelligence, the valkyrie exhibits prophetic vision and speech, and her words and relationship with the hero have important implications on the future of their world. From very early in her first season, Rose understands the vital role the Doctor plays in securing the universe. When she explains to Mickey that the 9th Doctor is not her boyfriend, but something far more important, is she preparing us for the 10th Doctor's "death" in "Turn Left," and all the ramifications that has on reality?[27] When the unthinkable finally occurs in Donna's alternate reality, due to her failure to meet the Doctor and prevent him from dying under the Thames, Rose appears from her parallel dimension in order to spur Donna into action and save all possible worlds from destruction. In doing so, she uses her knowledge of the proper timeline, which appears to Donna to be prophetic information of events that have not yet occurred. For example, Rose directs Donna to take her soon-to-be winning raffle ticket and be far from London on the next Christmas holiday. In doing so, Rose prevents Donna and her family from being killed in the Titanic's fall to Earth. This buys Rose and the universe more time to find a way to correct the damage that had been done by Donna's unwittingly destructive wrong turn.

Rose appears to Donna several more times, materializing in this alternate reality in a luminous flash of light reminiscent of the time-jumps in *The Terminator*. As she directs Donna's actions toward the inevitable act of self sacrifice (for as Jessica Burke's contribution to this book will argue, Donna is also a valkyrie-figure in her own right), Rose uses her knowledge of the future—of all possible futures—to make prophecies that finally rouse Donna to action. In her most powerful prophecy, Rose tells Donna that in three week's time, her grandfather will see something with his telescope that will make Donna finally ready to work with Rose, despite the fact that it will lead to her own death. All unfolds as Rose has foretold, and the Doctor is saved, and with him the fate of all universes, at least for the time being. For Rose has one final prophecy, undoubtedly her greatest of all, an outgrowth of her similar prophetic acts during her adventures with the 9th Doctor. As Donna lay dying, Rose whispers two words into her ear, which Donna relates to the Doctor when she awakens back in the original timeline—"Bad Wolf." With a look of utter horror on his face, the Doctor races out of the fortune teller's lair, to find that Rose's powerful warning has replaced all writing in Shan Shen. Her warning about the end of the universe has crossed universes, timelines, and alternate realities to finally reach her chosen hero.

What does our hero do when he receives a warning or plea for help from his valkyrie? As with all proper Norse-style heroes, he is immediately spurred into action, despite the fact that the action may very well end in grief, as well as his own injury or death. Perhaps the most obvious example is in "The Christmas Invasion," when Rose stands vigil over the unconscious regenerating Doctor. When a plastic Christmas tree attacks Rose and Jackie, Rose places the sonic screwdriver into the Doctor's hand and in an act all-too reminiscent of Princess Leia and Obi-wan Kenobi, whispers in his ear, "help me." The Doctor immediately wakes up and instinctively uses the weapon on the menacing flora. This act removes the immediate threat, but sets into motion the Doctor's later life-threatening interactions with the Nestene Consciousness. Later in the same season, Rose investigates the mysterious Magpie television repair shop and the "pretty little girl" has her face sucked off by "The Wire." Rose is brought to the Doctor by the police, giving the Time Lord the ultimate motivation to solve this crime. Grim-faced, he vows that there is "no power on this Earth that can stop me."[28]

Rose plays a more active role in driving the Doctor to act in "World War Three," in the scene when Mickey and Rose are threatened by the Slitheen. Hearing their urgent cries over the telephone, Rose begs the Doctor (who is uncharacteristically paralyzed with indecision) to save her mother. The Doctor responds by directing Rose and Harriet to share everything they know about the Slitheen, in an effort to discern their home planet (and hence their weakness). In the same episode, the Doctor is reticent to share with his companions the sole solution he can find to stop the Slitheen (which the viewer soon learns is a direct missile strike on 10 Downing Street) because it might endanger Rose. Without hearing the solution, Rose urges him to take action, even though the result might be his losing her (an admission accompanied by a lingering pained expression on the Doctor's face).

The horrifying thought of losing Rose is a recurring theme throughout the 9th and 10th Doctors' first seasons. For example, in "Dalek," an enraged Doctor lashes out at Henry van Statten when he believes Rose has been killed when she is trapped behind a bulkhead with the creature. The Dalek uses the Doctor's emotions against him in the following scene, when it is revealed that Rose is alive, albeit the Dalek's prisoner. The alien taunts the Time Lord, inquiring about the use of emotions if they prevent one from saving those they love. The Doctor submits to the Dalek's demand to open the bulkhead, explaining that he had already killed Rose once and could not bear to do it again. This painful choice again faces the Doctor in "The Satan Pit," where the Doctor makes the conscious decision to destroy the demon, despite the fact that Rose may very well be killed in the process. He explains his willing sacrifice to the demon as evidence of his unshakable trust and belief in Rose, and that they will either both succumb or Rose will "find a way" to save them all. It should be noted that Rose's loss is inevitable, as is the loss of all those the Doctor cares for, because as an immortal he is doomed to outlive all those around him. The Doctor explains to Rose in "School Reunion," this is the greatest sorrow of all. As a Time Lord his curse is to ultimately live alone, and to watch the death of those he loves, whether through old age or tragedy. Therefore, his relationship with Rose is doomed from the onset to cause him immeasurable grief.

This loss of that which is most precious is central to the Valkyrie Reflex. Both the valkyrie and her hero must suffer the loss of something central to their existence, in extreme cases their very lives (either in willing self-sacrifice or as the victim of murder or other catastrophes). Rose suffers increasing iterations of loss throughout her travels with the Doctor. As early as her second episode, Rose witnesses the destruction of the Earth, taking with it all its history.[29] Despite the Doctor's admonition to "be careful what you wish for," Rose asks to bear witness to her parents' past, and in the process loses her childhood illusions that their relationship was a fairy-tale one and that her father was a successful businessman and perfect father. She has to bear the pain of losing her father (more than once) when she experiences her father's death in person.[30] In "Rise of the Cybermen," Rose is faced with a reality in which she has never been born, and her cold and materialistic mother is transformed into a Cyberman. It is interesting to note that if Rose had been born into this parallel world, she would have more clearly met the valkyrie criteria of high birth and status. In the next episode, Rose faces the loss of Mickey, whom she does care about and relies on despite his inability to compete with the Doctor for her deepest affections, when he decides to remain in the parallel reality. Although they are reunited in later episodes (when Rose is banished to the parallel world), it is only temporary, as Mickey eventually chooses to return to the primary reality.[31]

Finally, Rose's willingness to sacrifice herself to save the Doctor (and/or her world) is evident in a number of episodes, for example the previously mentioned "World War Three." In "The Satan Pit," Rose demonstrates that she deserves the Doctor's unwavering faith in her. After the demon (speaking through the Ood) taunts the Doctor and Rose by prophesying that she—the "valiant child"—was doomed to soon die in battle, Rose does not back down in the face of what appears to be certain death. As the spaceship escapes the black hole, bringing with it the embodied spirit of the demon in the form of Toby, Rose uses the remaining ammunition in the bolt gun to fracture the windshield and unbuckle Toby's harness, simultaneously sealing the creature's fate and their own. In true valkyrie spirit, she meets her fate with bravery, noting that although they will all die, she unselfishly acted as the Doctor would have done, vanquishing the creature. Rose is visibly concerned about the demon's prophecy of her impending death (as evidenced in her later inquiry to the Doctor about it), yet this does not deter her from her heroic and ultimately self-sacrificing actions in later episodes (most especially "Doomsday").

While examples of each of these elements of the Valkyrie Reflex can easily be found in various episodes, certain episodes particularly highlight Rose Tyler's role as a valkyrie. Among these are the two-part installments "Bad Wolf," "The Parting of the Ways," "Army of Ghosts," "Doomsday," and "Stolen Earth," and "Journey's End." In these three pairs of episodes, it can be shown that Rose simultaneously embodies a number of the valkyrie characteristics, including the polar extremes of benevolent protectress and merciless mistress of the slaughter, as well as the themes of loss and grief. In the "Bad Wolf / "Parting of the Ways" arc, Rose is a source of loss and grief for the Doctor on several occasions. In the first episode, the Doctor believes Rose to be dead when she is apparently vaporized after attempting to escape from a murderous parody of "The Weakest Link." Later in the arc, after Rose makes clear her unwavering decision to stand with her hero (rather than run away and save herself), despite the odds, the Doctor makes the conscious decision to sever himself from both Rose and the TARDIS by sending Rose back to her own time and home in order to save his beloved time machine and companion from the Daleks and his delta wave weapon.

Once back on Earth, Rose suffers an unfathomable grief and sense of loss as well, noting that she cannot return to a normal, ordinary life after witnessing a more noble and meaningful existence. Rose has made the transition from ordinary to nobility, in keeping with the valkyrie tradition. She is determined to return to the Doctor of her own free will, at any cost, even her own life, as she explains to Mickey—"there's nothing left for me here." She uses her superior intelligence to reason that if she can access the heart of the TARDIS she can use its telepathic powers to force it to return to the Doctor. Her actions are initiated by the realization she is fulfilling a prophecy, namely the message "Bad Wolf," which has been surrounding her for some time (in this case, written in large letters on the asphalt).

Once committed to her willful, self-sacrificing course of action, Rose opens the heart of the TARDIS and the light pours into her eyes, the windows of her soul. In this way, Rose and the TARDIS are linked heart to heart, soul to soul, transfiguring Rose into a figure of golden light, an embodiment of the Time Vortex and all its powers. She has become divine, and has the ability to discern every atom in the universe at every moment in time—she is no longer limited in time and space. She and the TARDIS return to the space station and act as the hero's private protectress, explaining that she was saving him from "the false god," namely the Emperor Dalek.

In her divine role as TARDIS personified, Rose proclaims that she is the source of the very prophecy that drove her to this point—she herself is the Bad Wolf, who created her own being and scattered her own message throughout time and space. She becomes Brahma and Shiva, creator and destroyer, and is able to see everything that has ever been or could ever come to pass. In a terrible display of her power she commits what appears to be genocide, in destroying the Dalek Emperor and all his compatriots, and then in the next breath returning life to Jack Harkness, who becomes deathless (immortal). But she is not truly a goddess, and the power of the Time Vortex begins to consume her. The Doctor takes the power into himself through a kiss, but at the expense of his own present incarnation, resulting in his premature regeneration. Love becomes death, death becomes life, and none of the affected characters is the same for their experience.

In the episodes immediately following the Bad Wolf incident (the first season of the 10th Doctor), Rose appears weakened and diminished, less independent and more closely aligned with the stereotypical damsel in distress than a true shield maiden, as if the Doctor removed more than merely the Time Vortex and relevant memories from her mind. If she had been male, one would be tempted to call her temporarily castrated. Perhaps this was meant to parallel the rebirth of the Doctor (and all the changes and uncertainties that accompany a Time Lord's regeneration). Whatever the intent, it is clear that over this season of the series Rose regenerates as well, rejuvenating from her own personal nadir in "The Christmas Invasion," reclaiming her previous strength (physical, emotional, and mental) through "Rise," to "Satan," and culminating in "Army," and "Doomsday," where we again see Rose in her full valkyrie fury.

"Army of Ghosts" begins with the shot of a bleak landscape (which we later learn is Bad Wolf Bay in Norway), and a grim, black-clad Rose standing amidst the desolation alone. Her sorrowful voiceover explains that we are about to learn the tale of how she died. It appears that the demon in "The Satan Pit" was correct in his prophecy that the "valiant child" was doomed to die in battle, as any good valkyrie should. The unfolding episode is ripe with foreshadowing as well as philosophical reflection of past episodes and adventures. Jackie is reunited with her daughter, whom she barely recognizes. Rose admits that she has been greatly changed by her time with the Doctor, and that she is no longer the simple girl who worked in a department store. When asked if she will ever settle down, Rose ties her fate to her hero, the Doctor, explaining that since he will never settle down, neither can she (an ironic statement when considered after viewing the episode "Journey's End"). Jackie warns Rose that she will keep changing and eventually cease being Rose, perhaps even stop being human. The apparent apotheosis of Rose, which was temporarily achieved in "Parting," seems to have left a permanent mark on her, one which is evident to her mother. She has forsaken her ordinary birth as a London commoner for a rebirth as a true valkyrie.

Rose's effect on Mickey is also evident in this story arc. When Torchwood is threatened by the Daleks and Cybermen, Mickey and company travel from their parallel dimension into Rose's, the "stupid lump" now transformed into a warrior himself, whose charge is "defending the Earth." When Rose calls Mickey "the bravest man I've ever met" (quickly qualified to bravest human, after Mickey reminds her of the Doctor), we see a valuable gift Rose has given to her former boyfriend, the gift of personal growth. Although it has (and will once again in the future) necessitated her separation from him, her loss has been Mickey's gain.

When faced with the Daleks emerging from the Voidship in "Doomsday," Rose stands her ground, as we once again glimpse the divine Rose, the Bad Wolf, holder of superhuman knowledge, prophetic powers, and control over time and space. She sheds the white lab coat that was her previous disguise, and exudes an inner confidence and luminosity that transcends the visual. With the fury of a full-blooded valkyrie, Rose boasts that she not only faced down the Emperor and his army, but she "took the Time Vortex and pulled it into his head and turned him to dust." With a bloodlust reminiscent of the original valkyrie of Norse lore (as goddess of the slaughter), Rose adds with a laugh, "The god of Daleks, and I destroyed him." Less dramatic, but equally as willful, are Rose's acts later in "Doomsday," when she returns from Pete's world to her own reality, in direct opposition to the Doctor's wishes (and attempts to keep her safe). When the Doctor explains that once the breach between the universes is closed, it can never be reopened, thus forever separating Rose from her mother (who is now in Pete's world), Rose reminds her hero that she made her choice "a long time ago" and will never leave him.

The valkyrie and her chosen hero work as a team to open the time breach and destroy both the Daleks and the Cybermen, and then close the breach to save both worlds. Unfortunately, Rose loses her grip (after bravely pulling back the slipped lever to assure that all their enemies are sucked into the void), and is only saved from certain death by her parallel father, who safely catches her and brings her back to his world just before the breach closes. Rose and the Doctor are now separated, one assumes forever, in both time and space, their relationship ultimately bringing them both grief and loss. This loss is magnified in the episode's coda, where Rose follows prophetic visions in her dreams, and comes to Bad Wolf Bay in Norway for a bittersweet reunion with the Doctor. Using the power from a dying star, the Doctor manages a two minute projection of his image into Rose's new world (one she clearly sees as a prison), and tells her that she is officially dead in her primary world. Rose explains that she has aligned herself with this world's Torchwood, the valkyrie still active as "Rose Tyler - defender of the Earth."

The Doctor is doomed to live his life alone, in the grief of the last of the Time Lords. This grief becomes razor sharp, for both Rose and the Doctor, and the viewer, when Rose proclaims her love for the Doctor but his reply is cut short by the end of his transmission. The view of tears running down the Doctor's cheeks is potent, a fitting summary of the relationship of the valkyrie and her hero.

But the tortured relationship continues through the third season of the 10th Doctor, beginning with Rose's futile attempts to warn the Doctor of his impending doom in "Partners in Crime," "The Poison Sky," and "Midnight." In "Journey's End," Rose remains true to her Valkyrie Reflex, this time spurring a heroine instead of a hero to action, in this case Donna Noble. As previously noted, in "Stolen Earth" and "Journey's End," we see Rose as a "badass" weapons-bearing interdimensional warrior. The Rose of this arc is a complete battle-hardened valkyrie, in the tradition of *Alien*'s Ripley and *The Terminator*'s Sarah Connor, determined to defeat the alien enemy in order to save the lives of others, no matter the personal sacrifice it may entail. When chaos ensues on the relocated Earth, Rose appears, bearing a very large weapon and a grim attitude. She walks into a store, cocks her gun, and threatens two looters, adding with Freudian humor, "Do you like my gun?" When the Daleks reveal their identity, all of the Doctor's previous companions—Martha Jones, Jack Harkness, Sarah Jane Smith—falter in their confidence, with the exception of Rose, who responds by firing her weapon at a Dalek ship. Rose can see the other companions through Donna's parents' laptop, but initially cannot communicate with them (or the Doctor, or Harriet Jones), and even her reunion with Mickey comes to an end, as he decides to remain in the primary reality at the end of the arc. Thus we see that it is not only the Doctor who is destined to be alone, but his valkyrie as well.

Rose's use of Bad Wolf as a prophecy appeared throughout her first season, from the name of the Slitheen mayor's nuclear power plant (Blaidd Drwg) in "Boom Town" and the name of Henry van Statten's helicopter in "Dalek" (Bad Wolf One) to a defaced rave poster in "Father's Day," and graffiti on the TARDIS in "The Aliens of London" (among other examples). Even after the origin and initial purpose of the prophetic words were revealed in "The Parting of the Ways," Rose continued to come into contact with them, leading to the ultimate battle at the end of all universes in "The Stolen Earth" arc. The mythic meaning of the words Bad Wolf and their connection to the end of the universe are clear from a Norse perspective. In this tradition, the last battle, in which the gods battle against the forces of evil, aided by the human warriors whom they have drawn to their side over the ages, is called Ragnarök, the Doom of the Gods. The parallel with the Doctor and his companions fighting the Daleks over the fate of all possible worlds is clever if not predictable.

But the connection between the phrase Bad Wolf and Ragnarök is not as obvious to a modern audience as it would be to the original listeners of Old Norse poetry and prose. In "Tooth and Claw," the werewolf taunted Rose that there was something of the wolf in her, and as previously noted, the werewolf linked Rose to the sun and himself to the moon. In Norse myth, the chariots of the sun and moon were constantly chased by two ferocious wolves, Sköll (repulsion) and Hati (hatred), who desired to devour the luminous orbs and plunge the world back into utter darkness. While they were sometimes temporarily successful in swallowing one or the other luminary (creating eclipses), the wolves would not be successful until the beginning of Ragnarök.[32]

After a frustratingly long tease to the audience (nearly the entire episode), the Doctor and Rose are finally reunited, but not without the predictable sacrifice and grief. The Doctor is shot by a Dalek ray as he runs toward Rose, and begins to regenerate. While the regeneration is halted (by channeling the energy into his disembodied hand), the sacrifice is evident and begets an even larger sacrifice and sorrow to come. After vanquishing the Daleks, all the Doctor's companions are safely returned to their rightful homes, with the exception of Rose, who considers the parallel world an alien landscape. She protests her return, because she traveled through time and space (and dimensions) to be reunited with her hero. The Doctor explains that there is a cost to their reunion and their actions, in this case the Doctor 10.5. His crime is genocide against the Daleks (a crime that Rose herself committed as the Bad Wolf, and for which one could say she was ultimately banished to the alternate reality). The Doctor describes his part-human doppelganger as "born in battle, full of blood and anger and revenge," the male equivalent of a valkyrie. The Doctor reminds Rose that he himself was in this primitive state when Rose first met him, and that their relationship changed him for the better. It is now her charge to work the same metamorphosis on the Doctor 10.5.

Knowing that their separation is a sacrifice he will have to make, the Doctor resists the urge to complete his previously aborted declaration of love to Rose, instead leaving that to the Doctor 10.5. His grief is palpable as he explains that Rose and the other Doctor can have a normal life together, including the all-to-human experience of growing old together. He, however, is doomed to continue on alone, in his own sort of solitary confinement, free to travel in space and time, but nonetheless trapped in his ultimate loneliness.

And what of Rose's fate? On the surface, one might argue that she has transcended the tragic fate of the valkyrie, for the Doctor suggests his human version really is him, with all his feelings, memories, and reactions. But the audience, and Rose, knows better. Just as Pete Tyler refers to Rose as "the daughter of a dead man"[33] rather than his own flesh and blood, this human-Time Lord hybrid is not the Doctor. The resemblance is superficial, not only in its physical form. For as Sarah Jane warns Rose, the real pain of knowing the Doctor is not only the eventuality of losing him, but all that his and the TARDIS's companionship entails—"We get a taste of all that splendor, then we have to go back."[34] Although he and the Doctor share a face, he is merely a two-dimensional reflection of the Time Lord, trapped in time and space alongside Rose. And despite the depth of his love for her, and no matter how deep her feelings for this hybrid Doctor may become, he will remain a constant reminder of all that she has lost. In the dark of the night, in the silence before dawn, as the golden-haired valkyrie shares her bed with the man whose face mirrors that of her beloved hero, she will hear a single heartbeat, and be painfully reminded of every sacrifice she has made.

---

1 Damico, *Beowulf's Wealhtheow and the Valkyrie Tradition*, 41.

2 Davidson, 178.

3 Damico, *Beowulf's Wealhtheow and the Valkyrie Tradition*, 41.

4 Jochens, *Old Norse Images of Women*, 90.

5 The author wishes to emphatically thank Anthony Burdge and Jessica Burke for pointing out the relevance of Donovan's paper to the mythology of *Doctor Who*.

6 Donovan, 110-11.

7 Donovan, 111.

8 See note 6.

9 Damico, *Beowulf's Wealhtheow and the Valkyrie Tradition*, 48.

10 Damico, *Beowulf's Wealhtheow and the Valkyrie Tradition*, 79.

11 Damico, *Beowulf's Wealhtheow and the Valkyrie Tradition*, 42.

12 See note 10.

13 Donovan, 109.

14 "Aliens of London," 9th Doctor, Russell T. Davies (New) Series 2005-ongoing.

15 "The End of the World," 9th Doctor, Russell T. Davies (New) Series 2005-ongoing.

16 "The Impossible Planet," 10th Doctor, Russell T. Davies (New) Series 2005-ongoing.

17 Jochens, *Old Norse Images of Women*, 94.

18 "The Christmas Invasion," 10th Doctor, Russell T. Davies (New) Series 2005-ongoing.

19 "New Earth," 10th Doctor, Russell T. Davies (New) Series 2005-ongoing.

20 See note 18.

21 See note 12.

22 See note 15.

23 "Father's Day," 9th Doctor, Russell T. Davies (New) Series 2005-ongoing.

24 "Rose," 9th Doctor, Russell T. Davies (New) Series 2005-ongoing.

25 "The Girl in the Fireplace," 10th Doctor, Russell T. Davies (New) Series 2005-ongoing.

26 Clive in "Rose," Mickey in "World War Three," Queen Victoria in "Tooth and Claw," Elton in "Love and Monsters."

27 See note 14.

28 "The Idiot's Lantern," 10th Doctor, Russell T. Davies (New) Series 2005-ongoing.

29 See note 15.

30 See note 23.

31 "The Age of Steel," "Doomsday," "Journey's End," 10th Doctor, Russell T. Davies (New) Series 2005-ongoing.

32 Guerber, 8-9, 331.

33 "Doomsday," 10th Doctor, Russell T. Davies (New) Series 2005-ongoing.

34 "School Reunion," 10th Doctor, Russell T. Davies (New) Series 2005-ongoing.

Doctor Who and the Valkyrie Tradition, Part 2: Goddesses, Battle-demons, Witches, & Wives

Jessica Burke

The valkyrie image always appealed to me: a supernatural woman, marching to war, holding powers of prophecy at her fingertips. Pop-cultural images of an overlarge, metallically-bustiered woman with wings on her conical helmet is more than laughable. Leslie Donovan's "The Valkyrie Reflex in J.R.R Tolkien's *The Lord of the Rings*" linked Helen Damico's "The Valkyrie Reflex in Old English Literature" to the realm of Middle-earth, inspiring the "Valkyrie & the Goddess" theme for the Mythopoeic Society's 2008 conference, chaired by Anthony Burdge with coordination by Kristine Larsen and myself, where Donovan presented, "Brightly Shining and Armed for Battle: The Valkyrie Legacy in Tolkien's Middle-earth Fiction." The evening after the conference, while celebrating over several bottles of first-class hobbit wine, (mead being unavailable), my fellow conference coordinators and I caught up on Series 4 of *Doctor Who*. Using the criteria for the Valkyrie Reflex presented by Donovan, Larsen and I enjoyed some dynamic conversation about which character was more 'valkyrie-like,' Donna or Rose. Our companion essays and this volume were spawned from that discourse.

Without covering the same ground already discussed in "*Doctor Who* and the Valkyrie Tradition, Part 1" by Kristine Larsen, I intend to explore the Valkyrie Reflex as presented in the characters Martha Jones and Donna Noble, Companions to the 10th Doctor in Series 3 and 4 respectively of the New Series of *Doctor Who*. Yet, Russell T. Davies' regeneration of the BBC series has valkyries hidden around several corners. Other valkyries will also be discussed—from the benevolent Professor River Song ("Silence in the Library" & "Forest of the Dead")—to the dark valkyries seen in the Carrionites ("The Shakespeare Code"), Lucy Saxon ("The Sound of Drums" & "Last of the Time Lords"), and Sky Silvestry ("Midnight").

Please note, in this article I will concentrate on Series 3 and 4 of the New Who Series. Taking a leaf from Professor River Song's book, I don't prefer spoilers, so I'll refrain from referencing any conjecture about how the 10th Doctor's song ends, no 2009 Companions will be referenced, and these current explorations will cease with "Journey's End."

Valkyrie Reflex?

Related to Old Norse *valkyrja*[1] and Anglo-Saxon *wælcyrge*,[2] valkyrie means chooser of the slain. J.R. Clark Hall defines *wæl* as "slaughter," "carnage," and "field of battle... [field of] dead bodies," respectively, while *cyre* is "choice."[3] The chaos of the nineth through twelfth centuries in Northern Europe and the British Isles specifically, the fated fatal times when "Christ and his saints slept,"[4] reaffirmed a need to place blame outside the social norm; and, as usual in patriarchal societies, women were responsible:

> In the second decade of the eleventh century, *wælcyrian* and *wiccan* 'witches' are connected as baleful influences on society in Wulfstan's *Sermo Lupi ad Anglos* (A.D. 1014), which accuses them, in concert with murderers, slayers of kinsmen, and fornicators, of destroying the English nation.[5]

Unfortunately, this sinister seed bleeds into today's scholarship and pop culture as well. In *Shamanism and Old English Poetry*, Stephen Glosecki introduces *Wið Færstice* (Against a Sudden Stitch), calling the valkyries represented in this charm—and elsewhere in Germanic and Anglo-Saxon literature—as "vaguely female, unpredictable, mostly evil [earth spirits] able to materialize out of nowhere and then disappear, usually after causing or predicting trouble."[6] Glosecki's curious reading of these undoubtedly female entities supports misconceptions and dualities in the valkyrie image. Initially, we have the benevolent, golden-haired maiden, predominantly linked to Rose Tyler in Larsen's essay; however, on the convergent side resides the "fierce battle-demon"[7] characterized by the Carrionites,[8] and the

> ...*idisi* 'divine ladies'... [which refers] to the status of the creatures, rather than to their behavior ... baleful war-spirits, who bind and fetter the host, and, in essence, inflict a kind of paralytic terror upon the warriors.[9]

The grim valkyrie underlies the foundation of what a valkyrie is: Goddess unto herself. Many negative characteristics of the battle-demon are also "functions" of Oðin's valkyries.[10] Martha and Donna can be included in the *idisi*-aspect of the valkyrie, which portrays something much deeper than the sardonic view an Anglo-Saxon Professor of mine once had about all valkryies when he termed them "Oðin's Stewardesses." In *The Language of the Goddess*, a text crucial to Goddess studies, Marija Gimbutas reveals possible origins for the valkyrie, something before women who fetched and carried for a male deity. When discussing the vulture images from the Neolithic Çatal Hüyük, Gimbutas links these broom-like images with "the power of the Death Goddess," the "witch's broom of European folklore," the Celtic *an badb catha*—the Morrígan or the "battle crow"—and "the raven, the dark bird of the dead which is called *wælceasig*, 'corpse-choosing,' a term which exactly accords with *wælcyrge* or Valkyrie."[11] Clark Hall's definition for raven is *wælcēasega*, "carrion picker,"[12] which, in turn, links to the grim war-spirit. In Damico's "Valkyrie Reflex in Old English Literature," uniting the *idisi* (Old High German) with the *dísir* (Old Norse, plural) and the Mother Goddess Freyja,[13] Damico furthers concepts of the grim, baleful, war-spirit with Goddess worship lingering in other cultures resonated in the Celtic and Irish War Goddesses. The valkyrie as terrible-but-worshipful representation of the Threefold Goddess—Maiden, Mother, Warrior/Crone— reflects in River Song, Martha, and Donna but also in the Carrionites, Lucy Saxon, and Sky Silvestry, as we shall see.

What does this all mean for the women in *Doctor Who*? Much. This expansion of the valkyrie image does several things. While it might allow the viewer to apply Damico and Donovan's valkyrie traits –Valkyrie Reflex—to any and all female characters in the New Series, thereby resulting in a hodge-podge of elements equivalent to "the Bible Code" applied to *Moby Dick*,[14] when using the unambiguous criteria, identifiable valkyries are revealed, each of whom possesses *all* of the valkyrie traits. Larsen lists the fourteen major points, according to Damico and Donovan.[15] However, these traits don't necessarily—as listed— apply to the characters I will be examining. What is a valkyrie to do? Damico elucidates these criteria:

> ...Old Norse poetic tradition conceives of the valkyries as noble, dignified women...riding over land or sea. In the...mythological poems of the *Edda*, the valkyries are entirely supernatural with few individualizing attributes. With the exception of Freyja...the characters are stereotypes. Stripped of their religious potency, they have been reduced to serve purely as Odin's functionaries, and whatever narrative weight they carry comes from associative allusion rather than from action.[16]

These nameless valkyries are mute echoes of their religious past. From Damico's explication there are traits important to the Valkyrie Reflex not explored by Donovan. I wish to regulate the specific standards of eligibility. According to Damico's passage, a valkyrie:

- has dignified character
- rides over land or sea
- gives gifts
- possesses shining eyes and "thoughtful features"[17]
- comments on the hero's destiny
- exhibits great beauty (specifically fair-skinned and golden haired)
- exists as an "entirely supernatural" being (with "few individualizing attributes")
- maintains sagacity and wisdom[18]
- prophesies[19]
- links herself to a hero
- suffers grief or loss
- demonstrates an "unswerving desire to satisfy herself"[20]
- displays splendid adornment—most connected with "metallic and martial properties"[21] (*bēahhroden*[22] and *goldhroden*[23])

In the aspect as a grim war-spirit or battle-demon, many of these same characteristics apply. *Wið Færstice* and other Old English Charms depict the grim valkyrie in much the same terms as the benevolent ones, except she strikes fear in the hearts of men as well. Damico notes this aspect of being a "warrior-fetter" was attributed not only to the battle-demon, but Oðin's valkyries as well.[24] I would add another criterion:

- binds the hero in a kind of paralysis

The valkyrie is linked to the dead via her association with carrion. In much the same fashion as the Morrígan, the valkyrie chose which of Oðin's favorite heroes would die valiantly in battle, thereby adding another element:

- associates with Death/the dead

Above and beyond the ordinary association with Death inherent in traveling with the Doctor, as written, this list is problematic. Used to exclusion, Martha Jones and Donna Noble would be removed from any valkyrie list. Even Rose Tyler wouldn't be considered a valkyrie because she is not "entirely supernatural" and she certainly has many "individualizing attributes." However, I wish to mitigate such statements to open the field a bit wider, but not so wide as to adopt any strong female character into the valkyrie ranks.

First, consider the valkyrie's "noble social status."[25] Donovan was referencing valkyries in Tolkien's Middle-earth who were of aristocratic status, being sovereigns of realms and the children of princes. Even Shelob is of a kind of "noble" status; however, here's the key difference. Being the "last child of Ungoliant,"[26] Shelob isn't aristocratic, not according to our standards; however, because of her lineage, she is of a "higher station," her forebear being of supernatural ability and class.[27] The inclusion of Shelob in the Valkyrie Reflex—and under this criterion of "noble social status"— would unlock Damico's "noble or dignified character" to non-aristocratic women.

When tackling the stereotypical Aryan notion of beauty—blonde-haired and white-skinned—we can see that that was, most likely, the accepted social norm of Norse society. Without exploding any possible underlying biases, fair hair and unblemished skin was an ideal carried forward throughout much of Western society from Guinevere and Iseult, to Queen Elizabeth I and Gloriana[28], to Clarissa and Jane Eyre, and even forward into popular Western culture awash with "vanilla" icons. Nevertheless, we've challenged these notions to provide a wide variation on beauty. Instead of limiting this ingredient in the Valkyrie Reflex to Aryan blondes alone, as Larsen notes, this specific standard can be linked to "otherworldly radiance" and overall beauty. So, let us define this as radiant beauty.

The perception of "entirely supernatural" is tempered by Damico when she acknowledges that these are "stereotypes." I would like to question *what* is considered supernatural. Donovan deems the valkyrie as having "divine or semi-divine origins or ancestry."[29] Damico doesn't note the necessity of divine origins, delineating the concept of the purely supernatural valkyrie as a creature "not [being] limited by spatial and temporal considerations,"[30] hence linking the valkyrie to divinity through her connection to deity—but not in origin. Instead the valkyrie "stands on a plane midway between the human and the divine" and is "used by men for help and intercession."[31] Furthermore, the valkyrie, messenger for Oðin and favorite of the Goddess Freyja—the Chief Valkyrie and battle-Goddess—connected to the Norse Fates—the Norns— making them Goddesses in their own right, regardless of their lineage.

Particular to the Valkyrie Reflex is splendid, metallic adornment: *bēahhroden* and *goldhroden*. *Gold* is obvious, but *bēah* is linked to rings or a ring, while adorned is *hroden*. Damico notes, "the expression 'adorned with gold' is most commonly invoked to praise splendid military dress."[32]

The Old Norse equivalent of *bēahhroden* is *baugvarið*, which means "ring-bedecked woman."[33] The *baugr*, *bēag*, and *bēahhroden* have several possible meanings, from "an allurement for a man"[34] possibly via the physical adornments themselves, to a bent or spiral ring worn and "used primarily as treasure or currency,"[35] indicating generosity. *Baugr* has a martial reference—literally to the circular shields used by the Northern people—"a shield, the ring of battle,"[36] but I would posit another element: armor—specifically ring mail or lamellar, (armor composed of interlocking rings, circles, or scales), both of which were used at the time. Damico notes that the valkyrie would have been "adorned with shields, the jewels of the battlefield,"[37] but donning multiple shields isn't probable, being cumbersome, since these women may have been on horseback. A single shield alone would pose enough difficulty and wielding a weapon of any kind would necessitate having the weapon hand free.[38] Lamellar armor, composed of interlocking "shields," is a more likely interpretation. Furthermore, these intermingled terms *bēahhroden* and *goldhroden* refer both to the martial aspect of the valkyrie and their radiant beauty, linking them to "the shining brilliance of the sun."[39]

As a result, the Valkyrie Reflex I will examine can be shortened but intensified to include:

- dignity of character
- elevation, riding over land or sea
- generosity
- radiant beauty (with shining eyes)
- splendid adornment—linked to metallic, gold, rings, and/or military ornament
- intermediary between destiny and the hero—prophecy
- wisdom (in action and speech)
- suffering or loss
- unswerving desire or will
- paralysis or some binding of the hero (in body or will or both)
- link to Death

Battle-demons & Carrion Pickers

Working from a perverted view of the benevolent valkyrie with underlying correlation to Goddess-worship, we have the baneful, grim, battle-demon represented in the New Series of *Doctor Who*, but observed most keenly in the figures of the Carrionites, Lucy Saxon, and Sky Silvestry.

The Carrionites

The Carrionites of "The Shakepeare Code" represent some of the most stereotypically offensive views of women in the New Series. Granted, this wasn't Gareth Roberts' intent,[40] but it raises a concept noted by Jenny Jochens in *Old Norse Images of Women*: the idea that women transgressing the gender roles outlined by men must be humiliated and punished.[41] Roberts perpetuates vicious notions of women and witches stemming from Wulfstan and the very human desire to scapegoat.

Aside from her monstrous appearance, Lilith the Carrionite is connected to the mother of demons, Lilith, the first wife of Adam, the demonic mother of Cain, and the mother of succubae. In Kabala, Lilith has been coupled with the "demon" of Friday, an interesting association to the valkyrie because Friday's deity is, in fact, the Goddess Freyja. In succubus-fashion, Carrionite Lilith uses her radiant beauty to attract a young suitor. Looking down, Lilith is literally elevated above her suitor, face illuminated by a singular candle, giving an eerie red halo. This initial image, combined with the subsequent ones pairing Lilith with firelight and a malevolent red glow, hearken to Donovan's tie between the valkyrie and "battle-fires."[42] It's important to note two other elements of the sinister female depiction that would strike terror in the heart of men everywhere: the Carrionites physically tear apart Lilith's suitor for the purpose of eating him. This measures up to Damico's references to the *dísir* needing sacrificial appeasement.[43] Lilith wryly says, "A suitor should meet his beloved's parents," before calling on her Mothers Doomfinger and Bloodtide. Not only do these women eat men, they apparently procreate without the aid of any male of their species, so we are presented with man-eating lesbians who use magic against men.

Furthering this gender transgression, Lilith has an apparent insatiable sexual appetite noted in her interactions with Mr. Lynley. After she begs him not to "hurt that handsome head of his," he calls her a "wanton woman," leaving her with an apparent promise to return later, accordingly insinuating Lilith's tendency toward prostitution. She appears as a maid-servant in very good clothes, but how did she afford such fine things as a servant? Lilith is rather intimate with Lynley and the Doctor—caressing the heads and faces of both men. Lilith crosses class lines, another offense necessitating punishment: she appears as both a serving-maid and the only woman in the episode to wear Elizabethan finery (aside from Queen Elizabeth's brief appearance at episode's end). Lilith wears her ornate, gold-laden clothes, crowned and in her own private box in the Globe theater.

Converse to the valkyrie traits, Lilith and her Mothers aren't generous; instead, they take: the young suitor's life, locks of hair from Mr. Lynley and the Doctor, and even Shakespeare's own gift of words as the Carrionites need the final words of the Bard's lost play to release the rest of their people from "Deep Darkness." Lilith appears in the Globe, caressing a poppet,[44] fixating on Shakespeare, winding his hair from the doll around her fingers.

Lilith is the most prominent Carrionite, with dignified bearing but with profane intent. There isn't proof of her aristocratic lineage; however, because she is one of three Carrionites who escaped the Eternals' prison, she is of an elevated station. Also, her physical appearance, along with that of her Mothers, is more enunciated than the indistinct, swirling Carrionites emanating from the vortex. As noted earlier, she is the only woman to dress in Elizabethan finery, and the only one, aside from the Queen, to appear crowned. Lilith's manners are elevated, like the *idisi*—from rank instead of behavior. After all, her singular intent—her unswerving desire—is to resurrect the ways of her people; that alone raises her above the class of the humdrum Carrionite. While explaining her wish to release the Carrionites from their prison, she says:

> ...the human race will be purged as pestilence.
> And from this world we will lead the universe back
> into the old ways of blood and magic.

Lilith represents the unyielding desire to bring death. She is beautiful, but harbors the monstrous bearing of her Mothers, often shifting between the two facades. Despite her apparent radiance, we are reminded of the "horrific eyes of the Gorgons" noted by Damico.[45] This, combined with her eyes, lifts Lilith to a place above her Mothers.

The Carrionites can fly and are often seen suspended in air. As already noted, when we first see Lilith, she is elevated above the young man she is soon to devour. When casting her magic against Shakespeare and the Doctor, she is literally airborne, outside the window. Mother Bloodtide first appears plastered against the ceiling in their abode in All Hallow's Street, and the Carrionites fly through the whirlwind of the portal as it opens. In keeping with the bird images Donahue and Gimbutas link with the valkyrie, the Carrionites escaping the orb appear vulture-like, while Lilith and her Mothers don sable robes that mimic feathers of carrion birds.

Lilith displays a kind of wisdom, although she doesn't use it for positive purpose. Her people use words as their magic and weapon. Lilith's words not only bind Lynley, Shakespeare, Martha, and the Doctor, but she uses them to reveal hidden truths—from referencing that Death has been waiting for the Doctor "for a very long time," noting that Martha Jones is "out of her time." She hits a particular nerve with the Doctor when she says, "There's still one word with the power of the day" and that word, of course, is "Rose." This conversation binds the Doctor, but before using her "DNA replication module"—her poppet—her words resurrect the undercurrent of stereotypical fear that men had about strong women: "Behold, Doctor, men to Carrionites are nothing but puppets." This correlates the stereotype of the witch with the negative valkyrie as being a source for male horror. Lilith doesn't only bind the Doctor alone; she is also seen gleefully binding Shakespeare with the rhyme "Bind the mind and take the man," along with her attempts to use the final words of *Love's Labor's Won* to bind the human race.

While we don't see the Carrionites as properly *bēahhroden*, their word-spells take place within a circle, standing above a cauldron,[46] itself set over a vast iron ring over flames within an even larger spiked iron circle. In their perverted cottage, we see many variations on the ring-image in the background—rings from iron chains, circles of sundry torture devices, and a large, circular shield displaying heraldry from another world and time.[47] Another ring corresponds to suffering via the Carrionites' loss of freedom. As Jochens predicts,[48] punished for their crimes and gender transgressions, they are locked within the blue orb. Their punishment deserved, since the Earth was to be stripped of life, the Doctor stating that the Carrionites wanted "A new Empire, on Earth. A world of bones and blood and witchcraft." Lilith confesses that this new age would spread across the universe. If the Eternals deemed this race worthy of confinement, then there was a reason. Beyond being bound within this circle, they are further humiliated by being cast, screaming, into a trunk stored in the sub-levels of the TARDIS, tossed alongside Cyberman-related refuse, a bramble of wires, and a spare copy of Agatha Christie's *Death in the Clouds*, all of which we see much later in "The Unicorn and the Wasp." In the Doctor's defense, if I had to watch over a screaming blue orb for all eternity, then perhaps I'd find a faraway place to stash it alongside some other unneeded, but equally unforgettable items.

Lucy Saxon

Lucy Saxon, the wife of Harold Saxon—the alter-ego of the Doctor's chief nemesis, the Master—is seen in "The Sound of Drums" and "Last of the Time Lords." At first glance, Lucy doesn't seem like much. Barely having a handful of lines, she mostly stands in the Master's shadow, literally behind him, the dutiful wife. Yet, a complex creature, she may have ramifications in the future of the series, and her actions, regardless of how demure, designate her as a baneful, battle-demon in human form. As we first see Lucy, she is a radiantly beautiful woman, golden light casting a halo above her head. Usually a feature reserved for Donna, the light is particularly metallic, positively glowing golden. As examined by Larsen, Rose, too, has a golden light, but it is much softer—except when she is inhabited by the Heart of the TARDIS. Perhaps this golden quality to the backlight signifies that the woman in question is the Companion to a Time Lord specific to the New Series. When the Doctor realizes the Master has been elected Prime Minister, the camera zooms in not to the face of Harold Saxon, but of his wife. She appears as the classic, benevolent, Aryan valkyrie: blonde, fair skin, light eyes, wearing a trim, feminine suit, black embossed in gold, reminiscent of Jackie Kennedy, with golden pearls and modest gold ribbons, minus the hat and gloves. As the camera adjusts, we witness a kiss between the Master and his human Companion (the first of many), but not just a simple kiss of affection or celebration for Saxon's victory. Deeply passionate, Lucy is marked as an intensely sexual being, reflecting the polar opposite to our other Time Lord and human Companions. Despite Russell Davies' claim that "Man, woman, on screen = love story,"[49] this is only tangentially true for the relationship between the Doctor and Rose.[50] While Martha does have sexual desire for the Doctor, there is no love story there, nor is there with Donna. The Master and Lucy are in a kind of love relationship; she loves the idea of him, his power, his own sexual appeal, and her place with him. Bonded in a physical, sexual relationship, they are married. While the Master gives his first speech as Prime Minister, Lucy stands behind him positively radiant with sexual energy and the vigor of triumph, a look on her face that can only be described as orgasmic.

Lucy's comportment is dignified, but she is also of noble class. When reporter Vivien Rook corners Lucy, we learn that despite Lucy's not being "especially bright," Mrs. Saxon is of "good family." In order to marry a rising politician endeavoring to be the next leader of Britain, Lucy would have to have come from an upper-class family. Her appearance is certainly distinguished, and, like the *idisi*, we can say that her elevated status—her dignity—is connected solely to her station and not her behavior.

Lucy doesn't give gifts—not initially and not from generosity—but she does manipulate. We believe she may trust Rook, that far-off gaze giving us the sense that perhaps Lucy (like the rest of England) may have been held in a kind of thrall by the Master. However, we realize with Rook that Lucy was just beguiling the situation, the reporter, and us. This is confirmed when, in the following scenes, we think Lucy flinches because of Rook's prolonged, agonizing screams as the Toclafane attack. However, Lucy is more upset that the reporter "knew everything," and that if the Archangel Network wasn't "One-hundred percent" then, how much time until there were more questions for the Saxons?

When Lucy is generous, it's in her rapturous support for Harold Saxon—at least in "The Sound of Drums." Her final "gifts" are complex and, quite possibly, were part of some plan of the Master's. In the final moments of "Last of the Time Lords," as the Doctor explains that the Master will be imprisoned in the TARDIS, Lucy gifts her husband with death. By shooting the Master, Lucy has unwittingly gifted the Joneses with the knowledge that the Master is dead. This generosity becomes rather convoluted when we see Lucy's crimson nails pluck the Master's ring[51]—coincidentally encrusted with Gallifreyan symbols evocative of the Chameleon Device and the Ring of Rassilon—from the ashes of his pyre. The Master's laugh resounds and we wonder if her gift of death was in fact a gift of life. In this moment, Lucy is very much the Creator-Destroyer, and has taken on goddess-like proportions.

Important to our Valkyrie Reflex and concepts of adornment is Davies' use of color schemes in *Doctor Who*. In the Classic Series, the prevalent color array was confined to the Doctor. Each regeneration had specific "outfits" with a definite kaleidoscope. Classic Series Companions had no such color scope, with the exception of Leela, who, being a "noble savage" stereotype, wore animal skins in earth tones. Davies extended color motifs to the Companions. Lucy's initial color design is restricted to black and gold. Wearing cream-colored coat and matching gloves when meeting the American President, she follows in the exact shades of gold and black that she wore in opening scenes. In "Last," we have her red nails, lips, and the vivid crimson gown she wears to exclusion. Initially, her hair is decorously swept up, but in "Last" it lies loose in a cascade of gold that begins to look dull and unkempt. Lucy's colors symbolize death, fury, passion, and blood, being associated with the Goddess, the Norns, and the elements of Fire and Earth.[52] Colors have deep meaning and some meanings must've, in some way, been known to the creators and costumers of *Doctor Who*—even on a semi-conscious level.

Lucy first appears atop a staircase, elevated but descending to those eager to catch the first images of the British First Couple. When aboard the Valiant, she's literally airborne, riding above both sea and land in proper valkyrie form. While she doesn't bear any specific martial adornment, she does take up Francine's discarded gun; however, Lucy's colors and elegance are Lucy's martial adornment, in the same way Jackie Kennedy's prim debutante style became a uniform of sorts. Lucy becomes frenzied at the destruction of Earth. Ruin and desolation satisfy her appetite; and while she isn't appeased in a ritualistic sense, her passions are assuaged when observing death and pain. Her lust is her martial adornment because it goes beyond mere sexual passion; like a serial killer, Lucy gets her carnal arousal from devastation and not intimacy. When Saxon touches her in "Last," disgust flits across her face, which is further accentuated by her physical frailty, her limping, and her bruised face later in the episode.

Lucy stands behind Saxon in a numb, hypnotic state, eyes shining with the intensity of an addict. Saxon is her drug, her martial adornment, and even her weapon. Faithfully, she hangs on his every word, leaning on his chair, physically resting on her husband while watching the American President's attempts at speech with the Toclafane. While it may be a "snub" on the Doctor, I tend to view Lucy's sharing jelly babies with the Master as reference to the 4th Doctor being the "Evil One" eating babies in "The Face of Evil." Watching the subsequent action with familiar deadened expression, Lucy abruptly dances, touching her lips provocatively as the Toclafane descend. Her "I don't know" response to the Master's question is pure ecstasy, as is the gaze she fixes on him when he embraces the sound of the word "decimate."

Finally, we have Lucy's abilities of prophecy and binding. If we consider Saxon her weapon, she is successfully helping to bind England to his will. The dutiful wife is an essential element to any male politician's attempts at greatness, and without her physically embellishing him, we can question his success. Lucy does bind Vivien Rook into false trust. Believing she has earned the ear of Mrs. Saxon, Rook becomes manipulated and with her life forfeit. After Saxon reveals himself as the Master of Earth, it becomes evident that Lucy is also bound to him.[53] Despite her revulsion at his touching her, she displays anger and annoyance at his toying with the idea of adopting Tanya as his new Companion. Successive scenes show a physically weakened Lucy—blackened eye, staggering, diminished. She is his puppet, however, she still manages to kill him; in and of itself an action of binding. Lucy doesn't properly fetter the Doctor, already imprisoned, tortured, and caged by the Master. Yet, when she does give her prophecy about the ending of the universe, the Doctor is held rapt—and fettered by the weight of her words. Through Lucy, the Doctor realizes that the Toclafane are us, are our Futurekind.

THE MASTER
I took Lucy to Utopia. A Time Lord and his human Companion. I took her to see the stars. Isn't that right, sweetheart?

LUCY
Trillions of years in the future. To the end of the

universe.

THE MASTER
Tell him what you saw.

LUCY
Dying. Everything dying. The whole of creation
was falling apart. And, I thought, there's no point. No
point to anything. Not ever.

Since she traveled to the farthest reaches of space and time, she is transformed into more than a mere human. Like Martha, Donna, and Rose, Lucy is affected by the fundamental components of travel in time and space—what the Doctor calls "Void Stuff" in "Doomsday." This Void Stuff makes Lucy, and indeed any Time Lord Companion, more than human. In addition to linking her with the divine, preternatural abilities of the Time Lord, it makes her supernatural and no longer bound by spatial or temporal considerations. Her words are tantamount to prescience—or modern prophecy thanks be to time travel,[54] and she serves as a median point between the Master and the Doctor, as well as an intermediate between the Doctor and the fate of the Toclafane.

Sky Silvestry

One of the most disturbing episodes of the 4th series of the new *Doctor Who* was "Midnight." In this "Companion-light" episode, the Doctor is confronted by a classic, grim valkyrie. Despite the episode's plot—a human infected or overcome by an external, alien presence—in *The Writer's Tale* Davies describes Sky as a woman "with wild staring eyes" who is not an alien, but a woman possessed.[55]

Once the Doctor boards Crusader 50, Sky is the first passenger we see, passing the Doctor as he pleads with Donna to join him. After boarding, Sky is the first seated passenger brought to our attention, reading silently, wearing black. Her adornment—*bēahhroden* and *goldhroden*—are a bit more subtle. Obviously blonde with fair eyes, attractive, but not conventionally beautiful the way Rose, Martha, or Lucy Saxon are attractive. Middle-aged, Sky wears diminutive gold rings in her ears and glittering, jewel-like collar and cuffs on her sable blouse. Her only colors are black and a touch of red; her nails are dark, blood red but no truly golden light surrounds her. She principally appears in shadow and then the sickly, roiling yellow light of the entertainment system. Before becoming engulfed by the entity, she becomes hysterical, a nimbus of pale, barely gold light reflects off her blonde hair. Sky isn't backlit, but shrouded in obscurity and gloom. Surrounded by the golden floor lights, she backs into a corner, convinced the creature is "coming for" her, then becoming swallowed by a darkness punctuated only by the golden sparks of electrical mayhem. Once possessed, the light that she is illuminated by—the torchlight initially and later the cabin-lights—becomes bleak, white, cold, and glittering.

Complex before becoming possessed, reserved to a fault, it's difficult to see why Sky took the tour. When everyone talks, after she shares a private smile with the Doctor at the "Failure of the entertainment system," she keeps to herself. The Doctor befriends her, making a point of speaking with her over lunch. She makes a connection to our hero—albeit not a sexual one. The Doctor devours his food, whereas Sky spends time unfolding her napkin, arranging all her food items purposefully, and even questioning what kind of food they've been presented with. Her eating is ritualized and her manner is dignified, but we are without information concerning her past, her lineage, or indeed her place in society. Prior to her possession, all we have is her interaction with the Doctor, and the knowledge that she is not integrated into this microcosmic society of Crusader 50. She removes herself from the group and, in turn, is quarantined by them. We come to the lunchtime conversation in medias res. The Doctor discusses Donna being left behind in the Leisure Palace, then asks about Sky's history.

> SKY
> No it's just me.

> THE DOCTOR
> Oh, I've done plenty of that. Traveling on my own. I love it. Do what you want. Go anywhere.

> SKY
> Well, I'm still getting used to it. I found myself single rather recently. Not by choice.

> THE DOCTOR
> What happened?

> SKY
> Oh, the usual. She needed her own space, as they say. A different galaxy, in fact. I reckon that's enough space—don't you?

We know she's traveled in space, but she is yet another example of a woman without the need of a man. Contrary to popular perception, I see examples of female-centric sexuality in the current *Who*niverse being linked to the grotesque. Lesbians[56] often have been connected to alien infection or monstrous influence. Fodder for a paper unto itself, we can extrapolate a very male, very patriarchal view: female desire, grounded and centered on other women, may be held in contempt and feared. Male sexuality is embraced via the brilliant character Captain Jack Harkness; female sexuality tends to be castigated.

Being in Crusader 50, Sky rides over land and sea on this trip to view Midnight's Sapphire Waterfalls. Her name itself, Sky, is emblematic of elevation and lofty heights. The alien entity attacks her from above, and in her final moments, Sky is pulled into the Xtonic sunlight of Midnight by the Hostess, where they'll both be vaporized. Sky isn't generous but manipulative. Before being overcome by the alien presence, she is the first of the passengers to ask "What's wrong?" Her questions are hysterical without desire for knowledge or security. Other passengers vacillate between denial, whether the vehicle actually stopped, or whether it's simply a "pit-stop." Sky insists the vehicle stopped, and she is the first to become overtly harsh, barking at Professor Hobbes: "Evidently, we have stopped, so there's no point in denying it." Making the gift of derision and discord to the passengers, Sky is the first passenger to show a compromised mental state, which rapidly metastasizes even before the entity arrives. Asking "Is there something out there," she sows panic and terror. Self-centered and selfish, Sky contradicts beneficent valkyrie wisdom, emphasizing she's "on a schedule." Lacking regard for her fellow passengers, she shrieks: "It answered! Don't tell me that thing's not alive. It answered him!" Bestowing the need to blame, she shouts at the Hostess:

No! Don't just stand there telling us the rules!
You're the Hostess! You're supposed to do something!

We learn that Sky's tale about her lover needing "space" may've been just that—a tale; Sky's narcissism explodes as she cries: "She said she'd get me!" Vendetta superimposes panic. Pointing at Jethro, the Professor, Mr. Cane, and the Doctor—the men in the party— in quick succession, she frantically repeats the refrain, "It's coming for me" without regard for any of her companions; this repetition is a self-fulfilling prophecy, which nearly costs the Doctor his life.

Following Sky's possession, head in hands, she sits on the torn-up seats, torch-light creating a sinister halo. Red nails gripping her head, accentuated against her pale hair, give a dominant impression of claws while her shadow hands projected on the wall are evocative of Gimbutas' vulture-wings from Çatal Hüyük. Wicked, empty, feral, raptor-like eyes stare back at the passengers. Lizard-like, inhuman movements mark that Sky is no longer with us, compounding the losses Sky has hitherto suffered: loss of lover, place, self, calm, decency, and humanity. Sky isn't a simple battle-demon, becoming an echo of the Doctor, quite literally. Her clipped, unnatural movements accentuate her word-theft. Repeating, assimilating, and anticipating the passengers' words, she begins with the Doctor. Framed behind her, her shadow becomes larger and blacker as the passengers and the audience becomes more apprehensive. Stealing the first word—her own name— Sky's shadow overtakes her, her tone changes, her expressions move between blank disjointedness to ominous glee as the passengers become more unhinged and as the Doctor becomes more desperate.

Her word-theft is her prophecy; particularly when she anticipates, speaking before the passengers themselves. Connecting with malignant magic and further disturbing everyone, Dee Dee quotes Christina Rossetti's worrisome fairy tale "Goblin Market":

> We must not look at goblin men,
> We must not buy their fruits:
> Who knows upon what soil they fed
> Their hungry thirsty roots?[57]

The use of Rossetti's poem, itself an enigma, promulgates Sky's gender transgressions by presenting a tale of two sisters snared in a web of vicious enchantment by crafty goblins. Ripe with sexual imagery, the goblins captivate young, sexually immature women with delectable fruit and the power of their voice. One sister succumbs to the goblins' sorcery, while her sister resists. Adding to carnal descriptions of fruit and salacious imagery of eating, we're presented with a potentially incestuous relationship between the sisters. On the surface, Dee Dee may be linking Sky to the goblins themselves, but Davies may be linking Sky to negative, female-exclusive relationships.[58] Professor Hobbes brings us back around, reminding us Sky isn't an alien, "She's not a goblin or a monster; she's just a very sick woman."

Physically bound in place, Sky sits while the passengers' panic rises and while the Hostess initiates suggestions of throwing Sky out. Speaking with each of the passengers as they attack the Doctor's credibility, frenziedly planning to throw him out, Sky uses words as her weapon. As the passengers approach him to throw him from Crusader 50, Sky stops speaking. Sky marks her chosen victim: the Doctor. Her stance altered from suspension to taut anticipation, her gaze fixates on the Doctor as she prepares to pounce. As he asks why *his* voice, Sky's face appears golden, but as the Doctor speaks, Sky binds him.

> ... You've captured my speech... You need my voice in particular? The cleverest voice in the room. Why? 'Cause I'm the only one who can help? Oh, I'd love that to be true. But, your lies, they're saying something else. Listen to me. Whatever you want. If it's life, or form, or consciousness, or voice, you don't have to steal it. You can find it, without hurting anyone. And I'll help you. That's a promise. So, what do you think? Do we have a deal?

The Doctor speaks in a sing-song voice, echoed by Sky, but with each word, he is ensorcelled. With his final question, he is fettered completely. Pilfering his words and his promise, she twists them, further manipulating the passengers as her weapons against a paralytic Doctor. Her skull-like eyes darken as she unfreezes, moving fingers and face, she is radiantly golden but adorned with a simpering smile of death. Fixing her gaze on the passengers, looking past an ineffectual, drooling Doctor, Sky reaches up to the Professor, the oldest of the male passengers, and is lifted into a circle of golden light. Surrounded by men, Sky has her back to the Doctor, before Dee Dee and the Hostess shatter the frame—the only women to perceive the problem when the men cannot. Dee Dee pleads for them all to hear her, but, surrounded by Goblin Men, she melts into the background, pathetic against Sky's thrall. Val looks to men for guidance. Camera angles reverse to show the Doctor's face, with Sky standing behind, acting as *his* shadow. Weaving her words, she incites the passengers (her weapons) to remove the Doctor from the vessel:

> That's how he does it. He makes you fight. Creeps into your head. And whispers. Listen. Just listen. That's him. Inside.

Sky is now repeated by Val and obeyed by the men. Neither Dee Dee nor the Hostess takes part in the attack. Dee Dee herself bound, the Hostess remains unfettered. Upon hearing the Doctor's stolen word— "Molto bene"—the Hostess casts Sky into the oblivion of Midnight's raw sky.

Goddesses and a Wife

Without acquiescing to what Larsen called "cookie-cutter" valkyries, the following valkyries contest the baneful battle-demon, but so too do they challenge the benign valkyrie, Rose Tyler. River Song, Martha Jones, and Donna Noble represent a three-fold ultimate valkyrie, Freyja, the Goddess of the Valkyries.

River Song

River Song deserves special attention because, as Davies states, River appears to all intents and purposes to be the Doctor's wife.[59] Assuming his view is the correct one (since he's the mastermind behind the New Series), I won't examine or mention Internet rumor and surmise we may meet her again in the series future.

Shrouded in smoke following the flash-explosion that opens the Library, River Song is exceptional. Her face illuminated with silver light, she appears in a white spacesuit. Leader of the expedition, Captain of her crew, and Professor of Archaeology, River is of elevated status. Having come from her ship, she has obviously traveled in space and, being an archaeologist, she has also traveled over land. Her bearing is dignified, proving even nobler than whining Mr. Lux, patrician spokesman for his family's corporation. Her familiar, intimate posture with the Doctor—her greeting, "Hello Sweetie"—tells us we've not met with her like before. Without Davies' admission that River is indeed the Doctor's wife, hinting at this relationship, Mr. Lux exasperatedly shouts in the face of imminent death: "...you're just squabbling like an old married couple!"[60] Naming the Doctor privately so none can hear, she substantiates their relationship. We know his name would be given in utter trust, which is the ultimate bond between the Doctor and the Davies Companions.

The Doctor expresses this trust for them by granting unlimited access to the TARDIS via a key of their own, and by giving their cell phones the universal upgrade, technically termed by the 9th Doctor as a "bit of jiggery-pokery." The keys, in the old series, were occasionally given to companions, or hidden above the P in Police box, to cultivate storylines. While the Doctor trusted his companions, they were subsidiary and interchangeable, with only few exceptions—Leela, Sarah Jane, and Romana, who, in my opinion, are still flattened, disconnected stereotypes, mostly used as plot devices. We can't assume River Song has a TARDIS key, nor can we presuppose she would be unable to access it if presented with the opportunity. I'm particularly fond of the idea that she might enter the TARDIS with a snap of *her* fingers. Instead of depicting his unbound trust in her via a key, the Doctor's trust in her is expressed through the power to name him. Beforehand, expressing regret, she reflects even more intimate knowledge that his name isn't only a secret, but a source of pain for him. Apologizing, her hand on his heart, she momentarily fetters him in fear and disbelief. Pervaded with grief, face bathed in silver and red light, she names him, and he is speechless.

Matching the Doctor's intellect and ego, River swiftly calls the Doctor's bluff by asking why he didn't sign Lux's contract, relenting with a smile that she didn't sign either. Even in the face of death, she promptly but humorously checks him: "Oh, what? I'm not allowed to have a career, I suppose?" Radiantly but somewhat stereotypically beautiful, with large blue eyes, gold and brown ringlets, River isn't the golden child Rose is. Clashing with Rose's kaleidoscope of pink, black, blue, with white or red splashes, River is restricted to white, with accents of vivid spring-green (spacesuit communicator), silver (her diamond, tear-drop earrings after being "saved"), and silver-blue (space-suit and Library illumination, and her helmet's tinted visor). After she is "saved," she appears in a willowy white gown, ornate with glittering sequins, trailing wing-like sleeves, hair brilliantly golden, loose, and flowing in the soft, white light. While River doesn't wear red or gold, she is occasionally illuminated by these shades— when naming the Doctor, when remembering *her* Doctor to Anita, and when preparing for death. She is aligned with the three-fold Goddess— Maiden, Mother, and Crone/Warrior.

According to Jochens, River's age precludes her from being the strong maiden warrior; a woman's "role as warrior could be taken seriously" in the time before marriage.[61] However, it's apparent River is both valkyrie and wife. She's the only member of the expedition to carry and use weaponry, her Sonic blaster (a Squareness Gun) holstered on her thigh and her Sonic Screwdriver always at the ready. Ideas that valkyries can only be maidens[62] before marriage leaves no room for River, Martha, or Donna and would only intimate Rose as the singular valkyrie in the New Series. I don't believe Jochens considered the role of Freyja, or that the Goddess has many faces, only one of which is Maiden. Jochens' assertions, while true for Norse Society, may reflect women whose images were "formed in men's imaginations."[63] The virgin shield-maidens are seen as pure male fantasy that, when challenged, turned into the baneful battle-demon. Freya and the Morrígan weren't maidens but were clearly warrior women cultivating male fear centered on an unwillingness to appreciate, understand, or acknowledge raw, feminine energy.

Like Donna, River Song is older, past maiden-hood. Along with her intimate greeting, when she calls the Doctor into her "office," she slips into a banter we've only seen with recent Companions: "Should we do diaries, then? Where are we this time?" We can construe he's shared his story with her—something rarely done before. Rose shares no such on-screen intimacy. Martha begrudgingly pries our first proper glimpse of Gallifrey in the New Series from the Doctor's memory when she refuses to accompany him further without knowing more.[64] While Donna acquires all the Doctor's memories, this isn't by his choice. We get only snippets of him voluntarily telling her his story. While we can assume the Doctor shares his tales with Rose, Martha, and Donna *off-screen* in spaces between episodes, we haven't been privy to any sharing of "diaries" before. So, not only does River become his wife, she becomes his confidante, his Companion, and, in some ways, his biographer.

The Doctor's initial qualms have little to do with River's strength of will, but from her physical intimacy with him and from her use of Sonic weaponry. We all know the Doctor's distaste for guns and, when River reveals she has not just any Sonic Screwdriver, but a future version of *the Doctor's,* his alarm is apparent. The Doctor's underlying unease at River's familiarity with him is initially something he attempts to shrug off with, "Oh. *I'm* Pretty Boy." She takes a liberty with him imposed by a scant few—two being Lilith in "The Shakespeare Code," and Rose when possessed by the Lady Cassandra in "New Earth"[65]—touching his face. River's caresses are done with obvious love. Because the romantic attachment isn't yet realized by the Doctor who has never met this woman before, barely trusts her much less loves her, her adoration of him isn't reciprocated and serves as a source of grief for her. His trepidation arises not from male fear, but from River's familiarity, his realization that he doesn't know her but she knows him.

River's knowledge, her prophecy is exclusive to the Doctor[66]— our hero—in the form of her little, blue, book, uncannily similar in appearance to the TARDIS. She also is able to contact him, to "call" him via his Psychic Paper. This time, the message arrived too early in his timeline, but we don't rightly discover why she called him. In addition to her book of prophecy, her "spoilers," she grants us a picture of the future Doctor. Despite his current age, we know he's much older when she knows him because she remarks how "young" he is. We deduce that wearing a suit, for her Doctor, isn't a common-day affair. When talking to Anita, terrified that the Doctor won't return, she says:

> Well, yes, the Doctor's here. He came when I called, just like he always does. But, not *my* Doctor. Now, my Doctor, I've seen whole armies turn and run away. And he'd just swagger off, back to his TARDIS, and open the doors with a snap of his fingers. The

Doctor, in the TARDIS, next stop everywhere.

Companion aside, River is possibly the first with the audacity to call the Doctor "Pretty Boy," reflecting that she's an erotic being, much in the same fashion as the Goddess Freyja. Freyja was presented "as a voluptuous, sexually insatiable creature, and as *Vanadís*, 'goddess of the Vanir', she is one of the chief divinities among these gods of fruitfulness."[67] Unlike Freyja—also called the Norse Aphrodite—River doesn't direct her sexuality toward every male she meets. It's embraced as portion of her overall strength, and is obviously turned in the Doctor's direction. When the expedition appears, Anita asks how Professor Song knows that the Doctor and Donna "aren't androids." With a libidinous gleam in her eye, a pop of her helmet and a toss of her head, River quips, "Because I've dated androids and they're rubbish." Scant moments later, she orders, "Pretty Boy, you're with me" and when Mr. Lux, in frustration, asks why he's the "only one still wearing his helmet," she jibes, "I don't fancy you." The obvious implication is that she fancies the Doctor. Even in her final moments, she flirtatiously raises her eyebrows—"Spoilers"—in response to his question: "Why do you even *have* handcuffs?" We're permitted to ponder the notion that River didn't call the Doctor to investigate the Library necessarily, but that perhaps she used his Psychic Paper to request his presence for other purposes.

Being linked with Freyja and not virginal doesn't bar River from being a "valkyrie bride," who represents the erotic, lovelorn relationship between valkyrie and hero characterized by suffering and loss. In relation to the Doctor as hero, the only "valkyrie brides" we currently have in the New Series are Rose, Martha, and River. Larsen has already explored Rose's function as "valkyrie-bride," paying attention to the fact that Rose's Valkyrie Reflex, in some respects, centers on this unfulfilled relationship with the Doctor. But, Rose's only sexual connection to the Doctor comes in the form of awkward lustful tension and her final achievement of Doctor 10.5 in "Journey's End." River's romantic attachment is a source for the Doctor's misgivings as well as her own. When the Doctor answers her plea of "Please tell me you know who I am" with "Who are you," her pain is palpable. Despite Donna's protective bad-temper, River reveals, "This is the Doctor in the days before he knew me. And he looks at me, he looks right through me, and it shouldn't kill me but it does." Rivers final moments with the Doctor, full of anguish and tenderness, authenticate her relationship to him as "valkyrie bride," wife, and as goddess:

RIVER SONG
Funny thing is, this means you've always known

how I was going to die. ...All the time we've been together, you knew I was coming here. The last time I saw you... you turned up on my doorstep with a new haircut and a suit...Oh, what a night that was... you cried. You wouldn't tell me why, but I suppose you knew it was time. My time. Time to come to the Library. You even gave me your screwdriver. That should have been a clue. There's nothing you can do.

THE DOCTOR
Let me do this!

RIVER SONG
If you die here it'll mean I had never met you.

THE DOCTOR
Time can be rewritten.

RIVER SONG
Not those times. Not one line. Don't you dare. It's okay....it's not over for you. You'll see me again. You've got all of that time to come. You and me. Time and space. You watch us run.

THE DOCTOR
River you know my name. You whispered my name in my ear. There's only one reason I would ever tell anyone my name. There's only one time I ever could.

RIVER SONG
Hush now. Spoilers.

In the moments of death, River takes on another unique aspect of Freyja—weeping tears of gold—only achieved by Donna and Rose respectively. Damico posits that Freyja's golden tears are gifts—payment—to her warriors for service.[68] River gifts life—to the Doctor and all those "saved" by CAL—and the knowledge that some day the Doctor will, again, have a family. In addition, her determined will is evident in these final moments. Not only did she physically assault the Doctor with a steady right hook, she handcuffs him and ultimately dies to guarantee that she will one day meet him. Compounding her selfless will is her link to death. She is the one who recognizes the skeleton as Miss Evangelista, declares the woman is "ghosting," and demands "a little respect" for Evangelista when the other crewmembers would rather River remove the communicator and walk away. River gifts us and the Doctor with the knowledge that "4022 saved, no survivors" refers to the number of people last in the Library and she reveals the gravity platform, the means by which he can "save" the survivors, to the core of the planet. Her "unswerving desire to satisfy herself" isn't selfish but selfless.[69]

Martha Jones

Initially, I didn't consider Martha valkyrie-material. Her functionality in Series 4 places her amongst the dark valkyries, but reevaluation reveals Martha is a valkyrie at odds with Rose, and at a another phase in life.[70] Older than Rose, still a maiden, but at the cusp, we meet Martha as she moves into that next stage of becoming a doctor and soon-to-be-wife, thereby leaving maidenhood behind.

Grounded in the humdrum, a work-a-day girl, Martha opens "Smith and Jones," attempting to mediate familial discord. Yet, since Martha is the mediator, by solving her familial squabbles, she is elevated. Martha becomes the only Davies Companion to leave the Doctor voluntarily to care for *her family*. Aside from River, Archaeologist and Professor, Martha is specialized, scientific, a Doctor herself; by the end of Season 4, she becomes UNIT's Medical Director for Project Indigo. Martha exhibits elevation in her physiognomy as well. "Reset" (*Torchwood*)[71] tells us that Martha's lymphocytes have mutated, making her something rare and marvelous because of her exposure to time and space. While this is certainly because of her travels with the Doctor, it could have started when the Royal Hope was taken to the moon by the Judoon. Void Stuff notwithstanding, it is Martha's own dignified character combined with her exposure to time and space that truly elevate her beyond mundane life.

Contrasting Rose—whose opening scenes are bathed in radiant, golden light—Martha initially appears drab in blue denim. While radiantly beautiful, her luminosity isn't external; it's internal: her smile, her eyes, and her personality are what serve to illuminate her. Rose isn't only externally beautiful, but when we first meet her, she seems dull and waiting to be sparked into life by the Doctor, externalized through the lighting. River Song also is externally illuminated, although she does exhibit a certain golden glow when she recalls her Doctor. Martha's inner light exists independently from the Doctor. When Martha is externally illuminated, commonly she isn't lit in warm tones of gold and copper, but in chill silvered shades. Martha displays a kind of *goldhroden*, almost exclusively silver, *seolforhroden*,[72] with some brilliant blue or baleful red illumination, colors converse to the benevolent valkyrie, linking Martha to the battle-demon and to the original, powerful Valkyrie Goddess. In "Smith and Jones," Martha wears very cool tones (blue and black), almost no jewelry, except for unobtrusive gold hoops. Her most prominent adornment signals her profession—her white Doctor's coat. As she becomes the next Companion, her attire echoes with severity the Companion still very much on the Doctor's mind: Rose.

Entering the TARDIS, Martha is now bedecked and bejeweled— now prominent hoop-earrings, dazzling necklace and bracelet, with several glittering rings, and her pink and blue color palette unfairly places Martha in Rose's shadow. As Martha becomes more her own person, dusky-rose becomes red and black, with the most striking texture being leather. Indicating her maturity and associations with war, she is immediately seen wearing professional dress, but by "Human Nature," she wears a stylized, black, military coat. She dons similar garb in "Last of the Time Lords," and her position with UNIT is reflected by the Eisenhower-style coat in "The Sontaran Stratagem" and black uniform in "Stolen Earth" and "Journey's End." Her color scheme extends to her appearance in *Torchwood*, however, her professional dress tends toward black pantsuits. Martha has no other splendid adornments, never gaining an opportunity to dress up the way Rose and Donna do. While Martha does dress in period costume in "Human Nature" and "The Family of Blood"—as Mr. Smith's servant, it's for survival, not for amusement. The only reference to her "dressing up" comes in "The Poison Sky," when wearing the Doctor's coat, she remarks: "I feel like a kid in my dad's clothes." There's no opportunity for Martha to wear any beaded flapper gowns or poodle-skirts.

During Martha's first journey, to Elizabethan England, the Doctor is dismissive: "Just walk about like you own the place...." Not having Martha in period clothing to help her blend reflects a kind of unimportance. Debatably this was to be "one trip"—but even so she could've been allowed access to the TARDIS closets. There were times when Rose and Donna traveled in time, predominantly into the future, when their attire was of little to no importance or when it served to humorously underpin the banter.[73] However, both Rose and Donna were able to take advantage of traveling in a TARDIS with immense wardrobes. The only time we see Martha at all embellished, she wears a minimalist cocktail dress for the soiree at LazLabs.[74] It's doubtful that the Doctor even told her the TARDIS had a wardrobe, much less a swimming pool[75] or Cloister room.

Concerning the Valkyrie Reflex of riding over land or sea, Martha qualifies even prior to traveling with the Doctor; the Judoon take her hospital to the moon. Riding in space and time is added as she becomes Companion, but Martha often continues in this valkyrie function independent of the Doctor. "The Sound of Drums," sees her escaping the Valiant using Jack's teleport device, leading to her year-long walking-tour; in "The Doctor's Daughter," solitary, she travels the desolate planet surface; "The Stolen Earth" has her not only travel with Earth to the Medusa Cascade exactly one second out of time with the remaining Universe, but she travels via Project Indigo to Germany and into the foyer of her mother's home.

Martha is decidedly more sexualized than Rose. Her clothing throughout is more "fitted" than Rose's or Donna's, noted by Shakespeare with "Hey nonny, nonny." For the first half of Series 3, she displays more bare skin than the 10th Doctor's other Companions, and even when completely covered, her clothes are body-hugging. Martha is seen flirting or kissing—enjoying the genetic transfer/kiss in "Smith and Jones," evading a kiss by telling the Bard his breath "doesn't half stink," kissing Riley in parting after they were about to die together in "42." Martha's kiss to Riley, a gift of thanks unseen by the Doctor, was as deliberate an act as her telephoning Dr. Tom Milligan at the end of "Last of the Time Lords." Davies notes, "Martha ...rarely says what she's... thinking."[76] While not be as blunt as Donna, Martha does say what she means—but not to the Doctor. Bringing Tom's attention to his wanting to see her apart from the Perception Filter, she asks: "Is there a Mrs. Milligan?" Donna remarks Martha eventually does "get over" the Doctor,[77] because when we meet Martha in Series 4, she's engaged to marry Milligan. During her appearances in *Torchwood*, erotically-charged banter flows with Owen, marked in her reference to his recent death: "And...no stiffening anywhere?"[78] Her maturity is reflected in her lightening-quick jokes to Jack— "Still struggling to conquer your shyness, Jack?"—her challenges to Torchwood's resident doctor, "You never know, Owen, you might learn, something" —and her witty assertion to Gwen about both being "the only two people on the planet" not intimate with Jack.[79]

Martha's suffering stems from her inability to confess her feelings to the Doctor. Regardless of Martha's notice of his having kissed her, shown up in a "tight suit," traveled "all the way across the universe to ask [her] on a date," she yields prematurely, resulting in his not investing in her. Instead, the Doctor on rebound uses her to show off. Even Shakespeare notices the Doctor's failure to appreciate Martha, "The Doctor may never kiss you. Why not entertain a man who will?" David Tennant remarked:

Although they became very close and ... a good

team, that was always going to drive a rift between
them... the Doctor could never be to Martha what she
ultimately wanted him to be.[80]

Martha's parting comments to the Doctor in 3.13 force him to
acknowledge his insensitivity.[81] The Doctor does eventually trust her;
he unceremoniously gives her a TARDIS key at the end of "42," which
is overly-similar to a reversed cup-giving scene: her hands cupped to
accept his gift. Even Jack has a TARDIS key, and he only traveled with
the Doctor for the final five episodes of Series 1. Martha had to wait
until midway in her series to receive the Doctor's trust in terms of the
key. Her phone is also upgraded at the beginning of this episode with
"Universal Roaming" as a part of her "Frequent Flyer's privilege," which is
more about his machismo than his trust in her. His trust, however, once
given, goes beyond even what he has for Rose or Donna, and perhaps
rivals his trust for River. His life as John Smith, his existence as Time
Lord, and the fate of the Universe, are left in her capable hands when he
uses the Chameleon Device to escape the Family.[82] While her connection
to the Doctor is sexual, it morphs into the role as guide, intermediary, and
even savior.

Martha's unswerving willpower is reflected in her use of weaponry
and her steadfast ability to endure her mission notwithstanding personal
pain, or what suffering she might inflict. Martha is the only New Series'
Companion to wear armor— the byrnie or armored corset via Project
Indigo's teleport harness in "Stolen Earth," and "Journey's End." While
she doesn't carry a weapon like River, Martha quickly uses anything to
hand—especially her intellect—like the other Davies Companions. In
"Gridlock," Martha uses the gun Milo used to kidnap her and she doesn't
falter to use the Family's weapon to threaten them.[83] Martha gives
Operation Blue-Sky their marching orders.[84] Visibly affected watching a
black-clad Martha orchestrate military action, Donna incredulously asks,
"Is that what you did to her? Turned her into a soldier?" Not comfortable
with Donna's sagacity, the Doctor outpours his displeasure, retorting to
Colonel Mace, "I don't like people with guns hanging around me, all
right?" Martha mediates, but the Doctor's snappish rejoinder reflects his
anger: "People with guns are usually the enemy in my books. You seem
quite at home." Speaking directly to the truth, Martha doesn't predict the
future but interprets the present for the Doctor specifically. This gift—
her own prophecy—matured since her time as Companion. Addressing
the Doctor's "tetchy" attitude regarding her work with UNIT, she notes
that he got her the job, and that she doesn't carry a gun because she uses
her mind with the goal to "make them better" by working from within.

After all, she did "learn from the best." Martha advises Donna to inform her family because: "You know the Doctor—he's wonderful, he's brilliant, but he's like fire. Stand too close and people get burnt." Tempered by the Valkyrie Reflex of paralysis and death, Martha fetters the Master.[85] Bowing before him, intending to sacrifice herself, she explains her year-long intent to spread news of the Doctor using "No weapons, just words." No longer able to travel with the Doctor, Martha binds him in shame and silence as she exposes her feelings, leaving him under the controlling influence of her phone. After Earth is transported across the universe, Martha's orders to UNIT have changed; asking if anyone has been injured, she begins giving orders to get the lights on and the wounded medical attention. At heart a doctor and not a murderer, Martha, on occasion, does serve as executioner. Despite her refutation in a draft of Davies' script for "Stolen Earth,"—"I'm not a soldier. I'm a medic"[86]— Martha is armed with the Osterhagen Key, perhaps the worst weapon man crafted on Earth, making her executioner for the entire planet. In the English translation of Martha's exchange with the Old Woman in "Journey's End," the Old Woman remarks that Martha, unlike the soldiers, would not go home to die, calling Martha demon, "You are the nightmare! It's not them, it's you! I should kill you, right here, right now!"[87] Martha isn't merely any old night demon. Likened to the Nazi-like destructive power of the Daleks, the Old Woman curses Martha, "You're going straight to hell."[88] A concept furthered by Martha's *Torchwood* appearances: Martha as monster.

Martha wavers between Warrior and Crone, allied with life and death. She arms herself to fight the Pig Slaves, concocting the impromptu electrocution device to channel lightening that massacres the Slaves.[89] The Doctor as Mr. Smith vitriolically says, "So, your job was to execute me?"[90] After her year walking the Earth,[91] the legend of Martha hinges on assassination. Milligan meets her, saying: "Story goes...you're the only person on Earth that can kill him...you alone can kill the Master stone-dead." Martha propagates this tale for Professor Docherty's benefit, displaying a special weapon. From assassin to monster Martha is forcibly impregnated by the Mayfly larva, while her body becomes a battleground for the cannibalistic creatures.[92] She then becomes the third face of the Goddess—the Crone— with the second Resurrection Glove's touch. "The Poison Sky" sees Martha physically turned into a weapon by the Sontarans via cloning. The monstrous creature in the slime-vat becomes Martha's doppelgänger, itself a creature of death whose purpose was to stop the nuclear weapon strike, thereby allowing the Sontarans time to overwhelm Earth.

Counter to her destructive purpose, the Martha-clone unwittingly gifts humanity with life, echoing our Martha's generosity, which circulates around life, hope, and healing, particularly to the dead or dying. Offering sympathy and kindness to her dying clone, Martha regains what is hers: her engagement ring from the dead clone's hand. In "Smith and Jones," she takes a moment to close Mr. Stoker's eyes when the Doctor doesn't think twice about leaving the dead man behind. Martha is a fountain of safety, security, service, and ultimately sacrifice for Mr. Smith,[93] just as she becomes that someone to believe in for Riley.[94] She tries to revive Jack at the beginning of "Utopia," giving him a hand up when he reanimates of his own accord. Ultimately, Martha heals the Doctor so he's better able to move beyond Rose, and she gives the gift of recognition to many during her journeys—from Chantho (asking about Chantho's life) to Creet-as-Toclafane.[95] Martha sparks the chain of recognition in Professor Yana when asking about the watch.

Her gift isn't always positive, nor is the intent destruction. Her supreme gift and pivotal sacrifice grants hope to all humanity during the year-that-never-was. Martha gifts the Hath with healing and friendship, refusing to leave Hath-Peck in the face of danger, shouting to the armed Hath, "I'm Doctor Martha Jones. Who the hell are you?" This is who Martha has become since relinquishing TARDIS-travels for her family and for the sake of her own sanity. She sacrificed her love for the Doctor in order to live. Martha is the only one of the Davies Companions to do so, keeping her apart from the rest, and of any of the Companions called to arms in "Stolen Earth," and "Journey's End" the only two who don't falter (not counting Donna who was unaware of Earth's Dalek-situation) are Rose and Martha. When Jack and Sarah Jane are ready to give up, Martha's mission becomes crystallized, as she says to her mother, "I'm a member of UNIT. I've got to do my job." While not a soldier in the strictest sense of the word, as Davros stated of the Doctor's "Children of Time"—Martha was an ordinary person, fashioned into a weapon: a weapon for good, but a weapon nonetheless.

Donna Noble

"The Runaway Bride," Donna's first appearance in *Doctor Who*, begins with the exact concept—frame-by-frame— as did the New Series. Davies notes the New Series launch:

> ...had to start with Rose Tyler. Except it didn't...
> It started in outer space, zooming in on her flat....
> [giving] her whole world an outer-space context with
> the promise of weird things to come.[96]

Instead of the camera zooming onto her flat, we converge on Donna's wedding day. Davies remarked, "[Donna's] an equal to the Doctor, a friend, a mate, a challenge."[97] Luminous in bridal gown, adorned with a nimbus of golden sunlight and copper hair, Donna, enigma to the Doctor, is the most blunt, most mature—and most damaged— of all the Davies Companions. Marked as "Something terrible and new,"[98] Donna suffers the greatest loss of the other Davies Companions.

Immediately, the Doctor has to "slightly readjust to what he's used to in a Companion."[99] Treating him in a manner to which he's unaccustomed, she yells, slaps him, and accuses him of kidnapping other women, wielding Rose's abandoned jacket as proof. Donna Noble translates as Lady, or gift, of great celebrity. This translation derives from *Dona*, the Italian for "Lady" or *donnum*, the Latin for "gift," and from *nobilis*, Latin for celebrity. The Doctor qualifies this with: "*Dona nobis pacem*"[100]—give us peace—which reflects Donna's largesse, but also her association with Freyja the "peace-weaver."[101] This generosity, granting peace to the Doctor after his cyclical suffering, elevates her status well beyond her mantra: "I'm just a temp from Chiswick."[102] Donna matches the Doctor in ego, intellect, and wit, which serve to further ennoble her. Before their meeting, she's been physically elevated by the infection of Huon particles—the same particles at the heart of the TARDIS. About to walk down the aisle, screaming, she dissolves into a shimmering streak of gold as the TARDIS drew her into itself. Void Stuff becomes an addendum to the Huon particles, removed by the Empress of the Racnoss, as the TARDIS draws Donna in and from the Doctor taking her to see the creation of Earth. Physically elevated and riding over land and sea in the TARDIS, "The Sontaran Stratagem" opens with Donna actually flying the TARDIS, encapsulating his trust in her, their friendship, and their footing as equals.

Donna seeks acceptance,[103] despite her bravado, the first sign of her suffering, and serves as a leitmotif throughout her time as Companion. While not properly part of the Valkyrie Reflex, Damico notes that valkyries don't have "intimate relationships" with other women, "not even between mother and daughter,"[104] which lends to Donna's need for validation. Sylvia Noble surpasses Francine Jones in negativity and detriment. Francine, like a lioness, wishes to protect Martha from the Doctor, but Sylvia encourages the degradation of Donna, resulting in Donna thinking herself anything but brilliant. "Partners in Crime" gives witness to Sylvia's disappointed, barbed invective toward Donna, and with such injurious relationship, getting away from mundane-life becomes Donna's objective. By "Turn Left," Sylvia's pessimistic disapproval may

169 • Jessica Burke

have contributed to the literal destruction of reality if Donna did not outstrip Sylvia's distemper (with Rose's help). Initially, the Doctor echoes Donna's misgivings:

> It's weird. I mean, you're not special. You're not powerful. You're not connected. You're not important.

To which Donna replies: "This friend of yours, before she left, did she punch you in the face?" Donna parries as both a self-defense mechanism—to hide how utterly painful her lack of self-assurance is—and a kind of prophecy. Donna wears her suffering just beneath her radiant surface, but instead of using it to inflict harm—as Sylvia obviously does to her—she manages to push it aside to accomplish the task at hand, especially when that task involves the safety and well-being of others. Like Martha, Donna is a healer, but instead of using her hands, she uses words.

Donna's healing, her ability to save, often comes through her candor. Unlike other Companions, there to follow the Doctor's lead, Donna asks the difficult questions. Davies notes that not only does Donna ask the essentials like what makes time fixed and what makes history established, but that no other Companion has asked these hard questions.[105] Essentially, no other Companions has made the Doctor explain himself to such a degree as Donna has. She consistently gives the Doctor his comeuppance when he becomes too insensitive, too alien, and too bloodthirsty. Despite Donna's own inner turmoil, Davies notes: "There's an indestructible core to her... she's always determinedly at a right-angle to events."[106] She is self-centered, but not selfish,[107] often reflecting how we are, but Donna pushes conscience to the limit and forces the Doctor to examine his own actions.

Donna's vehemence about doing something to "warn" the people of Pompeii about the impending disaster is placed squarely before the Doctor when she says: "Listen, I don't know what sort of kids you've been flying around with in Outer Space, but you're not telling me to shut up."[108] This is her prophecy; while it isn't always caustic, she isn't afraid to remind him of his own transgressions. Donna's original plea— "Find someone.... sometimes, I think you need someone to stop you"[109]—becomes crucial as the 10th Doctor's song concludes. By pleading, "Doctor, I think you can stop now,"[110] she saves his life, keeping the entire Universe on proper course. Bluntly, she asks the Doctor about Rose: "That friend of yours, what was her name," offering him recognition and acceptance of his loss. When the Doctor realizes he is the cause of the eruption and the murderer of thousands, she shares his burden by placing her hand on the lever as well. In payment, he does go back to save Caecilius, admitting,

"Sometimes, I do need someone." After finding him again in "Partners in Crime," she stops him from holding two Sonic devices together, doesn't allow him to forget his slaughter of the Racnoss, and asks if he's just going to "blow up" the Adiposean newborns. Bantering about "mad Martha" and "Charity Martha," Donna mocks the Doctor being "fancied," thereby taking him off any pedestal. The Doctor, as Tennant confesses, shows great relief when Donna "couldn't be less interested in him as anything other than a friend."[111] When she barks, "You just want to mate," firmly grounds their relationship in camaraderie, not sexual attraction. Despite his attempts to gobsmack her with the bigger-on-the-inside speech, she dismisses him with, "Oh, I know all that bit, although frankly, you could turn the heat up."

Routinely throughout Series 4, the two are mistaken for a couple—"Dr. Noble and Mrs. Noble."[112] Donna is, however, a sexual being but her erotic focus isn't the Doctor. We see Donna in two relationships—with Lance, whom she's about to marry, and with Lee McAvoy, whom she does marry.[113] Donna flirts with Captain Jack,[114] yet, even in this her sexuality is mocked. While Jack is interested in anyone anytime, he doesn't seem interested in Donna, and the Doctor tells her to "save your womanly wiles for later, in case of an emergency."[115] However, of all the Davies Companions, Donna alone appears as Mother—married and with children.[116] Emulating Freyja—the Nordic Venus—Donna calls herself "the Goddess Venus" while modeling her purple toga for Evelina.[117] Her sexuality, coupled with her adornment, reflect her stage in life—mature well beyond maidenhood. Donna's clothes are adult, exhibiting more color—shades of purple, blue, and deep red with splashes of pink, black, or grey. Her adornments are earthy, spiritual, royal tones, Freyja's colors, paralleled as Wilf spies Venus, commenting: "The only planet in the solar system named after a woman"—to which Donna adds "Good for her" firmly grounding her in strong, actualized, unsubjugated feminine energy. Donna's Goddess bond is authenticated when Donna becomes true goddess as Caecilius' household deity, on par with Hestia—Mother Goddess of Hearth, Home, and Fruitfulness—harkening back again to Freyja.

Donna's *goldhroden* manifests in her radiant copper hair, dazzling earrings, pendants, and moon-like stone ring. Donna consistently has the opportunity to dress splendidly, from wedding gown to business suits, fur-lined parka to purple toga—a color reserved for the Emperor and the Divine. Donna is most resplendent schmoozing with Agatha Christie in metallic Flapper garb, hair swept into copper bands with Cinderella-like gold slippers.[118] While not wearing ringed-armor, Donna is known for spectacular golden hoop-earrings and wide, corset-like belts, the most notable in "Turn Left,"—gold circles overlapping metallic crescent-moons. The joviality of her golden, Christmas-crown radically changes, as she loses color, washing into glum shades, striking in long, 'hero-coat' she wears before donning the byrnie-like jacket to time-travel. The closer Donna comes to becoming the Doctor/Donna, she wears more brown, possibly emulating the Doctor's own brown tones.

Donna is habitually seen associated with fire—from the fire-consumed sub-basements of HC Clemens, to the obliteration of Pompeii, from the battle for supremacy over the Ood-Sphere, to the cleansing conflagration from Rattigan's Atmospheric Converter.[119] Donna unwittingly plunges into the midst of the Hath-Human war, survives the nuclear holocaust in London, and is engulfed in the inferno of the Crucible's Z-Neutrino core.[120] Donna exhibits another mark of Freyja: tears of gold. Donna's tears characteristically shimmer with golden light— notably while begging for the Doctor to "just save someone,"[121] while denying herself to Rose "I'm nothing special...I'm nothing!"[122] Absorbing the cannibalized-TARDIS' golden light, Donna accuses Rose of lying, eyes bright with golden tears and the realization her death is imminent. The golden whirlwind transporting her back is not unlike the Doctor's regeneration energy or the golden nimbus circling Rose as Bad-Wolf. As the Doctor's regeneration energy, stored in his spare hand, connects with Donna, she is surrounded by a "gold lightstorm,"[123] and when Davros activates her into the Doctor/Donna, her eyes shine golden.[124]

While not a professional like Martha or River, Donna displays intelligence on par with the Doctor's even before becoming the Doctor/Donna. Davies' intent for the opening scenes of "Partners in Crime," was to have Donna and the Doctor parallel each other.[125] Donna parallels the Doctor in sheer word-play, and frequently her words fetter him in a kind of disbelief—first seen in his stunned reaction to her mimed tale through the windows of Adipose Industries. Donna doesn't harmfully bind him as did the Carrionites or Sky. Donna's words stun him, shame him, force him to consider his actions. Her words serve to stop him when he needs reminding that if he crosses too many lines, he would become omnipotent. She does, however, properly bind him on three occasions: when telling him the blonde was "Bad Wolf," with the question "Doctor, what do we do" after the Tandoka Scale runs cold, and as her memories are stripped to keep her alive.[126]

The Doctor and Donna are verbose to the point of euphoria and, save for Romana, no other Companion has ever matched his shrewdness. While some Classic Series companions can banter, it's often irresolute and subservient to his dexterity. Rose, River, and Martha are quick with rejoinders, but Donna outshines them all. Her directness is both refreshing and at times distressing for the Doctor, sustaining her connection to him as valkyrie. The Doctor is callous in the face of her outrage at the Second Great and Bountiful Human Empire, but her reply, equally hard, reminds him his words wound:

> Is that why you travel around with a human at your side? It's not so you can show them the wonders of the universe. It's so you can take cheap shots.

The Doctor apologizes—something I don't believe he would've done in the past. It's hard to imagine the 4th Doctor apologizing for his cutting remarks about Leela's savagery or the 3rd Doctor expressing remorse at reprimanding Jo's foolishness. Donna wryly dismisses the Doctor's apology—"Spaceman"—affirming their vast difference that shouldn't be forgotten. Her sagacity, prophecy, and far-reaching actions do conflict with her underlying personal trepidations. Yet, Donna's confidence has shone during her time with the Doctor, as expressed to the Chief Constable's harsh query: "Donna, I'm a human being, maybe not the stuff of legend but every bit as important as Time Lords, thank you."

While Donna does give physical bounty—producing a second golden, parthenogenesis capsule in "Partners in Crime," the walnuts and kiss helping the Doctor detoxify in "The Unicorn and the Wasp")—Donna's intelligence combines with her perspicacity to forge genuine prophetic insight and recognition. Donna's selflessness shines in her first trip as official Series 4 Companion, to travel "Two-and-a-half miles that way," giving Wilf the blissful satisfaction of seeing his granddaughter contented, amongst the stars. Customarily, Donna is the first to recognize things for what they are—before the Doctor or us. She:

- recognizes the marble slab Caecilius crafted for Lucius is a circuit and that Evelina (and the Sybilline sisterhood) are turning into stone
- verbalizes that the Ood are slaves, that not born with Ood "spheres" (as Donna calls them) they're "born with their brains in their hands"
- names Jenny as the Doctor's daughter and Time Lady with two-hearts,
- understands the colony codes are dates
- questions the Library's books being alive—an unconscious foreknowledge about the Vashta Narada's source
- discerns the dead-faces on the information nodules
- connects the 24 displaced planets with Pyrovillia and the

lost Adiposean Breeding Planet that enables the Doctor to understand the planets were stolen from time *and* space
- grasps the disappearance of the bees
- distinguishes the second heartbeat of Doctor 10.5
- deciphers how to stop the Reality Bomb
- renders the Daleks and Davros impotent
- perceives how to restore the planets to their right place in space and time[127]

Donna's gifts revolve around death and a visceral need to do right—which may not always have positive repercussions. By confronting the Doctor's heartlessness in Pompeii, Donna propels him to save just "someone"—Caecilius—may have tragic end-results in terms of *Torchwood*'s "Children of Earth."[128] Pushing beyond her fear and revulsion, she attempts to comfort dying Ood Delta-50, even when the Doctor holds back.[129] She snatches the Firestone from Agatha's hand, tosses it into the lake, and drowns the Vespiform seemingly without conscience because it was the right thing to do in that moment.[130] Comforting Miss Evangelista in life—and death—Donna suffers the first of several of her own deaths, placing her face onto the Information Nodes' Flesh-Aspect and her consciousness into CAL's vast data-core.[131] Suffering from low self-esteem, Donna's manifest suffering surrounds her several deaths. Although Donna's goal is to remove the creature from her back, her decision to die—and ultimately correct the flow of the universe—isn't selfish; her inner confusion and distress are palpable. For Donna, in "Turn Left," Rose is her valkyrie. It takes Rose's intervention to make that version of Donna understand just how important Donna is. Donna's affliction is tormenting as she weeps: "You told me I was special. It's not me. It's this thing. I'm just a host!" Rose verbalizes Donna's importance—echoing the Doctor's own words to Syliva and Wilf at the end of "Journey's End": "Donna Noble, you're the most important woman in the whole of creation!"[132] Regardless of death, Donna never wavers, hitting the ground in a stance reminiscent of *Terminator*, realizing she's in the wrong location, she runs into action, golden light diffusing her face as she replays Rose's prophecy to her. Giving up her life, Donna offers a silent "Please" as plea to the universe to set things right. Meeting up with the Doctor again, her insecurity underpins her final interactions with him as Companion:

THE DOCTOR
Somehow I think there's way too much coincidence around you, Donna. I met you once then I met your

grandfather. Then I met you again. In the whole wide universe, I met you for a second time. It's like something is binding us together.

DONNA
Don't be so daft. I'm nothing special.

THE DOCTOR
Yes you are. You're brilliant.

In "Stolen Earth," Rose again notes how all the "time lines...converge" on Donna. Bringing the Doctor 10.5 into existence by helping to channel the regeneration energy from the spare hand, Donna is imitated— in tone and movement—by the Doctor 10.5, a reverse of her unconscious parallels of his movements in "Partners in Crime," again inverted as Donna becomes the Doctor/Donna, internalizing his techno-babble. Unlike the 10th Doctor, Doctor 10.5 fully understands and fully acknowledges Donna's suffering:

DONNA
But why me?

THE DOCTOR
Because you're special.

DONNA
But I keep telling you. I'm not.

THE DOCTOR
No, but you are though. Oh. You really don't believe that do you. I can see, Donna what you're thinking. All that attitude. All that lip, cause all this time you think you're not worth it.

Her jubilation at becoming his proper equal—the Doctor/Donna, as prophesied by the Ood—becomes physically uncomfortable for audiences to bear as it turns to utter despondency at the knowledge that there "can't be" a "Human-Time-Lord meta-crisis." Donna's fate, as noted by Catherine Tate, is a fate worse than death.[133] Personally, I would've preferred Donna to die with her memories of herself as not only the Doctor's Companion but as that woman whose praises are being sung "a thousand million light years away" because to dissolve into not much more than a caricature from *The Catherine Tate Show* is excruciating. Donna wasn't meant for that, hence her anguished final words on the TARDIS:

> I want to stay....I was gonna be with you forever.... The rest of my life, traveling in the TARDIS— the Doctor/Donna... I can't go back. Don't make me go back. Doctor, please! Please, don't make me go back... No, no, no, please!

While Rose suffered the loss of the man she loves, she gained a reasonable facsimile as the Doctor 10.5. Martha left the Doctor of her own accord and despite becoming a weapon in her own right, she has a fiancé who sacrifice himself for her (since he has during the year-that-never-was).[134] But, of all the Davies Companions, and perhaps of the Classic Series as well, I personally believe Donna suffers the most. She tells us in "The Runaway Bride:" "I missed my wedding, lost my job, and became a widow on the same day." Series 4 has her lose her life on three separate occasions, lose her husband and children,[135] lose her reality,[136] and lose herself as "the most important woman in the whole-wide universe."[137]

Blame It on Charley

Jochens observes:

> Men...had the last laugh. Even the most powerful maiden king was invariably overcome, often in humiliating ways, domesticated, married to the successful suitor, and curiously content with her new position. ...Icelandic literature taught...that gender roles should be obeyed and transgressors would be punished.[138]

We've seen this with dark valkyries—the Carrionites are subdued and shoved into a crystal ball, Lucy Saxon remains the Master's sex-slave/abused wife, Sky Silvestry was purged in the fire of an Xtonic Sun—but is this true for benevolent valkyries? Rose settles for the spare Doctor, a decision our Doctor manipulated her into. Benjamin Cook declares to Davies:

> You're hung up on the idea that Rose must be dumb to choose to stay on Bad Wolf Bay, but she

doesn't choose, does she? Not really. He does.[139]

While Davies rewrote the scene to give Rose more control—as examined by Kristine Larsen—Rose still opts for second-best. She fell in love with the Doctor, not the half-human, half-Time-Lord 10.5. River Song has no choice but to be content to live out a semblance of life inside CAL because, after all, she died. Martha may walk off in the best position, echoing her "Last of the Time Lords" rallying cry "This is me, getting out"—she strolls on with Jack, UNIT, and her soon-to-be married life to Dr. Tom Milligan, pediatrician. With openings in *Torchwood*, who knows what the future holds for Dr. Martha Jones. Granted a façade of life, Donna's "curiously content with her new position," hooting on her cell phone, blogging at her friend's romantic inclinations, she putters in the kitchen of her mother's home.

But, are they "punished" for some notion of gender transgression? Not in the same way as Jochens believes valkyries and Icelandic warrior women were. Davies' Companions had their path paved by an 8th Doctor Companion—established in the canon of Big Finish audio adventures—Charley Pollard. Davies acknowledged this in an email to Pollard actress India Fisher: "If it hadn't been for Charley, I wouldn't have been able to write a character like Rose."[140] Berry's article examines the delineation between Classic Series Companions and the route Davies' Companions took because of Charley. Opening the article he says:

> The role of the *Doctor Who Companion* has changed a lot in the past decade. You wouldn't catch Donna Noble dropping out of an adventure because of a twisted ankle, or Captain Jack running around in a short skirt...[141]

Davies' Companions progress and end because of this forerunner who spent a decade as Companion to the 8th and 6th Doctors respectively, thanks to timey-wimey goodness. While some gender stereotypes surface in New Series dark valkyries, if gender stereotypes hindered Davies' mind, then we would've had repetitions of Jo, Dodo, and Susan, whiners, shriekers, and mini-skirted little girls with no apparent individual will-power, no recognizable backbone, and no Valkyrie Reflex. In Davies' world—one soon-to-be inherited by Steven Moffat (creator of River Song)—possibilities abound and valkyries fly.

---

1 Donovan, 111.
2 Damico, *Beowulf's Wealhtheow*, 44.

3 J. R. Clark Hall, *A Concise Anglo-Saxon Dictionary* (Toronto: University of Toronto Press, 2000), 393, 80.

4 *The Anglo-Saxon Chronicles* portray a discordant England from generations of invasion and corruption:
"A.D. 1137: ...King Stephen came to England... every rich man built his castles, which they held against him.... They cruelly oppressed the wretched men of the land.... To till the ground was to plough the sea: the earth bare no corn, for the land was all laid waste by such deeds; and they said openly, that Christ slept, and his saints" (quoted in Killings).

5 Damico, *Beowulf's Wealhtheow*, 44.

6 Glosecki, 66.

7 Damico, *Beowulf's Wealhtheow*, 43.

8 "The Shakespeare Code," 10th Doctor, Russell T. Davies (New) Series 2005-ongoing.

9 *Ibid.*

10 *Ibid.*

11 Gimbutas, 189.

12 Clark Hall, 393.

13 Damico and Olsen, 176-177.

14 "Equidistant Letter Sequence in the Book of Genesis" by Witztum, Rips, and Rosenberg explored 'codes' found in letter arrangement of Biblical texts purported to transmit information in Nostradamus-like fashion.

15 Larsen, 122.

16 Damico, 41-42.

17 *Ibid.*

18 Damico and Olsen, 181.

19 *Ibid.*

20 Damico, 49.

21 Damico and Olsen, 181.

22 Damico and Olsen, 183.

23 Damico and Olsen, 179.

24 Damico and Olsen, 177.

25 Donovan, 110-111.

26 Tolkien, *The Lord of the Rings*, 707.

27 Ungoliant is posited to be one of the Maiar, or angelic creatures of Tolkien's mythos, who served the Valar, or divine beings. Ungoliant spawned countless generations, Shelob being the last.

28 While good "Queen Bess" is portrayed as a red-head—in particular see William Scrots' "Princess Elizabeth," Marcus Gheeraerts the Younger's "Ditchley Portrait," and our modern interpretations of the Queen— both Nicholas Hilliard's "Pelican Portrait" and Isaac Oliver's "Rainbow Portrait" along with Edmund Spenser's characterization of Elizabeth I in the guise of

Gloriana in *The Faerie Queene* (Book I especially) depict Bess with golden hair.
29 Donovan, 110.
30 Damico, 42.
31 Damico and Olsen, 187.
32 Damico and Olsen, 183.
33 Damico and Olsen, 184.
34 Damico, 33.
35 *Ibid.*
36 Damico and Olsen, 184.
37 Damico and Olsen, 185.
38 Having fought in medieval-style combat, I can attest that wielding a single shield isn't easy. Knowing about Norse-style armor from having worn a bit myself, no self-respecting valkyrie would be caught dead donning multiple shields.
39 Damico, 37.
40 In "The Good, The Bard, and the Ugly" (printed in *Doctor Who Magazine* #382, May 2007, pp.13-22), Benjamin Cook notes that there was a toss-up between what kind of monster would be featured in "The Shakespeare Code:" witches or fairies. Russell Davies' comment, "to be fair: who's going to win that fight," is representative of the deep-seated bias against the image of the 'classic' witch—the hag, crone, old wise-woman, or empowered woman.
41 While many feel no offense should be taken with Roberts' depiction of Witches, it must be noted that those who *do* take offense—namely Pagans, Witches, and feminists—have a right to be heard. Witches are one of the last groups it's socially acceptable to persecute and stereotype. Roberts' depiction of Witches is currently part of the 'accepted' world view, but is no less offensive than Shylock is to Jews, Uncle Remus is to African-Americans, Tonto is to Native Americans, or Sacha Baron Cohen's Bruno is to Gay men. As a writer, Roberts' should have pushed the boundaries of stereotype a bit more instead of presenting yet another tired view of Witches—and of women. See Anthony Burdge's comments on the Carrionites in his essay in this present volume, "The Professor's Lessons for the Doctor: The Doctor's Sub-creative Journey Toward Middle-earth."
42 Donovan, 111.
43 Damico and Olsen, 176-177.
44 A poppet is a doll used for magical purposes. Often used in modern witchcraft and pagan practices, the poppet has been 'popularly' but incorrectly referred to as the Voodoo doll. Poppets are crafted by the petitioner for sympathetic magic and are often used in healing spells, in addition to protective and defensive magic.
45 Damico, 44.
46 The Carrionites' cauldron displays two great, lidless eyes adorned with

stylized flames. This is undoubtedly a form of a ring, but perhaps is another Tolkienian nod to the lidless eye of Sauron, itself within a ring of fire.

47 The device displayed in the backdrop of the abode is similar to Gallifreyan written language. However, this "language" of the Carrionites is as angular as Gallifreyan is circular.

48 Jochens, 1996, 112.

49 Davies and Cook, *The Writer's Tale: The Untold Story*, 123.

50 While there is love between the Doctor and Rose, it's never properly professed, and when it is, it's not between our Doctor and Rose, but between Doctor #2 and Rose. In the end, Rose never actually gets the man she loves. She gets his carbon copy. So, while it is a love story *per se*, it is not a traditionally consummated one.

51 While we don't yet (at the time of composition of these essays) have specific news that it was, indeed, Lucy's nails taking up the Master's ring, logic dictates since Lucy was the only female in "The Sound of Drums" and "Last of the Time Lords" to don crimson nails, then we're led to believe she's the one to pluck the ring from the ashes. The debate will rage across the Whoniverse until the 10th Doctor's song ends and this notion is confirmed—or denied.

52 In esoteric practice, black equals death, rebirth, and Earth; red represents Fire, blood, fury, passion, raw female energy (menstruation), and destruction; gold associates with Earth or Air, resurrection, and can also stand in for black during magical ritual. Black, red, and white (sometimes gold) are also representative of the Triple Goddess, the Fates, and the Norns: black representing the Crone, red the Mother, and white (or gold) the Maiden.

53 As noted in Larsen's discussion, valkyries often lose much through their relationships with men—hence suffering as part of the Valkyrie Reflex.

54 Clarke's Law dictates: any advanced technology can appear as magic.

55 Davies and Cook, 291.

56 Davies notes Alice and May, the elderly women in "Gridlock"; they've essentially spent the last 23 years living in a box—along with the rest of the Motorway's residents—a grotesque form of living. Brannigan jokingly refers to them as "sisters," to which they reply, "We're married." This references past notions (particularly nineteenth-century sentiments) of female companions and the lessening of female-centric sexuality as platonic, which almost echoes the relationship of Laura and Lizzie, the "sisters" in Rosetti's "Goblin Market."

57 Lines 42-45.

58 Despite his being a pioneer in portraying non-traditional relationships, Davies may be shedding light on gender stereotypes by using Rossetti's "Goblin Market" or may be perpetuating those stereotypes unwittingly. Using a poem with such negative connotations of female sexuality coupled with a lesbian character turned monstrous—and punished for transgressions—questions gender roles. Was Davies' use of the poem subversive? Was he trying to hold up

stereotypes only to destroy them with Sky under the harsh glare of an Xtonic Sun, or has he been caught in a dangerous trap, having used a portion of a poem because it 'sounded good' without knowing the ramifications attached to using *this* poem? It remains to be seen...

59 Davies and Cook, 366.

60 "Forest of the Dead," 10th Doctor, Russell T. Davies (New) Series 2005-ongoing.

61 Jochens, 1996, 94.

62 Not synonymous with virgin, "maiden" refers to a woman's age, usually late teens to 20.

63 Jochens, 1995, *ix*.

64 "Gridlock," 10th Doctor, Russell T. Davies (New) Series 2005-ongoing.

65 Madame De Pompadour is another of note, but she deserves her own discussion.

66 While she may know about Donna—River Song falls silent when Donna petulantly demands to know what happens in the future—River Song doesn't reveal her knowledge, nor does she refer to it as "spoilers."

67 Damico, 48.

68 Damico, 81.

69 Damico, 49.

70 Damico, 51.

71 Martha appears in "Reset," "Dead Man Walking," and "Day in the Death."

72 *Seolfor* = silver in Anglo-Saxon.

73 Most notably in "Tooth and Claw" when Queen Victoria was clearly "not amused" by Rose's outfit.

74 "The Lazarus Experiment," 10th Doctor, Russell T. Davies (New) Series 2005-ongoing.

75 In "The Invasion of Time," the Doctor and Leela run through a TARDIS-room with an in-ground swimming pool empty of water. So, Doctor Who fans, yes, the TARDIS has a swimming pool.

76 Davies and Cook, 330.

77 "The Poison Sky," 10th Doctor, Russell T. Davies (New) Series 2005-ongoing.

78 *Torchwood*.

79 *Torchwood*.

80 "Doctor Who Greatest Moments: The Companions," 2009.

81 *Ibid*.

82 "Human Nature" and "Family of Blood," 10th Doctor, Russell T. Davies (New) Series 2005-ongoing.

83 *Ibid*.

84 "The Sontaran Stratagem," 10th Doctor, Russell T. Davies (New) Series 2005-ongoing.

85 "Last of the Time Lords," 10th Doctor, Russell T. Davies (New) Series 2005-ongoing.

86 Davies and Cook, 334.

87 Davies and Cook, 434.

88 *Ibid.*

89 "Evolution of the Daleks," 10th Doctor, Russell T. Davies (New) Series 2005-ongoing.

90 "The Family of Blood, " 10th Doctor, Russell T. Davies (New) Series 2005-ongoing.

91 *The Story of Martha* (BBC books; Abnett, Roden, Lockley, et al.), detrimentally relays Martha's year-long journey. The authors diminish Martha's importance—making her into a sniveling girl who wears heeled shoes and focuses on her own stupidity instead of her mission (Abnett et al, 37). The story is divided between Martha and the misogynistic tales of her being hunted. Here Martha becomes a slave in Japan, anticlimactically overrun by the Drast, never actually travels the world because other people pose as Martha Jones to tell the stories instead, and spends a deal of time remembering unconnected tales about the Doctor. Abnett and his colleagues devalue an otherwise complex valkyrie.

92 *Torchwood.*

93 "Human Nature," "Family of Blood," 10th Doctor, Russell T. Davies (New) Series 2005-ongoing.

94 "42," 10th Doctor, Russell T. Davies (New) Series 2005-ongoing.

95 "Utopia," and "Last of the Time Lords," respectively, 10th Doctor, Russell T. Davies (New) Series 2005-ongoing..

96 Davies and Cook, 221.

97 Davies and Cook, 197.

98 Davies and Cook, 349.

99 Catherine Tate; "Doctor Who Greatest Moments: The Companions."

100 "The Poison Sky," 10th Doctor, Russell T. Davies (New) Series 2005-ongoing.

101 Damico, 85.

102 Shouted at her most depressed, self-doubting times—specifically to Rose in "Turn Left" and to the Doctor in "Journey's End," and on variations throughout Series 4.

103 *Ibid.*

104 Damico, 20.

105 Davies and Cook, 72.

106 Davies and Cook, 310.

107 Davies and Cook, 330.

108 "The Fires of Pompeii," 10th Doctor, Russell T. Davies (New) Series 2005-ongoing.

109 "The Runaway Bride," 10ᵗʰ Doctor, Russell T. Davies (New) Series 2005-ongoing.
110 "Partners in Crime," 10ᵗʰ Doctor, Russell T. Davies (New) Series 2005-ongoing.
111 "Doctor Who Greatest Moments: The Companions."
112 "Planet of the Ood," 10ᵗʰ Doctor, Russell T. Davies (New) Series 2005-ongoing.
113 "The Runaway Bride" and "Forest of the Dead," 10ᵗʰ Doctor, Russell T. Davies (New) Series 2005-ongoing.
114 "Stolen Earth" and "Journey's End," respectively, 10ᵗʰ Doctor, Russell T. Davies (New) Series 2005-ongoing.
115 "The Doctor's Daughter," 10ᵗʰ Doctor, Russell T. Davies (New) Series 2005-ongoing.
116 "Forest of the Dead," 10ᵗʰ Doctor, Russell T. Davies (New) Series 2005-ongoing.
117 "The Fires of Pompeii," 10ᵗʰ Doctor, Russell T. Davies (New) Series 2005-ongoing.
118 "The Unicorn and the Wasp," 10ᵗʰ Doctor, Russell T. Davies (New) Series 2005-ongoing.
119 "The Runaway Bride," "The Fires of Pompeii," "Planet of the Ood," and "The Poison Sky," 10ᵗʰ Doctor, Russell T. Davies (New) Series 2005-ongoing.
120 "The Doctor's Daughter," "Turn Left," and "Journey's End," 10ᵗʰ Doctor, Russell T. Davies (New) Series 2005-ongoing.
121 "The Fires of Pompeii," 10ᵗʰ Doctor, Russell T. Davies (New) Series 2005-ongoing.
122 "Turn Left," 10ᵗʰ Doctor, Russell T. Davies (New) Series 2005-ongoing.
123 Davies and Cook, 425.
124 Davies and Cook, 467.
125 Davies and Cook, 186.
126 "Turn Left" to "Journey's End," 10ᵗʰ Doctor, Russell T. Davies (New) Series 2005-ongoing.
127 "Fires," "Planet," "The Doctor's Daughter," "Silence," "Stolen Earth," and "Journey's End," respectively, 10ᵗʰ Doctor, Russell T. Davies (New) Series 2005-ongoing.
128 See endnote 16 in Melissa Beattie's "Life During Wartime: An Analysis of Wartime Morality in *Doctor Who*."
129 "Planet of the Ood," 10ᵗʰ Doctor, Russell T. Davies (New) Series 2005-ongoing.
130 "The Unicorn and the Wasp," 10ᵗʰ Doctor, Russell T. Davies (New) Series 2005-ongoing.
131 "Silence in the Library," "Forest of the Dead," 10ᵗʰ Doctor, Russell T. Davies (New) Series 2005-ongoing.

132 "Turn Left," 10th Doctor, Russell T. Davies (New) Series 2005-ongoing.
133 "Doctor Who Greatest Moments: The Companions."
134 "Last of the Time Lords," 10th Doctor, Russell T. Davies (New) Series 2005-ongoing.
135 "Forest of the Dead," 10th Doctor, Russell T. Davies (New) Series 2005-ongoing.
136 "Turn Left," 10th Doctor, Russell T. Davies (New) Series 2005-ongoing.
137 "Journey's End," 10th Doctor, Russell T. Davies (New) Series 2005-ongoing.
138 Jochens, 1996, 112.
139 Davies and Cook, 497.
140 Dan Berry, "*Doctor Who Magazine* #414 (October 2009): 52.
141 *Ibid.*

The Doctor or the (Post) Modern Prometheus

Vincent O'Brien

The character of the Doctor has many similarities to the mythological cultural archetype of the Prometheus myth. The tale of Prometheus is essentially that of an ancient god imparting the gift of fire to the newly created human race. At a surface reading, this myth is essentially one of the noble rebel who wins the high ground but suffers greatly for it. Myths such as the Prometheus legend serve a purpose for society in providing explanations for events or situations that already exist. However, as with much mythology, the fluidic nature of interpretation allows for another viewpoint. Man created the myth, as man already had fire and had realized its potential to be a destroyer as well as a tool of creation. So if the myth were "true," then there was no noble sacrifice, no divine gift or indeed no choice. He is ultimately a heroic fictional figure who is bound by his story to make the noble sacrifice, a creation of his creation.

The Doctor in *Doctor Who* has from his very inception been portrayed as both teacher and savior (inside the Doctor's own universe) or as entertainer (in our "real" world). Yet like Prometheus, the Doctor has also been shown to be the bringer of death and destruction along with freedom. This paper will explore the inherent contradictions of these dual roles both in the context of the Doctor's fictional universe and the real one.

The characters of Prometheus and the Doctor have both obtained the status of myth, although it can be argued that the Doctor is only mythic within the domain of popular culture. This is not to say that the details or interpretations of each story are known to the general populous of the twenty-first century Western world, but the central characters and situations have transcended specifics and become archetypes. As with most archetypes, the essences of their tales can be distilled to a series of flashpoints or semiotic (having to do with signs and symbols and their meanings) triggers. The imagery and associations attached to the name of Prometheus have inspired everything from the subtitle to Mary Shelley's gothic masterpiece, *Frankenstein, or The Modern Prometheus* to the name of one of the first human starships built in the mythology-heavy sci-fi U.S. TV show, *Stargate SG1*.[1] In order to understand how these two disparate characters are connected, it is necessary to look at relevant flashpoints and examine how they compare and contrast.

The character of Prometheus is a figure from Greek mythology and is traceable as far back as the poet Hesiod's *Theogony* in the eighth century BCE[2]. Prometheus was born into a race of gods known as Titans, which were the forebearers to the Olympian gods of most of Greek mythology. The legends associated with Prometheus are essentially creation myths that portray his taking a role in the creation of the fourth race of beings to inhabit the Earth—humanity. Different interpretations of this tale exist, although the primary difference between the variants of this myth is solely concerned with the exact circumstances of his motivation. However, in all the variations, Prometheus defies his peers and gives humanity the hitherto unknown secret of fire. This act of balance or rebellion has the Titan then punished by his monarch, Zeus, to be chained to a rock whilst a bird of prey eats his liver by day. This organ is then re-grown each night, so the cycle can repeat the next day. This punishment is perpetuated until Prometheus is freed by the demi-god Heracles as part of his labours of atonement.

The comparison between the Doctor and Prometheus is most eloquently stated in the Doctor's sole canonical appearance outside of the main series, in the third series of *The Sarah Jane Adventures* spinoff. The quasi-mythic entity The Trickster describes the 10th Doctor in the episode "The Wedding of Sarah-Jane Smith Part Two," as "*a man of...fire, who walked among gods...now he is surrounded by children.*" Even though this depiction is stated when the Doctor is actually surrounded by three characters in their teens, it is equally possible to interpret "*children*" as any human, or in fact the entirety of sentient life in the universe from the point of view of The Trickster. This quote sums up the way that the Doctor occupies a special and rather nebulous position of being part god and part mortal, a stranger in both realms. It is especially ironic that this comparison comes from a being called The Trickster because Prometheus has often been presented as occupying the sub-category of trickster gods.[3] However, as opposed to the likes of Loki of Norse mythology, who reaps destruction upon reality as a whole, the true victim of Prometheus' actions are the Titan himself and arguably those of humanity who embrace his gift. The Doctor can also been seen to reap the joys but rarely sees the pain of his fiery existence. This stage of the Promethean gift or curse is expanded upon later in this paper.

Within *Doctor Who* itself, the 2008 season finale, "Journey's End," contains a line of dialogue that is significantly important in the relation to the Doctor's own mythical dimension.

Davros to the Doctor: '*I name you, forever, you are the destroyer of worlds.*'

This line of dialogue is expertly used, for to the casual viewer it seems merely to be the bitter last words of a dying madman. However, within *Doctor Who* fandom, and extended non-televisual fiction, there have long been references to a Dalek legend regarding the Doctor in which he is named the Ka Faraq Gatri. This title is translated from the fictional Dalek language as both Destroyer of Worlds and Bringer of Darkness.[4]

The notion that the Doctor had gained such a mythical aspect within Dalek history was first introduced in the novelizations of the Classic series serial "Remembrance of the Daleks" by scriptwriter, Ben Aaronovitch, and has subsequently been used in the licensed Virgin spin-off novels, as well as in the comic strips of Marvel UK/Pannini's *Doctor Who Magazine.*[5] Both definitions of the Ka Faraq Gatri can be applied with equal measure to the Doctor but can also be seen as being descriptive of the Daleks themselves, specifically the Bringer of Darkness interpretation. Nowhere is this expressed more clearly than in "Journey's End," where the Daleks' attempted use of the reality bomb would have had the effect of destroying all matter, essentially turning out the stars, bringing darkness, and ultimately destroying worlds.

It is necessary to realize that the ratification of this term within the television show is of importance, due to its status as the primary text whose canonicity cannot be questioned. However, as many of the implications of this term are gathered from the possibly non-canonical mythology that has arisen, they are therefore subject to individual interpretation.

Continuing to look at the Doctor specifically through the lens, or eyestalk, of the Daleks, the notion of the Doctor's own godhood is shown in greater clarity. Whilst the Daleks of the 2008 finale are quite literally the spawn of Davros, the creator of the Daleks is never treated with the veneration implicit in the role of creator. In fact, the history of the relationship between the Daleks and Davros within the show's own chronology demonstrates that the Kaled scientist is treated with the same lack of reverence for life by his creations as every other non-Dalek life form. This is in direct contrast with how the Daleks frequently treat the Doctor, as despite many assurances to the contrary, the Daleks have often not taken the opportunity to exterminate the Doctor when they have had the chance.

Examining the Daleks' contrasting relationship with their creator and their steadfast enemy, it seems on reflection that the Doctor is treated with far greater respect than Davros is. In the creation of their reality bomb, the Daleks can be seen to be seeking to emulate the "mythical" Doctor by becoming the destroyers of worlds and that Davros or the Supreme Dalek is seeking to be the bringer of darkness. Taking this textual extrapolation to its logical conclusion, it is possible to view Davros and the Doctor as having conflicting, yet interconnected, god-like roles with relation to the Daleks. Davros is obviously the creator god, but he is treated with scorn by his creations, and attempts, however unsuccessfully, to retain a measure of control over them. The Doctor contrastingly is cast as the destroyer god or possibly even in a satanic role. As the Daleks are ultimately destroyers themselves rather than creators, it would seem that they worship a destroyer god, even if his victims are themselves. The definition of destroyer god and the nature of his "destruction" is open to interpretation because whilst the Doctor can be in many cases seen as a physical destroyer, he can also been seen as wielding a spiritual devastation. Literally this can be seen as being expressed by his tampering with the Dalek mindset in "The Evil of the Daleks," but the mere presence of the Doctor has been shown to rally individuals to fight not only for life, but for ideals, contrary to the Daleks' stifling ideology.

The Doctor may be linked in Dalek mythology to the bringing of darkness, but the Prometheus myth is itself intrinsically linked to the significance of his gift to humanity: fire. Fire, whilst existing untamed under the right conditions in nature, has far more productive and destructive connotations under sentient manipulation. The nurturing aspect of regulated fire is one of the most basic yet necessary parts of human civilization, but it can be a destroyer. It is this destructive capability as well as its more productive industrial uses that make fire the metaphorical cornerstone of much of humanity's cultural evolution. Fundamentally fire is merely a tool as its power and purpose depends entirely upon its level of cultivation. Humanity can only really be said to be creators, and thus masters of their own destiny, when they learn to literally control fire, and to thus symbolically harness knowledge.

The metaphorical fire brought by the Doctor is again shown most clearly in his dealings with the Daleks. In all of his encounters with their race, the Doctor has been a foe of the Daleks, and on three separate occasions within the show's screened continuity held god-like power over their race.

The first of these in both the show's internal timeline and in respect to the real world occurs during the serial "Genesis of the Daleks." Within this storyline, the Doctor's 4th incarnation has been tasked unwillingly by the Time Lords to stop the creation of the Daleks. This is the story that not only elaborates on the stifling culture and xenophobic feud that spawned the Daleks but introduces also a previously unknown figure— the Daleks' creator, Davros. Prior to the introduction of this figure the Daleks can be imagined to be the product of evolution, albeit a warped one. Davros, however, shows the creation of the Daleks and their agenda and prejudices are the deliberate product of their creator's intent, showing the potential negative consequences of such creativity and knowledge

This serial has many iconic scenes in Doctor Who history; however, the most pertinent to the Doctor's godhood is when he has the ability to destroy the nascent Dalek race and chooses not to. The destruction the Doctor chooses not to unleash is signified by his refusal to connect two wires that would trigger an explosion, symbolically not acting as a Prometheus -like character, not bringing fire to the Daleks, thus ensuring their survival.

The second occasion of god-like power and destruction is in the serial whose novelization first mentions the Doctor's mythological status, *Remembrance of the Daleks*. This serial has the Doctor's 7th incarnation returning to 1960s era London to retrieve an item his 1st incarnation left there. The item in question is a piece of advanced technology from the Time Lords, the Hand of Omega. After putting up a show of defence of this item, the Doctor allows the Daleks to take it and pleads with them not to use its destructive force. However, as he knew they would, the Daleks refuse to listen. When activated, the Hand unleashes its power upon the star that Skaro, the Daleks' home-world, orbits destroying not only the Daleks' base, but much of their fleet. This directly contrasts with not only the 4th Doctor's choice not to destroy the nascent Daleks, but also with the same incarnation's begrudging actions due to the Time Lord hierarchy's manipulations as the fiery destruction is planned for and expected by the 7th Doctor. Furthermore, if we take Davros' point from "Journey's End" regarding the Doctor's displacement of guilt in the wake of destruction he leaves, it is possible to rationalize that although the plan was his, the activation was not. This indirect action reinforces the perception of the Doctor as a trickster god, for the Doctor wilfully manipulates the Daleks, turning their victory to literal ashes.

Symbolically, the Hand of Omega as a stellar manipulator can be viewed as truly divine as it tampers with and exerts influence over the primal fires of the universe and stars, yet can be seen paradoxically as representative of the most anti-Promethean technology possible. This manipulation results in almost god-like levels of power generation, which opened up avenues of technological exploration, including mastery of time travel. However, like the Promethean flame that has it consequences, so does stellar manipulation. The Hand is only able to grant these levels of power by collapsing a star into itself, thus generating a black hole. Such a phenomenon allows nothing to escape its gravitational pull, not even light, and as such can be symbolic of the ultimate in stifling god-like imagery.

This serial also takes place in a controversial era of the show, where the script editor, Andrew Cartmel, was attempting to restructure the show's internal mythology. Cartmel was attempting to return a large amount of mystery to the character of the Doctor that had been eroded by over twenty years of revelations regarding his people and his past. This "master-plan," as it became known after the initial run's completion, was never followed through to its climax. Cartmel's collaborator in the plan, Marc Platt, did write a novel for the Virgin New Adventures series, *Lungbarrow*, which completed this arc as well as bookending the 7th Doctor's literary existence[6].

Lungbarrow suggests that the Gallifreyan who would one day be called the Doctor was actually an even more mysterious ancient alien being reborn through the artificial reproductive system of the Time Lords, the Looms. This being, known simply as The Other, was an ally of Rassilon and Omega, the first Time Lord and his premier scientist respectively. This alien, whilst enigma even to his own allies, formed with them a triumvirate that moulded the Time Lord society seen in the show and to a greater extent, the novels. This same novel further suggests that it is the Other's influence that makes the Doctor steal the TARDIS and that Susan is not the Doctor's granddaughter, but rather The Other's.

The backstory contained within this piece of prose is supported by the inferences the 7th Doctor makes to be a contemporary of Omega in "Remembrance of the Daleks," as well as by the infamous deleted scene from this serial in which the Doctor claims to Davros that he is "far more than just another Time Lord." Further evidence is implied in the later serial "Silver Nemesis," where the Doctor tries and fails to keep another ancient Gallifreyan weapon out of the hands of another of his old foes. The weapon this time, a sentient metal statue, ends up following the Doctor's will and condemns his enemies, the Cybermen, to a similar fate to the Dalek fleet.

The implication taken from the hints dropped throughout the latter part of the McCoy era, that the Doctor is far more ancient than previously thought, further links the character to the myth of Prometheus. Although referred to as a Titan, Prometheus is in fact the son of a Titan, and in that regard shares a generational equality to the elder of the more commonly known Olympians: Zeus, Hades, and Poseidon; and ergo effectively only defies a generational equal who had elevated himself when stealing from Zeus. If the Doctor was a reincarnation of The Other, then he by virtue of being one of the triumvirate who established Time Lord society, would have a right to question, and ultimately defy, the laws set against him by the current ruling Time Lords.

The canonicity of both the novel, *Lungbarrow,* and the deleted scene is questionable as neither was shown in the original television broadcast. In fact the whole master-plan has its critics due to its secrecy and the fact that several sources, including a recent *Doctor Who Magazine* article, suggest that it was less of a structured plan and more a general movement towards a specific endpoint.[7] This retroactive continuity effectively fuels the mythic status of the Doctor and the master-plan in a similar way to that of the Prometheus legend. Both fulfil a need for explanation, although the Cartmel master-plan had a significantly smaller demographic.

As well as providing an explanation, the Prometheus myth also fulfils two important mythological and quasi-religious needs by portraying the Titan as being simultaneously humanity's benefactor/saviour and its persuader into damnation. The unending punishment can be viewed as being symbolic of a pessimistic view of the mortal struggle of humanity. The eagle represents time, consuming the insides of Prometheus. The choice of the liver, the organ that removes much of the poisonous by-products of life, can be seen as symbolic of the natural wastage of the human body and spirit through the cycle of life. Undue damage to this organ, even in the twenty-first century, would be fatal to a real human being. The reappearance of the organ at night can equally be seen as reproduction rather than regeneration, and thus taken to be Prometheus representing each day a fresh generation of Mankind, who are destined to experience the cycle again. In spite of this, the liver is also the only organ in the human body that is capable of regeneration itself, which can be seen as the possibility of regeneration of spirit or hope.

The nature of the punishment of the Titan demonstrates one of the subtleties of the Prometheus myth, in that it actually glorifies the mortal state of being. The torture of Prometheus by day, who regenerates his organs by night only to have them ripped from him again, presents immortality as a burden rather than gift or a prize. Whilst it is possible to read this as another attempt to justify the mortal lifespan that could not be explained by less enlightened science, it also presents a positive message of seizing the day or carpe diem. Within *Doctor Who* this message is also reinforced through both the character of the Doctor as well as other characters, usually other Time Lords.

This concept, and other Promethean themes, are demonstrated in *Doctor Who*'s most blatant homage to the myth of Frankenstein, the serial "The Brain of Morbius." In this story, the brain of a deposed Time Lord dictator has survived his execution and is transplanted by one of his acolytes onto an artificial monstrous body. Morbius, potentially already unbalanced by his sentence from his own people or from an extended period as a bodiless brain, is driven totally insane at the prospect of eternity in an aesthetically horrific if durable form.

Whilst this serial itself is something of a piecemeal affair with very obviously many design elements borrowed from the monster movie genre, it only truly displays the signs of the Frankenstein myth rather than those of Shelley's original tale. The symbolism of Promethean imagery it still retains is mostly in contrast. The obsession Solon has with the myth that is Morbius and their mutual dependence is in certain aspects akin to the relationship and distain between the Olympian gods and humanity in the Prometheus myth. Whilst these emotions may seem fundamentally contrasting they do in fact mirror each other. Morbius' acolyte, Solon, is the architect behind his god and his desire to resurrect his idol has no benevolent purpose. The obsession Solon has with Morbius is not with the reality of the mad but powerless brain in a jar, but rather with a mythic Morbius whom he has never actually met and who may never truly have existed. The return to life of Morbius, with full knowledge of his previous existence, makes his resurrection a direct contrast to the innocence of Shelley's creature and the nascent humanity that is gifted fire from Prometheus.

Furthermore, whilst this serial does in fact only feature one incarnation of the Doctor, his 4th, in the flesh, and his time-track is not divided through alternate means, his other selves are evident through a mental battle with Morbius. Each of the Doctor's other selves appears in profile during this battle as do several faces not seen before on screen. The implication of this is that the Doctor we believed to be the 4th incarnation, was in fact far older than the audience had believed. This potential facet of the Doctor's past has never been directly touched upon since, although it is possible to read one of those faces as The Other of *Lungbarrow*. The Doctor can be seen as mentally many different men, in contrast to the monstrous Morbius whose form is as piecemeal, but both are representative of interpretations of the nature versus nurture argument implicit in the Frankenstein story and more importantly the mortality-affirming message of the Prometheus myth. Morbius by his unnatural extension of his life is compelled towards monstrosity and insanity, whereas the Doctor as a construct of his own experiences is compelled towards the opposite. The need for fresh ideas and experiences to validate life is further demonstrated in this serial by the collection of mystics who oppose Solon, the Sisterhood of Karn. This coven worship a holy flame, but unlike the gift of fire presented by Prometheus, their flame stifles their evolution, extends their life cycle beyond and grants them superhuman abilities.

The most basic enforcement of this message is contained within the twentieth anniversary story "The Five Doctors." Within this special, several incarnations of the Doctor are manipulated into opening the tomb of Rassilon, the first of the Time Lords, and acquiring his secret of true immortality. However, when the mad Time Lord President,

Borusa, receives this gift, it renders him immobile and unable to interact with the active universe. Borusa had previously been portrayed as one of the Doctor's teachers and an influence upon his character, although this is unclear as to whether the effect was intended or more of a contrary reaction. As such, the punishment to be made truly immortal but to be frozen can be seen as either the result of his assimilation into the staid hierarchy of Gallifrey or as a counterpoint to the rebellious Doctor.

It is worthy of note that it is the Doctor's 1st incarnation that works out the pitfalls of Rassilon's offer, and realises it to be a punishment rather than a treasure. It is possible to read this as the wisdom of youth speaking, despite the paradoxically elderly appearance of the 1st Doctor. This special reinforces the idea that it was the Doctor's choice to leave his staid home-world, one he makes repeatedly through the Davison years.

The Doctor's decision to quit Gallifrey and the consequences of this choice are at the heart of the Doctor's tale, as much as the choices made by the Titan are the fundamental point of the Prometheus myth. One of the main elements of this myth that contrasts with other creation tales is it grants greater depth and ambiguity to the rebel Titan. Knowledge, as represented by fire in this Greek myth, is given by Prometheus to humanity as a true gift, one without intended consequences, although there inevitably are. The naivety of the Titan in not foreseeing the consequences of his actions is a flaw of the Doctor's as well. With the notable exception of the Doctor's 7th incarnation, whose manipulations are discussed elsewhere in this paper, the adventures and consequences resulting from the Time Lord's visits are neither prepared for nor fully realised. The Doctor rarely has to deal with the consequences of his appearances, although this has been a recurring theme throughout the era of the 10th Doctor. This has been evidenced by his meeting several characters more than once, such as Wilfred Mott, Francine Jones, and Harriet Jones, and seeing his unintended impact upon their lives.

Negative consequences are indeed possible from both the Doctor's and Prometheus' interactions with their environments, but out of the same metaphorical fire creativity and productivity, and even life itself can be seen to spring forth. It is in looking at the situation in this light that the Promethean gift can be alternatively viewed as a Promethean curse. Fire, seen as representative of independent thought, ultimately creates one of three identifiable stages of existence: the creation, the destruction, and the survival. These stages are symbolised by the Titan, his gift, and by humanity after his intervention.

The Doctor in his role as noble rebel, in defying the Time Lords' isolationist policy, is usually shown to be on the morally right side. Notable individual examples such as The Monk and The War Chief do, however, demonstrate the dangers of interference. The Time Lords within the show's continuity also provide another example of the Prometheus curse, with their interaction with the Minyans. The indigenous humanoids of the planet Minyos, it is revealed in the serial "Underworld," have made their world uninhabitable through a series of nuclear wars, similar to the fate of the planet Skaro. However, the Minyans did not create their weaponry solely from their own natural progress, but rather through technological assistance received from early explorers from Gallifrey. These technologies allowed the Minyans to advance technologically at a pace their sociological evolution could not match. Ergo, they ultimately almost destroyed their civilization. Therefore, the implication of this is that as well-intentioned as the Doctor's interventions may be, they have the potential to create as much disaster as they divert.

This can be countered by the presentation of a world without The Doctor in the episode "Turn Left." In this episode, global events take a drastic turn for the worst, due to a decision made by Donna Noble. Both of these storylines contain potentially dire consequences to actions, but the alternative, inaction, is not presented as being any more desirable. The alternative viewed in "Turn Left" is created by a being described by the Doctor as being one of *"The Trickster's brigade."* This is comparable to the uniting of the Doctor's companions in the following stories under the Davros given nickname "The Children of Time." The Doctor's metaphorical children all bring fire into the episode, be it the fire inside of Donna's mind, or the threats made by Captain Jack Harkness, Sarah Jane Smith, and Martha Jones. This is used by Davros to torture the Doctor by suggesting that the potentially murderous actions of the Doctor's companions reveal the Doctor's soul. Whilst death may be an inevitable consequence of their actions, the Kaled scientist ignores the fact that each of the companions has conceived of and is capable of achieving an inventive scheme to thwart the Daleks' plans. This level of self determination, to the point of choosing a fiery productive death over an oppressed wasted life, in fact shows the true gift of the Doctor.

The final time the Doctor holds power over the Daleks is in the dying minutes of "Journey's End," which is actually their most recent appearance on screen. For the purposes of this investigation, it is necessary to clarify that there existed three individual aspects of the Doctor on the Dalek station known as the Crucible at the conclusion of "Journey's End." Each of these differing versions of the Doctor acts out a different part of the Promethean story and curse.

The first of these is the true Doctor, in his 10th incarnation. The other two aspects are hybridizations of the Doctor and his companion Donna Noble. Due to the energy of an aborted regeneration, a previously severed hand of the Doctor's had been severed essentially to grow another body, which was part human, part Time Lord. This "meta-crisis," as the show branded it, resulted in a second Doctor who is half human and half Time Lord, and Donna undergoing metamorphosis into the Doctor/Donna, a being prophesied throughout the series, and her ultimate evolution. The Doctor/Donna possesses what is described as the best part of the Doctor—his mind.

The creative, productive aspect of the Prometheus myth is demonstrated by the Doctor/Donna's inventiveness in her solutions to the reality bomb. In dialogue, she proclaims to be able to come up with ideas that the Doctor couldn't, due to her inherent humanity. This over-abundance of creativity, borne of the unprecedented merger, is ultimately her downfall. Within the pseudoscience of the show such a meta-crisis is not possible, and by the end of the episode, after only a brief time in existence, this version of Donna ceases to be. The Doctor is forced to wipe her conscious mind, and bury the knowledge of the Time Lords deep within her unconscious, in order to save her life. The fundamental essence of the Time Lord, which has been symbolised on screen as fiery rebirth since the regenerative process of "Parting of the Ways," is burning out the shell of Donna Noble and must be contained. Donna, through this process, is made into being the first true equal to travel with the Doctor, albeit briefly, and one he is forced to part with.

In a further curious twist on the Prometheus myth, the end result of this process leaves Donna essentially a Pandora-like figure. One of the lesser well known parts of the myth is that the story is linked to the myth of Pandora, the first human woman created in Greek mythology. She is gifted a jar or box which when opened releases evils upon the world, leaving behind only hope in her box.[8] The comparisons to Donna can be carried further, as she can be seen to hold her own mental box of woes, with the potentially fatal knowledge buried within. Donna's mental box does though still contain hope, in more than one way. The first most literal interpretation is demonstrated on screen when members of the Master race attempt to attack her in "The End of Time Part Two." When threatened, and on the verge of remembering her past, an energy force is released that renders her assailants unconscious as well as Donna. This can be seen as a literal representation of hope remaining, by keeping Donna alive. The more poignant of the possible meanings is that the personality that Donna had, the person who she grew into whilst travelling the cosmos with the Doctor ,was not destroyed, but rather contained. Not only can that personality be seen to represent the hope left in Pandora's box, but it can also be seen as a version of Prometheus, trapped to a metaphorical rock, unable to interact with the outside world whilst the time ate away at Donna's lifespan.

The humanized Doctor is the bringer of fire and destruction as he chooses without hesitation to destroy the immobilized Dalek fleet. As the true Doctor states when leaving his doppelganger with Rose, he parallels the true Doctor's 9th incarnation by being "born of blood and fire and revenge." This situation also mirrors the connection between enlightened humanity and the Titan in the Prometheus myth, as well as the relationship between creation and creator in Shelley's *Frankenstein*.

The creation of the humanized Doctor does further mirror the introduction of the demi-god, or half human god, Heracles, into the Prometheus tale. Through the humanized Doctor, the perpetual torment that the true Doctor and Rose Tyler had to endure due to their unfulfilled love can finally be ended. Through this relationship between Rose and the humanized Doctor, and its potential consequences, it is possible to see the fiery connotation of Prometheus' gift as being part of the emotional growth of humanity and its ability to reproduce before death

This ending for the humanized Doctor and Rose Tyler is, however, forced upon them by the true Doctor, placing him in the final of the Promethean curse states: the survivor. It is the Doctor who sacrifices and he who is left alone, a composite end result of the other two stages. This stage is curious as it is can be seen, especially in this case, to be both the product of the actions of other parties as well as a consequence of the Doctor's own choices.

Within the text this is not always true of situations and roles the Doctor finds himself in, although it is possible to argue that from an external real world perspective, it is. Externally to the text, it can be accepted that an adventure drama without any adventure or drama would not succeed. Textually it is implied through much of the Hartnell era that the Doctor's exile is not voluntary, but from the Troughton era onwards, it is retroactively taken, that the initial decision to leave Gallifrey was his. The Doctor has made a conscious choice to become—and through much of his television existence, rejoices in being—one of the "wanderers in the fifth dimension." As such, it is not unreasonable to assume that the Doctor bears a measure of responsibility for all the situations he finds himself in within the text. The most extreme and emotionally charged aspect of the Doctor's responsibility is revealed in the serial "Dalek." In a confrontation with what he believes to be the last surviving Dalek, the Doctor's 9th incarnation reveals to it, his companion, and the audience for the first time, that he witnessed his people burn along with the Daleks during the Time War. Subsequently in "The Sound of Drums," the 10th Doctor informs the Master that it was by his hand that the Time Lords died, making his loneliness his eternal punishment administered at his own hand. This decision is once again the Doctor's to make in "The End of Time Part Two," as he ultimately is forced between the time-locked Time Lords and humanity. Like Prometheus, the Doctor puts the needs of humanity above the desires of his own people, a decision that costs him not only his people but also his 10th life.

The character of the Doctor, like Prometheus, can be viewed as existing both within and outside of the usual paradigms of conventional popular cultural myth, and like the Titan, his existence can been seen to be fundamentally concerned with the exploration of choices and their consequences.

At a surface reading, a god (with a lower case *g*) such as Prometheus and an alien such as the Doctor are polar opposites. However, it is possible to view them both as fulfilling a similar need in a differing population. The genesis of the Greek gods several thousand years ago can be attributed to the needs of that society to understand the world in which they lived, and when their science failed to provide adequate explanations, their culture filled in the gaps with myths of gods and goddesses. The aliens of science fiction, including the Time Lords and the Daleks, are not dissimilar to the Greek Gods in that they bring in from outside known society a distinctly "familiar unlike" set of principles and dynamics. This paradox of a familiar unlike, or quintessential alieness, is evident throughout science fiction and is what makes much of it the modern equivalent of myth. Their biologies may differ but fundamental emotions, hierarchies, and belief structures do not.

Prometheus the god acts in a far from divine, omniscient role; neither does his king, Zeus, act as a benevolent creator or as an experienced teacher/father. As the character of Davros points out in the 2008 season finale "Journey's End," the Doctor often leaves a trail of destruction and violence in his wake, regardless of his intention, and so contradicts the quintessential tenet of the medical doctor, to do no harm. All of these situations are created through actions and thus have consequences.

Yet in both his theft of fire and in his spontaneous tissue regeneration within his punishment, Prometheus does fundamentally achieve that which is beyond the mortal realm. The Doctor, despite the fact that the audience is never presented with any proof of the veracity of his claim to his title, is often shown in the light of a knowledgeable elder, and even a teacher. This is most definitely the role the Doctor's first incarnation assumed with his companions Susan and Vicki, and to a lesser extent to Ian and Barbara, within the show's original directive to educate as well as entertain. As the series progressed, the Doctor has, in both the shows' internal hierarchy and externally in regards the genre he inhabits, become less the direct educator and more the heroic lead, bound and cursed to sacrifice.

All of these myths essentially also grapple with the limitation of self, whether character and role is defined by nature or by nurture, and to what extent choice and consequence matter. The Doctor exemplifies this, whilst being presented as the rebellious hero, like Prometheus, and does in fact bring with him during his journeys a potentially marvellous and destructive gift, himself.

The Doctor is simultaneously the deliverer and the gift, the saviour and the destroyer.

1 Shelley, 1818.
2 Unknown, Prometheus, http://en.wikipedia.org/wiki/Prometheus.
3 Wilkinson and Philip, 327.
4 Aaronovitch, 1990.
5 Gray, *Doctor Who Magazine Summer Special*, 1993.
6 Platt, *Lungbarrow*, 1997.
7 "The Watcher's Guide to the Seventh Doctor" *Doctor Who Magazine*, 2009.
8 Wilkinson, 57.

"Mythology Makes You Feel Something": The Russell T. Davies Era as Sentimental Journey

Matthew Hills

Doctor Who has already outlasted "myth." This is true as long as the term myth is approached from a specific vantage point: it possessed currency in cultural studies of the 1970s and 80s. Theorists such as Roland Barthes and Claude Lévi-Strauss were frequently drawn upon, and myth was thought of as a universal structuring principle, or mental ordering of the physical world. Author of *Myth: The New Critical Idiom*, Laurence Coupe, points out that in vintage "cultural studies 'myth' is frequently used as synonymous with 'ideology'".[1] For John Tulloch, writing at the end of the 1980s, structuralist definitions of myth had "*defined* the preoccupation of Cultural Studies" up to that point.[2] John Fiske was one of the first to interpret *Who* in this way.[3] But such analyses of myth fell out of favour; academic fashion moved on, and by the time of *Science Fiction Audiences*, John Tulloch and Henry Jenkins were distancing themselves from "mythic" readings of *Doctor Who*.[4] The sort of "myth" posited by Lévi-Strauss was folded away as part of yesterday's theories. *Doctor Who*, though, went on unfolding anew.

Today's *Who* is self-consciously a "mythology" show. This is true as long as the term "mythology" is understood in a specific way: it possesses currency in contemporary industry, fan, and journalistic discourses. Chris Carter described his work on *The X-Files* as "a sort of 'mythology' approach, where you weave the serial in and out of your series."[5] And this series/serial hybridity has been traced through many TV shows:

> Like *The X-Files*, *Buffy the Vampire Slayer*, and *Twin Peaks*, cousins in the mythology genre, *Lost* has attracted a devoted following... A Boston Globe article... categorizes mythology shows as those that attract a "lively, game audience"; mythology shows make their "viewers into cosmic Sherlocks... Mythology writers expect rigorous... viewing".[6]

Bad Wolf, Torchwood, Saxon, the Medusa Cascade, the four knocks: all represent seriality woven in and out of new *Who*'s otherwise discrete episodes, attracting audience attention and speculation. Here, "mythology" becomes a genre of textual puzzle, an invitation to spot clues. However, Laurence Coupe is no happier with this meaning of the mythic, suggesting that in "entertainment... [myth] is frequently used as synonymous with 'fantasy'" and the creation of narrative worlds. In fact, he links cultural studies and industrial usages of the term: "In either case [myth] is being used to imply some sort of illusion, whether one is an academic exposing the hidden agenda of a... cultural text, or... a... manufacturer trying to attract customers."[7] In this argument, structuralist theories of myth and industry understandings of mythology are both improper uses of the concept. Like a hypothetical fan grouching that "Love & Monsters" isn't really *Doctor Who*, Coupe wants to determine what myth really is.

Contra Coupe, I will read TV-industry discourses of "mythology" back into an old-school cultural studies' discourse of structuralist "myth." I will argue that approaching myth as a set of binaries (e.g., alien/human; man/woman) continues to offer something useful to thinking about the Russell T. Davies era of *Doctor Who*.[8] I will also suggest that contemporary industrial mythology can tell us about how new *Who* plays with and complicates the binaries it sets out. Rather than these versions of the mythic being rejected *a priori* as wrong, what happens when they are brought into dialogue? One significant emphasis I'll explore is the emergence of emotional or *affective playing with myth*, on the part of *Doctor Who*'s media professionals and audiences. As Davies himself has argued, drawing on production discourses of the "mythology show":

> What you don't want is lots of... the Cybermen came from Telos and Mondas, you don't want the complication of it. You *have* to distinguish between mythology and continuity... Mythology is simple and *emotional*! Mythology makes you feel something. Continuity is... irrelevant... a drama in the year 2005 has got to have proper emotion.[9]

Theorizing the importance of sentiment in new *Who*, I'll first examine how the series has become mythic, in the cultural studies' sense of the word.

Time Lord Myth and Emotion: Playing with the "Human / Alien" Binary

Structuralism "stresses the intellectual coherence within myth... [for] Claude Lévi-Strauss... myth has nothing to do with emotions".[10] Instead, myth is a system of ordering and meaning-making, made up of binary opposites that are then resolved or ameliorated in some way. It represents patterns of thought through which the world can be understood. Edmund Leach points out that "Lévi-Strauss has argued that when we are considering the universalist aspects of primitive mythology we shall repeatedly discover that *the hidden message is concerned with the resolution of...contradictions.*"[11] Structuralism says that all myths can be analysed as made up of similar binaries, binaries which are central to cultural order and meaning. Writers such as Joseph Campbell are sometimes compared to structuralists, since Campbell argues for the uncovering of shared, deep structures of mythic meaning beneath the surface diversity of historical myths.[12]

John Tulloch and Manuel Alvarado offer a version of structuralist myth analysis when they argue that classic *Who* is marked by a "narrative quest... to prove that the intellectual law-giver is... 'spontaneously' human".[13] That is, through the character of the Doctor, specific binaries are magically resolved; law/freedom and machine/human are condensed onto the Doctor, who is figured as both law-giver (upholder of moral order) and as "humanly" spontaneous.

But unlike Lévi-Strauss's emphasis on myth as a system of thought, Tulloch and Alvarado bring emotion back into their analysis, noting that "the central emotional investment" of the show lies "with being human," and what this means.[14] They note how classic *Who* consistently values the Doctor as a source of "heroic discourse" opposing "Knowledge as centre of the universe: 'I think therefore I am' [to] Exploitation/defilement by aliens: "I will therefore I am." This contradiction of 'knowledge versus will' ultimately leads to, and is resolved by, "Liberation: the final (human) face of the Doctor."[15] Alienness and human spontaneity are hence resolved via the myth-form of the Doctor's character, suggesting that *Who* can be usefully analysed using Lévi-Straussian concepts.

Indeed, when discussing his 2005 reimagining of the series, showrunner Russell T. Davies actually uses binary oppositions to encapsulate the format: "you've got to keep it simple: man/woman, alien/human, ...it's brilliant."[16] But Davies is referring to the Doctor versus Rose here, and to the generation of story possibilities: as man is to woman, so alien is to human. He doesn't engage with any notion that these contradictions might be resolved via mythic mediation. However, I will argue that the 9th and 10th Doctors narratively mediate human/alien and masculine/feminine binaries, with the Doctor being represented as melodramatically carrying a "burden of feeling" more typically linked to female characters.[17]

Rather than exemplifying myth's "intellectual coherence," I want to consider how BBC Wales' *Doctor Who* focuses affectively on what it means to be human, and on how the Doctor's alien difference manifests itself. Co-writing with Anne Cranny-Francis, John Tulloch revisits themes from *The Unfolding Text* to argue that an "intense association of the Time Lord/hero/other with the most empathetic of human emotions, loneliness, and isolation, is one of the strongest emotional investments in the new *Doctor Who*."[18] The Doctor is again connotatively human, but by displaying lonely angst rather than grinning spontaneity. Losing his companions means "they break my heart," as he confides to Jackson Lake (David Morrissey) at the conclusion of "The Next Doctor." This seems inaccurate coming from a two-hearted Time Lord, yet the statement *humanises* the Doctor, representing him as subject to the most human of—loss. The character's humanity—and how this fuses with his alien otherness—is constantly narratively picked over and complicated. As early as "Rose," the Doctor returns to tell the titular character (Billie Piper) that his TARDIS travels in time as well as space; though the moment can be interpreted as a display of potency, alienness, and the meta-textual promise of visual spectacle to come,[19] it also humanises the Doctor's otherness. The character is shown as wanting Rose to travel with him, but refusing to display this emotional dependence. The last-minute return, when separation seems textually assured, is also a trope of romance fiction, intertextually representing the Doctor as a romantic male hero unable to articulate his emotional needs.

The Doctor's romantic life, never quite given voice by him in "Doomsday," is explored in more detail in "Human Nature"/"The Family of Blood," where he temporarily becomes the human John Smith, and falls in love with Joan Redfern (Jessica Hynes). Yet this state of affairs is shown to be unsustainable; the suppressed Time Lord dreams of his previous adventures—alien difference threatens to reemerge. And when restored to Time Lord identity, the Doctor seems uncharacteristically vengeful in his various imprisonments of Family members: the narrative reinstates exaggerated alien otherness hot on the heels of the Doctor's literalised, temporary humanity. From denotative human to a loss of humanity; these episodes imply that far from uniting or resolving human/ alien contradictions, the 10th Doctor switches between human/alien poles of his identity. Here, far from embodying a resolved contradiction, binaries of human/alien are pitted against one another as a result of the chameleon arch. In philosopher Noel Carroll's terms, the Doctor becomes a fantastical "fission" rather than "fusion" entity—the latter unites contradictory categories in one body, whereas the former shape-shifts between opposed categories over time, and hence these oppositions never mythically coexist.[20] Davies's vision of the Doctor is typically one of human-alien "fusion," but Paul Cornell's screenplay reconfigures this mythic aspect, with John Smith versus the fire-and-ice Doctor coding a splitting of human and alien.

At other moments, however, the human/alien binary is represented via pronounced "fusion" entities, e.g., the Time Lord-human metacrisis of the Doctor/Donna in "Journey's End." Whereas the Doctor is able to denote alienness and connote humanity (he's an alien who seems human), Donna's reconfiguration as a human who feels like a Time Lord is too narratively threatening to be sustained. Like the Bad Wolf version of SuperRose who incorporates the Time Vortex, the Doctor/ Donna is promptly narratively expelled. It seems curious that two of the Doctor's female companions have saved him by taking on alien, "othered" superpowers, only to be restored—or in Donna's case, restricted—to norms of human identity. However, the Doctor's position of narrative uniqueness would be compromised by a partner of equal standing: he alone mythically mediates human/alien. To vary this defining aspect of new *Who*'s format would transgress its core concepts. A problematic outcome of gendering the mythic mediation of human/alien as denotatively and singularly masculine (the lone Doctor) is that female candidates are subordinated as characters. Rivals for the Doctor's human/ alien status are either expelled from the series (we can add the villainous Cyber-Hartmann and Cyber-Hartigan to this list), downgraded to the merely human, or given their own spin-off show, in the case of the immortal male (anti)hero, Captain Jack. Human/alien binaries can be temporarily condensed and magically resolved via supporting characters or companions, but it would seem that, in the Russell T. Davies era, the Doctor alone is permitted to carry this binary as an ongoing structuralist myth.

Alongside crisis and metacrisis, the Doctor is more generally humanised through his displays of passionate knowledge, revelling in the universe's marvels. Ken Chen observes that "it is astonishing to watch Doctor Who—he's so much happier to be alive than you are! Happiness is... an active engagement with the world."[21] Whether admiring the beauty of a werewolf ("Tooth and Claw") or appreciating how "special" a meal of chops and gravy can be ("Planet of the Dead"), the Doctor loves life, conveying a vitality shared by his 9th and 10th incarnations. Christopher Eccleston has alluded to this *philia*:

> The thing which sticks out for me is the Doctor himself and the mystery of, you know, who *is* he? Where does he come from? What's he thinking? What does he feel? *How* does he feel? He's got two hearts, so does that mean he cares twice as much? [laughs].[22]

Alien and human are articulated in Eccleston's character reading: the 9th Doctor is more human as a result of his very alienness, intently feeling the losses and gains of life. By the time of series two, this linkage of heightened human feeling with the Time Lord non-human had progressed to the 10th Doctor being described as a "Lonely God" ("New Earth") and a "lonely angel" ("The Girl in the Fireplace"). But rather than simply feeling the human emotion of loneliness, the Doctor is *alone* in sensing and feeling the universe as a Time Lord. He can see the fixed and fluid points in the web of time ("Fires of Pompeii"), thus literally feeling in a way that's unlike any other being. As Eccleston asks: "*How does he feel?*" Davies's version of the Doctor doesn't just emote human-seeming guilt or loneliness; rather, he is constructed as feeling in ways that separate him from all other human and alien characters. Such is the Time Lord's narrative elevation and burden—sensing and feeling that which nobody else can perceive. The character's affective life doesn't just range exaggeratedly from angst to zest; the Doctor's alienness produces a different alphabet and grammar of emotion, where human meanings and perceptions are displaced.

As Greg M. Smith has noted, any given "serial cannot take care of all its narrative business by staying solely within the bounded world of core characters. It needs guest stars. ...guest appearances provide conflict in ways that the core ensemble cannot."[23] Given that new *Who* has rarely functioned as an ensemble-cast show (some episodes involve the families of Rose, Martha, and Donna, but only the Doctor and his companion feature in every episode) it has an even more pressing need to involve guest casts in its exploration of key, mythic binaries. And as Cranny-Francis and Tulloch point out, "the exploration of difference through encounters with alien life-forms, including the Daleks and... Cybermen" has been a repeated theme.[24] By confronting a changing rota of monsters, the Doctor's mythic human/alien resolution of binaries can be tested, celebrated, and further complicated.

The Cybermen pose a particular challenge to the Doctor's mythic identity, as they are humans who have been transformed into inhuman, alien others.[25] The Toclafane, and Daleks created out of genetic material from a human lumpen-proletariat have also functioned narratively in this way,[26] as do the Cult of Skaro—Daleks humanised by virtue of their individuality and imaginative capacity to scheme. Just as some of the Doctor's companions mediate human/alien, so too do monstrous others. Cranny-Francis and Tulloch suggest that Daleks and Cybermen both represent humanity swamped by technology:

The Daleks are based in a kind of biotechnology; the

Cybers in a version of information technology... both cyborg creatures can be seen as configuring the dangers for embodied human subjects who are subsumed by their technology; that this technology effectively overrides or excises the sensory-emotional complex that characterizes human being. It is this... that the Doctor repeatedly describes—gleefully—as the essence of the human.[27]

Humanity is extinguished or erased by typical Daleks and Cybermen, though with the distinction that Cybermen retain sufficient human perception to be horrified by their own monstrosity. "The Age of Steel," "Doomsday," and "The Next Doctor" involve Cybernised characters sacrificing or destroying themselves as a result. And the Cult of Skaro similarly judge Dalek-kind to be monstrous; hybrid Sec opposes his fellow Daleks, and dies as a result, and Caan ultimately plots against Davros in "Journey's End." The humanisation of these monsters thus culminates in their self-destruction; far from human/alien being mythically resolved as a contradiction, the binary is depicted here as irresolvable. Again, seemingly only the Doctor—as mythic hero—is able to successfully bear the categories of human/alien. Other Time Lord characters emerging across new *Who* are variously shown to be inhuman in their pursuit of power: the Master is coded as a power-fixated version of the Doctor, compelled to greedily own or possess the Universe rather than appreciating its beauty. And Rassilon is depicted as another monstrous Time Lord other, fascistically and inhumanly proposing a Final Sanction that will destroy all of creation, leaving chosen Time Lords to become Godlike, transcendent beings.

Along with human/alien, the Doctor also mediates masculine/feminine in a Lévi-Straussian manner. As Dee Amy-Chinn reminds us:

...the Doctor has always been an ambivalent hero... with feminine as well as masculine traits. Indeed, despite the critiques of various companions, the Doctor does care—for the human race in particular... and for 'others' in general... Through caring he embraces his 'feminine' side—but one thing he does well in a 'masculine' way is to see the bigger picture.[28]

And Ken Chen interprets the Doctor as resembling "humanity's nurturing mother, always giving pep talks about mankind's special potential."[29] Rather than a Time Lord patriarch, Davies's version of the Doctor stands for feminised, maternalised masculinity; he's dedicated to helping human protagonists realise their potential, and refuses to wipe out absolute others such as the Daleks.[30] Where he is, unusually, repositioned as paternal ("The Doctor's Daughter"), then this twist leads to considerable narrative unease, and a sense that the paternity, because techno-fantastical, is somehow invalidated. It remains easier to view the Doctor connotatively as humanity's "nurturing mother" rather than a patriarchal figure.

However, Amy-Chinn argues that new *Who* is problematically gendered: Rose's caring causes problems, e.g., reactivating the Dalek in "Dalek" and saving her own father, Pete Tyler (Shaun Dingwall) in "Father's Day," whereas the Doctor's ethical concerns are purely rational rather than relational.[31] This argument is, if not invalidated, at the very least destabilised by developments in "The Waters of Mars," for here "the Time Lord Victorious" emerges. The Doctor transgresses new *Who*'s established format, taking on a patriarchal role, and assuming the right to change the time-line of Adelaide Brooke (Lindsay Duncan). Moving closer to a God-like status than ever before in the series, at this moment the Doctor represents pathologised, patriarchal masculinity rather than valued, nurturing and feminised masculinity.

This is, though, a lapse; the Doctor realises he's "gone too far" after Adelaide commits suicide to restore the fixed point of her death. A lingering close-up on David Tennant's distraught face emphasises the emotional impact of this narrative transgression and unusual reconfiguration of the Doctor's character. The moment's emotional fallout continues to be stressed in "The End of Time, Part One," as the Doctor confesses to Wilf (Bernard Cribbins) that he "did some things— it went wrong." Rather than poeticised dialogue, melodramatic emphasis falls on the mute, visual coding of the Doctor's emotional distress, as tears well up in his eyes, and he can say no more to Wilf. *Contra* the "Lonely God" label, the Doctor cannot violate the laws of time that bind him; though he is a special Time Lord, linking human/alien unlike Time Lord others (the Master/Rassilon), he cannot assume a position of total power, but must accept his limits.

And yet there is one character in the Russell T. Davies era who has unlimited powers to appear and disappear, imparting crucial narrative hints seemingly at will (and outside a time-lock assumed to be operating): the Woman (Claire Bloom) in "The End of Time." This character is textually implied, and extra-textually stated, to be the Doctor's mother: "It could only be his mother, really. If I can't imagine a world in which our mothers are there, at the end of our lives, in our time of need... then what's the point?"[32] This maternal figure represents unfettered potency and knowledge, knowing more than Rassilon, the Master, and even the Doctor himself. The Woman's white dress codes her as ethereal, transcendent, heavenly, and whilst the Doctor's apotheosis is censured diegetically—that is, within the narrative "space" of the story—the Woman's Godlike capabilities are valued as leading to the 10th Doctor's salvation and destiny. Omnipotence, for Russell T. Davies, is negatively coded in its patriarchal form and positively coded as an image of maternal care. The Woman, like the Doctor, unites alien/human, albeit this time in a female form—something his companions are unable to achieve. Yet her format-threatening similarity to the Doctor's distinctive mythic role again leads to immediate narrative expulsion, this time in a white-out of presumed annihilation.

Against views of myth that see it as a static or closed system of meaning, such as Campbell's "monomyth," I'm suggesting here that the developments in an unfolding text enable key binary oppositions to be continually reconfigured. The Doctor doesn't simply resolve human/alien contradictions, but rather carries these in a variety of shifting ways: sometimes splitting into human and alien identities ("Human Nature"), sometimes lending Time Lord-like—or even more omnipotent—powers to others (e.g., Rose and Donna), and sometimes confronting different versions of human-alien hybridity (the Cult of Skaro; the Cybermen). As a result, I would argue that new *Who* fails, ultimately, to correspond to a structuralist or Campbellian template of myth.[33] It is *stereomyth* rather than monomyth—a mythic tale that revises its crucial binary oppositions and reworks them through new and altered character relations, for example, the Doctor/Donna being created; the Doctor becoming the Time Lord Victorious; the Doctor's mother appearing; and so on. Where monomyth follows a set sequence of phases, stereomyth circles back over its mythic binaries, periodically moving off in new narrative directions (humanised Daleks; returning Time Lords) and complicating its diegesis or internal primary story. The "mythology" emphasised as emotional by Russell T. Davies achieves its affective impact on viewers precisely by reconfiguring and varying Lévi-Straussian-style binaries. Big reveals in new *Who*—a returning lone Dalek; a Dalek army; Cybermen; the Cult of Skaro; the Chameleon Arch; the Master; Gallifrey's return; the four knocks—all provoke reconfigurations of the Doctor's human/alien binary. Right down to the 10th Doctor's demise, what it means to be "ordinary" and human versus "special" and Time Lord-like undergoes (re)interrogation. Finally, the Doctor puts ordinariness above his own "special" life, refuting any hierarchy of the Time Lord Victorious versus "little people." Humans, he avers, are "giants" in his eyes.

As Greg Smith has argued, serial TV narratives "create a set of compelling... character relations.... Once these relations are established, the serial must somehow undo them.... Narrative incidents alter old relations."[34] This "mythology" results in a shifting, unfolding "set of multiple, intersecting binary comparisons [which] asks us to stage a series of comparisons among... characters, evaluating their relative differences and thus creating a long-running moral balancing act."[35] In other words, rather than the human/alien binary being magically resolved in new *Who*, it is constantly opened out and restaged. Each restaging is linked to emotional impact, often textually stressed via lingering close-ups on the Doctor's tremulous face, as when the "he will knock four times" prophecy is first spoken, or when the Doctor realises he's "still alive" after confronting Rassilon.

My articulation of TV-industry "mythology" with academic discourse on structuralist "myth" is indebted to John C. Lyden's work. Lyden observes that a Lévi-Straussian approach to popular culture "views myths as essentially irrational attempts to unite contradictory views.... [It]...cannot allow that myths may actually empower people to...deal with contradictions in positive ways."[36] The Russell T. Davies era constitutes a meditation on what it means to be "ordinary" or "special," human or alien. Ignoring the narrative twists (losses/reunions/ goodbyes) and accompanying effects of new *Who* in favour of static "myth" means converting an emotional experience into a cognitive set of facts—it means problematically transforming "mythology" into "continuity," in Davies's own terms.

Having thus far sought to explore production "mythology" as a type of serialised, periodically reworked and unresolved Lévi-Straussian "myth," in the closing section I want to move on to address in more detail the affective dimensions of this textuality. How has the Russell T. Davies era used *Doctor Who*'s status as a "mythology show" to emotionally engage audiences? Considering this will involve drawing on Robert Segal's thoughts on the future of myth study.[37]

Time Lord Mythology and Emotion: Playing with the Inner / Outer Boundary

If pushed to propose a single Tone Word for the Davies era, "emotional" would be my choice. This has been Davies's continual watch-word, not just in the distinction between continuity and mythology, but in the very grain of storytelling: "Every story has got to make sense emotionally... that's when regeneration works. When you feel it."[38]

Indeed, the degree of control that Davies has exerted over this project is shown in a revealing discussion in *The Writer's Tale: The Final Chapter*. The showrunner recounts how he requested a re-edit of "Waters" in order to emphasise the emotional story beats, and impact, of the Doctor's decision to contest the laws of time:

> Graeme Harper and the editor... they'd...refined...a tight
> action thriller about Water Monsters on Mars...but that's not
> what the story is about. ...The worst bit was when the Doctor
> goes to leave the base, and everyone is dying. This had been
> edited as the story of Adelaide and her crew fighting the
> good fight...intercut with the Doctor walking away...but that's
> completely wrong. It's the story of the Doctor turning his back
> on dying people, so Adelaide and the crew should become just
> voices in his head; he's hearing their screams...until he decides to
> break the fundamental rule of the Time Lords, and go back.[39]

As Davies points out, an edit can involve "the same images, the same
events, the same order. But the emphasis tells a completely different
tale."[40] Televisuality is thus crucial—not only how scenes are acted, but
when do we cut to a close-up of the Doctor? Which characters are the
audience aligned with emotionally as a result of this focalisation? Davies
clearly altered the presentation of "Waters of Mars" to make it less about a
'realist' or external, objective diegetic world—a thriller following a set of
characters—and more about representations of the Doctor's subjectivity:
we stay on him as he's tormented by the colonists' deaths, and as he decides
to act. The audience are thus granted a sense of access to the Doctor's
internal feelings, coded via events becoming "voices in his head."

Davies's vision of *Who* is one where characters' internal feeling-states
televisually blend into representations of external narrative events. In this
sense, new *Who* is a sentimental or "emotional journey."[41] As sentimental
culture, its ongoing, developing mythology affirms a series of credos:

> "...the ideals of sentimental culture [are] the affirmation
> of community, the persistence of hopefulness and...the belief
> that everyone matters".... These 'good ideals'...are what make...
> programmes popular.... The notion that 'everyone matters' is
> clearly an enjoyable message for viewers, but is also reflective of
> sentimental concerns.[42]

Whilst conveying meanings such as "everybody matters"—
something so fundamental to Davies's work that it eventually permeates
the 10th Doctor's regeneration—the series' mythology blurs internal
character emotion-states and external narrative realities at the same
time. Series finales, and the 2009 Specials, do this especially intently:
"Doomsday" is as much about the defeat of Daleks and Cybermen as it is

about the Doctor and Rose's separation, culminating in the Bad Wolf Bay sequence—and another lingering close-up on the tearful 10th Doctor, alone in his TARDIS. "Last of the Time Lords" is as much about the Doctor's separation from the Master, dying in his arms and refusing to regenerate, as it is about the fate of the human race. "Journey's End" fuses Donna's fate with the defeat of Davros, and "The End of Time" allows the 10th Doctor to visit his companions one last time, after having saved all of creation. The blending of feeling-states and external events is repeatedly encapsulated in a single image; that of the Doctor unable to say what he really feels, as tears brim in his eyes. This image is structured into almost every series' finale, and into the majority of the 2009 Specials. The Doctor becomes not only the mythic hero, but also a melodramatic one:

> [W]e can identify melodrama's pathos of the 'too late!' In these fantasies the quest to return to and discover the origin of self is manifest.... In these fantasies the quest for connection is always tinged with the melancholy of loss. Origins are already lost, the encounters always take place too late, on death beds or over coffins.[43]

The defining irony of new *Who* is that in a show about time travel, the Doctor is always "too late!" Too late to save Gallifrey as point of origin; too late to reach Madame de Pompadour; too late to be united with Rose; too late to live a life with Joan Redfern; too late to redeem the Master; too late to allow Donna to remember him; too late to understand the prophecy of the four knocks. And throughout all this, the Doctor is blocked from saying what he feels, in another melodramatic coding of emotion as non-verbalised, and coded audio-visually through acting, camera close-ups, and swelling incidental music:

> [M]elodrama utilises narrative mechanisms that create a blockage to expression, thereby forcing melodramatic enactments into alternative and excessive strategies to clarify the dramatic stakes. ...Melodrama's recourse to gestural, visual and musical excess constitutes the expressive means of what Brooks calls the 'text of muteness'. Devices such as... spectacle reach 'toward...meanings which cannot be generated from the language code'.[44]

Nowhere is this combination of "too late!" and "too mute" more expansively present than in the 10th Doctor's pre-regeneration goodbyes. When asked if he was happy, the character merely gives a "little smile" to Verity Newman (Jessica Hynes). He exchanges glances with Martha (Freema Agyeman) and Sarah Jane Smith (Elisabeth Sladen); they are represented as wordlessly sensing an ending. And where no ending is sensed—in the 10th Doctor's final encounter with Rose Tyler—then the scene is pregnant with what cannot be said. Time travel itself (going back to see Rose before they've otherwise met) creates a melodramatic "blockage to expression," again flooding external narrative events with codings of the Doctor's internal emotional state. This version of *Doctor Who* conveys its crucial moments of internal-external fusion through the Doctor's often tear-filled or melancholy gaze. And through the lingering look. For instance, the battle between the Doctor, the Master, and Rassilon effectively ends with *a wordless exchange of looks between the Doctor and the Woman*. Much can be said about Davies's writing and dialogue, but his version of *Doctor Who* is consistently about the unsaid, the can't-be-said, and the never-was-said; about time travel imprinted by loss. These "emotion cues" may be skilfully read by long-term fans, as Kristyn Gorton notes: "only a faithful viewer will experience the full emotional impact of a well-crafted story arc."[45] But establishing melodramatic televisual possibilities is simultaneously "one of the sure ways to develop new viewers/fans. It also suggests the way in which television...must construct itself for faithful *and* casual viewers."[46]

The blurring between characters' internal emotional states and external science-fictional events creates a sense of "intimate epic,"[47] but it also draws *Doctor Who* ever closer to psychoanalyst Donald Woods Winnicott's specific concept of play. Intriguingly, this idea is drawn on by Robert A. Segal in *Myth: A Very Short Introduction:*

> I propose applying to myth the analysis of play by... psychoanalyst D.W. Winnicott. For Winnicott, play is *acknowledged* as other than reality...[but] is more than fantasy or escapism. It is the construction of a reality with personal meaning...the adult recognizes that the myth is not reality yet adheres to it as if it were. Myth is 'make-believe'.[48]

Winnicott's work dealt with the way in which young children can become intensely attached to a physical object—a blanket or comforter of some kind. This "transitional object" is unusual for being experienced as powerfully personal (feeling like a part of the self) and at the same time recognised as objectively in the world, i.e., as separate from the self. For Winnicott, this first not-me possession enables the child to begin distinguishing between internal feeling-states and external reality. But by bridging the two zones, by being "transitional," such objects fall in-between inner and outer, merging them in emotionally-significant artifacts. Winnicott went on to argue that art and religion are a sort of adult, cultural equivalent of the child's "transitional object":

> ...the task of reality-acceptance is never completed, ...no human being is free from the strain of relating inner and outer reality, and...relief from this strain is provided by an intermediate area of experience which is not challenged (arts, religion, etc.).[49]

Cultural objects and texts that work for us in this way take on an exceptional personal significance and vitality. We feel a sense of ownership over such things; they are emotionally ours (belonging to inner feeling-states) and also recognised as out there in the world, being potentially shareable with others, provided we don't attempt to impose personalised, inner sense of emotional significance:

> If...the adult can manage to enjoy the personal intermediate area without making claims, then we can acknowledge our own corresponding intermediate areas, and are pleased to find areas of overlapping, that is to say common experience between members of a group in art or religion or philosophy.[50]

Or, we might say, the "common experience between members of a group" in *Doctor Who* fandom. Though Segal uses Winnicott's model of play to think about how "myth accomplishes something significant for adherents,"[51] others—myself included—have previously applied Winnicottian theory specifically to television,[52] and to fan cultures.[53] If myth can become personally significant for "adherents" then so too can the contemporary "mythology show" for its fans. These pop-cultural stories are experienced within "a region of 'personalised' culture,"[54] which makes them akin to transitional objects, though not necessarily rooted in childhood psychodynamics. Objects of fandom are not the same as blankets or comforters that children carry around with them: for one thing, the child cannot share its object's inner meaningfulness with others, even though that object exists in the physical, outer world. The child's teddy bear or rag carries significance for just that one person; it cannot sustain a community of overlapping interests. By contrast, *Doctor Who* fandom is both intensely personal and capable of being shared intersubjectively. We therefore need to distinguish between childhood transitional objects and cultural artifacts that carry highly personal significance in later life, and often across the fan's life—these I have termed "secondary transitional objects."[55] They are in no way regressive or child-like, but form part of life's ordinary creativity and vitality.

What is important about these types of objects is that they bridge "inner" and "outer," allowing internal emotional states to be managed and related to outer reality. They remain "transitional," in a third space of personalised culture where the tissue of the "inner/outer" boundary is suspended and played across (but not abolished altogether; players always know what is real and what is fantasy). Hence "make-believe" or "as-if" culture: fantasy treated as if it is real, fictional characters responded to as if they are real people; mythology experienced as if it refers to actual events.

Of course, it can be argued that *Doctor Who* has always worked in this way for its fans. As a "secondary transitional object" the classic series has been carried through life by long-term devotees or "Whovians." Texts that work in this way tend to be child-adult crossovers or "family" entertainment—they have sufficient double-coding to appeal to younger fans and older audiences alike, hence not inevitably being abandoned as fans age.[56] Indeed, Lance Parkin has argued that, in a sense, "*Doctor Who*... noticeably grew up with its audience,"[57] being aimed less at children as its initial 1960s child audience matured into adults in the seventies and eighties. But the reverse is also true: fans have grown up with *Doctor Who*, responding differently to it at different stages of their lives:

> [T]exts [that tend to become used as secondary transitional objects—MH] also have a degree of openness that allows them to do different things for a person at different points of the life course depending on their shifting...interests. Thus, I watched *Doctor Who* differently in the 1960s, as a sometimes frightened child, from how I watched as a teenager in the 1970s with friends, to how it engages me now with my own sons.[58]

The "mythology" of popular TV can hence be akin to "myth" in Segal's Winnicottian sense—both carry personalised significance for "adherents," and both can be related to across the life-course, as well as being passed on from generation to generation, as in the example given above (and in my own experience, given that I first watched 1970s *Who* with my own father).

My argument, however, is that new *Who*'s mythology offers itself up even more clearly as a suitable secondary transitional object for viewers. It is "family entertainment," obviously. But more than this, it dramatises and mimics the transitional object's blurring of inner/outer, by recurrently—and melodramatically—coding characters' inner emotional states (usually the Doctor's, but also his companions') as saturating outer narrative realities. In professional discourse, this may simply be "good drama"[59] but it is also a mimetic representation of personalised culture—of those objects that hold our captivated attention, and cross experiential lines between "inner" and "outer." It has been argued that representations of love, or "limerence," can hold intense, personalised audience emotion and Winnicottian play.[60] My argument is a variation of this: "mythology" TV can become affectively significant to audiences by imitating the experience of (secondary) transitional objects. Such audiences may then become fans, playing with the text's meaning, and playing across fantasy/reality via the "make-believe" culture of fandom.[61] Indeed, other highly successful mythology shows such as *Lost* also blur character's internal feeling-states with external narrative realities, creating fantastical amalgams hovering diegetically between subjective/objective. As Porter and Lavery note, the very title *Lost* can be read "not just geographically but psychologically,"[62] again textually condensing and representing the transitions of the transitional object. So, too, does BBC Wales' *Doctor Who* give rise to external diegetic questions and internal psychological ones. "Doctor Who?," from 2005 onwards, has been at once a question of "continuity" (diegetic fact) *and* a question of "mythology" (how does it feel to be that character, sensing the laws of time as the last of the Time Lords?).

In this chapter I have sought to do two things, *contra* Coupe's suspicion of "improper" usages of myth. Firstly, I revisited structuralist "myth," arguing that as a contemporary TV "mythology" stressing shock reveals, the Russell T. Davies era has dwelt on binaries such as human/alien, not to resolve these, but rather to continually re-open and complicate them. Secondly, I explored new *Who* as a "mythology show," where melodramatic codings of the "unsaid" and the "too late" generate a televisual excess of diegetically permeable inner/outer states. This renders new *Who*, even more than its Classic Series predecessor, a prime candidate to be embraced by (fan) audiences as personally significant culture. In Robert Segal's terms, this is a key attribute of the mythic experience— that which affectively fuses fantasy/reality in "make-believe" without cognitively confusing their difference. BBC Wales' *Doctor Who* plays with defining binaries, and plays with inner/outer boundaries. In both "mythic" and "mythological" dimensions, then, it "makes you feel."

---

1 Coupe, *Myth*, 2009, 1.
2 Tulloch, *Television Drama*, 8.
3 Tulloch and Jenkins, 30.
4 Tulloch and Jenkins, 41-2.

5 Cited in Abbott, 21.

6 Porter and Lavery, 268-69.

7 Coupe, *Myth, 2009,* 1.

8 It being understood that this is an analytical short-hand for *Doctor Who* (2005–10). Despite his powerful production role as showrunner, Davies obviously remained part of a wider creative team.

9 Davies, quoted in O'Brien and Setchfield, 38.

10 Silverstone, *The Message of Television*, 51.

11 Leach, 58 (my italics).

12 See Campbell, 1993.

13 Tulloch and Alvarado, 77.

14 Tulloch and Alvarado, 76.

15 Tulloch and Alvarado, 95.

16 Davies in O'Brien and Setchfield, 38.

17 See Modleski, 331.

18 Cranny-Francis and Tulloch, 349.

19 Schuster and Powers, 27.

20 See Carroll, 1990.

21 Chen, 57.

22 Eccleston in Hickman, 11.

23 Smith, 145.

24 Cranny-Francis and Tulloch, 350.

25 While new series Cybermen are explicitly identified as humans who have been rendered alien or inhuman, this is less clearly the case for Classic Series Cybermen. Arguments made here are hence specific to BBC Wales' *Doctor Who*.

26 This blurring of Dalek and human is specifically introduced in "The Parting of the Ways." Otherwise, the Daleks can be considered to have mutated from humanoid forms, but Russell T. Davies specifically plays up Dalek-human hybridity in his reimagining of *Who*.

27 Cranny-Francis and Tulloch, 353.

28 Amy-Chinn, 241.

29 Chen, 59.

30 Amy-Chinn, 243.

31 Amy-Chinn, 232.

32 Davies in Davies and Cook, 622.

33 See Rafer, 125.

34 Smith, 73.

35 Smith, 77.

36 Lyden, 63.

37 Segal, 138-42.

38 Davies cited in Gorton, 76.

39 Davies in Davies and Cook, 668–69.
40 Davies in Davies and Cook, 669.
41 Kay Mellor quoted in Gorton, 91.
42 Gorton, 95-6, drawing on Robyn Warhol.
43 Williams, Linda, 279.
44 Gledhill, Christine, drawing on Peter Brooks, 30.
45 Gorton, 80.
46 Gorton, 118-9.
47 See Hills, *Triumph of a Time Lord*, 102-3.
48 Segal, 138-9.
49 Winnicott, Donald Woods. *Through Paediatrics to Psychoanalysis: Collected Papers*. London: Karnac Books, 1992, 240.
50 Winnicott, 241.
51 Segal, 6.
52 Silverstone, 20-47.
53 Hills, *Fan Cultures*, 2002.
54 Hills, *Fan Cultures*, 109.
55 Hills, *Fan Cultures*, 108.
56 Hills, *Triumph*, 118-23.
57 Parkin, 21.
58 Longhurst, 113.
59 Davies in O'Brien and Setchfield, 38-9.
60 See Harrington and Bielby, 1995.
61 Segal, 142.
62 Porter and Lavery, 55.

Afterword

"...We're about to interfere in something that's best left alone."

I have to laugh, recalling that dread pronouncement of the fearful Miss Wright in the *Doctor Who* pilot episode, "An Unearthly Child," written by Anthony Cobrun in 1963. That first Doctor, spookily played by William Hartnell, was pretty testy, with a dim view of humans, as I recall. His equally mysterious traveling companion, granddaughter Susan, quips, "I know these Earth people better than you. Their minds reject things they don't understand." Happily, that first noir appearance of our indomitable time traveler sucked legions of daft humans into the Whoniverse, such that Doctor Who has been "interfering" in our universe ever since.

Zoom forward to 2010. Seasoned Whovians can now speak with authority on the intricacies and nuances of the many episodes of the Classic Series, while neophytes and new recruits continue to join us, thanks in no small part to the 21st century SFX of the brilliantly written and acted New Series begun in 2005. Although Doctors 9 and 10 have pushed the series to new dramatic heights under the inspired guidance of Russell T. Davies, my heart still belongs to Tom Baker's loopy, scarf-flinging Doctor. But I digress.

What started as a little noir scifi show has bloomed into an epic universe brought to life with gravitas by many actors of high caliber. What draws them to the series? Undoubtedly an important factor is the quality of the scripts. In fact, the entire *Doctor Who* saga has been blessed with some of the best writers in the business. People who know their stuff—literature, mythology, history, physics, cosmology, and fabulous wordsmithery. The amazing level of talent and scope of vision that underpins *Doctor Who* elevates the series to material worthy of scholarly discussion and dissection.

Enter the clever folks from Heren Istarion (The Northeast Tolkien Society). Discussing the good Doctor and his many companions while at Mythcon 40, Anthony Burdge, Jessica Burke, and Kristine Larsen hatched an ambitious idea, and then tossed it to me (fellow Tolkienista and Mythopoeic Society member), who pitched it to small press Kitsune Books (who published the second edition of my *Dragons* book and were looking to expand their literary commentary line), and, well... finally you have the amazing book you're holding in your hands (or possibly reading on your digital e-reader device). We Whovians are a demanding and discerning lot, and this volume represents some of the best thinking available about the series as it now stands.

The Doctor has come a long way. Miss Wright, the disbelieving schoolteacher of that long-ago first episode, on entering the TARDIS, exclaimed, "Maybe we've stumbled upon something beyond our understanding." That may have been true for her, but now that you've read the carefully researched, meticulously documented, and imaginatively discussed topics in *The Mythological Dimensions of Doctor Who*, you may find your own understanding of this wonderful series "kicked up a notch."

So, as this virtual TARDIS of information is launched into the Whoniverse, you may find yourself returning to these well-crafted essays again and again. I know I will.

—Anne C. Petty

Contributors

Melissa Beattie is currently a postgraduate researcher in Ancient History at Cardiff University, where she is studying Roman desert warfare. A new but surprisingly ardent fan of Doctor Who and Torchwood (with a fondness for The Sarah Jane Adventures and PROBE), in 2008 she ran the successful "'Whoniversal' Appeal" academic conference on the various series, the proceedings of which are soon to be published. She hopes to continue in the field of 'Whoniverse' studies in the future, and is currently engaged in a combination contemporary archaeological and media/cultural study of the impromptu memorial to Torchwood's Ianto Jones in Cardiff Bay.

Anthony S. Burdge, an Independent Scholar, was first introduced to fantastical, mythological worlds by his parents who claim to have read The Hobbit to him while in utero. Since childhood Anthony has traversed the roads of Middle-earth, studying the history and literature that inspired its creator J.R.R. Tolkien. As a voracious reading appetite was created via Tolkien and related tales, Anthony vividly recalls the days of Doctor Who on PBS and WLIW. In particular is the glowing ring of Eldrad upon the hand of a possessed Sarah Jane Smith ("The Hand of Fear,") and the Sherlock Holmes-ian 4th Doctor in "The Talons of Wang Chiang." Anthony is co-chair, with his wife Jessica Burke, of The Northeast Tolkien Society and a proud member of Doctor Who New York.

Jessica Burke was born in 1974 in Brooklyn, New York. Planning on attending a doctoral program next year, Ms. Burke is a self-professed Geek with studies ranging from anthropology, myth, and folklore, to Anglo-Saxon, Arthurian, and Medieval literature, to Abrahamic and Pagan theology, to vampyres, faeries, monsters, and much in-between. Influenced by the works of J.R.R Tolkien, Ms. Burke first experienced the realm of Middle-earth after a quest to the N.Y. Public Library, at the age of five, where she discovered a recording of Professor Tolkien reading "Riddles in the Dark" from The Hobbit. As her childhood opened into a world of dragons, Ms. Burke fondly recalls being terrified of the Daleks and fascinated with Tom Baker's scarf, yet confesses that her first in-depth journey with the Doctor didn't come until the airing of Russell Davies' re-envisioned series in 2005.

Neil Clarke "Despite the show having gone off air four years after he was born, Neil Clarke nevertheless managed to grow up with Doctor Who – thanks to whoever plugged a mid-Nineties scheduling gap with repeats of Planet of the Daleks, The Green Death, and Pyramids of Mars. From then on, a life of rampant geekery was pretty much inevitable - the evidence of which can be seen at his Doctor Who reviews page, Shall We Destroy? http://shallwedestroy.blogspot.com. Back on planet earth, he is an aspiring failed-artist-cum-writer, in the process of moving from London to the much prettier Bath with his equally pretty girlfriend, Sophie."

Barnaby Edwards was born in London, and now resides in New York City. He's been a fan of Doctor Who ever since Julian Glover ripped off his face revealing the one-eyed Scaroth underneath at the cliffhanger to episode 1 of City of Death. This led to devouring every Target book and DWM he could lay his hands on! Today he runs a fan group in Manhattan (Doctor Who New York), and runs Doctor Who events there under the banner of Who York. His favorite story is Nightmare of Eden, and someday he'll finish his own contribution to Doctor Who non-fiction writing. Someday!

Melody Green received her Ph.D. in English Studies with a specialization in Children's Literature in 2008 from Illinois State University. Currently, she is a lecturer at Illinois State, teaching children's literature and composition classes. She has read papers on J. R. R. Tolkien, George MacDonald and fantasy literature at several academic conferences, and her essay "The Riddle of Strider: A Cognitive Linguistic Reading" was published by the Tolkien Society in The Ring Goes Ever On: Proceedings of the Tolkien 2005 Conference in 2008.

Simon Guerrier is the author of the *Doctor Who* novels *The Time Travellers*, featuring the 1st Doctor, and *The Pirate Loop* and *The Slitheen Excursion*, featuring the 10th Doctor. He's written numerous Doctor Who short stories and audio plays for Big Finish Productions as well as an episode of the new *Blake's 7* and novels for *Primeval* and *Being Human*. Simon is currently working on a short film and his own, original novel. He lives in London with a bright wife and a dim cat.

C.B. Harvey is an award-winning science fiction and fantasy author, journalist and academic specializing in transmedial storytelling. His gothic short story The Stinker won the first SFX Pulp Idol award in 2006. Colin's fiction work includes contributions to two BBC-licensed Doctor Who short stories for Big Finish, the magazine Steampunk Tales and the second episode in the Highlander audio series, published by Big Finish under license from MGM. His academic work includes material on Battlestar Galactica and a book about Grand Theft Auto. He teaches creative writing at London South Bank University and is currently writing a fantasy novel.

Matt Hills is Reader in Media and Cultural Studies at Cardiff University. A lifelong fan of *Doctor Who*, he's been a professional academic as well for the past decade or so, and has recently written the first scholarly book devoted to BBC Wales' re-invention of the show, entitled *Triumph of a Time Lord: Regenerating Doctor Who in the 21st Century* (I.B. Tauris, 2010). Being in Cardiff offers opportunities to watch location filming, and Matt has seen the 9th, 10th, and 11th Doctors in action. Sadly, though, he was in a University Committee Meeting whilst Cybermen stalked the city centre, and so missed out on that. Worst. Meeting. Ever.

Kristine Larsen has inhabited the space-time of Connecticut since her birth in 1963. An aficionado from an early age of equal parts world mythology and religions, science fiction and fantasy, and scientific literature, Dr. Larsen was first drawn to *Doctor Who* in graduate school. Her long career in astronomy education and outreach draws heavily upon her diverse intellectual interests, including numerous publications and presentations on the intersection between science and science fiction/fantasy. She is currently Professor of Physics and Astronomy at Central Connecticut State University.

Leslie McMurtry has a BA from the University of New Mexico and an MA in creative writing from Swansea University and edits The Terrible Zodin (www.doctorwhottz.blogspot.com), a Doctor Who fanzine. She has been published in a number of small poetry magazines and has had her radio drama performed in the UK and France. Recently she won the Elizabeth George Foundation Grant to research the life of John Milton. She is happy to have met so many great people through shared interest in Doctor Who and is especially grateful to her mom for introducing it to her in 1984.

Vincent O'Brien is a graduate of the University of Wales, Aberystwyth; Willamette University, Salem, USA and the Open University. He holds an undergraduate degree in American Studies (specialising in film studies) and a Masters degree in Popular Culture. He was born and raised upon the Rift in Cardiff and has fond memories of the original series, which dutifully nurtured his unknowing fear of the Vashta Nerada. He does find himself haphazardly coming across filming for the current run, whilst going about his daily routine and tries to bear the burden with dignity.

Bibliography

BOOKS:

Aaronovitch, Ben. *Remembrance of the Daleks*. London: W. H. Allen & Co, 1990.

Abbott, Stacey. "How *Lost* Found Its Audience: The Making of a Cult Blockbuster." In *Reading Lost*, edited by Roberta Pearson. London and New York: I.B. Tauris, 2009.

Alkon, Paul K. *Science Fiction Before 1900: Imagination Discovers Technology*. Genres in Context. London: Routledge, 2002.

Amy-Chinn, Dee. "Rose Tyler: The ethics of care and the limits of agency." *Science Fiction Film and Television* 1.2 (2008): 231-47.

Barnes , J. *The Presocratic Philosophers*. London: Routledge, 1979.

Barthes, Roland. *Image – Music – Text*. London: Fontana Press, 1977.

Beatty, Scott. "Batman." In *The DC Comics Encyclopedia,* edited by Alastair Dougall. New York: DK Publishing, 2008.

Bendis, Brian Michael, Bob Kane, and Bill Finger. *Batman: The Greatest Stories Ever Told, Volume 2*. New York: DC Comics, 2007.

Bolter, David J. and Richard A Grusin. *Remediation: Understanding New Media*. Massachusetts: MIT Press, 2000.

Brittain, Constance. *Strong of Body, Brave & Noble: Chivalry and Society in Medieval France*. Ithaca: Cornell University Press, 1998.

Bucher-Jones, Simon and Kelly Hale. *Grimm Reality*. London: BBC Books, 2001.

Burke, Jessica and Anthony Burdge. "The Maker's Will....Fulfilled?" In

Tolkien and Modernity, Volume 1 Cormare Series 9. Switzerland: Walking Tree Press, 2006.

Campbell, Joseph. *The Hero with a Thousand Faces.* US: Fontana Press, 1993.

Carpenter , Humphrey. *The Letters of J.R.R Tolkien.* New York: Houghton Mifflin Company, 2000.

Carroll, Noel. *The Philosophy of Horror.* New York and London: Routledge, 1990.

Chapman, James. *Inside the TARDIS: The Worlds of Doctor Who.* London: I. B. Tauris, 2006.

Chen, Ken. "The Lovely Smallness of *Doctor Who.*" *Film International* 32 (2008), 52-9.

Clark Hall, J. R. *A Concise Anglo-Saxon Dictionary.* Toronto: University of Toronto Press, 2000.

Cohen, Gillian. *Memory in the Real World.* Hove: Psychology Press, 1996.

Cook, Benjamin. *Doctor Who: The New Audio Adventures – The Inside Story.* Berkshire: Big Finish, 2003.

_____. "1989: It's Not Me, It's You." *Doctor Who Magazine Special Edition: In Their Own Words* 5 (2008): 1987-96.

Cook , J. *Morality and Cultural Differences.* Oxford: Oxford University Press, 1999.

Cornell, Paul. *Human Nature.* London: Virgin, 1995.

_____, Keith Topping, and Martin Day. *The Discontinuity Guide: The Definitive Guide to the Worlds and Times of Doctor Who.* Texas: MonkeyBrain Books, 2004.

Coupe, Laurence. *Myth: the New Critical Idiom.* London/New York: Routledge, 1997.

_____. *Myth: The New Critical Idiom.* 2nd ed. London and New York: Routledge, 2009.

Cranny-Francis, Anne and John Tulloch. "Vaster Than Empire(s), and More Slow: The Politics and Economics of Embodiment in *Doctor Who.*" In *Third Person: Authoring and Exploring Vast Narratives,* edited by Pat Harrigan and Noah Wardrip-Fruin. Cambridge and London: MIT Press, 2009.

Damico, Helen. *Beowulf's Wealhtheow and the Valkyrie Tradition.* Madison: University of Wisconsin Press, 1984.

_____ and Alexandra Hennessey Olsen. *New Readings on Women in Old English Literature.* Bloomington and Indianapolis: Indiana University Press, 1990.

Davidson, Hilda Ellis. *Roles of the Northern Goddesses.* London: Routledge, 1998.

Davies, Russell T. and Benjamin Cook. *Doctor Who: The Writer's Tale: The Untold Story of the BBC Series.* UK: Random House, 2008.

_____. *The Writer's Tale: The Final Chapter.* London: BBC Books, 2010.

Davis, Gerry and Allison Bingeman. *The Celestial Toymaker.* UK: Target Books, 1986.

Donovan, Leslie A. "The Valkyrie Reflex in J.R.R. Tolkien's *The Lord of the Rings.*" In *Tolkien the Medievalist,* edited by Jane Chance. London: Routledge, 2003.

Dowden, Ken. *The Uses of Greek Mythology.* London: Routledge, 2000 [1992].

Duncan , Randy and Matthew J. Smith. *The Power of Comics: History, Form, and Culture.* New York: Continuum Books, 2009.

Finger, Bill. *The Joker: Greatest Stories Ever Told.* New York: DC Comics, 2008.

Fiske, J. *Television Culture.* London: Routledge, 1987.

Flieger, Verlyn. *Interrupted Music: The Making of Tolkien's Mythology.* Ohio: Kent State University Press, 2005.

_____, ed. *Smith of Wootton Major: Extended Edition.* London: Harper Collins, 2005.

Fountain, Nev. "The Five O'Clock Shadow." In *Doctor Who: Short Trips: Snapshots,* edited by Ian Farrington. London: Big Finish, 2005.

Geoffrey of Monmouth. *The History of the Kings of Britain.* London: Penguin Books, 1966.

Gillatt, Gary. *Doctor Who: From A to Z.* London: BBC Worldwide Ltd, 1998.

Gimbutas, Maria. *The Language of the Goddess.* New York: Thames and Hudson, 2006.

Girard, Rene. *The Scapegoat.* Translated by Yvonne Freccero. Baltimore: John Hopkins UP, 1986.

_____. *Things Hidden Since the Foundation of the World.* Translated by Stephen Bann and Michael Metteer. Stanford, CA: Stanford UP, 1987.

_____. *Violence and the Sacred.* Translated by Patrick Gregory. Baltimore: John Hopkins UP, 1979.

Gledhill, Christine. "The Melodramatic Field: An Investigation." In *Home is Where the Heart Is: Studies in Melodrama and the Woman's Film,* edited by Christine Gledhill. London: BFI Publishing, 1987.

Glosecki, Stephen. *Shamanism and Old English Poetry.* New York/ London: Garland Publishing. 1989.

Gorton, Kristyn. *Media Audiences: Television, Meaning and Emotion.* Edinburgh: Edinburgh University Press, 2009.

Gresh, Lois and Robert Weinberg. "A NonSuper Superhero." In *The Science of Superheroes.* Hoboken: John Wiley & Sons, 2002.

Gross, Larry. *Redefining the American Gothic: From Wieland to Day of the Dead*. Ann Arbor: UMI Research Press, 1989.

Guerber, H. A. *Myths of the Norsemen from the Eddas and Sagas*. New York: Dover, 1992.

Harrington, C. Lee, and Denise Bielby. *Soap Fans: Pursuing Pleasure and Making Meaning in Everyday Life*. Philadelphia: Temple University Press, 1995.

Harvey, Colin. "But Once a Year." In *Doctor Who: Short Trips: Ghosts of Christmas*, edited by Cavan Scott and Mark Wright. London: Big Finish, 2007.

_____. "The Eyes Have It." In *Doctor Who: Short Trips: Snapshots*, edited by Joseph Lidster. London: Big Finish, 2007.

Hickman, Clayton. "Revolution #9: The Christopher Eccleston Interview." *Doctor Who Magazine* 343 (2004): 10-13.

Hills, Matt. *Fan Cultures*. London /New York: Routledge, 2002.

_____. *Triumph of a Time Lord: Regenerating Doctor Who in the Twenty-first Century*. London /New York: I. B. Tauris, 2010.

Homer. *Iliad*. Vol 1, translated by A. T. Murray. Cambridge, MA: Loeb Classical Library, 1971.

Howe, David J., Mark Stammers, and Stephen James Walker. *Doctor Who: The Eighties*. London: Doctor Who Books, 1997.

Jenkins, Henry. *Fans, Bloggers and Gamers: Exploring Participatory Culture*. London: New York University Press, 2006.

Jochens, Jenny. *Old Norse Images of Women*. Philadelphia: University of Philadelphia Press, 1996.

_____. *Women in Old Norse Society*. Ithaca/London: Cornell University Press, 1995.

Jones, Gerard. *Men of Tomorrow: The True Story of the Birth of the*

Superheroes. London: Arrow Books, 2006.

Keenan, Dennis. *The Question of Sacrifice.* Indianapolis, IN: Indiana UP, 2005.

Kinder, Marsha. *Playing With Power In Movies Television and Video Games: From Muppet Babies to Teenage Mutant Ninja Turtles.* London: University of California Press, 1993.

Leach, Edmund. *Lévi-Strauss.* London: Fontana Press, 1970.

Leavis, F. R. *The Great Tradition.* London: Pelican, 1972.

Long, A. A. *Hellenistic Philosophy.* London: Duckworth, 1974.

Longhurst, Brian. *Cultural Change and Ordinary Life.* Maidenhead/ New York: Open University Press, 2007.

Lyden, John C. *Film as Religion: Myths, Morals, and Rituals.* New York/ London: New York University Press, 2003.

Miles, Lawrence. *Doctor Who: The Adventuress of Henrietta Street.* London: BBC Worldwide Ltd, 2001.

Miles, Lawrence and Tat Wood. *About Time, The Unauthorized Guide to Doctor Who, Volumes 1-6.* Illinois: Mad Norwegian Press, 2004– 2007.

_____. *About Time, The Unauthorized Guide to Doctor Who, 1975 – 1979, Seasons 12 – 17.* Illinois: Mad Norwegian Press, 2004.

_____. *About Time, The Unauthorized Guide to Doctor Who, 1985 – 1989, Seasons 22 – 26, The TV Movie.* Illinois: Mad Norwegian Press, 2007.

Misztal, Barbara A. *Theories of Social Remembering.* Maidenhead: Open University Press, 2003.

Modleski, Tania. "Time and Desire in the Woman's Film." In *Home is Where the Heart Is: Studies in Melodrama and the Woman's Film,* edited by Christine Gledhill. London: BFI Publishing, 1987.

Moore, F. and A. Stevens. "The Human Factor: Daleks, the Evil Human and Faustian Legend in Doctor Who." In *Time and Relative Dissertations in Space: Critical Perspectives on Doctor Who*, edited by David Butler. Manchester: Manchester University Press, 2006.

Moser, K. and T. Carson. *Moral Relativism: A Reader.* Oxford: Oxford University Press, 2001.

O'Brien, Steve and Nick Setchfield. "Russell Spouts." In *SFX Collection: Doctor Who Special.* Bath: Future Publishing, 2005.

O'Mahony, Daniel. *Doctor Who: The Cabinet of Light.* Surrey, England: Telos Publishing Ltd, 2003.

Parkin, Lance. "Canonicity Matters: Defining the Doctor Who Canon." In *Time and Relative Dissertations in Space: Critical Perspectives on Doctor Who,* edited by David Butler. Manchester: Manchester University Press, 2007.

_____. "Truths Universally Acknowledged: How the "Rules" of *Doctor Who* Affect the Writing." In *Third Person: Authoring and Exploring Vast Narratives,* edited by Pat Harrigan and Noah Wardrip-Fruin. Cambridge/London: MIT Press, 2009.

Pavlac Glyer, Diana. *The Company They Keep: C.S. Lewis and J.R.R. Tolkien as Writers in Community.* Ohio: Kent State University Press, 2007.

Platt, Marc. *Battlefield.* UK: Target Books, 1981.

_____. *Lungbarrow.* London: Virgin Publishing Ltd, 1997.

Porter, Lynnette and David Lavery. *Unlocking the Meaning of Lost: An Unauthorized Guide.* Illinois: Sourcebooks, 2007.

Rafer, David. "Mythic Identity in *Doctor Who.*" In *Time and Relative Dissertations in Space: Critical Perspectives on Doctor Who,* edited by David Butler. Manchester/New York: Manchester University Press, 2007.

Richards, Justin. *Doctor Who: The Legend Continues.* London: BBC Books, 2005.

Rojek, Chris. *Cultural Studies*. Cambridge: Polity, 2007.

Rose, Steven. *The Making of Memory: From Molecules to Mind*. London: Vintage, 2003.

Scheffler, S. *Human Morality*. Oxford: Oxford University Press, 1992.

Schuster, Marc and Tom Powers. *The Greatest Show in the Galaxy: The Discerning Fan's Guide to Doctor Who*. Jefferson: McFarland, 2007.

Segal, Robert A. *Myth: A Very Short Introduction*. Oxford: Oxford University Press, 2004.

Shelley, Mary. *Frankenstein, or The Modern Prometheus*. London: Harding, Mavor & Jones, 1818.

Shippey, Tom. *J. R. R. Tolkien: Author of the Century*. New York: Houghton Mifflin Company, 2001.

Silverstone, Roger. *The Message of Television: Myth and Narrative in Contemporary Culture*. London: Heinemann, 1981.

_____. "Television Myth and Culture." In *Media, Myths, and Narratives: Television and the Press,* edited by John W. Carey. London: Sage, 1988.

Simpson, Paul, ed. *The Rough Guide to Superheroes*. London: Penguin Books, 2004.

Smith, Greg M. *Beautiful TV: The Art and Argument of Ally McBeal*. Austin: University of Texas Press, 2007.

Stone, Dave. *Doctor Who The New Adventures: Sky Pirates!* London: Virgin Books, 1995.

Tolkien, J. R. R. *The Lord of the Rings*. New York: Houghton Mifflin, 1994.

_____. *The Monsters and the Critics and Other Essays*. UK: HarperCollins Publishers, 1997.

Tulloch, John. *Television Drama: Agency, Audience and Myth.* London/ New York: Routledge, 1990.

Tulloch, John and Manuel Alvarado. *Doctor Who: The Unfolding Text.* London/Basingstoke: Macmillan, 1983.

Tulloch, John and Henry Jenkins. *Science Fiction Audiences: Watching Doctor Who and Star Trek.* London/New York: Routledge, 1995.

Wheatley, Helen. *Gothic.* Manchester: Manchester University Press, 2006.

Wilkinson, Philip. *Myths & Legends: An illustrated guide to their origins and meanings* . London: Dorling Kindersley Limited, 2009.

Wilkinson, Philip and Neil Philip. *Eyewitness Companions: Mythology.* London: Dorling Kindersley Limited, 2007.

Williams, Graham. *The Nightmare Fair.* UK: Target Books, 1989.

Williams, Linda. "Film Bodies: Gender, Genre and Excess." In *Feminist Film Theory: A Reader*, edited by Sue Thornham. Edinburgh: Edinburgh University Press, 1999.

Winnicott, Donald Woods. *Through Paediatrics to Psychoanalysis: Collected Papers.* London: Karnac Books, 1992.

PERIODICALS:

Barnes, Alan. "Battlefield." *Doctor Who Magazine* #402 (November 2008).

_____. "The Celestial Toymaker." *Doctor Who Magazine* #408 (April 2009).

Berry, Dan. "Charley Says..." *Doctor Who Magazine* #414 (November 2009).

"DVD Poll Results." *Doctor Who Magazine* #332 (July 2003).

Gray, Warwick. "Bringer of Darkness." *Doctor Who Magazine Summer*

Special (Summer 1993).

Kibble-White, Graham. ". . . But Is It Art?" *Doctor Who Magazine* #216 (2009).

"The Good, the Bard, and the Ugly." *Doctor Who Magazine* #382 (May 2007).

Morris, Jonathan. "The Changing Man." *Doctor Who Magazine* #409 (2009).

Mulkern, Patrick. "Blink." *Doctor Who Magazine Special Edition 200 Golden Moments* (2009).

Pritchard, Michael. "The Time Team." *Doctor Who Magazine* #409 (May 2009).

The Watcher. "The Watcher's Guide to the Seventh Doctor." *Doctor Who Magazine* #413 (September 2009).

_____. "The Watcher's Guide to the Eighth Doctor." *Doctor Who Magazine* #414 (2009).

TELEVISION:

"Bringing Back the Doctor." *Doctor Who Confidential*, 2005.

"Doctor Who Greatest Moments: The Companions." *Doctor Who Greatest Moments*. BBC, 2009.

PODCASTS:

Doctor Who Podshock. Episode 7 NY. Gallifreyan Embassy: 9/21/2005. http://www.podshock.net

ONLINE SOURCING:

BBC Online. "Interview: Lawrence Miles." *BBC: Doctor Who – The Official Site,* January 1, 2004. http://www.bbc.co.uk/doctorwho/news/cult/news/

drwho/2004/01/01/13690.shtml

Cornell, Paul. *Canonicity in Doctor Who,* February 10, 2007. http://www.paulcornell.com/search?updated-max=2007-03-28T23%3A04%3A00%2B01%3A00&max-results=50

Doctor Who TARDIS Index file. "Canon." March 2007. http://tardis.wikia.com/wiki/Canon

"Morality." *Stanford Encyclopedia of Philosophy.* http://plato.stanford.edu/entries/morality-definition/

"The Outpost Interview: Lawrence Miles." *Outpost Gallifrey.* http://www.gallifreyone.com/interview.php?id=miles

Shorthand for the decade 2000-2009. "Top 100 defining cultural moments of the noughties." *The Daily Telegraph,* 30 October 2009. http://www.telegraph.co.uk/culture/6466684/Top-100-defining-cultural-moments-of-the-00s-noughties.html.

FILM/TV CITATIONS:

Bill & Ted's Excellent Adventure. Los Angeles: De Laurentiis Entertainment Group, 1989.

Frankenstein. Los Angeles: Universal Pictures, 1931.

The Bride of Frankenstein. Los Angeles: Universal Pictures, 1935.

CONFERENCES:

Beattie, Melissa (moderator), et al. 2008. "Who's Morality?" Panel at "Whoniversal" Appeal: An Interdisciplinary Postgraduate Conference on Doctor Who and All of Its Spin-Offs.

Index